Tsarina

B.W. ATKINS

Copyright © 2016 B.W. Atkins
Cover design © 2016 B.W. Atkins
All rights reserved. No part of this book may be reproduced in any form or by any electronic or mechanical means – except in the case of brief quotations embodied in articles or reviews – without written permission from its publisher.

The characters and events portrayed in this book are fictitious. Any similarity to real persons, living or dead, is purely coincidental and not intended by the author.
Copyright © 2016 B.W. Atkins
All rights reserved

For all my friends who kept me insane during these years.
Nostrovia!

∞∞∞ *Vigilant*

"Do you think he's following us?" Shelby asked.

Tsarina glanced back and the albino's eyes shot to the ground. "Come on, girl. He's definitely following us."

Bounding into the subway on 66th Street, Tsarina pulled the MetroCard from her pocket and swiped it through the reader. As she passed through the turnstile, her eyes flashed to the top of the stairwell, searching for the stalker. A thin silhouette of the man loomed on the platform, then advanced. She wrangled Shelby onto the boarding platform, pressing toward the front of the line, peering into the void. A horn blasted from inside the corridor and a headlight beamed through the darkness.

"Where'd he go? Dude just vanished!" Shelby gasped.

"Great," Tsarina responded, inhaling the malodorous air flooding the tunnel.

"But seriously, it was like he just disappeared when he hit the turnstile."

"Awesome. Hope he couldn't get through," Tsarina maintained, pressing closer to the edge of the platform.

Seconds later, the *1* train screeched to a halt inside the station, stifling the debate, and Tsarina yanked Shelby inside. Forcing her way through the crowd, she scanned beyond the collage of faces for the vagrant's alabaster hair and crimson eyes. Shelby's report of his disappearance seemed accurate for the moment. Tsarina puffed a short breath of relief through the lone, auburn ringlet, resting in the middle of her raven locks.

She wondered, *Who was that man—and why on Earth was he following us?* The albino's features were striking, and a faint memory seemed to be trapped inside lingering fear. She was sure she had seen him before. The disconnect gnawed on her psyche as she pressed deeper into the sea of passengers. Struggling to balance as the train lurched forward, she tossed backward into Shelby's unpadded chest. Like a drunken ballerina, she tiptoed forward and felt the golden links of her mother's anklet cutting into her skin. Mindlessly, she shook them into a manageable position.

    For twenty years, she had borne the anklet like a crown of thorns, and on more than one occasion, she had wanted to heave it as far as she could into the Hudson River and just be done with it. The artifact was an incessant and painful reminder her mother was no longer a part of this world. However, despite its useless and uncomfortable presence, she could never let go of the heirloom. Anastasia had touted the auburn gemstone as the *Eye of Istia*—a magical sunstone imbued with wondrous powers. Tsarina had grudgingly respected her mother's wish to keep it safe, even if she didn't believe in its magic. She also knew her older sister, Tasha, would absolutely kill her if she ever lost it.

    "Aw hell, he's back," Shelby drawled, disrupting Tsarina's thoughts. "You see that? He just came through that door! Can't that little sunstone make us disappear or something?"

    "No. It can't! It's just a stupid friggin' rock, ok. Come on, we gotta keep moving."

    "I'm just saying, it would be nice is all," her waifish friend huffed.

    Stalking closer, the mysterious vagrant slithered into the center of the car, directing a bony finger toward Tsarina. She turned and ripped the connecting door open to a wave of clacking sounds. Screeching metal wheels shot golden sparks at her feet as she swayed back and forth. With a miscalculated hop, she lunged into the next car, and as she landed the train engaged its brakes, taking a corner. Momentum tossed her into a short, chiseled teenager. Immediately after, Shelby bumped them from behind. Tsarina spun off the boy's white tank top and apologized, "Sorry, bro."

The Puerto Rican youth glared at her with seedy black eyes and licked his lips provocatively. "Yo mama. What's yo hurry?" he asked.

Tsarina recognized the gang tattoo on the side of his face as the insignia for the Brujos Majestuosas and apologized again. "Sorry, man. My bad," she replied, turning away.

"Yo, *qué coño, puta?*" he hissed, and grabbed her arm, pressing his long fingernails into her skin. "Where do you think you going?"

"Let go of her, asshole!" Shelby snipped.

The boy's friend, who was a foot taller, with a similar tattoo on the opposite side of his face, stepped into the middle of the aisle next to Shelby and grinned. "You kinda sassy, *chica*. I think I love you."

Shelby cowered and took a step back. During the exchange, Tsarina struggled to wriggle free and noticed the connecting door open behind Shelby. The albino stepped through, and his eyes immediately shot to Tsarina. Shelby shrieked in his direction, huddling with Tsarina, clutching at her arm.

"Who the fuck are you *esé?*" the taller boy woofed.

"Who I am is of no concern of yours," the albino responded, his voice low and soothing. "Now step aside. I must have a word with that girl," Inexplicably, the boy loosened his grip and pressed Tsarina into the arms of his abettor then stepped forward in an apparent daze, blocking the albino's path.

"Now, you will let me pass," the albino cautioned, his voice rumbling like distant thunder.

"I will let you pass?" The boy echoed, shaking his head as if trying to toss the thought from his mind. "What, you think you can play mind tricks on me, Obi-Wan? You'll pass, when I say you pass, *puta.*"

"Insolent cur!" the albino growled, stepping forward.

In that moment, the train's wheels began grinding to a stop, and the albino grabbed the boy by the shoulder. As the outer doors sprang open, the three combatants seemed to be frozen in time, their eyes locked on each other with deadly intent. Tsarina took advantage the distraction and elbowed her captor in the stomach then yanked Shelby out of the car onto the platform. Synchronously, the albino pursued, shoving the gangbangers aside as he lunged off the train.

"Tsarina! Wait, child!" the stranger howled, contorting in pain, grabbing his lower back with one hand. The unexpected sound of her name from his lips forced her to pause, and she turned to face him. As he staggered forward, he reached for her arm, and she witnessed his eyes dimming. He pulled a bronze necklace from inside his shirt and displayed it in the palm of his hand. A tarnished, eight-point star, formed exactly like the links on her mother's anklet, dangled from the chain, and the pendant flashed a meek spot of light at her as it gently swayed back and forth. With a choked grunt, the man in the threadbare suit collapsed to one knee, gazing deeper into Tsarina's eyes. She noticed gentle warmth in his expression, and then mysteriously heard his voice inside her head like a floating like a whisper. *Listen to me, child—you mustn't open the portal. Some wounds should never be reopened.* The words weighed on her as the strained voice faded from her mind. She watched, frozen, as the albino slumped onto his stomach, a red and black switchblade sticking out of his lower back.

"What?" Tsarina asked, kneeling, afraid to touch him, her mind welling with questions.

"Tsarina!" Shelby called from behind. "Let's go!"

"We gotta help him," she argued.

"Forget it! That dude is dead. Come on!"

"But—"

"The cops are gonna be here any minute, girl!"

Ignoring Shelby's warning, Tsarina placed her fingers on the man's carotid artery but felt no pulse. Guilt swelled in her throat, suffocating her. She took a deep breath, steadying her hand, and ripped the chain from the albino's neck. Stashing it inside her bra, she rose to her feet. Blood began pooling onto the floor from under the man's stomach. She quivered at his wan, lifeless expression, and a feeling of helplessness washed over her. For an instant, she wished the anklet *could* do something magical—that it truly was some supernatural force that could save him, but it wasn't, and it couldn't.

Several feet away, a Jamaican woman shrieked, "Oh my God! That man's been stabbed!"

Tsarina felt a strong tug on her arm. Shelby was jerking her up the stairs.

"Excuse me! But if you don't mind, what the hell just happened back there?" Shelby crowed, as they entered the bright cityscape.

"I don't know," Tsarina mumbled.

"You don't know? Really? Who the hell was that guy?"

"I don't friggin' know!" Tsarina snapped, struggling to place his image—the albino's pale face and blood red eyes were pressed against a cover of cellophane, blanketing her memory. Her temples throbbed. "Look it, whatever just happened back there, you're right, we gotta forget about it and catch the 2 before it gets too late, or all this shit will be a total waste. We can worry about that dude after we find my mother's grimoire and cast the friggin' spell."

∞∞∞∞*Old School*

Monotonous thumping sounds from the train's wheels rocked Tsarina into a trance as they rumbled through the Bronx, the albino's face haunting her thoughts. She pulled the pendant from her bra and examined it, hoping it would spark a memory. The word, *vigil* was engraved on her back.

Her mind raced with questions. *Who was that guy? And why the hell did he risk his life with those gang bangers just to warn me not to open the portal? How could he even know about that? About me? What did he mean by - some wounds should never be reopened?*

"You got a clue yet?" Shelby asked, breaking Tsarina from her internal rant.

"Not really."

"I mean, not to sound like a whiny little bitch or nothing, but we almost ate it back there. That dude was a full-on psychopath. Did you see how he attacked to those gang bangers? It was like he was possessed or something."

"Yeah, but I don't think he was crazy." Tsarina shook her head. "I think he was trying to protect me."

"What? How do you figure that? Shelby scoffed.

"He warned me not to open the portal."

"When did he do that?"

"When he was falling to the ground."

"I didn't see him say anything."

"He didn't say anything. I just heard it," Tsarina explained.

"What do you mean, you just heard it?" Shelby questioned.

"I just heard it in my mind…I don't know."

"Like telepathy?"

"Yeah, I guess."

"Ok then, but how'd he even know about the portal in the first place?" Shelby asked with a crooked frown.

"I don't know."

"Maybe he read your mind. He could have been trying to steal your mother's anklet for himself if he was a warlock."

"I guess," Tsarina muttered.

When the train stopped, the tempest of questions subsided, releasing her from her guilt, and she tucked the dull pendant into her bra. As she exited the train and stepped off the platform onto the familiar streets of Mott Haven, a sweltering mist hovered inches above the asphalt, flowing back and forth like a confused spirit seeking a host. The humidity frizzed her tight curls into a ratty nest, and she groped at them, scanning the alleys for would be stalkers.

The dilapidated buildings on Willis Avenue hadn't changed much, different owners perhaps, but they still pressed tight against one another with loose bits of trash tumbling around their foundations. Tsarina felt a wave of nervous excitement toss her forward when she saw her old supermarket, and she wondered why her mother had chosen to live in Mott Haven, as a single parent with two little girls. It wasn't the safest neighborhood to rear a six year old, and Anastasia wasn't poor by any means. Her ample trust fund was a testament to that fact. Maybe her mother had been hiding from someone. Maybe it was the man from the train.

"Is this really the first time you've been back up here since your mom died?" Shelby asked, dabbing her forehead with a black handkerchief.

"What? Yeah." Tsarina nodded, trying to repress the caustic memories of her mother walking the streets alone at night. Those memories only rekindled her feelings of desertion, loneliness, and self-pity. They were always hiding somewhere in the back of her mind, but here, in this place, it was impossible to overlook them. Striding forward, she glanced at the facades of the familiar buildings and tried to focus on happier times: double Dutch in the street with her sister, riding her bike to the beauty shop, water balloon fights, splashing in open fire hydrants.

The brick structures, red and tan, framed by thick metal bars and green awnings, rose up through the black asphalt into the light blue sky like giant fingertips of concrete golems. When Tsarina mustered the strength to look back, she noticed Shelby gawking up at the rooftops. "Hey, chill out with that tourist shit," she chastised. "You want to get us mugged?"

"No, I'm just taking a mental picture of the area, so I can remember it," she explained, then her face contorted. "Dang, chill out girl—and it doesn't seem all that scary. As a matter of fact, I'm liking it a lot better than midtown right now. At least we don't have some freaky ass albino stalking us. Besides, this is going to be hallowed ground for all us witches some day."

Tsarina shook her head and laughed, "What are you talking about?"

"You know, once you go and open up that portal, you're going to be a famous witch around here, and they're going to build statues of the *Priestess Tsarina* on this street."

"Whatever." Tsarina rolled her eyes. "I'll leave the witching fame to you. I just wanna find ma's grimoire, cast the spell, and then when it doesn't work, be done with this friggin' nightmare. At least then, I'll know I'm just crazy wack psycho and need to check myself into the loony bin."

"Well, from all the stuff that's happened today, it's sure looking more and more like you ain't crazy wack psycho and there is something to your dreams," Shelby persuaded. "I'm telling you, you should embrace being a sister of magic as I have. Shit's real. And it ain't all that crazy."

"I know," Tsarina relented, "I'm not saying you're crazy, but what if I'm just a freakin' nut job, and this is all in my head?"

Shelby shrugged. "Honey, I know you're guarded and jaded and have some real social issues with all this, but you have got to start believing in yourself. You can see the future. You have a gift."

"Or a curse," she countered.

"Well, I don't see it like that. It's all a part of your spiritual connection to the world, and I think it's pretty cool."

"Yeah," Tsarina grumbled to herself, realizing Shelby's belief in magic was unwavering, and it was pointless to argue.

When she lifted her eyes to the red arch overhead, she recognized the address, *413*. Stepping onto the cracked steps of her old stoop, she scrolled the hand-written list of names inside the door panel, and the tarnished brass buzzer for her old apartment was now marked "*Sipp.*" She recognized the name, *Mr. Marcel*, a kindly old man who had lived directly below when she was a child. With a tentative breath, she depressed the scorching button, and her finger tingled with the vibration.

A moment of eternity passed then a deep voice, softened with age, crackled from the speaker. "Hello? Who's it out there?"

Tsarina cleared the rasp from her throat and pressed the intercom button. "Mr. Marcel? It's Tsarina. I used to live here with my mother, Miss Anna, and my big sister, Tasha."

The metal speaker box crackled at her, "Tsarina? Oh my word, Little Miss Mini Muffin? What gives? What are you doing back around here?"

"It's kind of a long story. Can I come in? I need to talk to you, if you don't mind. It's about ma."

A few seconds passed in silence. Shelby's brown eyes rolled under her straw-like bangs, squinting for a sign, and she tugged at the bottom of her white blouse. Tsarina nodded when the bronze latch buzzed. With a confident pull on the handle, she opened the door and pressed into the entry hall then clomped up the first flight of tile stairs to the second, Shelby galumphing close behind. At the top of the deteriorating staircase, a senescent, Jamaican man stood wavering in the doorway of her old apartment, puffing on a Newport.

"Well now, Miss Tsarina, look at you all grown up," he marveled, then discarded the half-smoked butt onto the floor, squashing it with the heel of his oxford shoe. "Who's your friend?" he asked.

"This is my roommate from college—Shelby."

"Very nice to meet you." He extended his leathery hand.

Shelby fashioned a glowing smile and shook his hand, her collage of silver bracelets jingling.

Mr. Marcel looked at Tsarina and remarked, "Dang. College? You must be doing alright."

"Yeah, I guess." She allowed a humble smile.

"What you studying?"

"Pre-Med."

"Mercy, I'll bet that's some serious stuff. Where you studying at?"

"Fordham, and yeah, it's definitely a challenge."

"Dang, that's alright," he chuckled and wrapped his arm around her shoulder. "Well, come on in with you now. It's hotter than a two-dollar pistol out here. Got me a new air conditioner from Morale's Hardware, little baby works like a dream."

When he opened the door, a wave of cool refreshing air engulfed Tsarina. She crossed the narrow foyer of her childhood, walking past two waist high, Chinese vases, ferns sticking out of the top, each painted with a different scene depicting regal Asian men standing in council. She recognized them from her cat chasing visits downstairs as a child. That was the excuse she used whenever she wanted to visit Miss Mika's apartment and have teatime with the worldly lady. She surmised the vases were kept in tribute to Mr. Marcel's deceased wife, a beautiful, petite, Chinese lady with an infectious smile, who always allowed Tsarina to sit and ask questions and partake in her afternoon tea sessions. She remembered the day the ambulance came to take Miss Mika away, red lights and the doleful expression on Mr. Marcel's face.

Canvassing the transformed apartment, Tsarina noticed the once navy and purple interior of the kitchen had been repainted in soft apricot and yellow hues, olive accents trimming the edges. The arrangement of the furniture was basically the same, there were only so many places a table and chairs would fit in the confined space, but Mr. Marcel's version of the decor was a fusion of sixties and seventies memorabilia interspersed with an ancient Chinese motif. As the old gentleman shuffled across the room, he offered a seat on the vinyl and chrome chairs with a casual wave of his hand. "You ladies thirsty? I got fresh lemonade or water."

"Lemonade would be wonderful," Shelby replied.

"Yeah, that sounds great, thanks," Tsarina agreed.

The kitchen table and chairs were the only recognizable pieces of furniture from Tsarina's past. They reminded her of her childhood: quick morning conversations; bowls of cereal; games of dominos and checkers; scrabble; puzzles; laughter and tears. Mr. Marcel pulled up a metal stool for himself and placed two lemonades with ice on the table, then asked, "You look so serious child. What's going on with you? I'm guessing you didn't come all the way out here just to see this old face."

With an abashed smile, Tsarina set aside her initial reaction to verbally vomit about her dead mother, who had been pleading with her in her dreams to find a secret book of spells that might open a magical portal to some other planet. She realized it would only be regarded as insanity. Instead, she explained, "You know,

Mr. Marcel, this may sound sort of crazy, but I have reason to believe ma might have stashed a diary of hers somewhere in this apartment. The thing is—she wasn't able to tell me exactly where she hid it before she died." Tsarina took a sip, chewing on a piece of ice, awaiting his reaction.

The sexagenarian's face scrunched, sealing the cracks around his eyes as he leaned back and folded his arms. "Yeah, well, you know, I was sure sorry to hear about your mama—damn crazy ass punks—pardon my French." He blushed. "It just makes you wonder what's wrong with the world when bad stuff like that happens to good people. Miss Anna sure was a good-hearted lady. You was always good people."

"Thanks, Mr. Marcel," Tsarina responded.

"So, you think she hid something in here, you say?" he asked.

"Yeah. It was a black leather book with gold stars on it. I just remember her talking about it and saying it was really important that I read it one day."

"If you don't mind me asking, what made you think of it now, after all these years?"

"I had a dream about it the other night and it made me wonder."

"Well, I spent a bunch of years up in here, and I ain't never come across no book like that in all my messings around. Sorry, but I can't imagine where it could be."

Tsarina gave an understanding smile. "I know it's a long shot, but I thought I'd try."

"Never hurts to try," he smiled and looked at her with a glow in his eyes. A genuine smile blossomed under his wrinkled cheeks, and he brimmed with childish enthusiasm, "You know, this actually sounds kind of exciting. I'd be more than happy to poke around this old place with you." Then he squinted, as if he had lost his train of thought. "So, where do you think it could be?"

"I guess it could be like a secret panel in the floor, or a space in the wall, or something. Something hidden…like a little safe maybe?" she said.

"Got it, nooks and crannies. Messed with a lot of them back in my day," he mentioned.

"Yeah, nooks and crannies—and ma used to say, *at high tea the light will show you the way.*

"The light?" he asked.

"Yeah, ma told me the sun will light the way," she recalled, intentionally leaving out the part that it had come to her in a dream.

"Well, the only light that's going to come in here would be in the kitchen or the bedroom, through them side windows, and come to think of it, it do get pretty bright on the walls this time of day, in the summertime." Mr. Marcel glanced up at the miniature grandfather clock sitting on top of the refrigerator. "We should be seein' it soon then. It's almost five."

"Cool. I guess I'll take the bedroom if that's okay?" Tsarina proposed.

"Alright, good luck then." He winked. "Me and Miss Shelby can split up the kitchen and the bathroom," he said, looking to Shelby, who nodded approval.

Tsarina loped into the bedroom where, as a child, she would sit and watch her mother preen in front of a large antique mirror. Scanning the room, she searched for a clue to spark her memory, but now the walls were different shades of yellowish-orange and the mirror was gone. The sound of wooden cabinet doors, opening and closing, clattered from the kitchen, and Tsarina plopped onto Mr. Marcel's squeaky brass bed. She stared at the bare yellow wall reflecting the glow of the sun. A thick beam radiated through the small barred window across from the bed, illuminating a memory from her childhood and she imagined herself as a six-year-old, gazing into her mother's gold-framed mirror. Innocent blue eyes glared with a wanting stare as her child-like image struggled to brush out the thick, black, knotted curls resting upon her head. The sturdy metal bristles always seemed to detangle the crapulent web of nightmares that suffocated her, releasing them from the confines of her memory. The memory comforted her, but with the mirror absent, her reflection was only an illusion replaced by a flat wall and thin rays of sunlight. The radiant heat warmed her face and grounded her thoughts as the light steadily crept across the room. *Even if I find this grimoire, it doesn't prove anything. Ma still could have been some crazy person who just thought she was a witch, and now I'm just following in her footsteps. If I don't try to cast this spell tonight— Another year of this will drive me insane.* She shook her head, trying to keep her hopes in check.

Golden rays began pouring through the window as the clock ticked seconds into oblivion, and the light gradually engulfed the space in front of her. When the hands fell on the five and the twelve, she noticed the light consume the space where the mirror had once hung. Unable to fully break from her daydream, she continued staring at the apricot slab. The warmth of the reflection flushed her cheeks. Sliding off the bed, she moved toward the glowing spot on the wall and wondered if the light was signaling a secret compartment behind the wall. She tapped the space with her knuckles, and a solid thump reverberated from the wall instead of the hollow sound she had hoped she would hear. Pulling her switchblade from her pocket, she stabbed the wall but only the tip of the blade made it through. She stabbed in several places up the wall where the light would travel with the passing of time, but the wall was solid behind each poke. As she raised the knife above her shoulder, the light reflected off the blade and flashed past her eye. The flash landed across the room, and she wondered where the sunlight would fall if the mirror were still in place. She placed the blade flat against the wall and a thin shaft of light pinpointed a large faceplate on the opposite wall without a light switch or electrical outlet. With the tip of her switchblade, she unscrewed the plate and found the faint outline of a large box, etched into the wall behind. Touching the thin layer of cracked paint covering the raised lines of the box with her fingernails, she switched and began scraping at the edges with her blade. The dry paint flaked off the wall like a chilled shell of a hard-boiled egg. Beneath the first layer, she felt the hard sensation of metal, and inside a minute, she had unearthed a silver box with a gold escutcheon, the shape of an eight-point star, surrounding the tiny keyhole. Holding it in her hand, she tried to open the lid, but it wouldn't budge.

"Awesome, it's locked," she groaned and placed the box on the edge of the bed. Returning to the recess of the wall, she foraged around inside with her fingertips, feeling for a key, but only made contact with the cool brick housing. After closer examination of the box, she abandoned her efforts to open it and called into the kitchen for assistance, "Hey you guys, come here. I found something!"

Shelby bounded into the room first, eyes wide. Mr. Marcel ambled behind.

"Is that it?" Shelby asked.

"I don't know. I found this box in the wall, but we're going to need a key, or a locksmith, or something," Tsarina explained, pointing at the keyhole.

Mr. Marcel took a long look at the chest, as if it were an alien artifact, and asked, "Now where did that come from? Has that been in here this whole time?"

"Yeah, it was behind this faceplate. Sorry about the hole." She frowned apologetically. "I guess ma used the plate to hide the recess in the wall, and this box probably has the diary, but there's no friggin' key."

The old man's lips pursed. "Hmm…interesting. You know what? Wait here a minute. I think I might just be able to help you out with that." Then with a slow pirouette, graceful for his age, he smiled and loped into the kitchen then started dialing numbers on the mustard-colored, rotary phone hanging on the wall. When an answer came, he responded, "Hey George, what's up amigo? It's Mr. Marcel up here in 206. You still got that old lock pick set of mine I left down there?" The reply spawned a frown. "Aw, hell no man, I ain't back into that mess. That's why I gave it to you. I ain't about to go there no more, but listen, I done locked myself out of a box up here, and I need to get at it. Could you bring it up?" His eyes rolled with the answer. "Yeah, I got Miller or Bud…Sure…You got it *amigo*. Just come on up here *pronto* and bring that bag with you."

∞∞∞Hidden Talent

    Mr. Marcel entered the bedroom with two frosty cans of Budweiser secure in each hand and a confident grin on his face.
    Shelby's eyes locked onto the beverages. "Aw, Mr. Marcel, you shouldn't have."
    "What?" the old man questioned with a curious squint, then asked, "You girls old enough to drink?"
    "In Europe," Shelby replied, accepting the cans from his wrinkled hands before he could muster a second thought to deny her. She then handed a beer to Tsarina, and they both thanked him with innocent smiles, tipping their cans.
    "You know, we ain't in Europe." He frowned. "Aw hell, just don't tell nobody." Defeated, Mr. Marcel shuffled to the refrigerator, and as soon as he began extracting the next set of brews from the bottom shelf, three raps sounded at the front door. He kicked the refrigerator shut with his foot then sauntered down the hall to greet his visitor.
    Outside, a wiry Puerto Rican fellow wearing a pristine Mets cap cocked to one side and a crisp pair of blue jeans hanging low off his butt fidgeted with his free hand in the hall. His street wear, especially his pressed denim shirt buttoned to the top, gave Tsarina the impression he had recently been incarcerated, or maybe he just wanted people to think that.
    "Come on in George." Mr. Marcel invited the pug of a man inside and swapped a beer for a black leather bag.
    "*Gracias* for the *cerveza amigo*." The man gave a wide, gold-toothed smile and popped the top on his beer then took a long swig as he followed Mr. Marcel into the kitchen. With the white

froth settling on his moustache, he licked it with his pointy tongue and grinned at Shelby.

"No problem George. Thank you for this," Mr. Marcel replied, caressing the thin bag softly with his fingers.

"So, what's goin' on in here man?" the neighbor pried, surveying the room like a swinger in a singles bar.

"These girls—well, this one—" Mr. Marcel pointed to Tsarina with his beer hand. "She used to live here with her mom and her sister. You remember that nice Russian lady, Anna, right?"

George nonchalantly shook his head in the negative, as he took another sip off his beer. "Before my time, man," he replied. "Was she hot?"

Mr. Marcel rolled his eyes then turned to the girls unfazed and continued, "Well, this is her daughter, Tsarina, and that's her friend from college, Shelby. Girls this here is George—best Mexican cook in the haven."

"Puerto Rican, man," he corrected, then turned to the girls, "and everyone but *pinche* Marci here calls me, *Jorge*. Damn man, how many times I gotta tell you that?"

Mr. Marcel shrugged his shoulders indifferently and raised his can in front of his nose.

Tsarina lifted her beer along with everyone else, honoring the introduction, as Mr. Marcel took a quick swig and finished, "So we think her mom left something locked up in this box here, and we need to get it open, hence the lock picks, *amigo*."

"Well, you definitely the man for that, homie," Jorge remarked and took another swill.

Mr. Marcel frowned, as if his skills were an insult to his upstanding character. Tsarina related to his humility, and wondered how many times he had done this type of work and what kind of life he must have led in his youth. It was hard to imagine him as a delinquent, or a thief of any sort. He seemed like such a kind, gentle old soul. *But you don't just learn how to pick locks for the fun of it*, she thought, as she watched him deftly slide the zipper across the top of bag then unpack a set of metal lock picks and place them on the kitchen table. After selecting two small picks,

Mr. Marcel began digging around inside the golden keyhole, and Tsarina watched as his steady hands manipulated the latch with the grace of a veteran thief. A moment later, he popped it loose and pulled open the latch.

Tsarina hovered over his shoulder while he reached into the metal frame and extracted another box. The flat, antique mini-chest was fitted with four short s-shaped legs, and an eight-point star was melted in gold onto the center of the cedar lid.

"What the hell is it that?" Jorge blurted.

"Well it's obviously a little treasure chest," Shelby huffed.

"Here ya go," Mr. Marcel said, placing the box in Tsarina's hands.

Twisting it in her palms, she examined it from all angles. Confused, she saw neither a latch nor a keyhole, and before the imbecilic feeling overwhelmed her, she surrendered again. "Ok, I give. How do you open this stupid thing?"

Mr. Marcel chuckled, as if he'd seen a thousand of them in his lifetime. "Well, it looks like a Polish secret box."

"A what?"

"A puzzle box. You see, back in them olden days, them dudes didn't use no keys. They just made them boxes into puzzles, so as only the maker of the box could open it. They's pretty simple, really, but if you never seen one before, I imagine you'd be in a heap of trouble trying to get at it," he explained.

"So, how do you open it?" Tsarina asked.

Mr. Marcel extended an open hand. "Mind if I have a crack?"

"Please." Tsarina gladly handed the frustrating coffer over and watched his fingertips caress the edges like a blind man reading Braille. Focusing on the s-shaped legs, he slid them into different positions until the lid eventually succumbed and fell open. With an abbreviated smile, he returned it to her.

"You see? It was them ol' legs. You just got to put them in the right positions, is all."

"Cool. Thanks."

Tsarina took a breath, lifted the lid, and anxiously peered inside. A thick, but compact, black, leather bound book, rested on bed of crushed red velvet, waiting for her to accept it into her quivering hands. The actual presence of the grimoire connected her dreams with reality, validating her repressed childhood visions. She recalled her mother's moniker for her—*my little oracle.* Tsarina had refused to accept it all these years and the responsibility she would have to bear along with it. Responsibility, guilt, excitement, and apprehension gripped her all at once as she slid her fingers over the rough cover.

With a curt smile at Shelby, she removed the tome from the box and lifted it to her chest. The weathered binding crackled under her thumb when she opened the front cover. As she began reading the text on first page, she recognized the language as some form of Latin. The cryptic words sparked a hazy memory of her last night with her mother:

She recalled watching, secretly, or so she thought, in her pajamas from behind the bedroom door. Her mother seemed focused on something far away and unaware of her immediate surroundings. Surrounded by candles, with the faint scent of a man looming in the air, she chanted strange Latin words, over and over, in an endless stream. When she finished, Anastasia surprised Tsarina by summoning her into the living room, and then she explained that her efforts were for all the family's benefit. With the casting of the spell, she would open a door to a safer place, a world far away from the dangers of the city, a place where they could be free and unafraid of their extraordinary powers.

Tsarina's dream melted from the heat of the prying eyes focused on her, and she inadvertently slammed the cover shut. "Yeah, this is it. It's ma's diary," she announced. "Thank you Mr. Marcel. This really means a lot. I think I'll finally be able to get some closure with this."

The old man gave the concerned look of a parent who knew he had just been deceived, but remained respectful of her privacy and made no mention of it. Tsarina internally appreciated his discretion, and she sincerely wanted to sit and reminisce. It pained her to leave so quickly, but the day was getting long, and the window for her to cast the portal spell was closing. Her mother had been very specific regarding the urgency of performing Istia's spell on the day of the Summer Solstice, and Tsarina was determined to perform the ritual perfectly, according to the instructions from her dream. She needed to leave no room for doubt in order to put an end to her torment, once and for all, crazy or magical. The spell's success or failure would serve as final proof of her sanity, and if nothing else, she knew it had to be cast before the day's end.

Tsarina tucked the book under her arm and said, "I don't wanna to be rude, but if you don't mind, I'd really like to go home and give it a read. I've been waiting to do this so long, you know."

"Sure thing little miss mini muffin, I understand. I'm just glad I could help you out with that. But you got to promise me, you won't be a stranger now, will ya?"

"I won't. I promise."

"Good. Well, I sure hope you find what you're looking for in that old book." He winked. "Come on then, let's get you home now."

Blushing, she gave Mr. Marcel a firm hug and pecked his cheek then glanced at Shelby and asked, "You ready?"

Shelby rushed to her side with an excited nod, and Mr. Marcel escorted them into the hallway, bidding farewell with a wave. Tsarina gave a halfhearted smile and vowed to send him a token of her appreciation after the tribulation was finished.

Out on the street, Tsarina secured the small black grimoire under her arm, while scouring the shadows of the buildings for signs of anyone following.

"So? My god! What does it say?" Shelby squawked, her eyes fixed on the grimoire.

"I couldn't read much. It's all Latin crap," she replied, bracing for the reaction.

"That's a freaking grimoire alright!" Shelby began bouncing as they walked. "I knew it! You see, your mother was a real witch! I always told you. I knew you were a sister of magic."

The glow on Shelby's face made Tsarina's stomach churn. "Calm down. People could still be following us," Tsarina reacted, stifling her own excitement and anxiety with a frown. Wading through the thinly scattered pedestrians bustling on the street, she wished her mother were alive to explain the significance of the book of spells, and its connection with the sunstone attached to her anklet. Thousands of questions flooded her mind. She wished she had allowed the man on the train a chance to explain. The spell, the grimoire, and the Eye of Istia were all a part of a grand puzzle she now had to piece together without any help and all before the day's end. It seemed an impossible task.

"What the hell?" Shelby yipped. "Aren't you just a little bit excited? This is the answer you've been looking for your whole life, and now you're acting like it ain't no big deal. That little grimoire validates all your prophetic dreams and everything you thought was you just being messed up in the head. It also means your mama wasn't just some crazy freak either. Anastasia was a bona fide witch, and you are too, whether you want to accept it or not."

"Stop saying that!" Tsarina snapped. Her words hit harder than intended. She watched Shelby's face slump into disappointment and instantly she felt the need to apologize. "Look it. I'm sorry. It's just—I just want to get home and process everything, okay? I am gonna try and make it work…for ma."

"And for yourself." Shelby shrugged. "It's ok. I get it. Your whole crazy world is about to get real. It's just going to take some time for you to accept the fact that your family is gifted and magical. But once you open this portal, you won't have any reason to deny it and neither will Tasha. Your sister has been trying to keep you from this truth your whole life, but that grimoire, right there, is pure, undeniable evidence. And I'm sorry, but Tasha is wrong, Tsarina. You have to face the facts: you come from a line of powerful witches." Shelby tapped the binding of the black book with her knuckles, curling her lips, accentuating her point. "And how about if this spell works? What are you going to say then?"

Tsarina scrunched her cheeks. "If this spell works, I'll make dinner for a week."

Shelby chuckled. "I'm not sure if chicken nuggets and warmed up pizza sauce in the microwave is a real prize, exactly, but I suppose I'll take it."

∞∞∞*Playing With The Boys*

The late afternoon sun hung high, lingering in the Summer Solstice, as Shelby drew the shades in the bay window of their apartment. Tsarina plopped down on the hard fuchsia couch at the rear of the living room and lit a circle of candles on the coffee table. She cracked the front cover of the grimoire, and as she peered inside the weathered pages of the black leather book, she felt Shelby's warm breath on the back of her neck. Her Wiccan roommate, dressed in a black lace shawl, sat peeking over her shoulder at the ancient text like an excited child on Christmas morning. She was thankful she had Shelby to help her with the details of casting the spell and wondered for a brief moment if fate had brought them together through some sort of magical synergy. She recalled the moment their eyes met in the new student orientation meeting, and how eager Shelby was to approach her.

"Well, what does it say?" Shelby interrogated.

"Dang girl, chill. I haven't even looked at the first page."

The grimoire looked much older than something her mother would have created, and she wondered about its origin. The edges were frayed, and the pages were yellowish-brown and brittle. A red signature on the last page read, *Istia*. Tsarina handled the grimoire with kid gloves, fearing the pages might disintegrate at the slightest touch. The first spell, *Somnium Ostium,* was inked in elegant black calligraphy, but the words were not in her mother's handwriting. Tsarina made an effort to recall the few Latin phrases she had learned as a child, but it only took a few scans for her to realize she was going to need a Latin translator to decipher the cryptic passages. She cursed herself for not having paid more attention to her mother's teachings and turned the page. The only truly decipherable information was a crude drawing of a horse-like figure inside a sea of stars etched on the second page. She recognized the symbol as a constellation. "I think this is Pegasus," she said.

"Pegasus? How do you figure?" Shelby questioned.

"It's a constellation," she explained, pondering its significance to the spell. "Ma was big into astrology."

"Does it mean anything to you?"

"Well, in astrology, Pegasus is a cluster of stars and planets, pretty close to us by galactic standards, actually. This drawing looks like a map. And you see these markings highlighted on his chest? They appear to designate a specific planet inside the system."

"You think that's where the portal opens up to?"

"That would make sense, but it doesn't help if I can't translate the words. Here—" She handed the grimoire to Shelby. "I need to grab my iPad."

When Tsarina returned from the bedroom, Shelby was turning the grimoire at different angles and holding it up to the light, as if trying to place the drawings in certain positions. "You got it figured out yet?" Tsarina teased.

"No, but these drawings are super cool. They're like *3D*, almost."

"Girl you're trippin'." Tsarina laughed and placed her tablet in her lap and crossed her legs, perching on the couch. "So what was that website you use to translate your spells?" she asked.

"Google. They got an online translator. It's pretty awesome, you just type the words in English, and it spits them out in Latin or vice versa." Shelby answered.

After a quick search, Tsarina found the translator and began entering the text from the first page. The translation brought her to a disturbing conclusion, and she questioned the accuracy of the *Google Translator*. "What? No way," she gasped. "This can't be right. And if it is, I don't know if I'm doing it tonight."

"What do you mean you don't know if you're doing it tonight? What does it say?" Shelby pried.

"There's no way my mother would expect me to do this. This is bullshit."

"What's bullshit? Do you have to burn somebody at the stake or something?"

Tsarina puffed, "No, nothing that extreme, exactly, but it seems like it says I have to *absorb* the *life essence* of a man before I start chanting."

"Life essence?" Shelby cocked her head to the side. "Like his—"

Tsarina's face grew red. "Yeah, that's what it sounds like."

"So…do we have to get you *fully* laid tonight, or can you just—"

"Whatever! All that is friggin' wack. I'm not having sex with some random dude for this crazy ass experiment. There's nobody I'd even think about doing it with anyway."

"Nobody?" Shelby questioned.

"No—body."

Shelby's lips pursed, and her head cocked toward the ceiling. "What about Avi? He'd probably get back with you for a night, if you worked it."

"Are you fucking kidding? It took me three months to get rid of that little bitch."

Shelby's brown eyes sparkled in the candlelight, and Tsarina felt their sting when they shot a look. "Ok then. What about a nice, nerdy, little ol' law student?"

"How about we forget all this shit and call it what it is—insanity. This shit is stupid."

"Stupid?" Shelby's brow furled. "Girl, I'll tell you what's stupid. What is stupid, is you not wanting to finish this. Are you really going to quit now, after all we went through today?"

"It's not gonna work. This is ridiculous—"

"Really? So you think that dude that spoke to you telepathically was just following us by coincidence?"

"He could have been a random stalker."

"That knew your name? And all that shit about the portal? Come on, honey. You're lying to yourself now. The question you gotta ask is, do you really want to spend the rest of your life wondering if your mother was a witch—if you're a witch? You already can't sleep because of all this, and you're always running around here, dodging every effort I make to include you in my magic because you're afraid somebody will think you're weird. This ain't ancient Salem. There ain't no witch-hunts going on. People just think magic is quaint bullshit nowadays."

"I know, but this spell is too much." Tsarina retreated.

"It ain't like you have to sell your soul to the devil or anything. All you have to do is spend one night with some nice gentleman caller of your choosing—and I hate to tell you honey, but you ain't no damn virgin. We'll even try and pick you out a cute one." Her eyes sparkled deviously. "Personally, I think it'd be a lot of fun."

"That's because you don't have to bang some random douchebag in the next 6 hours." Tsarina closed her eyes and took a deep breath. When she opened them, Shelby was giving a cold stare.

"Okay. Assuming I do this, and I'm not saying I'm going to, but if I do, how am I gonna lure my victim into the apartment and force him have sex with me? Any dude that would do that is going to be a complete jerk off. I mean, if we find a nice guy, what am I supposed to do, give him a roofie and straight up rape him?"

"Seriously?" Shelby asked incredulously.

"Yeah, seriously. A nice guy is not just going to walk in here and take his clothes off like some sex crazed Chippendale and start grinding all over me."

"Honey, what planet are you from? All you have to do is play the sweet little ol' damsel in distress—works for me every time here on Earth. You are a beautiful girl in the prime of her sexuality. Unless we screw up and pick some gay dude, all we have to do is come up with something our Mr. Right-Now has to help you with tonight—like doing your homework. Then, you play it as a dinner-slash-study date here in the apartment with some booze, of course." Her face flattened. "These are law school nerds, college dudes. I guarantee if you ask any one of them for sex, they will more than willingly abide."

Tsarina frowned. "Seriously, what if Mr. Right-Now doesn't want to do it? How are we going to force him on me before midnight?"

"Well, worst case, I guess we could hire somebody. I'm sure we could find a service—"

"Screw that!"

"I'm just playing," Shelby giggled impishly. "Come on, honey, you're a sexy coed with perfect boobs and a sweet little ass. What man in their right mind wouldn't want a good old roll in the hay with you?"

"I don't know."

"Exactly. You know as well as I do, that college boys, or any man for that matter, will screw anything with a pulse, especially if you get them drunk enough. Just in case, I can whip you up a love potion." Her eyes rolled to the ceiling. "I think I have all the ingredients, not sure about the rose hips though…" She tapped her fingers to her lips.

"Yeah, I guess. I just don't know if I can go through with it. I mean, I know I can flirt, but I don't know about having random sex."

"Girl, this ain't random. You need to get that nonsense right out of your head. You have to treat this like a biology experiment."

Tsarina chuckled. "Yeah, ok. But there aren't that many students on campus right now. How are we gonna find this dude?"

"Yeah, like I said, the only ones I know are here are getting ready for law school, which is fine. Law nerds are easy prey. They always come in early and stay through the summer—good, clean, disease-free students. You might even luck up and find you a little virgin. I wonder if they're more powerful?" she mused. "Well, we just have to find something they can help you out with." She put a finger to her lips. "All those biology words you deal with in pre-med are in Latin, right?"

"Yeah, a lot of the roots are derived from Latin."

"Well there you go. We just have to say you have some crappy old Latin text you need to translate for a stupid elective class, and then we get a nice boy to translate it for you in here with a bottle of wine and some shots of tequila. Presto, safe nerd sex."

"What makes you think he'll be able to translate Latin?"

"Hello." Shelby's head bobbed side to side. "*Caveat Emptor* and *E pluribus unum* and all that mess."

Tsarina laughed. "Girl, you are crazy." She allowed a sigh of relief, and the churning feeling in her stomach subsided for the moment.

"And honey, it ain't gonna be about the Latin once I get through making you up," Shelby boasted.

"Okay, screw it. What do I gotta wear for this disaster?"

"Now you're talking!" Shelby leapt from the couch and grabbed Tsarina by the hand. "This is gonna be fun."

Thirty minutes later, Tsarina tugged at the V-neck of her yellow sundress, standing behind Shelby in the foyer outside the law school library. Adjusting it low around the center of her bosom to promote her curves, she prodded Shelby for a compliment. "Look good?"

"Oh yeah, honey. You are absolutely going to destroy those little law school nerds looking like that. Now, what about me?"

"Of course, your butt always looks tight in those jeans."

"Wrong answer. I'm supposed to look plain and frumpy."

"It's kind of hard for you to look plain and frumpy," Tsarina complemented.

"Well thank you, sweetheart, but remember, this is not about me. This is all about you."

Tsarina nodded with a half-smile and watched Shelby's thin hips swaying left to right, as her friend sashayed into the first floor study room. She followed with a confident, flirtatious smile and arched her back, surveying the small groups of students huddled around their massive texts at the mahogany tables. One group, wearing wrinkled oxford button down shirts and tan slacks, stood out; their eyes were darting around the room with only occasional glances toward their books. Shelby must've noticed them as well, Tsarina thought, because her friend gravitated to them with a mischievous smile. When Shelby approached the table, the skittish boys buried their heads in their textbooks.

"Hey guys," Shelby whispered. Her sultry southern drawl melted their jaws, and they looked up at her simultaneously like a high school chorus line. Tsarina locked eyes with the shortest of them sitting in the middle. The stout, curly-haired student nudged the bridge of his glasses toward his overgrown eyebrows, and they immediately slid back down.

"I wonder if one of ya'll could help us out with something?" Shelby asked.

"I certainly hope so," the tallest boy answered and closed his book without marking the page. His chubby-faced buddies swapped amused glances, seemingly amazed he had mustered the courage to speak, much less make a statement so arrogant.

"Great! So, can one of ya'll translate something from Latin to English for us? You see, we got this little Latin project here, and we just need a couple of pages translated. I'm sure it wouldn't take too long for such fine scholars as yourselves." Shelby's smile beamed with the warmth of the midday sun.

"Latin? Who reads Latin?" the lead boy asked.

Immediately, his walrus-shaped friend gave a swift elbow to the ribs and blurted, "Probably a real law student, dumbass."

The tall boy shot a look of frustration at his peer and blurted, "I told you this shit wouldn't work, dude."

"So, let me guess," Tsarina asked, "you guys are undergrad, and here to pick up on law school chicks, right?"

The boys looked incredulously at one another, then back at her.

"Awesome. Screw this!" she hissed, then whipped around and marched toward the spiral staircase on the other side of the room.

Shelby stopped her in the middle of the chamber, sliding her hand around Tsarina's shoulder. "What the hell are you doing? Those guys would have jumped your bones for a wooden nickel."

"And they probably all had gonorrhea. Those dudes were friggin' creeps," she huffed. "I don't know if I can do this."

"Okay, I understand your concern here, but in order for this to work, we have to stick to the plan. There has to be a nice boy in this library, somewhere. We don't have time to be all that picky, so let's just keep on looking, okay?" Shelby rubbed Tsarina's shoulder and gave it a little pinch. "You might have to lower your standards a bit, Miss High and Mighty—just for tonight. Okay?"

"Right. Yeah, okay."

"Now let's get out of this room. It's probably safe to say we've drawn a tiny bit of unwanted attention in here."

Tsarina lifted her head and scanned the faces of the students in the room, which all seemed to be focused on her. She desperately wanted to sprint to her dorm room and stay hidden for the rest of the year. Instead, she straightened her dress and looked to Shelby for their next move.

"Don't worry honey," Shelby whispered, "I know where the good boys are. Let's go upstairs."

"How do you know all this?" Tsarina asked. "Never mind, I don't really want to know."

Rounding the top step of the spiral staircase, she followed Shelby into the alcove where students were entrenched in their books and had intense focus dripping from their brows. Tsarina scanned the stuffy room, searching for a gentle, trustworthy face, and inside the vacuum of silence, a set of hazel eyes resting over a five o'clock shadow lifted, focusing into her gaze, pinning her hand to the top rail. As the tan boy peeked over the top of his thick book, she struggled to regain her balance, poise fluttering away. Upon second glance, she recognized him from his dark ponytail. "Hey, isn't that the kinda shy dude from across the hall?" she asked in a low whisper. "You talk to him, right? What's his name?" Tsarina asked.

"Oh yeah, that's Bud. He's actually pretty cool." She grinned. "Is he the one?"

Tsarina felt her cheeks warming.

"Nice. I invited him over a couple of times last year when you were out clubbing with Avi, but—" Shelby waved to him with hushed excitement and smiled. Bud returned the gesture nonchalantly and gave a faint smile. "And I don't think he's really that shy. You just never talk to anyone outside of your little NYC club kid circle."

"I talk to people," Tsarina protested. "I just didn't know he was a law student."

"Me neither," Shelby grinned sheepishly, "I just thought he was a cute Carolina boy when I first met him."

Tsarina had seen him coming and going in the halls, but he was usually wearing baggy basketball shorts and some sort of a concert t-shirt, not exactly her cup of tea. His shoulder length ponytail, juxtaposed with his athletic attire and frame, had always confused her, so she hadn't paid him much attention. He didn't seem to conform to any set of standard social patterns, and now, to see him sitting in the Law School Library, grinding over a huge textbook, the guy was a complete enigma.

"Wait, I thought you said you knew him."

"We've talked a couple of times—shootin' the shit about nothing, but that's about it. I didn't get a real charged vibe from him, so I didn't pursue it. I don't think he's weird or gay or anything. I just assumed he wasn't into blondes. I do know he's from Asheville, and he loves Tarheel basketball. He's always giving me a bunch of mess when Tech plays them. He seems pretty smart too, but not like, socially awkward, you know, he's cool."

"Do you think he can translate Latin?" Tsarina wondered aloud, glancing toward the floor after she spoke, sure that her swooning eyes had given her away.

"Uh oh. I know that look, honey. I think somebody's in trouble," Shelby teased.

"Me or him?" Tsarina countered with a mischievous smile, tossing her head to the side to dissuade any further teasing.

When her eyes made contact with Bud's, his unabashed stare weakened her knees, and she reminded herself she was in control. Drifting toward him, she felt his iron gaze pulling her across the room like a tractor beam, and her feet felt as if they were treading over a bed of fluffy clouds. As she approached the table, his hazel eyes widened, as if to inquire her intentions telepathically, but unlike the man in the subway, she heard nothing. Bud sat his book down, marking the page with a red tassel, and maintained eye contact. Tsarina suddenly found it hard to breathe, and when she opened her mouth to speak, a frantic vision of the two of them racing through a colorful forest hijacked her train of thought.

Shelby broke the awkward moment by stepping in front of Tsarina and asking, "Hey, Bud, what're you doing up here?"

"Hey…Shelby, nothing too exciting. I'm just reading over this civil procedure mess. What're ya'll doing up here? This ain't exactly party central." His gentle drawl pried with an uneasy jocularity.

"Oh, well…we were just…you know, checking the place out for information."

"It is a library." He lifted an eyebrow.

"Yeah, you know, Latin…stuff." Shelby's chest collapsed. "Okay, you got us. Actually, Tsarina needs some help translating her Latin homework, and well, she can't exactly read Latin so great. Basically, it's going to take her forever if she has to translate it all by herself, and it's due on Monday, and we ain't got time for all that."

"Ah, I see. And so, I'm guessing this is Tsarina with the Latin problem?"

Tsarina stiffened at the mention of her name.

"Nice to meet you." Bud stood and extended his hand.

Shelby giggled and leaned into Tsarina's shoulder with a playful bump and blurted, "Oh, heck, look at me. I am so sorry ya'll. Yes, this is my wonderful roommate, Tsarina. I thought ya'll might have met already."

The blood in Tsarina's palm turned from ice to fire when his hand touched hers.

"No. Never officially had the pleasure," he confessed.

Tsarina inhaled tiny bits of oxygen through her nose and produced a cordial smile, staring deeper into his eyes. She almost forgot to let go his hand when he pulled away.

"So, you need some dead old language translated, do you? And you figured all these law school nerds were easy prey?" he razzed with a wink.

Well..." Shelby started.

Tsarina nodded demurely, and her cheeks flushed as she struggled to find a response.

Bud released her from her guilt with a funny, warped face. "Well, I suppose I can help you out with that. I was just about to pack up and get out of here anyway. How long is it, and when do you want to do it?"

Tsarina hoped her voice would be audible when she muttered, "I think the first part is about two pages—"

Shelby finished, "And she needs it done tonight, because she has to join me upstate for a festival tomorrow."

"Okay. Well, I have to drop off an outline for this girl in my study group, and I'd really like to shower first, if that's cool?"

"Sure. Of course." Tsarina nodded with a smile.

"Cool. How about I meet you back up in the dorms in like an hour an a half?"

"Yeah, great. Just come across the hall to our place," Tsarina replied.

"Oh crap, I'll be heading out by then," Shelby complained facetiously, then strutted away, concealing a smirk. Bud chuckled, seemingly oblivious to their ploy, and began stuffing his book along with several loose papers into an old Army backpack.

"Hey, thanks. You want me to order some food or something?" Tsarina offered, "It's the least I can do."

"Sure, sounds good."

"Thai okay?"

"Perfect. I'll bring the wine."

"Oh...sweet."

∞∞∞Budding Relations

Three hips of precious pink rose
Under the summer sun it grows
Three wooden spoons of honey gold
Awaken thy power of old
Three wooden spoons of fruity wine
Golden time will make you mine
So shall it be, 'til I set you free
So shall it be, 'til I set you free

Tsarina sat cross-legged on the couch chanting and stirring the ingredients of Shelby's attraction spell. The rose hips floated to the top, bubbling inside a small silver pot situated over a blue flame. Shelby gripped her hand, squeezing tighter with each phrase. When Tsarina finished the chant, she opened her eyes and asked, "Is that it?"

"Almost." Shelby's eyes popped open. "Now you must choose a word to activate the spell. When Bud takes a sip you have to look into his eyes and speak the word. Pick the word and say it three times into the pot."

Tsarina thought for a moment for a word that would be appropriate in the moment and decided on *Nostrovia*. "*Nostrovia, Nostrovia, Nostrovia,*" she pronounced into the bubbling liquid.

"Good. You have completed the spell and imbued the potion with your will and the essence of your being. Now, transfer the Lover's Mark into the vial," Shelby instructed, holding up a hand-blown glass vial with blue and orange colored tendrils wrapping from the bottom to the top. Removing the cork, she positioned the vial in front of her chest and placed a small funnel into the top. As Tsarina poured the liquid into the container, Shelby said, "Now all you have to do is slip a couple of drops of the Lover's Mark into his drink, say the word, and he'll be all yours." She pressed the cork into the top of the vial and handed it to Tsarina.

"And you really think this is gonna work?" Tsarina asked.

"Billy Roberts?" Shelby reminded.

Billy Roberts had inexplicably fallen in love with one of their friends, after Shelby had given him the Lover's Mark.

"I think he liked her anyway," Tsarina contended.

"Are they together or not?"

"Okay, whatever. You're right."

"You must believe, sister. After tonight, you will know your power."

Tsarina wasn't convinced her roommate's logic was solid, but either way, she would finally be able to put an end, or a beginning, to her days of being a witch. The outcome of the spell was going to be a life-changing event either way. "Yeah, if the spell works," she said.

"It will, if you believe."

"I wish you could be here with me."

"You know I'd love to be here, but this is something you have to do own your own. Besides, I'm not really into threesomes all that much," she teased. "I mean, you're cute and all but—" The sound of Bud's door slamming shut across the hall halted her jesting. "Damn girl, he's ready to go. Put on some music." Shelby sprang from the couch, clearing her red-laced book of spells from the table.

With her heart fluttering, Tsarina scurried across the room and selected her ambient playlist. She lowered the volume then shuffled over to the front door. As she passed Shelby, she felt a tap her on the shoulder.

"Remember, only a couple of drops of this stuff, or else he'll be asking to be your eternal slave. And make sure he's looking at you when he drinks it and you're saying the word," Shelby reminded.

"Yeah, I got it." Tsarina nodded.

"Good luck, sister," her roommate beamed then disappeared through the hemp-woven bead curtain into their bedroom.

Seconds later, at exactly seven forty-five, Bud rapped on the metal door. Tsarina pressed her eye to the peephole, quietly observing him for a moment. He was holding a large Latin dictionary and a bottle of wine in his hands, as he banged the chrome knocker against the door again. The discordant sound resonated through the metal frame into Tsarina's nose, causing her to recoil. Gathering herself, she pressed her eye against the peephole again and watched him fidget with his starched sleeve. Bud's black hair, slicked into a tidy ponytail, and his well-pressed white oxford shirt checked with light blue stripes were a promising sign of his interest in her. She smiled impishly at his attempt to make a good impression and felt a tinge of excitement flash inside her chest when she opened the door.

"Hi." She smiled. "*Entrée.*"

A balmy draft blew in from the hall, ruffling the bottom of her Indonesian wrap pants, disturbing her thoughts. Vibrant shades of red, green, and white blossomed out of her black skirt, and the matching top hung softly around her shoulders. She felt loose and natural in the garb, hoping it would help settle her body into the role of seductress. When his gaze shifted to her thigh, she grinned at the subtle victory.

"Thanks," he replied, sliding the bottle of wine from under his arm. "Here, I thought this would go well with the Thai. It's a rosé. They're supposed to be the best fit for Thai. Really, I read it's beer, but I thought that might be a little inappropriate."

"What? You think I don't drink beer?" she teased, her Bronx accent in full throat.

When he fell mute, she felt empowered for the first time and quickly snatched the bottle, pointing her back firmly in his direction as she led him into the living room.

"No, I…" he stammered, following like a puppy.

"Come on…I'm just foolin'. This is perfect. Trust me, I love wine. It's one of my favorite buzzes. This one looks pretty sweet. I like the label with the little spaceship throwing down that tractor beam. Aliens are cool."

"Right. Well yeah, this is supposed to be a really good one, Bonny Doon. I don't normally drink rosé, but I do like a good wine buzz myself."

"Our first thing in common." She smiled and pointed toward the wooden bar stools under the pass through window that separated the kitchen from the living room. "Have a seat." *What a little charmer. This might not be so terrible,* she thought. Her confidence swelled as she walked the bottle into the kitchen.

"So what's up with this Latin homework?" he asked, taking a seat.

"It's on the table over there, but we don't have to hit that right now—not unless you've got a hot date lined up or something."

"Actually, I do," he replied.

The statement stung her chest like a swarm of bees. "Oh…really?"

"Yeah, I just met this beautiful girl, and apparently she needs my help translating some boring old Latin text or something. I've already told her yes, so—"

"Oh, and so you consider that a date?"

"Literally, I would say yes—and I believe figuratively as well—but I guess we'll have to wait and see. Oh, and she asked me, by the way," he reminded.

"Sounds like a clever girl. But, what if she's just using you for your mind?"

Before Bud could answer, the clattering sound of beads slamming against the bedroom doorframe blasted her jesting out of the air, and Shelby shot into the living room. "What's up, ya'll," she sang, as she fought an insubordinate strap and a pentagram necklace around her neck that seemed to be choking her. She looked like a sinister, elegant version of Little Red Riding Hood: dark mascara, black fingernails, black and red cape, short, flowing black skirt, and a fire-engine, red backpack, also bearing the mark of a black pentagram. "All right, I got time for one shot of tequila!

Break out the Cuervo, girl."

Tsarina giggled as she watched Bud's eyes grow wide.

In a flash, Shelby tossed her backpack on the floor and grabbed three shot glasses from the overhead cabinet, slamming them onto the counter. Tsarina unscrewed the bottle of Cuervo and sloshed the gold liquid into the glasses.

"No time for limes," Shelby chirped, raising her shot in the air. "Cheers! Here's to new beginnings and to new worlds unknown." She winked at Tsarina.

Bud gave a quizzical look, and after they all clinked glasses, Shelby tossed back her shot and slammed the glass down on the counter. "Ok, you know I'd love to stay and chat with ya'll, but I have a somewhat fine boy downstairs, waiting for me to do devilish things to him."

"Whatever." Tsarina rolled her eyes. "Just be safe out there in the woods with that dude. There's all kinds of weird shit can happen in the wilderness. People get crazy out there."

"He's cool," Shelby replied, waving her free hand as if to dispel the negative thought. "Besides, there's going to be plenty of decent people around, *mom*. Okay, I'm out!" Then, like a black and red tornado, she blew out the front door, leaving a trail of hot, perfumed air in her wake.

Bud flashed the two finger peace sign at the closing fuchsia door and asked, "Where's she going again with that tiny backpack?"

"A park near Saratoga."

When the door slammed shut, Tsarina's heart fluttered. The vacuum of the silence suffocated her slightly, and she turned her gaze into his eyes. The ambient music in the background sounded as if it was coming from another room, and then she noticed the clock, which read 8:15. Breaking from the trance, she said, "We should probably eat this food before it gets too cold," then she turned and dug into the large white plastic bag with the Pad Thai.

"You need any help?" Bud offered.

"Sure. If you take the food to the table, I'll bring the wine."

"Yes ma'am." He grinned, and awkwardly grabbed his

book along with the bags of food, transporting everything to the coffee table.

Tsarina slinked behind the kitchen counter and slipped a few drops of Lover's Mark into Bud's glass when his back was turned. *I've only got a couple of hours to get him in bed, this better work.* The thought pressed her forward as she sat the vial on the counter. Rushing to the couch, she sat next to him, absorbing warmth of his smile, unable to control her own. As she placed their glasses on the table, she gently pressed her knee into his, probing for a reaction, and he fidgeted like a spooked kitten. When she popped the cork, she watched his hazel eyes sparkle in the candlelight.

Breaking from his gaze, she glanced down at his thick Latin dictionary, and instantly, a vision of a classroom filled with high school boys dressed in khaki pants, button down shirts, and wrinkled ties materialized in her mind. A portly woman with curly white hair had her back to the students, and she was pointing to a chalk drawing of the structure of the DNA double helix. Several boys were whispering in the background, and when she turned to chastise them, a gold cross around her neck flashed on her white blouse.

"Let me guess, Catholic prep school?" Tsarina asked, attempting to verify her vision, as she placed the cheap wooden chopsticks in front of Bud.

His eyebrows dipped. "Wow, that's amazingly perceptive. How'd you—"

"Oh, I had a vision—I mean, it just seemed logical. You know, Latin books, preppy clothes." Fearing she had exposed her freakish ability, Tsarina quickly changed her train of thought. "Oh! It's pink," she blurted, hurriedly pouring wine into the glasses.

"What?"

"The wine—it's pink. I just didn't expect it to be so pretty in the glass," she said. "So where was this high school?"

Bud looked confused by all the jumping from one subject to another then answered, "Asheville, St. Stephen's. All boys prep. Technically, we were nondenominational, but we still had brothers, and mass, and all that jazz—if you wanted to participate, you could." He gave a devilish grin and raised his glass. "I just went for the fake wine. Cheers."

"*Nostrovia.*" She replied with a smile and stared deep into his eyes.

"*Nostrovia?*" He squinted.

"It's Russian for cheers," she informed.

"Oh. Cool. Then by all means, *Nostrovia,*" he echoed.

They shared the required moment of staring into each other's eyes and sniffed the wine, before taking the first sip. Tsarina felt confident she had collected his gaze long enough for the word and the tincture to take effect. Bud peered over the stained rim of his glass, and his eyes tangled her thoughts. Clawing free, she continued, "Those gendered schools always sound so stuffy. I mean, you didn't have *any* girls on campus?"

"Not a one. Well, that's not entirely true. We had three women on campus—the principal's secretary, the librarian, and Mrs. Gilbert, but that was it. Mrs. Gilbert was the only one we ever saw on a daily basis, though. And of course, she taught biology of all subjects. You can probably imagine how the Sex Ed classes went—that was a total free-for-all."

"I can imagine," she giggled.

"And she wasn't a looker by any stretch of the imagination—about sixty, big fluffy white hair—she looked like a gnome that ate a half-deflated beach ball."

Tsarina choked a laugh, almost spitting wine all over him, and he rocked back in his seat.

"The only times we ever had girls our age on campus were at pep rallies or dances. Friday was the big day, the girls from all our sister schools would come onto campus for the pep rallies. We had about a half hour to hit on them and get them out for the parties. Needless to say, it was pandemonium."

"No doubt. I bet you went wild when you hit college?" she pried, digging for a little insight into his moral code. Part of her hoped he would say no, but she knew it would be better for her immediate situation, if the answer was yes. She grimaced as she poured the yellow coconut curry soup over their mounds of brown rice, awaiting his response.

"Naw, not really. College was a lot easier than high school, believe it or not. Undergrad studies were pretty much a cakewalk after that hell, but this law school curriculum—things are a little more like high school. I think I'm going to have to actually start studying again," he stated.

"I wasn't talking about the academics. I was talking about girls."

"I know," he replied with a furtive grin.

"Ok. So, how many years you got in law school?" she asked, appreciating his diplomacy.

"None. I haven't started yet. I'm just taking a prep course this summer to try and get a head start. I start my first full semester of law school in the fall."

"No offense, but you don't really look like a law student," she mentioned, picking up a pair of chopsticks and jamming them into his mound of brown rice.

"Oh, really? And what's a law student supposed to look like? Clean shaven, short hair, glasses, maybe a bow-tie?"

"Yeah, something like that, I guess," she said.

"Thanks. Well, you're right on a certain level. I'm definitely not your stereotypical law student, if that's what you're getting at."

"No, I didn't mean to—"

"It's alright. This whole long hair thing wasn't a big deal when I was an undergrad. People just thought I was some weird philosophy major with an affinity for Jack Daniels, but now that I'm in *law school*, everybody seems to have the same reaction when I tell them I'm a law student." He plucked his chopsticks from the mound and waved them around like magic wands, as if they would dispel his disdain for other peoples' convoluted opinions.

Tsarina grabbed her chopsticks and retreated. "I guess…it's just…well, how are you supposed to get a job with a law firm looking like that? Are you going to work for Greenpeace or something?"

"Hardly," he chuckled. "I plan on taking what I learn and applying it to my own business ventures or possibly my own practice—maybe even politics—but I'm not worried about any of that right now. I still have to graduate first, and if you haven't noticed, Fordham ain't no joke."

"I feel you on that." Tsarina struggled to accept the fact that this easygoing enigma was interested in any type of law. *He'd probably end up being a personal lawyer to someone like Hunter S. Thompson*, she chuckled to herself. "So what kind of law do you want to practice—if you do?"

"Entertainment law, specifically within the music industry, and it's cool, because I already have a leg up when I get out. I got a couple of hook-ups back home who would take care of me if I want to get started down that road. It's like anything else—it's not what you know, it's *who* you know, so all I have to do is graduate."

"Sounds like you have a solid plan at least," she said, handing a ceramic soup bowl to him, noticing it was 8:45. "Here, let's eat before it gets too cold."

"*Nostrovia*," he said, as he plunged his spoon into the soup.

"*Nostrovia*," she echoed, studying his reaction to the dish, sipping on her spoon.

"Wow, that's good."

"Yeah. It's my favorite." She licked her lips and gave a seductive look.

Bud fell silent and began eating the soup a bit faster. Between bites he asked, "So what about you? What are your plans after college?"

The inquiry shocked her into a somewhat coherent state, and she answered like an automaton, "I'm focusing on microbiology because I think I want be a doctor. But who the hell knows what they want to do at our age? I'll probably end up as a Tarot card reader, or a witch, or something totally insane."

"A doctor?" His head cocked backward. "You really want to have to deal with a bunch of sick people? All that blood and gore?" He shuddered.

"Yeah. I like helping people, and I don't mind all that blood and gore. I find it kind of interesting, actually."

"To each her own, I guess. I sure as hell couldn't do it. The sight of blood and innards and dying people makes me ill to the stomach. I don't even like watching those doctor shows on TV."

"Oh, really? I love those shows. And the documentaries—where they go in and film the operation—that's what I'd really like to do, be in the ER."

"The ER? Wow, that's hardcore—more power to you. You've got a stronger stomach than me."

"For some things, maybe." She blushed. "But if you put me in a courtroom full of people, you wanna talk about sick?"

"Yeah, see, I would have no problem with that."

"Perfect. You can do all the talking when we go out."

"Solid plan." He grinned and cheers her glass.

Tsarina surprised herself with the insinuation of another date. She certainly didn't want to scare him off with any plans for the future and refocused on the mission at hand—get him into bed, soon. "Well, I hope you don't need a strong stomach for the rest of this food," she said, touching his wrist playfully then began sorting the last of the Thai food onto their plates.

"Are you kidding? This is awesome. Where'd you get it?"

"A little place called *Thai Market,* up on 107th and Amsterdam, but you got to know somebody for them to bring it all the way down here."

"Oh yeah, and how'd you swing that?"

"I know somebody." She smirked.

Bud laughed and then prodded the remaining noodles with his disposable wooden chopsticks. "So does Shelby really think she's a witch, or does she just enjoy freaking people out?"

"Well, you know, she's really into all that Wiccan stuff, and of course, this guy, Wesley, thinks he's Harry Potter or something. He's taking her to the Summer Solstice festival upstate for a couple of days."

"Summer Solstice?" Bud stammered, clearly baffled by the reference.

"Yeah, today is the Summer Solstice."

Bud gave a blank stare.

"Ha." Tsarina laughed. "Ok, it's the longest day of the year. Supposedly, for witches, it's the day when new life springs forth, and the earth harnesses the power from the sun," she proclaimed, repeating Shelby's words verbatim—a script she had heard every morning for the past two weeks. "Sun worshippers, like Shelby, believe they can charge up their energy on this day, more than any other, because they absorb the sun's energy all day. It's like the extra time in the sun gives them more strength to cast spells."

Bud smiled. "And run around naked in the woods and get all freaky with each other."

Tsarina giggled and raised her glass over her forehead then continued like a Shakespearian thespian, speaking in regal tones. "Quite. Basically, if thou wants to cast wicked spells and turn frogs into princes and suck on their slimy tongues, today is quite a most excellent day." Returning to her normal Bronx rasp, she continued, "But seriously, they do all these wild rituals and dance around bonfires and chant incantations. It's a big friggin' deal. There's literally hundreds of people from what Shelby's says."

"Sounds…interesting," he concluded.

"I just hope this dude ain't no crazy, friggin' mass-murdering creeper, you know?"

"She seems like she can take care of herself," he assuaged. "You're supposed to meet her up there tomorrow? Are you taking your boyfriend?"

"What boyfriend?"

"You know, that short, frumpy dude with the black cloak I always used to see you with. What's his name?"

"Avi? No way, he's a waste of friggin' life. We broke up last semester. He was just one of those stupid high school carry-overs."

Bud's unexpected line of questioning thrilled her, and she sipped her wine, struggling to hide the glow flushing her cheeks.

He had obviously been paying attention to her from afar, which meant he was interested, and had been for some time. "What about you? You got a girlfriend?" she pressed.

"Naw, I gave up the girls for law school. They're really bad for focus, if you haven't heard. You know, I've been thinking about trying the whole monk lifestyle thing. Buddhism's pretty hip, from what I hear."

Tsarina assumed he was teasing, but with his flat tone, it was hard to tell. She concealed her anxiety with a titter and took another sip of wine.

"So, what kind of magic does she do?" he asked.

"Who?"

"Shelby?"

"Oh. Well, I guess she regards herself as spiritual with her usage of the arcane arts. She claims she can affect the outcome of things like relationships or whatever. You know, she makes potions and chants spells and all that junk."

Tsarina then recalled an image of her roommate. Shelby was staring into a candle, and it was four in the morning. She was trying to sear evil spirits out of her mind by staring into the fire and chanting.

Be gone words of ill fate.
Leave thy mind and clean the slate.
Winds take the ills of remorse
Still thy mind and alter thy course

The *evil spirits* were the result of a botched English test, Shelby had explained, and her aunt had suggested that she try a spell to clear her thoughts. Tsarina recalled her friend's brown eyes, staring intently into the flame, while she chanted the extraction spell, over and over. Shelby was waving her hands in the air, and the evil spirits were supposed to evaporate with the process.

Tsarina chuckled at the memory and shook her head as she elaborated for Bud. "You should've seen her with all those candles and incense and crystals—dancing around like a lost bird." She fluttered her hands mockingly to illustrate her point, eliciting his laughter, prompting her to continue. "You know, it's all a trip until I'm ready to go to sleep, and then it's like, enough with the friggin' chanting already."

A tinge of guilt pricked her skin for poking fun at her best friend, but it truly was a hilarious image. She chuckled one last time then washed the guilt down with another swill of wine, her head buzzing with anxiety, as she checked the clock again. 9:45pm.

Bud echoed her laughter. "Yeah, I had a roommate freshman year who was a magician, but he was a *real* magician—card tricks and sawing girls in half and all that. Jerry Staples—that dude was a trip.''

"Jerry Staples? That name sounds familiar."

"Probably, he's got a pretty good act here in the city. I think he travels places too—AC, Vegas, Reno. You know, he did a show in the cafeteria a couple of years ago. You might have seen him then."

"I don't think so, I don't hang out in the caff too much."

Taking notice of Bud's empty glass, wavering in his hand, she grabbed it and placed it on the table alongside hers. Careful not to tip it over, she emptied the bottle, filling their respective glasses as evenly as possible and felt the intoxication swelling inside of her, freeing of her inhibitions. She hoped he was feeling the same.

"That dude could pull off some crazy tricks," Bud continued, accepting the glass as she handed it back to him. "This guy would have you pick a card out of the deck, and then he'd tell you to go to the bathroom—which was upstairs mind you—then low and behold, your card would be sitting there, floating in the toilet, staring up at you like Moby Dick. Now that's some real magic."

"Really, how'd he do it?" she asked.

"Hell, if I knew that, I wouldn't be in school sifting through acts and propositions. I'd be out on the road freaking people out," he joked, then swallowed a mouthful of wine. "So, does it ever work?"

"What?"

"Shelby's magic?"

"Well...I can't say for sure." She stalled, sifting through her muddled memories of Shelby's antics, angling to find proof of her friend's arcane abilities. She needed a plausible anecdote to protect Shelby from complete humiliation and decided on the Dicky Roberts episode.

"I guess, there was this one time—Dicky Roberts, one of Shelby's study partners, hooked up with this girl Danielle after Shelby gave him a *love* potion to slip into her drink."

"I think those are called roofies," Bud quipped.

"Probably." She stifled a giggle.

"What about you?" he asked. "From what Shelby tells me, you're like Nostradamus or something. I remember she once told me you predicted a bus flipping over?"

Tsarina bowed her head humbly, acknowledging the accusation. She was wary of anyone's perception of her after they were made aware of her gift. *Freak,* was the most popular reaction.

"So, she wasn't just making all that stuff up?" Bud asked.

Tsarina shrugged, debating whether to disclose her dark secret. She didn't want to spook him with insane tales of prognosticative dreams and portals to other worlds, but something in her heart told her to continue, and she admitted, "No, it actually happened."

His silence and pressing eyes begged her to continue.

"Ok, I had this dream where I was following her. She was going to this job interview at that restaurant across the street from the Met, and it was one of those frustrating dreams where I couldn't catch up to her no matter how fast I walked, and then bam! Out of nowhere, I see this bus hit a curb and fly up into a newsstand. It flipped right over in front of her, and then I woke up before I could tell if she had been hit or not. Of course, when I told her about it, she freaked out, as you can imagine. She's obviously always been receptive to my gift, or whatever you want to call it, and so anyway, she didn't go to the interview. Then later that day a friggin' bus flipped over out in front of that restaurant." Tsarina swallowed the lump that had formed in her throat with a swill of wine.

"That's pretty awesome." Bud affirmed.

"It weirds me out sometimes, but it's been happening to me since I was a kid, so I'm kinda used to it, I guess. I like to think of it as reverse déjà vu. That's what it feels like anyway, and actually…" She paused and took another sip of courage before confessing, "they've been getting weirder lately."

"What do you mean?"

The effects of the wine coursed from her heart to her head like a hot geyser. She wanted to properly manage her emotions, and exactly what she would allow him to know, but with every glance into his eyes, her guard fell, and she started to believe his interest might be the key to his cooperation. "Are you sure you really want to hear this stuff? I mean, it all sounds crazy to me."

"Yeah, no, it's interesting actually."

"Okay, I think I'm going to need another shot of tequila. You down?"

"Sure."

"Careful what you wish for," she advised as she looked at the clock and walked over to the kitchen bar window to grab the bottle of Cuervo. 10:15 pm.

"Normally my dreams are about everyday stuff like the thing with Shelby's job interview or whatever, and I usually know whether it's going to be real or not as soon as I wake up, but recently, I've been having these weird dreams that don't come true—but they seem real, like the ones that do come true, but these ones don't. Does that make sense? Shit, I sound crazy already."

"I think I get it," he said.

She settled on the couch and handed Bud a shot glass then poured two shots and toasted him. "Here's to you not thinking I'm super weird after this."

"*Nostrovia*," he offered.

"*Nostrovia*," she replied.

They clinked glasses, and as the warm tequila hit the back of her throat, a spark of brash courage shot through her. "Okay, so the dream last night was abnormally weird, and super real."

Bud seemed unfazed, so she continued, pouring the last bit of wine. "Anyway, I'm sitting with Ma in the kitchen of our old apartment, having a bowl of cereal, and she leans over and whispers to me to find this black book." She picked up her mother's grimoire from beside the couch and handed it to him for inspection. "Ma described it exactly: gold stars, black leather bound, gold lock, but she never mentioned exactly where it was hidden, like I was just supposed to know or something. Then ma said, *Find the grimoire and chant the 'Dream Door' with the power of the Eye to open the portal*—freaky shit, right?"

Bud nodded and grabbed his glass of wine from the table.

"She also said it had to be done on the day of the Summer Solstice and nothing else mattered," Tsarina explained. "And today is almost over."

After taking a sip, Bud asked, "So, what did she mean by the eye?"

"It's my mother's sunstone. This—" She lifted the bottom of her pant leg to reveal the anklet. Flecks of gold sparkled from the dancing candlelight inside the reddish orange gemstone, seemingly giving the artifact a heartbeat of its own. *I'm friggin' drunk*, she thought as she allowed the edge of her pant leg to fall over her feet; then she stabbed Bud with her eyes. "Ma strapped me with it when I was little. She called it the Eye of Istia. It's supposed to be a magical pendant from ancient Siberia, imbued with the powers of these ancient shamans."

"Shamans? I thought Shamans were Indians, not Russians."

"Indians have Shamans too, but the first shamans were from Siberia. They lived on this island called Olkhon, in the middle of Lake Baikal."

"Damn. History lesson." He smiled. "That's pretty interesting, but so, you're saying she told you all this in a dream?"

Tsarina worried she was losing him by the look on his face, and she slowed her speech. "No, she told me all that stuff about the shamans when I was a kid, but in the dream, she explained the spell and the grimoire. The dream part was messed up because my mother has been dead for over thirteen years, but in my dream, ma looked like she had aged—like what I think she would look like today, if she were still alive, you know? But how could I know that? You think I'd remember her like the last time I saw her, or what I remember from pictures. The lines on her face—it was really disturbing."

Bud's mouth straightened, and his voice quivered a bit. "I'm sorry—"

"No, it's okay. I mean, not really, it pretty much sucks losing your mother, but my big sis is still around, and she's always watching out for me." Tsarina gave a half-hearted smile and took her last swill of wine.

"You mind if I open another bottle?" she asked.

"Not at all."

"Cool." As she rose from the couch and made her way into the kitchen, she chided herself for destroying the sexual vibe she had created earlier and unbuttoned another button on her blouse.

"So, I'm guessing you want me to translate this spell then?" Bud asked.

"Actually, I already kinda did," she admitted, grabbing the bottle of Merlot from the counter.

"If you've already translated the spell, then what do you need me for?" His eyes studied her intently, as she walked into the living room. Remaining silent, she blinked, unsure how to respond until he offered, "Look, if you need some virgin's blood or bats wings, I don't roll with that kind of stuff."

A faint giggle escaped from her lips. "No, it's nothing like that…exactly," she said, sitting down close to him, uncorking the bottle of wine. "But yeah, I got to do some crazy stuff tonight—I'm sorry." She steadied her nerves for rejection, as her trembling hand poured the wine into their glasses. Her blood felt like concrete, drying in her veins.

"So what is it you need me to do?" he asked.

She licked her lips nervously and picked up her glass. "You see—that's the thing. Part of the spell requires the caster," she pointed her wine glass to her chest, "me. I have to absorb the life essence of a man. Translated literally from the grimoire." The words scorched her throat on the way out, and she suppressed the cough that followed with a swallow of pasty red saliva.

"Okay." He blinked mindlessly. "So wait—you mean—"

"Exactly."

"*Oh.*" His mouth pursed.

Blood flushed her dimples. "I'm sorry, I should have never tried to do this. It's friggin' stupid anyway. I don't know what I was thinking—"

He stared at her for a moment. "Well…do you have to chant the spell before, or after the…you know, absorption?" he asked with a concerned tone, as if trying to solve a calculus problem.

"After, I guess."

"Ok. Well, this is some pretty wild shit, but look, you don't have to pretend with all this magic stuff. I'm not gonna lie, I noticed you a long time ago, back when you were working down in the medical center. I just figured you were with that dude, so—" He edged closer.

An electric charge surged into the pit of her stomach as she ingested his words, and then it released, pouring out from her limbs. She felt like a succubus out of control as she dropped her glass to the floor and ran her fingers up his chest toward the arteries in his neck. She strangled his lost expression with a wild stare, knocking the glass from his hand, and as it shattered on the table, a mind-altering tension encircled her. She felt his flushed skin with the tips her fingernails and sniffed his stiff neck. The aroma of her perfume mingled with his cologne, and the aphrodisiac filtered into her nose as she walked her fingers behind his ears, pressing her lips to his.

Embracing more passionately with each kiss, her charged body sparked, and in the midst of her wicked assault, he took her breast in his hand.

"I want you so bad," she whispered, gently biting his ear, securing his hand tighter in hers. Raucously, he lifted her into his arms and carried her into the bedroom, tossing her onto the bed. Bouncing on top of her plush white comforter, she exchanged a frolicsome, seductive look, as he slid onto the bed over her. His enamored smile was a vision she knew she would remember forever.

∞∞∞*Morning Enlightenment*

Virtutem meam
Vim sanguinis
Virtus mea
Aperi mihi somnium

      Bud listened to the arcane phrase repeating from Tsarina's lips like a solemn prayer. She was holding her mother's grimoire loosely against her chest, and there were candles in the shape of a pentagram aligned upon the floor. The candles had burnt out sometime during the early morning by the look of it. Tsarina had obviously attempted to cast the spell. Bud felt a bit of guilt for taking advantage of her vulnerable state of mind, but took comfort in the fact that their night of passion was completely her idea—for the most part.
      Tsarina's eyes twitched in the soft light as he brushed the black ringlets from her face and placed a gentle kiss on her forehead. Inside the cloud of his morning fantasy, she resembled a Russian princess, her porcelain face framed by fluffy white pillows. The humidity of her breath faded from his face as he rolled over to check the clock—oddly, the digital numbers were unlit. It seemed as if he had only been asleep for a short while. The effects of the wine and tequila were still lingering like a fog in his head.

Stretching his hamstrings over the edge of the high-framed bed, he stepped onto the floor and scrounged around in the waning darkness for his clothes. His button-down shirt, now missing most of its buttons, was tucked under the foot of the bed, and his best pair of jeans were crumpled in the middle the floor. Clumsily, he shot legs and arms through cloth holes as he passed through the bead curtain into Tsarina's living room. Melted candles, small white boxes, and two empty bottles of wine shook when his shin made solid contact with the rounded corner of the coffee table. A sharp pain shot through his leg. He stumbled onto a tiny shard of glass and spit, "Son of a—!" After plucking the shard from his arch, he limped into the bathroom to take care of the morning's business and positioned himself over the toilet bowl. Jeff Buckley's version of "Hallelujah" played like a soundtrack in his mind. It was the last song he remembered from the glorious experience with Tsarina.

He anticipated the inevitable "morning after" conversation with her and tried to compose his thoughts. *This could be awkward,* he thought, as he pressed down on the chrome knob. *Don't be an idiot.* The cold lever flopped up and down like a dead chicken's neck, and he noticed there wasn't a single drop of water in the porcelain bowl. Thinking this more or less odd, he decided to perform a test on the defunct plumbing by washing his hands in the sink. Similarly, no water fell from the faucet, even when he cranked the chrome knobs to full.

Reeling inside the fog of a pre-coffee daze, he shrugged off the annoying lack of creature comforts and shuffled out of the bathroom, across the common room, where the first rays of auburn sunlight were beginning to filter through the tiny slits in the thin fuchsia venetian blinds. The warm shafts of light infected every molecule in his body with their radiant heat, as he ran his fingers along the smooth grain of the faux oak dining table—the table was exactly like the one in his room across the hall and exactly like everyone else's for that matter, however the sterility of the Fordham University dormitory was more than tolerable, to say the least. The layouts were gaudy in size by Manhattan's standards, and the views from all sides were equally astounding.

From his bay window, he could watch the tall ships, ferries, tankers, sailboats, and yachts trolling up and down the Hudson River. His favorite spectacle was watching the *QE2* come into port, but she wouldn't be in for another couple of months, and then the busy season would begin for him. As a first mate on a tall ship that did harbor tours, he normally worked weekends, but this weekend happened to be his captain's son's birthday, so no parties were booked. He felt fortunate to have the weekend off, allowing him time with Tsarina.

On this glorious Sunday morning, the bustling streets of Manhattan seemed amazingly tranquil. There were no galling horns, or angry voices, or obnoxious sirens billowing up through the windows. The city soundscape was eerily reminiscent of his woodland home in North Carolina, quiet and peaceful. So much so, he almost forgot where he was for the moment.

With a firm twist of the plastic rod, he opened the venetian blinds and witnessed an amber-coated prairie, full of head-high, yellow and green grasses. A strange auburn sunlight bathed the vegetation, producing vibrant colors over the landscape. Trolling the sky, thick, white, cumulonimbus clouds floated across the auburn-magenta background like giant balls of cotton. He blinked.

What the hell?

Immediately Bud slammed his eyelids shut for several seconds to reset the incongruous view, but when he reopened them, the alien landscape remained. Thunderstruck, he yanked the thin cord, sending the blinds crashing to the top of the windowsill. The unobstructed sight of the pristine valley bored deeper into his psyche with each blink, and he staggered from the anomaly like a drunken sailor. Placing his hand on the back of the couch for support, he spied a yellow pack of American Spirits on the coffee table. He paused for a moment, then vaulted over the couch and ripped open the top of the pack, extracting the lone cigarette with a shaky hand. He grabbed the pink lighter from the ashtray and put the cigarette to his lips. As he struggled to fire up the cheap lighter,

Tsarina clattered through the bead curtain, draped in a worn bathrobe. The gold moons and stars stitched into the purple terrycloth robe, along with her tossed hair, gave her the look of a frazzled magician from a children's television show.

"Morning babe," she muttered, scratching the back of her head.

Bud placed the lighter closer to the cigarette, struggling to hold his hand steady.

In passing, she barely seemed to notice his awestruck expression and mentioned casually, "I didn't know you smoked." With an arched eye she warned, "That better not be my last one."

The tan filter stuck to his lower lip as he pulled it from his mouth and said, "I just...well, you're the New Yorker. When you get back out here, take a look outside and tell me if I'm not crazy as a bat." He waited several seconds for a boggled response that never came then finally managed to light the cigarette.

While Tsarina was in the bathroom, he sucked down half of the cigarette, pacing the room. Eventually, she emerged from the unlit bathroom and asked, "What's up with the plumbing and the lights? And why is there blood on the floor?"

"That's just it. I don't know—None of that shit works." He puffed the cigarette. "I stepped on a piece of glass on my way to the bathroom."

"Are you ok?" she asked.

"Yeah, it's no biggie, but that's not the disaster. The disaster is this—" He pointed with the smoldering cigarette toward the window.

"So what's it I am supposed to be looking at over here?" She scrunched her cat-eyes at the light.

"You tell me. Just look out the window."

As she peered through the bay window, over her tiny collection of pink and white orchids, he watched her eyes flutter intently. Then they grew wide. "What the hell is that?" she asked.

"I don't know. This must be one of those dreams you have, right?"

"I've had some freaky dreams, but I've never shared them with anybody," she said, then snatched the cigarette from his hand. "Holy shit. You think the spell worked?" She inhaled a long drag.

"Are you serious?" He searched her eyes for the answer, but her unyielding stare disturbed him further. "Come on, you were just trying to get me in bed with all that witch stuff last night, right?"

"No. I really wanted to see if it was real, or if I was crazy or not."

"You were the one saying it was crazy last night," he charged.

"It is crazy."

"Right. So, something's up. I think it's more likely that your little Wiccan roommate went and slipped us some roofies or something, and then she drug us way out here in the country."

"The entire building?" Tsarina argued.

"Hell, I don't know. Maybe she put some LSD or something in the tequila." He reclaimed the cigarette to give it a quick puff, but the tobacco did little to comfort his raging nerves. Thinking they were both insane, or in some drug induced dream-like reality, he searched for a way to prove he was still in a dream. "Here, let me call my friend, Martin. I think he stuck around this weekend. Maybe someone else is seeing this shit, or not."

After a bit of trouble with the fold in his pocket, Bud ripped his cell phone out of his jeans and looked at the screen. "Awesome, I got no service. Where's your phone?"

"On the counter over there…" Her finger wavered in the air for a moment then pointed toward the kitchen bar top.

Bud crossed the room and grabbed her phone. "Shit. No service. What carrier are you with?"

"Sprint."

"I'm with AT&T. Both of them down—"

Bud watched her jaw stiffen as she walked toward the house phone perched on the wall next to the bar. With a beleaguered smile, she glanced at him and lifted the handset off the receiver, placing it up to her ear; then her shoulders slumped, and her head shook deliberately in the negative. She placed the phone on the receiver.

"Okay, this is ridiculous." Bud's mind raced in circles. "I'm not trying to belittle your *gifts* here, but this can't be real. There's got to be a logical explanation to all this. There's no such thing as magic portals. Come on, let's go see if anybody else knows anything."

"Hey, I'm with you. I don't want to believe any of this shit either." Then, Tsarina's raspy morning voice lowered as she took the dying cigarette butt and puffed it deep. "I think everyone on our floor went home this weekend except Mary and Jenny," she informed, before taking the final drag.

"Okay, great. Let's go see if they're there."

"I hate those bitches," Tsarina muttered, as she crushed the soiled filter into the coffin-shaped ashtray.

Bud dropped his head and thought of a compromise. "Alright then, let's go downstairs to the front desk and ask the guard what's up."

Tsarina nodded, signifying compliance then solemnly gathered her keys from the kitchen-bar countertop, and with an abbreviated swipe of her hand motioned him out into the dark hall. Tiptoeing toward the elevators in the shadowy light, Bud heard the thick metal door shut behind them. Ahead, tiny dust particles sifted through the golden slivers of sunlight that were beaming in from the windows at the end of the hall. The rest of the hall was veiled in periwinkle darkness. Bud felt Tsarina's hand trembling, as she slipped it into his with an ever-tightening grasp. He spread his fingers wide to calm her.

"I guess we're going to have to take the stairs since that elevator ain't going anywhere without power," he said.

"Awesome." Tsarina frowned. "Are we really gonna do this?"

"Yeah—you ready?"

"No, not really. This is actually beyond stupid. Maybe we should go back and get a flashlight or something."

"Okay. You got one?"

"I don't know." She blinked. "No."

Her understood her fear. Logical answers were not forthcoming, and the darkness in the stairwell was going to be hard to navigate. Bud remembered her lighter and slipped his hand into the front pocket of her robe. Rummaging near her hip, he felt the horn of a switchblade and pulled it from her pocket. "Damn, what the hell is this?"

"That's *Mama*," she replied, swiping it from his hand. "Here—" She slipped her hand into her pocket and swapped it for the lighter. "You were looking for this?"

"Yeah. Guess I know now not to mess with you."

"Smart." She flashed a curt smile.

Sparking the lighter with a flick, Bud gazed down into the stairwell and said, "Just follow me and hold on to the rails. We'll be fine."

Tsarina's wide eyes questioned his plan.

"Come on. We'll be fine," he comforted.

"Famous last words," she muttered.

With soft steps, Bud landed on the sixth floor platform—Tsarina snug to his butt. The one-foot perimeter of light, flickering around the pink lighter, was hardly worth the burning sensation he felt on his thumb, and he released the flame. The darkness inside the concrete shaft engulfed him, and he heard a door creak open below. He took a knee, and Tsarina mimicked his posture, placing her hands on his shoulders, nails digging lightly into his skin. He waited in the darkness without a breath, listening for footsteps, but the black pit beneath offered no further sounds of life.

"You see anything?" she asked quietly, pressing two fingers against his neck.

Squirming, he tapped her hand away, as the faint noises caromed off the concrete walls, sounding as if someone were sporting muddy galoshes that stuck to the floor with each step. "No, but you hear that?" he asked.

"Yeah," she gasped, grabbing his arm. "What're we going to do?"

"Well, we can go down there and meet them—"

"Whatever! Are you friggin' nuts? There's some serious weird shit going on here, and you want to go meet whoever it is down there in the dark? I say we hide somewhere and watch them come up the stairs."

"Or we could do that."

He gave a final bend of his ear to the stairwell below, and the clomping, sloshing sounds grew louder. Tsarina latched onto his belt loop with two fingers, as he began creeping down the last few steps to the next floor. After slipping through the metal door into the hallway, he positioned himself below the slim window to gain a bead, but Tsarina slid under his armpit and proceeded to root him away from the view.

Outside the door, slimy footsteps echoed off the walls, and he watched streams of panic ebb and flow through Tsarina's facial expressions as she bobbed in and out of the window, trying to steal a glance. Once the slithering noises faded, he pressed his head to the glass to see for himself, but before his eyes could adjust to the darkness, Tsarina popped up again, peeking through the window. She gasped and slid to the ground.

"Well, Miss, I got to have a look, what did you see?"

"I don't know." Her eyes fluttered. "Maybe we are trippin'. It was too dark to make anything out for sure." She hesitated. "It looked like some kind of slimy frogman or something with a bloody axe tied to his hip. It looked like some kind of mutant creature you'd see in a sci-fi movie—" Suddenly, a crazed smirk grew on her face, and she looked to the ceiling as if witnessing an angel. Bud assumed she was losing her last shred of sensibility and touched her forearm.

"That's it!" she proclaimed, stopping his advance.

"What?"

"Check it out. They're probably shooting a movie or something in here today, and we just missed the postings."

"Oh. Yeah. They do that kind of thing all the time, right?"

"Yeah. I've seen it a couple of times, not in this building, but yeah, they take over big buildings like this and shoot movies in them or whatever. Happens all the time."

Bud continued her train of thought by adding, "And the scenery we saw outside your window could have just been some elaborate backdrop, and if we were half-asleep, or whatever, and—"

"Right! And that thing was probably just some stupid actor going up to the floor they're shooting on…"

"…They probably tripped the power with all their lights and equipment," he finished her sentence and blew out a sigh of relief. "You see, now that all makes sense. I knew there had to be some sort of logical explanation. As much as it would be cool for magic to exist, I still ain't never seen it in person. Jesus, we about lost it there for a minute. Can you imagine us trying to explain to the RAs how we opened a magical portal to another planet and saw alien frogmen in the building?"

"Yeah," she expelled a breathy laugh, "that's friggin' crazy."

"They would have sent us straight to the counseling office and tested us for drugs."

"No doubt. Ok, I feel a lot better, now. Let's go down to the guard stand and ask how long they're going to be shooting." She blinked. "That was some pretty awesome makeup. Must be a big budget film. I wonder if anybody famous is here?"

∞∞∞*Noctiss*

The concrete floor in the stairwell cooled the soles of Bud's feet as he made his way deeper into the void. Sliding his hand along the metal handrail, he felt a gooey film sticking to his palm and wiped it onto his jeans. When he reached out for the door handle, Tsarina latched onto his arm like a viper.

"Careful," she urged, peeking over his shoulder, curls brushing against his neck.

He nodded, and she let go.

Quick and silent, Bud opened the door and tiptoed the L-shaped corridor, past the elevators, toward the security desk. When he approached the edge of the hall, he stopped to glance around the corner. Three, humanoid, frog-like creatures were milling behind the security desk, slapping each other's slimy backs with long curled fingers. Their bony spines flexed up and down, as they bobbed around the desk. Bud quickly ducked behind the corner, pressing Tsarina against the wall with his arm.

The hissing creatures smelled of blood and river bottom muck. Their grey skin, stretched taught over their bony frames, revealed sinewy muscles that rippled as they lurched across the floor. Flat slender heads housed two deeply recessed metallic purple eyes. The muculent creatures stood almost five feet tall with arms disproportionately short to their long frames, and they lacked any hair whatsoever, save for a few wiry whiskers twitching around their mouths. Two small holes serving as nostrils sprayed a thin film of mucus each time they exhaled.

After a horrid crunch, one of the creatures popped up from behind the counter with its fingers clamped around a severed human arm. The frogman swung the appendage over its head in a violent arc, raining blood down upon the frenzied pack. Hissing for approval from his mates, the creature revealed two rows of razor sharp teeth that bit into the limb. Further primal hissing erupted from the others, groping for a taste. At the height of their ebullience, a deep voice boomed across the foyer, disrupting the ruckus.

"NOCTISS!"

From the shadows, a tall, pale-skinned man stepped into the sunlit hall. White dreadlocks coiled around the base of his black hood and slithered over his shoulders like a nest of albino snakes. The tail of his black cloak, trimmed in red, pranced about his heels as he walked. As he strode toward the pack, the despotic figure tapped the end of his mahogany staff into the floor. Two of the alien creatures, slightly darker than the others, flanked him, carrying wooden short bows over their shoulders with black hand-axes tied around their waists.

The pale man stopped in front of the chastened pack and spoke deliberately. "Control your hunger! We must pay attention to the matter at hand. Find the Eye of Istia, and the girl—alive and unharmed. These other humans are of no matter."

"Butss thisss meatss isss soss goodss, Master Agni." one of the creatures hissed, dangling the guard's half-eaten femur in front of its foaming mouth.

The cloaked man glared manically at the creature and turned his free palm upward. As the wide sleeve around his wrist slid down to his elbow, he produced an orange and blue plume of flame that hovered inside his grasp. With a sharp flick of his wrist, the energy hissed through the air, engulfing the creature like a fiery wraith, and the oily coating covering its body fueled the flames. As its skin boiled and bubbled, the Noctiss writhed, hissing and flailing its arms, attempting to smother the fire. Draped in a blanket of flames, the doomed creature melted into a glowing ball on the floor, until all that remained was a smoldering pile of ash. The remaining Noctiss cowered and immediately discarded Jadu's half-eaten body parts onto the floor.

"If one lock on the girl's head is so much as frayed when I find her, know that I will hold each of you responsible. Now find the witch! Quickly! We haven't much time."

After the stern command, the Noctiss began slopping toward the stairwell.

Bud summoned Tsarina's attention with his gaze and whispered, "That looked pretty fuckin' real."

"That shit was real," she affirmed. "Come on, they're coming this way. We gotta head back to the room and get behind a locked door." Tsarina's eyes darted toward the stairwell behind them.

"Ok, let's move out," Bud said, waving his finger like a military scout.

Before his words landed, Tsarina was already halfway to the stairwell, firing a shrill hiss at him, "Come on! What the hell are you doing?"

"I was trying to be quiet," he muttered, tossing his hands in the air as he darted to catch up with her.

Upon reaching the eleventh floor, his thighs and calves burned, and he was gasping for breath. He stopped behind Tsarina who was hunched, transfixed, peering through the rectangular glass window. "Well?" he asked.

She glanced back and huffed, "Come on," then slipped through the door and sprinted down the hallway toward her room. Her head bobbed up and down in rhythm with her breath as she leaned forward, fumbling with her keychain in search of the key to her apartment.

Bud fought the urge to take the rattling mass from her hands while she attempted to line the key up with the lock. "Calm down," he urged.

Tsarina responded with a seething look and then tried jamming the key into the keyhole. "This thing is—shit!"

"Take it easy."

After watching several botched attempts, he made a calculated play for the keychain, but as he slid his hand over hers, the key slid into the lock with a pronounced click, and Tsarina ripped the door open. Bolting inside, she hurled the keychain across the room, and the metal keys bounced off the back pad of the couch, falling to rest between the middle seat cushions.

While Tsarina clattered through the bead curtain into her bedroom, Bud collected the keys and stashed them in the front pocket of his jeans. As he followed her into the bedroom, he watched her rip off her housecoat. Inked on the small of her back, her chalky skin displayed a tattoo of a Pentagram. The azure outer ring was speckled with shimmering white flakes, giving it a crystal-like appearance, and the inner star housed two, light blue clouds. Around the outer points of the star, a midnight blue, serpentine dragon glared at Bud with fiery purple eyes. The peripheral scales and tipped wings were of the same hue, and a blue light was etched, beaming out from the center of the glyph. The daedal artwork quickly sunk below the waistline of a pair of maroon sweat pants that read, "*Fordham*," printed in white lettering across the butt.

During the transformation, a glimmer of golden-orange light reflected off her sunstone. "That's what he is looking for isn't it?" he asked.

"What?"

"That guy downstairs, Agni—he wants you and that stone around your anklet, right? That's the Eye of Istia?"

Her eyes dimmed, and she nodded hesitantly. Turning her back on him, she slipped into a white sports bra then continued pacing the room.

"So who is he?" asked Bud.

"Beats me."

"Then how the hell does he know who you are?"

"I don't friggin' know, okay," she spat.

"Whoa, sorry." Bud was almost convinced she wasn't providing full disclosure, but he decided to cease and desist at any rate. Arguing wasn't going to speed up their escape, and she didn't seem to be in a reasonable state of mind to respond to any form of interrogation. "Look, it's cool. You just chill here and do your thing and pack. I'm going to head across the hall and get some supplies from my room—be right back."

"What? No frickin' way!" She barked and turned to face him, a purple bra swinging in her hand. "Are you completely insane? Have you ever watched *one* frickin' horror movie? That is exactly how we die. We split up, and bam! It's over. One of those lurker dudes pops up around the corner, and we are dead."

"Did you just call that thing a lurker?" he chuckled, surprised to find humor in spite of their situation.

Tsarina nodded with a shrug, as if he should have known all along that *Lurker* was its proper name. "Just wait a minute and let me pack my shit. Chill dude."

Acknowledging her remarkable, newfound sensibility, Bud took a seat in the tan papasan chair beside the couch and watched her forage around in her bedroom like a crazed ferret.

"Okay, this is going to be just like camping right? So what, we pack some warm durable clothes and canned food? Hey, do you got a tent or anything?" she asked.

"Um, no. I never really needed a tent in the city," he jabbed. "I do got a big ass knife though, and besides, it's the middle of summer. It's not really that cold."

Tsarina shot an irked look as she grabbed a backpack from her disheveled closet and tossed a pack of gum in the front pocket. "I get cold easy," she huffed, packing a pair of cargo pants and a couple of t-shirts into the backpack. With the pockets wide open and bits of clothing hanging out of the sides, she skittered over to the coffee table and stashed her mother's grimoire into the main pocket. Next she made her way into the kitchen, where she grabbed a small bag of pita chips, two cans of tuna fish, and four plastic bottles of water. After cramming the rations into the side pouches of the overburdened backpack, she turned to face Bud and stammered, "Oh wait," then crossed into the bathroom. Reemerging with a pink toothbrush, a roll of toilet paper, and a white tube of Crest, she asked, "Can you think of anything else?"

"You put the sink in there?" he jabbed.

"Hilarious." She smirked. "I'm serious, what else?"

"How about a can opener?"

"Oh yeah."

Tsarina scurried into the kitchen and pulled a hand-held can opener from a drawer next to the sink. "I guess that's about it," she calculated, scanning the rest of the apartment.

"Alright." Bud shrugged then clapped his hands together like a high school football coach preparing for the big game speech. "Let's go get my knife then get the hell outta here."

"What about everyone else?" she asked, trailing him out the door.

"Well, it's like you said, seems like most people went home this weekend, but as far as I'm concerned, it's every man for himself right now. I ain't about to go around here like Paul Revere banging on doors and ringing bells if that's what you mean.

Anyone who was here is long gone by now, or else they were breakfast for those frogs."

"Right." Her eyes lost their sparkle as she looked to the door.

"Don't worry, we'll be fine," he assured, then opened the front door and walked across the hall.

When Bud entered his apartment, a bright light beamed through the room, illuminating the disastrous state. Along the back wall, a giant pyramid of multi-national beer cans rose up like a shrine underneath a black and white poster of Jim Morrison's face. Dirty boxers and boxer briefs hung off the cigarette branded furniture, and a pair of grimy pink panties lay crumpled in the front corner of the open bathroom. Playboy and Maxim magazines littered the floor of the common room, covering one law journal, and the mangled carpet served as a giant ashtray with piles of ash standing like anthills.

"Wow. Do you guys own a vacuum?" Tsarina asked.

"Whatever, it was Tim's turn to clean this week." he retaliated, rushing off into his bedroom.

"What about last week and the week before that and that?"

Disregarding the flippant remark—as it wasn't the time to give her the grand tour and explain his distaste for his roommates' sanitation habits, or lack there of—he abruptly slid out of his jeans and hopped into his favorite pair of olive cargo pants. He then laced up his dark brown, steel-toed hiking boots and stuffed several plastic lighters into his pocket. Next, he reached under the bed for his backpack and extracted the nylon rucksack. Tossing it onto his bed, he packed two dark-colored t-shirts, ten feet of nylon rope, a full roll of duct tape, and an unopened first aid kit in the main compartment. With a solid pull on the drawstring, he secured the items then crossed over to the nightstand where he plucked the black combat knife from the top drawer and felt the edge of the blade with his forefinger, hoping he wouldn't have to test its bite. As he secured it to his belt loop, he looked into the common room to see if Tsarina was watching. She had taken a seat on the couch and was thumbing through one of the Playboy magazines. He chuckled at his need to be noticed in this perilous situation and refocused on more important matters, like ramen noodles and saltine crackers.

    Scrounging the kitchen cabinets, he stashed as many dry rations as he could into the side pockets of his backpack, then removed the plastic bag from the box of Captain Crunch, rolling it into the backpack to preserve space. Lastly, he tossed in a couple of knives, forks, and spoons before fastening all the clasps.

    "Ok, let's double check all our supplies," he said.

    "Oh, soap!" she blurted.

    "Ok, soap," he echoed, then rummaged through the cabinets until he found a slimy green bar hidden underneath the kitchen sink.

    "Wow, you guys actually have soap," she teased.

    "Hilarious," he muttered, as he tossed the bar into a plastic zip-lock bag and jammed it into one of the outside pockets of his backpack.

    An awkward silence stood between them for a moment, and he noticed the fear buried in her eyes. When she glanced away, he assumed she was trying to ward it off. "Come here." He beckoned with his fingertips. When he touched her skin, time seemed to stop, and he felt her shallow breath hovering over his lips. Then, as if she were searching his eyes for a visible soul, her gaze enveloped his. The warm tips of her fingers slid over his jaw and the stale aroma of her day old perfume crept into his nose. Her trembling fingernails slid behind his ears, and when her lips pressed softly to his, they tasted sweet, like watermelon candy with the texture of warm rose petals after a light summer's rain. He lost all thoughts of fear.

    "What are we going to do?" she whispered, her lips tickling his as she backed away.

    He took a moment then said, "We should get out of here. Those things are eventually going to find us if we just sit around. We need to get outside and try to figure out where we are. Like you said, I don't really want to stick around and hang out with those dudes either."

After a humble smile, she pecked his lips, releasing him into the world of reality. He gently stroked the hair from her cheek and scanned the fields outside the window for a direction. Across the vast prairie, the reflection of a bright auburn sun sparkled inside a translucent stream. Water meandered into a dense forest of white-trunked trees covered with lime-green leaves. Pointing toward the rippling current, he proposed, "I say we just follow that stream into those woods and see where it leads. Civilizations are usually built around water. So wherever we are, if there's people, they're going to need water."

∞∞∞∞*Creeping Out*

After checking the peephole twice, Bud inhaled a quick breath of courage and cranked on the handle of his front door. As the bolt slid across the metal frame, it sounded like nails on a chalkboard to his adrenaline soaked ears. A slight change in air pressure gently sucked him into the hall when he opened the door, and he scanned the dimly lit corridor for the creatures. After listening for several seconds, he took his first calculated step toward the stairwell. "Okay, let's go. We can take the other set of stairs and be closer to the back of the building when we get down."

"Okay." Tsarina nodded.

The floor was quiet when they approached the stairwell. Bud tiptoed down several flights until the spiraling descent eventually became routine, and at the penultimate step, a faint echo of metal banging on metal resounded from above.

Tsarina gasped, glancing up through the railing. "Shit! Go!" she whispered the command.

Darting out of the stairwell, past the R.A.'s office, Bud spied one of the creatures gnawing on the thigh of their Resident Assistant, Hannah. The abomination had the appendage half in its mouth and was shredding it like a giant turkey leg—her blood dripping down its jowls like red barbecue sauce. He cringed at the sight of his disfigured classmate and looked toward the exit. A few steps ahead the metal-framed glass doors leading to the atrium beckoned with the sight of head high grasses on the other side of the fence. Bud sprinted the length of the hall, slamming into the aluminum crossbar, and the latch budged just enough for a proper tease then braced against his weight. Bouncing off, he took a step back and slammed his shoulder into the glass again. The Noctiss raised its head and dropped Hannah's thigh to the floor.

"Shit!" Bud cussed.

Suddenly, he felt a strong tug on his arm, and Tsarina spun him from the doors, dragging him across the hall toward another exit. In that same instant, the office door flew open with a bang, and the Noctiss leapt forward, hissing through its spiked, blood stained teeth. Tsarina slammed into the crossbar with her arm, and to Bud's surprise, the door swung wide. He took a deep breath of humid air and sprinted into the courtyard. Instead of the streets and the structures of Lincoln Center, a vast prairie lay just beyond the iron fence, cofounding him under a sky of luminous purple hues.

As he raced toward the black gate, Bud felt his legs propelling him forward with unnatural alacrity. It seemed as if gravity had become slightly lazy, and when he stamped his foot into the ground, the ensuing bound was a feat he had never matched. He marveled at his newfound strength, but upon glancing back, he saw the frenzied Noctiss closing with leaping strides of their own.

Along the edge of the courtyard, a line of wrought iron stakes, six-feet tall and tipped with sharp fleur-de-leis, stretched toward the purple sky. The fence blocked him from the open field beyond, and the gate was always locked. Bud watched Tsarina tug at the handle, jerking violently with her body.

"Forget it." He grabbed her by the shoulder. "Step up on my hand," he said, clasping his hands together, forming a footstep.

"What about you?" she cawed.

"I got it. Just jump!"

Nodding, she stepped onto his hand. With a full body heave, he hurled her over the iron bars like a human caber. Up and over she flew, but he miscalculated of the force of his throw due to the lack of gravity, and she shot a foot higher than intended over the top. Grabbing a bar with her hand, she flipped, and as she redirected toward the ground, her inner thigh snagged the tip of the fleur-de-leis. The honed iron tore through her cotton sweatpants, ripping into her flesh, and she fell to the ground with a thud, landing on her backpack. Bud saw her head snap against the ground, and he clutched the bars. "Are you okay?" he asked.

Groggily, her watery eyes rose to his then suddenly darted behind him. Her wan eyes and wide expression warned of the approaching Noctiss. "Behind you!" she wheezed.

Whirling blindly, Bud drew his knife and drove the steel blade deep into the unsuspecting creature's stomach. A low hissing howl spewed from the Noctiss as its razor-like fingernails pierced the back of Bud's neck. Streams of blood trickled down his shoulders while he sliced his blade sideways, releasing the creature's bowels onto the ground in a gelatinous heap. Seconds later, its long bony fingers relaxed, and it slumped like an empty potato sack onto its own innards. Bud stood hovering over his victim, and his head felt as heavy as a bowling ball.

Across the courtyard, silhouetting the open doorway, the black-cloaked albino stood motionless, seemingly content to watch them escape, and Bud wondered why the warlock wasn't following. Suddenly, a raspy female voice filtered into his ears.

"Hey! Bud! Come on! What the hell are you doing, baby? We got to go! Move it!" Tsarina's voice seemed to be echoing from another dimension. A nauseating wave of energy erupted from the pit of his stomach into his throat as he searched for her voice. The strange inanimate creature at his feet retained his focus. Tsarina's voice sounded again. "Bud! Come on!"

Three of the creatures burst through the glass doors into the courtyard, and Bud leapt backward, grabbing for the fence, but the iron bars began to dissolve into golden evanescent flecks rising up and away like millions of electrified butterflies. As his hands passed through the evaporating particles, a tingling sensation pulsed beneath his skin. He stepped through the veil and ran into the field, in search of Tsarina. She was plowing through the head high grasses when he found her and, he looked back to measure the distance they had created from the creatures. Behind, he witnessed their building evaporating into tiny golden particles, and a golden green field sprouting up in its wake. The Noctiss exploded from the sparkling motes like grey-green demons, hissing as they leapt toward him.

Bud raced to threshold of the forest, Tsarina chugging steps ahead, toward a line of rotund bushes that served as a natural fence to the viscera of gigantic white-trunked trees. Haphazardly he swatted at one of the leaves and felt a sting inside his palm.

"Ow shit!" he spat, retracting his hand.

"What?" Tsarina scowled.

"These damn bushes got thorns all over them. That one just stuck the hell out of me."

With the Noctiss bounding closer, he rummaged through Tsarina's backpack in search of something to protect his hand from the thorns. Inside the main pocket, he found a pink t-shirt and wrapped it tight around his palm, then readied his combat knife and resumed hacking into the thick vegetation with wide slashes. The dark green stalks of the bushes bore velvety leaves, outlined in purple, concealing their underlying thorns. Bright crimson flowers, shaped like mission bells sat atop the brambles and released a pleasant rose-like smell as Bud hacked and slashed them from their perches. Hundreds of iridescent-winged bugs erupted from the falling leaves, swarming in tornado-like circles around his head.

"You think they're still following us?" Tsarina asked, swatting wildly at the swarm.

Bud looked incredulously at her for a split second and then kept hacking forward.

Tsarina continued, "Well, we were going pretty good until now, and—"

Crushing her hope, the crimson flowers behind them parted, and one of the frog-like faces poked through the coppice, purple eyes focused on them. Tsarina lunged forward, pressing her weight into Bud, slamming him through the thorny mass. Shaking his head, he widened his stance to stabilize. Pricked and tired of retreating, he figured the creatures would eventually catch them, especially since they were being so nice as to forge the trail. He stabbed his heels into the ground and gripped the knife sideways in his hand. "I'm done running from these bastards," he said. "You keep on going. I'll catch up.

Tsarina remained like a statue.

"Go on! I got this," he barked.

"I'm not leaving you!"

"Trust me. This is the best place for an ambush. Go keep trampling the path for us. They won't know I'm here."

Tsarina backed away with a scowl and began pressing deliberately into the thicket, using her backpack as a shield, while Bud refocused on the Noctiss. Once he was certain she was committed to her task, he slid off the path and squatted under the thick canopy of leaves.

Hissing sounds crescendoed inside the walls of the forest as the creature drew near. Bud worked the soles of his boots into the mossy ground and poised the knife for a throat-cutting strike. When the lone Noctiss passed, Bud stepped from behind and grabbed its head, slicing the blade across its throat. The gurgling corpse dangled in the barbed vegetation like a puppet, and Bud slithered down Tsarina's path.

When he drew within shouting distance, she spun, seemingly feeling his presence. "Keep going!" he bellowed, slipping on the turf. As he threw his arms forward to regain his balance, he glanced down at the velvety green moss growing in patches along the forest floor. The viridian carpet gradually thickened while the bushes thinned, allowing unrestricted movement into the heart of the forest. Thin shafts of banded auburn light pierced the canopy of leaves, spotlighting two slimy heads poking through the brush.

"Go! Run!" he howled.

A low hiss rumbled from the Noctiss as they leapt diagonally across the mossy ground. He raced forward, but the first Noctiss lunged, landing on Bud, wrapping its arm around his shoulder, spinning them both to the ground while the other leapt past toward Tsarina.

Bud's head bounced off the turf, blurring his vision, as the Noctiss clawed desperately with its pointed fingernails. The thrashing creature unhinged its jaw and let out a vengeful hiss, revealing hundreds of triangular yellow teeth crowded inside its mouth. Bud tossed the slimy arm to the side and sank his knife into the Noctiss's spongy back. Scrambling for a dominant position, he continued puncturing the creature's sinews, stabbing relentlessly into its chest as he pressed his knees into its hips. Geysers of purplish-red blood spouted from the fresh openings.

The overwhelmed Noctiss grabbed the back of Bud's neck with its curved fingernails, and its thin lips curled, as if they were about to tell a secret. It spewed a fine mist of white saliva at Bud's face. He turned away, but his ear and neck absorbed the brunt of the acidic foam, which sizzled upon impact. Berserk from the pain, he wrapped his fingers around the creature's neck and pressed his thumbs into its throat, puncturing the soft flesh. The Noctiss fell limp in his hands.

As Bud rolled onto his back, he felt the chipped blade of the Noctiss's hatchet brush against his shin and grabbed it, as a scream from Tsarina forced him to his feet. Scanning the tree line, he spotted her wrestling with the Noctiss. As it dragged her into a patch of golden-leaved trees with dark reddish trunks, he raced toward them.

"Get off me!" she screamed.

"Tsarina!"

"Bud!"

Tsarina thrashed and kicked at the Noctiss as it tried to pin her arms behind her back. With a burst of speed, Bud closed the gap on the creature and buried the hatchet into its shoulder. The Noctiss hissed, clinching the muscles in its back as it fell to its knees. Bud quelled the sound, driving his knife into its temple.

Tsarina whipped her head around as she broke free and wrapped her arms around him.

"Are you ok?" he asked, absorbing her embrace.

She nodded, as he squeezed tight around her waist, enjoying the comfort of her body. "I think that was the last of them," he offered.

"Good. Can we stop running now?" she asked.

"Yeah, I think so, but we should cover our tracks just in case."

Sounds of the water cascading along the rocky bottom of the riverbed released a bit of pressure from the air as Bud held Tsarina close. She buried her head into his chest, and he placed a kiss on her curls. High above, perched somewhere in the golden leaves, a hidden bird cooed with a low, haunting, *hoo waah*. Another answered, in a slightly higher pitch, deeper inside the forest.

∞∞∞*Grounded*

Bud searched for signs of civilization through the hallway of crimson and gold trees. If they were to have any chance of finding a way home, he knew they would have to ask someone for directions. The extent of those directions seemed to be the bigger issue. He scanned the inner forest for fire pits or old campsites. He looked overhead for man-made stands or perches. He examined the trunks of the trees for markings or bits of cloth, but the forest was devoid of any signs of human life. A few dried hoof prints, most likely some type of deer judging by the size, and several strands of coarse, grey and tan hair stretched over some of the lower bushes marked the path as animal territory.

Tsarina broke his concentration. "Look at all this stuff. Everything is so shiny and clean," she marveled then bent to take a closer look at the pink lilies growing along the edge of the river. "It's like all these plants are on some kind of nuclear miracle-grow or something." As she started to crouch, she grabbed her thigh and quickly returned upright.

"You alright?" Bud asked. "Here, let me take a look at your leg."

"It's cool. I wouldn't want you to pass out or nothing."

"Hilarious. Take off your pants—"

"Really? You gonna buy me dinner first?"

"Been there, done that," he boasted, eliciting a solid punch in the arm. "Hey! Watch it there killer."

Tsarina simpered as she wiggled out of her sweatpants and took a spot on the ground, while Bud grabbed the first aid kit from his backpack and dug out an alcohol prep pad. First, he sterilized her wound, covering it with a thick piece of gauze then secured the fluffy square of cloth with several pieces of duct tape. As he severed the tape, he feared he had wrapped it too snug and asked, "How's it feel?"

Tsarina pressed on the bandage with her forefinger and said, "Excellent work, doctor. Nice and tight." She smiled, then placed her hand on his neck and pecked his cheek. Immediately, she backed away, shoving his head to the side. "What the hell is this?"

"What the hell is what?"

"This friggin' second degree burn on your neck." She brushed back the hair covering the spot.

"Nothing. One of those frogs spit on me."

"And it did this?" She ran her fingertips over the bubbly surface, and his neck surged with hot pain. Gritting his teeth, he fought the urge to flinch. Tsarina shook her head at his lack of concern and prodded the bright red center with the pad of her forefinger. Another sharp pain ripped through his ear, forcing him to wince.

"Damn. Take it easy there, doc."

"This burn is rough," she stated clinically. "What do you have in your first aid kit? You got any burn cream or Aloe Vera?"

"I don't know," he moaned. "It was a Christmas gift from my aunt."

A disgruntled sigh puffed from Tsarina's nose as she reached for the kit. "Go rinse the area clean in the water. Gently," she instructed and started digging through the kit.

Bud obliged and walked to the stream, dipping his hands in the cool water, he splashed the wound several times then wrung his hands together and shook them dry in the warm air. Sanguine water dripped from his fingertips into the lazy current, and his mind flooded with the images of the brutal stabbings he gave the Noctiss. Killing them with such crude and intimate methods weighed heavy on his soul. Maybe it was the proximity of the kill. Maybe it was his sense of self-preservation. Maybe it was their similarity to humans. It seemed different from hunting animals for food somehow. As he squeezed the last drop of bloody water from his hands, he pondered the difference and then tossed his shirt and Tsarina's sweatpants into the river. Watching them float down stream, he wished his thoughts would swim away as well. Instead, they turned homeward, and he feared he would never see the skyline of Manhattan again or feel cool rain in the mountains of North Carolina.

Suddenly, a sharp pain hemmed through his nerve endings, and he winced as Tsarina began applying a clear cream to his neck. "Thanks," he grunted.

"No problem. It'll start to feel better in a couple of minutes," she informed. "Just don't scratch it off. You gotta let it soak in. We need to keep reapplying the aloe every couple of hours, but there's not a lot of it, so hopefully we can get somewhere and resupply"

"Not sure there's gonna be a CVS around the corner," he said, touching the wound.

"Sir." she stopped him with a scowl. "And you should wash that area every time before we reapply," she finished.

"Got it. Thanks doc," he smirked, pulling an olive t-shirt from his backpack.

"Wait a minute. I'm not done with you," she nagged. "We gotta wrap it with something. Where's your bandana?"

Reaching into his back pocket, Bud pulled out the blue and white bandana that his mother had given him when he was eight years old. She had given it to him to keep the mosquitoes from biting his neck and face on his first camping trip, and it was something had used for hundreds of purposes over the years. This was the first time it had ever covered an alien spit burn. He handed the faded cloth to Tsarina, and felt the warmth of her touch as she took it from him. She slipped the makeshift bandage into place, and he pulled his shirt over his head and listened to the strange clicking sounds resonating from the bushes beneath the trees. He speculated some type of insects must have been inside, producing the noise.

"You hear that?" he asked.

"What?"

"That clicking noise, like metal grasshoppers."

"Yeah, it's coming from the bushes," she noted.

"I know. I wonder what it is?"

"Do you really want to know?" she asked.

"Yeah, I think I do. And you know, you're right about all these plants. Look at those bent stalks on that bush over there."

"Which one?"

"That one with the big yellow flower on top." He pointed to the tallest one in the row. "Looks like it could just up and walk away with those legs there on the bottom. They're like little knee joints and feet." He bent down to have a better look. "This one's clicking."

"Man, you're trippin'."

"Are those eyes?" He inched forward. "This thing is so weird," he said, reaching out to touch the flower. At his touch, the plant's extremities began to quiver and several purple petals detached and floated to the ground. When the last petal landed, the plant howled a banshee-like shriek from somewhere deep inside the yellow bell-shaped flower sitting atop its stalk. The sound reverberated throughout the forest as the plant's flowery mouth spewed a golden cloud of pollen into Bud's face. Asphyxiated, he crumbled to his knees, covering his burning eyes and throat with his hands. Struggling backward, he gasped for breath, and the howling flower lifted its bamboo-like arms, waving them over his head. Bud tossed his forearms over his face to block the attack and braced his neck for impact. Inexplicably, the animated plant spun around and scampered into the woods like a spooked ostrich.

Bud spit the honey-flavored pollen from his lips and broke the thin seal of pollen crusting his eyelids. He tried to see through the yellow glaze, but only saw a muddled vision of Tsarina rushing toward then everything went dark.

"Bud! Wake up! Are you okay?" A faint voice snuck in his ears. He felt a hand gently slapping the side of his face and cracked his eyes open.

"Oh thank God. Baby, are you okay?" Tsarina asked, leaning into him, lightly stroking his face with her fingertips.

"What?" He expelled a deep breath and began assessing the damage. "I think so." Everything seemed to be working properly, except for his blurred vision. "What the hell just happened?" he rasped, rising to his feet, dusting the sticky yellow residue from his pants.

"I don't know." Tsarina shrugged noncommittally. "But whatever you did, scared the crap outta that thing."

"I didn't do anything." He rubbed his eyes; worried his vision would never return. "Damn it! Why is everything here spitting up shit on me? Look at all this crap." He dusted his arms, tempering his voice, veins popping in his neck. "I mean seriously, what the hell was that thing? And what were those frog sombitches I killed earlier? Noctiss! I mean, really, Tsarina. Noctiss? What the hell is is a fucking Noctiss?"

"I don't know," she offered softly.

"Here we are trying to act like all this shit is par for the course. Well, I got news for you honey—it ain't. Look at me! I'm covered in purple blood and yellow dust. This shit is fucked, and it ain't getting any better!"

Tsarina recoiled slightly from the outburst then spoke with an unexpected inner peace. "You're right. We're definitely out of our element at the moment, but we gotta take it one step at a time, you know? We gotta keep our heads until we get some answers. There *are* people here—we know this. And that guy leading those Noctiss spoke English, so when we do find civilization, we're should be able to communicate with the people there, no problem. Then we can figure a way home. But baby, this all hell is breaking loose attitude isn't doing us any good, right?"

After a moment of incertitude, her words landed and began to carry weight.

"Yeah, sorry. You're right. It's just—killing all that shit—" Bud started.

"Hey, it's cool. I get it," she comforted. "Don't worry, we're gonna be fine." She smiled.

"Famous last words." He struggled to grin.

"Touché."

∞∞∞*Never Being Boring*

The auburn sun crept toward the pinnacle of the trees, leaving only a few remaining shafts of light to penetrate the forest in a reddish hue. A slight chill of dusk sifted through spaces in the canopy of golden leaves, and Bud watched Tsarina shiver. The black-pebbled path weaved in and out of the white trunked trees, and the steady plodding of the last several hours had sapped most of his energy. He was getting hungry, and it seemed as if Tsarina was feeling the same, judging by the relentless growling sounds that were emanating from her stomach. He rubbed her shoulders and wrapped her in his arms. "I'm guessing we got about an hour of light left. You want to stop here?" he asked.

"Okay." She met his eyes and placed her head against his shoulder.

"Cool. This looks as good a place as any to set up camp for tonight and get some rest."

"Sure, but I'm not gonna be able to sleep," she relayed.

"Yeah, I know, but we have to try. We're gonna need our energy tomorrow. We can take turns on watch. I'll take the first watch."

"Okay, I'll try."

"That looks like a good spot over there." He pointed to a tight circle of trees. "We can set up inside those trees. That should keep us out of sight, if more of those *Lurkers* come looking for us."

Tsarina remained unfazed by his subtle jest, her mood unshakably grumpy and glum. "Sounds great," she replied. "Who knows, maybe if we go to sleep tonight and wake up in the morning, we'll be back in the city." She closed her eyes, fighting tears.

"Anything's possible," Bud comforted.

The events of the day had brought neon metal bugs, a berserk plant, a massive auburn sun, disappearing buildings, an albino wizard, and a pack of alien frogmen. There was also the slight lack of gravity and strange sounds inside the forest. Bud begrudgingly began accepting the unimaginable. Tsarina's spell had worked.

Haunted by the realization, he dropped his pack onto the ground and began rummaging for food. He began the task of preparing a meal with Tsarina's help, and took comfort in the familiarity. After spreading the shredded chunks of fish between crackers, he stood and surveyed their surroundings for loose tree branches and the makings of a lean to. The forest seemed endless in every direction, so he arbitrarily chose a path of grey and blue rocks and began traipsing into the forest, brandishing the bloodstained hatchet he had taken from the Noctiss.

"Where are you going?" Tsarina spat pieces of fish and cracker on her shirt.

"I'm just going over there to get branches for a lean to," he responded, pointing into the forest with the wooden handle of the hatchet.

"What's a lean to?" she asked.

"It's a tent you build on the side of a tree. It'll keep the bugs off us, and hopefully hide us from those *Lurkers*."

"Oh, okay…Southern man."

"Hey, they got stereotypes for a reason."

"Really? That's funny, the last thing I thought you were was a stereotype."

He flashed a curt smile.

"So while you're gone, what should I do?" she asked.

"Well, if you're up to it, you could find us some leaves to use for the roof. I think I saw a bush back there that would be perfect—looked kinda like a rubber tree. It had long, wide leaves. Those would work pretty good."

"Yeah, I think I remember it," she said, munching her last fish cracker.

"Cool. I'll meet you back here in a few." Bud issued a warm smile and marched away. Noticing the sound of his boots crunching against the forest floor, he softened his step in case there were any weird creatures hidden in the trees or the bushes. He searched the ground for loose branches that could act as poles to create the frame for the lean to. Buried under a patch of leaves, he spotted a tree branch covered with lime green mold and grey moss. When he picked it up, it crumbled in his hand, full of rot. Tossing it to the ground, he searched overhead for live branches, but even the lowest boughs on the gigantic trees loomed thirty feet above his head. Even with the slight absence of gravity, he knew he would not be able to jump and reach them.

He continued on, and after several minutes of tramping deeper into the forest, he came upon a clearing. The last shafts of sunlight poked their way through the thinning canopy, lighting a small circle of young trees with several branches hanging low. Leaping with both feet, he missed the closest branch only by a few inches and landed awkwardly from the extra height of his jump.

After gathering himself, he turned and walked several paces away to get a running start. He missed again, inches closer. Determined, he made another pass, and his hand clasped onto the branch. With his free hand, he drew the hatchet from his belt and began chopping at the base of the branch. After several clean whacks, he dropped it to the ground and fell along with it. Repeating the process, he gathered four branches of similar length and then began dragging the future trestles to the campsite. Chest swelled with pride, he felt a sense of how a simple life and simple work could be just as rewarding, if not more than the hustle and bustle of city life and electronic devices ruling the world.

    The serenity of the forest at dusk reminded him of hunting trips in the Blue Ridge Mountains, walking and talking with his father. Albeit the sounds and the trees here were alien, the overwhelming feeling of tranquility carried the same vibe. Gentle humming noises lined the inside of the forest with an occasional, *ca caw*, and Bud almost felt earthbound. As he looked up into the trees to see if he could find the boisterous ravens, or whatever they were, three opossum-like creatures with red baboon faces and long crimped tails scurried across the wide branches overhead. Stopping above, they squatted, hawking down at Bud. He maintained his gait and placed his hand on the handle of his hatchet, hoping they would sense his lack of fear and decide not to attack. After several steps, he realized the large rodents were content to simply watch and follow.

    On his way back, Bud came upon a set of vines with velvety tendrils, and he stopped to harvest them. As he severed the intertwined vines, he noticed the rodents stagger backward, trembling with fear. Chuckling, he made a low grunting sound, shaking his axe high above his head. The strange opossums scattered higher up into the trees, shaking the branches, sending leaves falling to the ground. In the wake, a scream pierced the nippy air like an icepick. *Tsarina*, Bud recognized. Turning to find her voice, he dropped the vines and branches and sprinted toward the campsite.

Tsarina's sporadic outbursts provided a general sense of direction. Several hundred yards outside the perimeter of their campsite, Bud caught a glimpse of her legs. She was hanging ten feet off the ground with her legs and arms wrapped around one of the lowest branches of a golden brown tree.

"Go away," she howled at a giant black boar stalking her from below. Snorting and scratching the ground, the bristly creature shook its white chest, rippling the crimson stripes running down its side. Four mustard colored horns, curved like sickles, sat atop its head, two of them angling forward and two of them back. Yellow bone spikes protruded out of its back as it turned its gold eyes toward Bud and snorted a thick breath of steam.

"Careful! There's more of them!" Tsarina warned, as she pulled herself up on top of the branch. Suddenly, five of the beasts circled around from the backside of the tree, snorting, and scraping the ground with their mustard hooves. Bud knew he would not be able to best them all at once at ground level, so he took a giant step toward the pack, howling and raising his hands above his head. The prickly hair on their backs stiffened, and steam blasted from their noses as they stamped their hooves into ground. Charging in unison, the beasts closed quickly, and Bud responded, sprinting toward them at full speed. As the boars surged closer, they opened their jaws wide, exposing yellow tusks. Tsarina's scream echoed off the tree, and just before impact, Bud leapt off one foot, soaring over the confused the animals. Squealing and spinning in circles, the boars stabbed their hooves into the soft soil, and black dirt and rust colored leaves erupted from the ground. They sniffed the air over their heads, trying to track his scent. Bud surged toward Tsarina's tree, leaping onto her branch, grabbing it with both hands. He pulled up and out of the boars' reach. As he settled next to her, he asked, "Are you okay?"

"Yeah." She blinked. "That was frickin' awesome! How'd you jump like that?"

"Haven't you noticed the gravity?"

"What are talking about?"

"It ain't the same here."

"Really?" She paused for a moment. "I guess I just thought I was light headed or something. Weird. So, you think that's what's going on?"

"Pretty sure. I don't see any other explanation. I noticed it once we got out of the dorm. I think that's why I threw you so far over the fence."

"Oh. I just thought you were amped."

"I don't think so. I feel it all the time. You think you can make it up to that next branch?" he asked.

"Yeah, why?"

"Cool. Head on up, I'm gonna need some room."

"What are you gonna do?" she asked. "They have us surrounded."

"Nothing yet. Let's just wait here a minute and see if they leave."

"And if they don't?"

"Then they have a problem, because I'm going to light the handle of this knife and toss it into one of their fat ass hides. Maybe we'll have bacon for breakfast."

"Mmm. Let's do that anyway," she purred and began climbing up to the next branch.

After a chuckle, he asked, "Hey, did you find those leaves?"

"Yeah, I but I only got about five of them before these frickin' pigs showed up. I never saw pigs look like that. What the hell are they?"

"They look like demonic razorbacks."

"Yeah. Now you see why I've never been camping."

"Aw come on, this is nature at its finest, straight up Darwinism. You must've studied all that shit. You just gotta remember, we are smarter than they are. All we have to do is scare them off—with *magic*."

"Magic? Who's doing magic?"

"I got the magic this time," he informed.

Tsarina cocked her head to the side, perplexed.

He pulled the lighter from his pocket and gave it a flick. "You ain't the only one with a trick up your sleeve."

She frowned and gave a cold, worried stare.

"What's up?" he asked.

"I don't know," she replied, a tremble in her voice, then her eyes flashed toward the boars and back up at him. "I'm just trying to piece everything together. I mean none of this makes sense, I know. I guess I'm just finally going full on crazy."

"Going?" he teased, then immediately wished he hadn't.

"Yeah whatever, forget about it," she grumbled, turning from him.

"Aw shit. I'm sorry. Come on, I was just messing with you. Seriously, what's wrong?"

Her eyes dimmed, begging for understanding, and an uneasy breath slipped from her mouth as she looked down on him. "After you fell asleep last night, I went ahead with the spell. I aligned the candles and began the chant, but I must've passed out while doing it. I don't remember anything except my dream. I heard my mother's voice again last night in the dream. And it was so real. It was—"

"—like the thing with the bus flipping over?"

"Yeah. But last night, I kept repeating the phrase from her grimoire. I couldn't stop. It was like she was chanting the words with me, for me—like she was inside my head, forcing me to speak the words."

"I know. I saw the candles and figured—"

"What?" She scrunched her nose. "Why didn't you say something?" she asked and her eyes fell to her mother's anklet.

"I don't know. I don't think you're crazy."

Tsarina looked at him in a way he hadn't seen before. It was the look of a scared child talking to a stranger, and it spooked him a little. Her eyes fell to her chest, and she mumbled, "I'm sorry." A tear rolled down her cheek as she looked up. "I'm sorry I did this to us. I just didn't think the spell was going to work. I mean—"

"Hey, it's okay."

"I just didn't want to believe it. It's crazy."

He took her hand in his, gently massaging her knuckles. "It is crazy. So, how could you believe the spell would work? I'd be worried about you if you did, honestly. Nobody in their right mind believes in magic portals."

"Shelby does. I obviously should have. I'm a real frickin' witch." She looked lost in the realization. "And there's more I never told you about, more than just the book."

"Like what?"

She jerked her hands from his. "Like, how my mother was a crazy witch, and a freak, and nobody said anything when she disappeared. I mean, I never understood why they wouldn't look for her? It was like she just vanished off the face of the Earth and nobody cared."

"What are you talking about? I thought you said your mom died."

"Yeah—I don't know."

"What do you mean? Didn't you see her body at the funeral?"

"No. She was cremated, supposedly. After the ceremony, we tossed her ashes off the Statue of Liberty. She loved going up there, so it made for a believable, fitting end, but I remember different."

"Different how?"

Tsarina sat forward and rearranged her legs on the branch. "On the night ma died, I had a dream—if it was a dream. Tasha swears it was a dream, but I never really believed her. It was all too real. I mean, I was only six, but I could tell something was up with our family. I think Tasha lied to herself to stay sane all this time. Tasha used to talk about ma, and how she was crazy because she was practicing witchcraft after we'd go to sleep. On the night ma was murdered, she took the anklet and told us to go to bed, but I stayed up and watched her. I saw her holding the Eye in her hands like it was a wounded bird or something. It almost looked like it was glowing, kinda like last night. I think over the years I convinced myself it was just the reflection off the candles, you know."

Another tear rolled down Tsarina's cheek, gaining momentum as she looked up. She wiped it away with the back of her hand and continued, "Ma caught me watching from the shadows. I guess she knew I was scared, so she called me into the room, and that's when she told me, Tasha was afraid of magic, and that I wasn't because I had more of the gift like her. She said we were descendants of a woman named Istia, who was a gypsy shaman that used the constellations to guide her movements. So then, I went to sleep with all those fairytales buzzing around in my head, and in the middle of the night, ma wakes us up, and she's got our backpacks full like we were going on a trip somewhere. She put the anklet on me and took us outside. It was just like today. Everything outside was wilderness—no streets, no buildings—just that grassy field where our courtyard should have been. There was this pale man in a black cloak waiting there, just like today, but it wasn't exactly the same dude. He walked out of the grass, and then he and ma started arguing about something—" Tsarina grabbed her forehead. "Wait—was it him?" She looked out into the forest as if searching for him in the trees.

"You think it was the same dude with those creatures?" Bud asked.

"No. I think it was the man from the train." Her brow furled.

"What are you talking about? What man from the *train*?"

"When me and Shelby were going out to my old apartment to find ma's grimoire, this weird dude was following us." Her face relaxed. "Yeah, that was him. He looked like the man from that night."

"So what happened to him? He died?"

"He was…he was killed getting off the train."

"Damn. How?"

"Some gangbangers were messing with us, and he pissed them off trying to talk to me, but I just ran from him. Now I think he was trying to help me—trying to warn me not to open the portal."

"He told you that?"

"Kinda."

Bud gave a quizzical look.

"Yeah well, he didn't actually say anything." She looked Bud straight in the eye. "He spoke to me telepathically. I heard his voice in my head," she explained.

"What?" Bud began to think she was getting delirious, but took one look at the boars still circling below and realized where they were and how they had gotten there. He suddenly didn't find it so hard to believe.

"Yeah, I thought I was frickin' crazy. I guess now I know it was real at least." Her face soured. "Shit! I forgot to grab the necklace."

"Jesus, a necklace? What does that do?"

"I don't know, but he was trying to give it to me when he died, and I frickin' left it on the desk. Damn it."

"Ok, wait. Forget about the necklace since we don't have a clue about that, but let's backtrack a bit to the night that your mother died. If you're right—let's assume all that really happened—one thing doesn't make sense. You said he was arguing with your mother outside the building that night, but you and your sister obviously returned to your apartment. It sounds like he and your mother stayed here in this wilderness, right?"

"Yeah. That's the last I saw of them, but I guess it's possible he could have come through the portal before it closed."

"Why would he do that?" Bud questioned.

"I don't know. For me. For ma. Maybe he's been watching me all these years. The last thing I remember was Tasha got really scared. She took us inside the building and hid me under the bed. I remember ma screaming from somewhere for us to stay inside, and of course, Tasha swears all this never happened." Tsarina lowered her voice mockingly. "Muggers killed ma. That's all she would ever say about that night."

"That's the story she gave you, then?"

"The story was: ma was on her way home from work that night, and she was jumped by two muggers who took her money and stabbed her to death."

"Why would your sister lie about that?"

"Probably to keep us both out of the psych ward. People can convince themselves of anything, and I think that's what Tasha did to herself. I know I've repressed it by pegging it as a dream all these years. I think she knows what really happened, but she just can't let herself believe it."

"Why didn't you ever say anything to anybody? Especially after you started having the dreams?"

"Are you mental? I didn't want anybody, including myself, to think I was a witch. It's like you said, that's insanity, right?" She cackled, "Lock me up! I'm a crazy ass witch who can see the future."

"Well, the good news is you aren't crazy," he reassured. "Look, I'm not going to sit here and tell you I know exactly what's going on. All this shit is...*interesting* to say the least. And I honestly don't know what's happened to us. It obviously doesn't make any sense coming from our world of science and logic. I'm generally all about logic and rational thinking myself, so all of this shit is way off the charts for me, and I keep hoping we'll find some shred of evidence that proves that we're wrong and that we're still on Earth, but—" He locked his eyes to hers, pressing his point. "All I know right now is I'm glad we're together, and whatever's happened, wherever we are, Earth or...wherever, I know you kept me sane back there, more than once, and I should be thanking you for it."

She shook her head. "Yeah but, if this is real, if we are really stuck on this planet, I did this to us."

"You couldn't know. It ain't your fault. You can't blame yourself."

The affection in her eyes grounded him and he began to slice a piece of cloth off the bottom of his shirt. "Come on, you're the rock. I'm the one who lost it after that plant-thing threw up on me."

A tiny giggle sputtered from her lips as they curled into a grin. "You were a little out of control," she admitted.

With a grin Bud, sliced the bottom half of his shirt with his knife and wrapped the frayed piece of cloth around the handle.

"What are you doing?" she asked.

"Magic," he said, shaving a few tiny strips of dry bark off the tree. He placed them inside the newly formed pocket of cloth and lit the makeshift fuse with his lighter. The tinder gradually crackled to life, and once the knife handle was ablaze, he hurled the blade into the boar's hide directly below. With a thump, the flaming knife buried itself deep into the hindquarters of the animal, and the massive beast kicked its back legs in the air wildly then bolted into the forest, spewing a frightened melody of squeals. The rest of the herd panicked, grunting and squealing chaotically, fleeing in all directions.

"That was dope," Tsarina applauded.

"That should keep them busy for a while. Hopefully, the one I hit will collapse, and the rest of them will eat him and forget about us."

"Eat him?"

"Yeah, boars don't give a shit. They're cannibals."

"That's sick." She grimaced.

"Yeah, well, that's why they're called pigs."

∞∞∞∞*First Night*

After helping Tsarina down from the thick tree, Bud marched her to the campsite and began organizing the materials for the lean to. Tsarina had a noticeable limp. When she took a seat on the mossy ground, she stretched her wounded leg out straight and rubbed the wound. He wondered how much pain it was causing her, and he pulled a packet of ibuprofen from his first-aid kit. "Here, take two of these."

"And call me in the morning," she chuckled, taking the packet from him.

"Yeah, how is it?" he asked.

"It's ok." She feigned a smile. "I just need to rest and keep it clean. Same with you and that burn."

"Alright," he agreed.

Tsarina held two of the four-foot wide rubber fronds, poking their integrity with the tips of her fingers. The dried mud, caked underneath her fingernails, didn't seem to bother her as she sat stroking the veins of the leaves. Looking at Bud, she asked, "I was thinking—are we gonna need firewood? That would keep the pigs and the bugs away, right?"

"Normally, I would say yes, but unfortunately, we can't do that. The smoke would lead those frogmen, and everything else right to us."

"Right." Her lips pursed. "I almost forgot about them. Good thing I got John frickin' Rambo over here." She smiled.

He raised one side of his lip and mumbled, "They drew first blood, not me...*They* drew first blood."

Tsarina shook her head disparagingly, laughing despite his horrible impression. Her gentle laughter rejuvenated his aching muscles and his taxed mind, allowing him to continue constructing the lean to with a renewed sense of purpose. As he placed the branches up against the thick, rust colored tree and bound them using the sinewy vines, he smiled at her and finished the structure by securing the rubbery leaves across the top. Once the final lash was tied in place, he sat next to Tsarina, admiring their handiwork. She rubbed his back and gave him a peck on the cheek before rising gingerly; then strolled over to her bag with a slight limp, she was obviously trying to downplay.

Bud sensed her pain even in the darkness. As she slid out of her bloodied sweatpants, his eyes wandered across her curvaceous silhouette. He noticed the dressing on her leg was stained with blood. "Hey, let's redo that bandage," he offered.

She batted her eyes. "You know, you're not so bad of a nurse. You're sterile and observant."

"Uh, thanks. I guess. But if it's all the same to you, I'd like to leave the gory stuff up to the professional. It'd be much better for both of us if you'd just stay out of trouble."

"It wasn't my idea to fly over the fence like Super Girl. You know, I could have fought that lurker dude with you." She made a loose karate chop motion with her hand.

"Uh, yeah. I don't think that would have worked out much better," he argued, as he pulled the first aid kit from his backpack.

"Hey, I pack a mean punch mister."

"I'm well aware of that, ma'am." He rubbed his shoulder and smirked.

Bud found it easier to treat her wound this time around. He reapplied the antibiotic cream much faster and taped the new dressing over the gash confidently. Tsarina smiled as he tore the last bit of tape from her leg, and she thanked him with a long kiss. When she slinked away, he sat mesmerized, watching her slip into a fresh pair of black sweat pants. He couldn't dissuade the grin blossoming on his face.

"I guess we should get to bed early and get a fresh start with the sun tomorrow. Guess there's no telling how long this night's gonna be."

"If I sleep at all." She frowned.

"We should be fine. This lean to is pretty good camouflage."

Her face remained clouded with a skeptical look as she nestled her head into his chest and said, "I just understand how this is possible, but those Lurkers were real as shit. I mean, right, those things were real? That portal was real? It just goes against everything—"

"I know," he comforted. The warmth of her touch soothed his raging nerves, and he stroked her hair, trying to provide a similar feeling. "There are plenty of things out there that are beyond our comprehension—we'd be fools to think otherwise. So, yeah, I guess all this shit is real. Hell, I've read stories about shamans who could meditate themselves into a dreamlike state, and then astral project themselves over to other places. Perception is reality," He stated, tapping his temple with his forefinger.

"Yeah, I'll bet those dudes were on Peyote or licking frogs' butts or something," she quipped.

"Ok, probably," he admitted, "but you never know what you think you know. I mean, for instance, you think my name is Bud."

"What are you talking about? Your name is Bud." Her silky curls caught the stubble on his chin as she sat up abruptly, questioning his eyes.

"Yep. You see, all this time you thought my name was Bud, but on my birth certificate, it's Taylor—Taylor Hawke Christiansen—perception is reality."

"Really? So if your name is Taylor, then what's up with Bud?"

"Short for Buddha," he snickered.

She muffled a laugh of confusion. "How'd you get that name?"

"Some weird kid back in the fourth grade dubbed me with it."

She looked at him suspiciously. "Some Carolina kid was into Buddhism in the fourth grade?"

"Damn, I'm beginning to think you are a serial stereotyper—but yeah, the kid's mom was a hippie from California or something, and they were all into Eastern culture and medicine."

"So, just 'cause they were into that shit don't tell me how you became Buddha," she said, extracting a couple of bottled waters from her pack.

"Well, you want the whole story?" he asked.

"Yeah, maybe it'll help me relax, she intimated, as she twisted off the cap and handed an open bottle to him. "So weird. Taylor huh? That's kinda sexy. Taylor—" His name rolled softly off her lips.

"Alright." He blushed and took a swig from his bottle.

Tsarina curled next to him rested her head onto his shoulder as he began, "I was in science class back in the fourth grade, and our teacher, Ms. Overwood, was conducting an experiment on reaction times. Her little reaction test was to sneak up on me and slap her ruler on my desk, thinking I would freak out. I guess she figured I would jump out of my seat like some wild ape or something. Stupid. But I just sat there, cool as a cucumber, and she had to alter her scientific conclusions a bit, as you can imagine. You could tell it wasn't the reaction she was looking for because she went on to explain, 'you see, everyone jumped at the unexpected noise.'" He mocked her excited teacher tone and fluttered his hands around his chest.

"Then she made up all this mumbo jumbo about reaction times and shit, but at the end of her little thesis, she pointed at me and said, 'Well, everyone jumped except for Taylor. Now, can anyone explain why?' That's when this kid, Richard, raises his hand and says, 'Cause he's Buddha,' and we were all like—what's a Buddha? Mrs. Overwood even giggled a little at him. Then she went on to explain all the possibilities for my lack of reaction time, and all this other mess, but you see what she didn't know was I was one step ahead of her the whole time." He tapped his temple. "I saw her coming with that silly ass ruler from a mile away and figured out her plan before she ever got close to popping the table with it. After that, all the kids started calling me Buddha. Pretty sure nobody knew who the hell Buddha was. They just thought the name sounded funny, and back then it was funny—didn't take much in the fourth grade. Then somehow, it just got shortened to Bud."

When he looked down, Tsarina's head was nestled around his side, her eyes half closed, her soft ringlets draped over his lap. He thought she was asleep until she rubbed his belly in a gentle circle and whispered, "My little Buddha."

∞∞∞Do Not Cross

Tsarina awoke, lying on the cold tile floor of the dormitory mailroom, confused and excited by the familiar surroundings. When she sat up, her head throbbed, as if her heart had been repositioned at the base of her skull.

"What the hell?" she wondered aloud.

A bright beam of sunlight splashed over the Dutch door separating her from the foyer and stung her eyes as she peered across the hall. Once her pupils adjusted to the light, she spied a squad of Navy clad police officers investigating the guard desk where Jadu had been mutilated. Men in blue were sectioning off the entrances in the area with long yellow *Do Not Cross* tape.

Tsarina remained on her knees behind the counter, observing a scrawny man with orange, curly hair, dressed in a white lab coat. The mortician was crouching over Jadu's body, what was left of it, poking and prodding with latex gloves. Tsarina felt the urge to run out and help with the examination, but she resisted her medical instinct long enough for a stocky man in street clothes to stamp through the main entrance. He stopped in the middle of the foyer, surveying the scene. The man, in his late forties, was dressed in a tan, single-breasted suit, a white striped shirt, and a crimson tie. His wispy blonde hair, faded grey around the temples, along with his chiseled facial features, gave him the look of an old movie mogul, while the rough lines on his face narrated a different story of hardship and pain. Several of the beat cops rushed to greet him before he reached the mortician. The tallest one initiated a conversation.

"Detective Morris, sir, I'm officer Young. I was first on the scene here, sir," the thin cop announced.

"Ok, Young. So what do we got here?" Detective Morris asked flatly. His accent, Manhattan rough, was slightly more articulate than the others.

"Well sir, that guy over there in pieces is—was Rajah Jadu. He was the overnight security guard on duty here."

Detective Morris focused his attention toward the lab technician and asked, "How long has he been dead Mort?"

"I'd say about eight to ten hours Dave."

"All frigging day?" Detective Morris raised an eyebrow. "Bullshit, how does this guy lay here dead, stinking' up the joint for ten hours, and nobody even notices? You called this in?" He glared at Officer Young.

"Well…uh…yeah, that's the weird thing sir," he stammered. "When we got here, we found the building all sealed up, late this morning, at approximately eight-twenty in the morning, sir. A student tried to enter the building and noticed it was locked. That's when we got the call. So then me an' Louie here," he tapped the short officer next to him on the chest, "we tried to get in touch with somebody inside the main office—to see if we could try and have them open up the doors from the inside. But all the phone lines was dead, and the lights was out. So that's what took us awhile, sir. We didn't know what to do. That's when we called the boys over at fire department and figured we'd just have them crack her open, you know?"

"Do you have a point officer Young?" asked Morris.

"Sir? Uh, yes sir. So that's what took us a while sir. I mean, we tried to hack the door open, but we got nowheres. I mean nutin'. The freaking glass wouldn't break. The locks wouldn't budge. It was like they had been welded shut or something. I'm telling you it was like Fort friggin' Knox over here. So at that point, we decided to put it to bed and let the demolition guys set up first thing in the afternoon, and that's what we did. So then they show up, and just before they was about to set off the explosives, Louie, over here, pulls on the door—for a laugh, you know—to show the all guys what they was up against, and *viola*! The freaking door opens up like we was all idiots—freaking weird, sir." Detective Morris nodded impatiently, pressing Officer Young to finish. "Ok, so that's when we found the dead security guard—about an hour ago—and now I got the rest of the men sweeping the building for survivors, but it's gonna take some time sir, there's twenty-two floors here, but the RA lady, the live one—"

"What? There's another victim?" Detective Morris interrupted.

"Oh yeah sir, there's a bunch of them. We keep finding bodies all over the place. Same thing, mutilated, half eaten—most of them next to piles of ash."

"Jesus Christ! So, what does this R.A. know?"

"She told us they only have students on a couple of floors in the summer—so that's good, but this could be real bad, sir. We've already found a couple of students dead on the fifth and sixth floors."

"Well, we'll want to bring her down to the station for questioning, so send somebody for her. What have you got on the killer, or killers?"

"That's the thing, sir. Nutin' yet."

The detective's chiseled jaw clenched as he echoed, "*Nutin*? You got a crime scene here that looks like something out of the *Texas Chainsaw Massacre,* and you tell me you got nothing? No fingerprints, no hairs, no footprints—nothing? Is that what I'm supposed to tell all those reporters out there, Officer Young?"

The young man held his head low as Detective Morris questioned the lab technician in disgust, "Mort, please tell me you got more than nutin', and please don't tell me this guy mutilated himself."

Mort looked up from the bloody carcass and answered stolidly, "No, he certainly did not. There are bruises on his wrists and forearms, which suggest his arms were ripped and hacked out of his body, and it seems like something sharp and light, maybe an axe or a hatchet, was used to lop off his head, from the lacerations there. Also, there are fragments of a strange metal embedded in his skin, and then there is this interesting dried slime and piles of ash everywhere. I'm about to tag this one and go see if the others are similar. All I know is, I would hate to run into whoever did this. This was not exactly natural."

"Ah, it was probably some freakin' nut job hopped up on PCP—watched too many episodes of the *Highlander.* Crazy bastards." He straightened his tie. "All right, it's time for me throw these frigging vultures a piece of meat." He turned to Officer Young. "Then we'll head up and check the other victims." The detective reluctantly sauntered over to the front of the building, and when he opened the door, dozens of flashbulbs exploded, popping off all around him as reporters began launching questions from every direction.

∞∞∞Funky Meters

At first, it seemed as if the flashbulbs were blinding Tsarina, then she noticed a set of rose-colored rays sifting their way through the cracks in the leafy roof of the lean to. She felt the soft mossy ground beneath her back and sat up, rubbing her eyes as they adjusted to the light. When she was able to open them without squinting, she realized she was in the forest with Bud. He was sitting cross-legged several feet away, outside the lean to, scraping methodically at something. The massive, white-barked trunks of the forest trees bled into her vision as she blinked the remnants of the dream from her eyes.

"Morning. You sleep all right?" She heard him ask.

Groggily, she examined her leg then replied, "Yeah, sorta. I don't know. I feel…different today."

"You're different alright," he joked.

The jab sparked her senses, and she realized he was sharpening a blade, either the knife or the hatchet, she couldn't tell which. Maybe he was scraping one against the other. "Whatever. What time is it?" She blinked.

"Uh, gee, I don't know. I forgot my sundial."

"Jerk."

He grinned smugly. "But we should probably get a move on—just in case there's more of them creatures out there, *lurking* us."

"Right," she agreed, refusing to acknowledge his teasing any further. It was too early for witty banter, especially without coffee. She tried not to think of the rich aroma, and the smooth taste, and the pleasant warmth it would have brought to her lips. Woozily, she rose to her feet with a giant, cat-like stretch, yawning, inhaling a large dose of the virginal morning air into her lungs.

Bud gave her a mischievously sexual look and said, "Somehow I don't think they're just going to let us just slip off into the mist, unless you can bat those pretty eyes and make us disappear or something."

Before she could respond, a tinny voice bounced off the trees. "Ah, disappearin'. Yes, disappearin'. 'Tis easy. Been at it all day, I have. 'Tis reappearin' what's the hard part."

Tsarina whipped her head around to locate the chuckling voice. A diminutive man, slightly under four feet tall, with limbs proportional to his body, stood at the edge of the trail, puffing on a honeycomb pipe. He was draped in a brown wool suit, which fit loosely around his waist and shoulders. His feet were dressed in sandals that tied around his ankles like boots. His speckled fingertips took his patched, multicolored, top hat from his head, and he placed it over his heart as he explained, "You see this ol' hat here? Well, I'm gonna throw me eyeglasses in and they's gonna disappear right before your very eyes, they will. Promises, promises. Now watch 'ere closely now."

Squinting, the tiny man removed his brass-rimmed eyeglasses and dropped them into the hat as predicted. Next, he waved his hand back and forth over the hat, shaking it gently, while muttering something inaudible that sounded like botched Latin. Upon flipping the hat upside down, he revealed that the article had miraculously vanished, and finally, in order to validate his efforts, he offered the magical hat to Tsarina for inspection. Wary of his touch, she made no motion to obtain it, which seemed to baffle the little magician for a moment. Abashed, he rolled his eyes and firmly placed the hat on his head.

"Well then, you see, there be nothing to it. Like choking a big fat Slogger at dusk. Oh me, o' my, so sorry. Where's me manners? Name's Rosel. Rosel Meters, at your service," he offered, extending his minikin hand.

Tsarina accepted his offering, and as she made contact with his skin, a jolt of cold, static electricity shocked her palm and spread into her wrist and forearm. She recoiled. "Whoa, you shocked me!"

"I beg your pardon milady," he said, rubbing his hand, "but 'tis quite to the contrary. 'Twas you who did'st shocked me. Not the other way 'round. Guess you be a fledgling witch then. Not be knowin' your own strength with ye magic, or ye just be showin' off. Either way, I must advise, you needs be careful wit' that energy in ya, milady. Don't want to go around bragging your talents to everyone like that. Never know whom ye might be talking with. Ah, but with the transfer of our energies, however, well—" His seductive look begged approval.

Wondering if she still might be in a dream, Tsarina looked at Bud in disbelief.

The little man continued. "Rules the world it do, whether it be real or imaginary—matters not. A spark between us, 'twas no fuss at all." He beamed a wink and puffed out his little chest with a quick arch of his back. "You see, I be a well trained cunning man me self, and I kindly offer me services of the arcane to all the poor unfortunate souls in need. I can find your buried treasures and protect ye from them evil spirits—for a nominal fee, of course. I also dabble in the illusions, and I have a certain knack for invisibility, as you can plainly see, or maybe ye can't." He chortled at his own little joke, then squinted one eye and asked, "So ya wanna be disappearin', do ya?"

"Oh…yeah," she replied. "What do we gotta do?"

"Well, um, let me see." He began counting his fingers and stopped on the pinky. "For that magnificent, one of a kind trick, I'll be requirin' fifty Adytum coins say—nothing more, nothing less. 'Tis me offer. Take it or leave it." He folded his arms and looked away.

Tsarina responded with puppy dog eyes. "Oh, well, I'm sorry but we don't have any of those coins sir. Actually, I was only asking because I believe we are all in great danger here, and I was hoping that those creatures don't find you here with us. We really should all disappear as quickly as possible."

The little man's voice raised an octave. "Creatures? What creatures be that?"

"Dark, slimy creatures with flat faces and no noses," Bud warned, as if spinning a ghost story to a group of small children, corroborating Tsarina's ploy.

Rosel shivered, rubbing his lower back nervously. "Noctiss! Here? What say, where? How that be? Crossed the gorge did they? How far they be?"

"We saw them in the field outside of the forest." Tsarina pointed behind Rosel. "What are they?"

"What are they? What are they? They's the meanest devils walkin', they be. Foul minions from the depths of the Obsidian Sea!" Rosel yelped, and began backing away toward the trail. "So, I was just walkin' up from Splinter there, goin' to have a gander at Istia's Field to pick me some shroomies for the day, but with this news—Ah, 'twas such a nice dawn for me walk, you know?" he stammered, all the while continuing to slink farther away. "Oh well, I really must be off. Truly, 'twas quite nice to meet you both and do have a most pleasant day." Tipping his cap, he crept farther down the path. "'Tis quite a ways for these tiny legs. Cheers!"

"Wait!" Tsarina pleaded.

Beset in the middle of the road, the little man spun around, stamping his feet together, a reluctant frown upon his face.

"Sorry sir, but we're sorta lost," she explained.

Rosel arched his back, cocking his head to the side, and waved a finger behind her, then instructed, "Well, since the world be round, you always be on top of it."

"Right." She pursed her lips. "Then could you at least give us directions to Splinter from the top of the world here?"

"Ah well, yes. I'm sure I could. In this case, you'd be just a half-day out of Splinter, as the bees buzz—down the path, right over there. Buzz, Buzz…"

Tsarina turned to find the path, and several indigo birds with yellow wings darted in and out of the trees, dodging the incoming shafts of sunlight. When she returned her attention to Rosel, he had vanished. "Where'd he go?" She looked to Bud.

"Don't know." He shrugged. "Little dude must have walked off when our backs were turned."

"Or he used magic," she suggested.

"How you figure?"

"I don't know. His touch was electric—" She rubbed the top of her hand.

"Well, he ain't no Jerry Staples," Bud stated in her silence.

"What's it with you and Jerry Staples?"

"I've seen better is all I'm saying."

"I guess," she allowed, continuing to rub her hands, trying to shake off the icy feeling still residing underneath her skin, "but when I shook his hand, it was really cold—gave me this chilly little shock. He did point us toward a town, at least."

"Yeah, if he wasn't messing with us. Hopefully we can find a halfway normal person there," Bud complained. "What was that about Adytum coins, though? You ever heard of anything like that?"

∞∞∞*Splinter*

After a dry, Captain Crunch breakfast, Bud repacked the rest of his gear, rounded up Tsarina, and headed toward Splinter—the direction given to him by a four-foot tall man who claimed to be a magician. He shook his head at the outlandish thought as he walked the path. Pebbles with wavy irises of brown and burnt orange rolled beneath his boots like marbles as he trekked beside the stream. Curling through the gigantic white trees, covered with viridian moss, he went out of his way to pass through the small shafts of sunlight that were plummeting to the ground in order to absorb their heat. The beams warmed his face and hands as they sifted their way down through the cracks of the lime and olive leaves, and where they touched the soil, orange, long-stemmed flowers, much like giant poppies, reared their heads to capture the precious energy as well. Purple lilies, lime ivy, multi-colored mushrooms, and the crimson, bell-shaped flowers flourished along the water's edge. The scenery made for a glorious hike and would have been immeasurably enjoyable except for the fact that he had no home, his destination was unknown, and a pack of slimy frogmen were possibly still lurking somewhere in the trees. "These trees look like white oaks, kind of," he mentioned, gazing up at the massive hardwoods, "but they're bigger than Sequoias. You ever seen a Sequoia?" he asked Tsarina, remaining hopeful he would see one again.

"No," she answered solemnly.

"Oh wow. We gotta do that. When we get back, we should plan a road trip out west. You got to see the Redwoods."

"Sure...sounds cool."

Her despondent agreement weighed like a wet sack of flour on his enthusiasm, and he forced an encouraging smile. "Hey, like you said, we got here, so there must be a way back, and this is just a little admission, but I'm starting to believe that it might be entirely possible this ain't Earth."

She looked at him crossways.

He continued, "But I still don't see why we can't believe that one day, we're going to wake up in the Redwoods and be laughing at all this like it was just a wild dream." He spoke partly to lift her spirits, and in the process, bolster his own.

"Yeah, I guess." Her tone remained melancholy.

It was apparent nothing was going to cheer her up. Plodding along in silence for several minutes, Bud found solace in a more mundane task. He slid the hatchet he had taken from the dead Noctiss and began examining the workmanship. The thin haft was lightweight and whittled from a cream-colored wood. The obsidian head of the hatchet was chiseled with jagged angles, honed for slicing. Bud stroked the tip of the blade of his forefinger and thought of how easily it had pierced the flesh of the Noctiss. He wondered aloud, "How intelligent do you think those things are?"

"What, those Lurkers? Intelligent enough to track us to our building and almost kill us," she reminded.

"Yeah, but they had that dude leading them."

"So?"

"I don't know. I guess I'm trying to figure out what they are. Aliens?"

"Or maybe, we're the aliens," she proposed.

"And that little dude, and the man in the cloak, are they aliens too?"

"Maybe." She swatted at a bug. "They certainly weren't normal."

Bud had to agree with her assessment, but he continued questioning his surroundings all the same. He surveyed the yellow, waist-high flowers shaped like diamonds as he marched up the large knoll. They were like nothing he had ever seen. Thin green stalks of foot high grass swayed chaotically in the wind like paper bamboo, wilting underneath his the stamp of his heavy boots. He felt the strain on his legs as the grade of the hill gradually increased. Grainy pebbles rolled under his feet, occasionally causing him to slip and slide like a drunken sailor, and as they traipsed through the flowers and the grass, Tsarina's progress was almost as graceful—she grabbed onto his hand several times for balance.

Climbing the hill took the better part of the day and eventually lead them into a sparse forest of conifers filled with wide flat branches and arrow-sized needles. By late afternoon, they had reached the summit, where atop the vast plateau, a diminutive conifer sprouted out of a rust-colored rock. Bud expanded his chest, inhaling a huge gasp of air as he strolled over to the tiny tree. The level ground relieved his burning thighs and lungs, and he quickened his pace.

A short wall of orange and yellow flowers guarded the roots of the tree, and when Bud placed his foot over them, it found no purchase. He caught his misstep with a swift grab of a tree branch, and when he looked down, the tops of the white and green trees were poking through the mist, thirty feet below. Pulling his foot back, he placed his palms into his hips, preventing Tsarina from making the same mistake. Her body pressed into his back, and she gazed over his shoulder, wrapping her arms around his waist. "Don't worry, I got you," she whispered in his ear.

Beneath their feet, a bluish-grey cloud masked the view of the narrow path leading down into the chasm. It looked like a deer-trail, Bud thought, due to the dry hoof prints embedded in the rocks and dirt. Farther down the line, thatched roofs with hard sheets of striped wood seemed to float on top of the mist like capsized rafts, and the hazy moisture wafted across the valley toward a stone tower situated at the far end of the village. The imposing structure presided over the other houses like a Puritanical chapel guarding its disciples. A circular, stained glass dormer, stationed underneath the pointed golden top, refracted brilliant rays of rose-colored sunlight spiraling down through the mist. The awe-inspiring spectacle overwhelmed Bud, and he almost didn't hear Tsarina when she asked, "You coming?"

Once he broke his gaze, he spotted her plodding down the crusty trail several yards ahead. Bud jogged for a moment to catch up then slowed his gait to admire her sultry hips, swaying back and forth. Satisfied, he shuffled even with her as they approached the blue mist, and they shared a smile of anxious expectation before wading into the fog.

Mindful of his footing, he marched down the treacherous path, and after several long switchbacks, he eventually saw the lower halves of the cottages, and the silhouettes of townspeople.

"Hey look—people," Tsarina announced.

"Yeah." Bud frowned, concerned how they would be received. Their foreign attire would alert anyone that they were outsiders, he thought.

Halfway down the trail, he took his eyes off his footing to scout the town, and saw a middle-aged man promenading like a peacock toward a violet and gold cottage. The man was dressed in a purple tunic laden with intricate patterns of white birds in flight. His bristly, brownish-grey locks, tucked deep inside his hood, spilled out in thin strands over his shoulders, and he used a tall, bone staff to prod himself forward.

"This place is a little different," Bud observed.

"Really, captain obvious." She stuck the tip of her tongue out of the side of her mouth. "It looks kinda like an old Amish settlement in Pennsylvania."

"What? Just because there's a cart in the middle of a gravel road? I don't know about that. I don't think the Amish paint their houses bright purple and gold.

"I'm just saying it kinda *resembles* that, with the little cottages—and yes, the cart." Tsarina turned her palms to the sky in protest and started walking toward the purple and gold cottage. "Whatever," she puffed. "I'm gonna go find out. You coming?"

"After you, milady," Bud allowed, flopping his hand in the direction of the violet cottage.

Tsarina followed the spindly man as he ambled into the vial shaped cottage, and Bud watched the thick wooden door shut behind. The creaky sign overhead hung from two gold hooks in the ceiling and rustled in the wake of the impact. It depicted several multicolored vials bubbling over with foam and read, "Althea's Apothecary." The elegant lettering was scribed in purple tempera calligraphy and set against a background of gold.

When Tsarina stepped onto the porch and opened the carved door, a sage-like fragrance with hints of jasmine burthened the air around them. Sunlight filtered through the tall narrow windows and provided ample visibility inside the shop along with a few candles that were sitting on top of the bookshelves. The brilliant rays shimmered off the hand-blown glass containers, illuminating their intricate, colorful tendrils, and as the door opened fully, dust particles formed miniature tornados with the change in air pressure, sparking chaotic refractions of the orange light.

In the corners, faint splashing sounds dribbled from various waterfall fountains, echoing throughout the rafters, drowning some of the more disturbing sounds that were coming from the lively bottles and vials on the lower shelves. Bell jars contained body parts from a multitude of different types of otherworldly insects, reptiles, and amphibians, and some of the concoctions in the vials sporadically gargled and popped. Tsarina jumped, muffling a yelp, as one bubbled over next to her in passing.

As they moved closer to the center of the room, Bud admired the unique collection, taking particular interest in the shrunken heads that were dangling from the shelves on rigid strands of vines laced with white flowers. Long, skeletal snouts on the skulls suggested that they were a type of rodent. The musty room was reminiscent of voodoo shops in New Orleans, and Bud questioned if they could have possibly ended up in Louisiana, or what a voodoo shop would be doing in upper state New York, or worse, and more likely, another planet called Adytum.

Toward the back of the room, the thin man in the purple tunic stood in front of a waist-high counter made of cerulean and emerald swirled crystal. He leaned against a bone staff that outstretched him by a foot, and it had a large sapphire inset at the top perched inside two golden wings. The man was smiling slightly at a portly woman sitting behind the counter who had his full attention. The proprietor was promoting a crystal ball in one hand and gesturing politely with the other. Her braided, burnt orange hair hung past her broad shoulders and slid back and forth as the clear orb sparkled in her hand. The client's razor-sharp nose bobbed up and down with each gesture, and a refraction of light sparked off his metallic tunic into Bud's eyes. He blinked it away as he followed Tsarina into the center of the room.

When they approached the counter, a large, orange and tan cat, belly sagging low, hopped up and paraded in front of the saleswoman, swishing its tail, meowing for attention.

Tsarina swapped glances with the square-headed lady then interrupted with a soft voice. "Excuse me—"

The woman nodded with a gentle smile, begging Tsarina's patience, then stroked the cat's back, arousing it to arch its long sangria tail into the air and purr contentment. The proprietor's purple and gold, v-neck blouse displayed a gold, heart-linked necklace inset with a large amethyst that rested comfortably between her substantial bosoms. The brilliant stone gently rolled out of the crevasse as her attention turned away from the cloaked man. Clamoring in a slight British accent, he stopped his query about the origin of the crystal ball, turned and scoffed.

"May I help you two dearies?" the woman asked politely, resting the orb on the counter.

"Well, yes. I hope so." Tsarina smiled then continued nervously, "Sorry, but we're kinda lost. We met this little man in the forest. He said his name was Rosel, Rosel Meters, and he directed us here. Well, not to your shop exactly, but to this town. Splinter?" She paused and the pair simply blinked and waited for her to continue, so she did. "Basically, we just wanna find out where we are and how we can get back to Manhattan. I mean, we've never heard of Splinter, so—"

The mercurial diatribe obviously flabbergasted the old woman, and she deferred to her patron. "Indimiril?"

The rat-faced man gave a confident nod and closed his eyes, solidifying his arrogance. "I see, so thou art friends with Mr. Meters art thou?" he asked.

"What? No." Bud scowled. "We're lost. Didn't you hear a word she said?"

Indimiril cleared his throat, pointing his nose above Bud's gaze. "Quite, and thou art trying to find a region by the name of Manhattan, as thou sayst?"

"Right!" Tsarina exclaimed. "You know it?"

"Of course not. There exists nothing of the sort," he responded with a frown. "Trust that I have traveled to the black base of Viduata's peak in the east and deep into the ice of Cairn Rose to the west, and this, *Manhattan*, is neither here nor there. Althea dost thou concur?" He looked to the proprietor who agreed with a blink and a nod. "And might I inquire whose province wouldst house this village?"

"America," Bud grumbled. "You know, the United States of America, on planet Earth?"

Indimiril's eyes grew wide. "Earth, thou sayst? 'Tis been many a day of sunshine, rain, or snow since I've spoken with anyone on such a fairy tale." He stroked his long peppered beard with his bony finger. "People who oft speak of Earth are either scholars, or those misfortunate souls whose eyes see a different picture from what is reality, and since thou art not dressed as scholars, nor speak as such, I must deduce the latter to be fact."

"Then deduce this Shakespeare—we're not a couple of nut jobs, okay? Earth is real, and the fact that you think it's some sort of fairy tale makes you the deranged one in my book. If this ain't Earth, then where do you suggest we are, exactly?"

Indimiril's frail jaw stiffened. "I assure thee, 'tis not I who art deranged, dear boy. I am the Archon of Splinter, and if there is anyone here who might be deranged, 'tis strangers who come babbling of mythical places such as Earth."

Bud gritted his teeth. "If you really think there is no such planet as Earth, then what planet are we on?"

"Why…Adytum, where else?" Indimiril spoke grandiloquently then shared a chuckle with Althea. "Now, if thou dost not mind, I have far more important matters to discuss with madam Althea."

"Ad-it-um?" Bud breathed. "Well, in fact, I do mind, sir. We have been running around here on Ad-it-um from these slimy-ass creatures for two days now, and all we keep getting from the few people we have run across are ridiculous answers to simple questions. Matter of fact, it's been absurd actually, and you appear to be no different."

Tsarina's face grew pale, and she bowed her head. Leaning toward the door, she grabbed Bud by the arm, apologizing along the way. "Excuse us. I'm very sorry. We are just really, really tired and a little confused right now. Really though, thank you for your time. We're just gonna go now. Thanks."

With a perturbed grunt, Indimiril shook his head then refocused his attention on Althea as if Bud and Tsarina had never entered. Bud fought the urge to turn around and punch the arrogant bastard straight in the eye, while Tsarina continued dragging him toward the exit like an unruly child. Shaking from her grasp, he stomped toward the door and ripped it open. Outside, the light stunted his vision. Panicked screams resounded from across the street.

Squinting, he took a step toward the commotion, and Tsarina immediately seized his hand. Bud watched several young villagers skittering into the small cottages. He scanned the length of the road to find the source of their distress. Groups of frogmen emerged from the azure mist on the outskirts of the village. Their viscid feet slithered over the cobblestone street toward a young man in a royal blue tunic.

"Noctiss!" the boy cried.

The crier, who appeared to be slightly younger than Bud, stood in front of a thin doorway, a long wavy-shaped dagger quivering in his hand. His bright tunic flashed its sheen as he whipped around to usher several women and children inside the cottage. The lead Noctiss hurled a black hatchet at the last woman, and she clutched the child she was holding to her breast. As she ducked inside the doorframe, the crude weapon tumbled head over handle and embedded itself into the seam of the wooden door. The young man ripped the hatchet from the seam and slammed the door shut, but his efforts left him open to the ensuing attack. Bud lurched forward instinctively, but could only watch in horror as the blade of a second hatchet plunged deep into the young man's chest. His blue tunic did nothing to dampen the impact of the serrated stone. The silver kris and the hatchet fell harmlessly from his hands onto the wooden planks, clattering to silence. The boy mustered a few weakened steps toward the Noctiss then collapsed to his knees. Shuddering, he grasped the hilt of the hatchet and feebly attempted to dislodge it from his chest, but his strength waned with each tug, and the weapon remained.

"Get back!" Bud shouted, pressing Tsarina deeper into the apothecary. Slamming the door shut, he stumbled backward. Tsarina backpedaled directly into the mahogany cases, hips and arms flailing, knocking over a wide row of glass vials. Amidst the crashing glass, Bud found a four-by-eight board stationed next to the door, seemingly made for keeping things out. He slid it between two iron hooks that were situated on either side of the doorframe and hurried to the counter where he overheard Althea ask Indimiril, "Noctiss? Here? They've never come this far into the woods? What could they be wantin' with us?"

"Could be for quite a number of reasons—" Indimiril contemplated.

"They're after us," Bud snipped. "They've been chasing us since yesterday. Do you believe us now?"

"Well, this most certainly does not provide thine tale with any more credibility, however—"

Before Indimiril could finish, a shattering blast ripped the front door off its hinges. Wooden shards whizzed across the room like darts, sending everyone ducking for cover behind the counter. As Bud hunched low, the cat sprang off his back and bounded into a small hole on the floor. Sawdust swirled in the fresh entryway, and a small pack of Noctiss filtered into the store, black hatchets poised over their shoulders. Bud stiffened and drew his hatchet and combat knife, preparing for the worst.

A silhouette of a stocky warrior emerged from the haze like an apparition—a dwarf, outfitted from head to toe in well-worn silver chain mail armor. Black and auburn braids slid back and forth across his cuirass, which consisted of four round metal disks, reflecting like mirrors. As he surveyed the room, his eyes eventually locked upon Tsarina, and he took several steps forward out of the sawdust cloud.

"There'll be no need for violence lad." His bristly eyebrows pressed down as he spoke, and his gruff voice belied his attempt at diplomacy. With a pronounced swipe of his charred gauntlet, he commanded the Noctiss to lower their hatchets. "Seems to be bit o' confusion here," he continued. "Allow me to introduce myself. I am Sükh Endrim, Dwarven ambassador for Master Agni. In addition, I kindly apologize for my unpolished cohorts here. They be not quite as well mannered as we would like—little more than a pack of wild dogs really."

Several of the Noctiss hissed at the degrading remark, glowering in the dwarf's direction.

"But things aren't as dastardly they seem, I assure you," he explained. "Please allow me to set it straight."

"Set it straight?" Bud crowed, a firm grip on his blade.

"Excuse me sir," Indimiril interjected. "Sükh was it?"

The dwarf nodded with a grunt.

"Yes, well I am Indimiril, the residing Archon here in Splinter, and I must inquire as to the meaning of this intrusion. That door will be quite expensive to replace. I say, are you of a mind to thieve us?"

The dwarf bellowed a genuine laugh. "Well, sorry for that, but 'taint no intrusion of thievery, sir Archon of Splinter—quite the opposite. Truth of the matter is—"

Bud cut in, "Truth of the matter here is those things tried to kill us—not to mention the fact that they ate everyone in our building for breakfast."

"I don't know about that," Sükh countered with a perplexed look. "What I do know is, I was hired by Master Agni to track down these two thieves here and take 'em back to Viduata, and as far as these Noctiss here are concerned, they was provided to help me track 'em. Been with me ever since we left Viduata's Peak, and by the look of them, you can tell they ain't had much to eat. Simple as that."

Althea nudged Indimiril and gave a subtle look of disapproval.

Indimiril nodded then questioned, "Then might I ask, what does Agni want of these two?"

"That be none of your concern schoolmaster. Now, enough slapping tongues. Stand aside. It's time I be taking these two with me."

"That ain't gonna happen," Bud stated, raising his hatchet, stepping out from behind the counter.

"I got a bag of Adytum coins in me pocket says different boy." Sükh sneered and took two deliberate steps forward. His dark beady eyes did not waver when Bud matched his stare.

Amidst the standoff, Indimiril lifted his hands to his chest, and the Noctiss raised their hatchets for attack. "Oh my," the magister gasped at the incensed reaction and lowered his hands to his side. "Pardon me," he entreated, "but if thou wouldst simply allow me to know why 'tis Agni requires these two villains, I would be more inclined to hand them over freely. Pray tell, what was't they stole? Thou canst surely understand where we might harbor a certain sense of mistrust, with thou busting in here like marauders, as thou hast done."

"Fair enough schoolmaster. If ya must know, it has to do with that little rock wrapped around the girl's ankle. She stole it from the old witch Viduata, and she wants it back."

"What? This was my mother's," Tsarina contended. "I've had it since I was kid—"

Indimiril blinked at Sükh. "I see, and what proof dost thou have of this crime?"

"A sack of Adytum coins waiting for me at Viduata's Peak is all the proof I need."

"This is a matter of justice. 'Tis truly something Madam Viduata should take up with the Council."

"There be no council in the black mountain. We don't need a council of senile old warlocks to tell us what's what. Now you'll be wise to hand over those two before I'm forced to show you a bit of justice."

Althea stiffened and shook her head disapprovingly. "No, I think not. You will not threaten us. In Splinter, we are governed by the council."

"Witch, I'd advise you to hold your fat tongue," Sükh warned.

Indimiril stood immobile, eyes darting toward Tsarina. Althea fixed a frigid stare upon the dwarf.

"Ah, so be it," Sükh said and then clamped his gauntlet around Bud's wrist. The stabbing pain from the vice-like grip choked the blood from Bud's hand, forcing him to release his knife to the ground. With his free hand, he swung the hatchet at the dwarf's head, but Sükh blocked the attack with his gauntlet. Sliding his hand down Bud's wrist, he knocked the hatchet to the ground and commanded, "Take the girl!"

The Noctiss hissed in unison as they leapt forward, hatchets held high. Althea countered, raising her hands into the air, shouting, "*Vereor incendia!*" They hissed at the witch like baby snakes being prodded with a burning stick then, inexplicably, the creatures dropped their weapons and fled through the gaping hole that was once the front door.

"Curse you, witch!" Sükh roared, and the pressure around Bud's wrist relaxed. The dwarf slipped a wide flat knife from his belt while stomping Bud's shoulder to the ground. With a flick of his wrist, Sükh launched the blade from his hand. It sparkled twice in the candlelight then disappeared as the honed tip buried deep into Althea's forehead. A single line of blood streamed out of the entry point down over her nose, dripping onto the countertop. Her head fell backward, and her body followed, tumbling down into the dark shaft behind the counter.

In that moment, another man entered the building and shouted, "Sükh! What has happened?"

"*Fulgor!*" howled Indimiril, slamming his staff into the ground. Upon impact, a brilliant flash of blue light erupted from the crystal in the top of his staff, blinding everyone in the room. Indimiril latched onto Tsarina's arm and jerked her toward the large hatch behind the counter.

"Ethan!" Sükh called. "Grab the boy." The dwarf pressed his boot heel harder into Bud's shoulder and waved a dagger at his head. Within the span of a breath, the tall brawny man rushed to his side, allowing Indimiril to flee with Tsarina down the ladder into the darkness below the floor.

"Take this boy and tie him to the back of your wyvern," Sükh ordered. "He's coming with us to cover our arses. We'll not be returning empty handed."

"Aye, sir," Ethan responded.

"I'll be after the little witch. If I do not return in the hour, take the boy to Viduata's Peak and toss him in the dungeon. Alive."

"Aye, sir."

Ethan grabbed Bud by the neck, shoving him to his feet, and pulled the silver mace from his belt, prodding him toward the door with the spiked tip. Outside, the cobbled street was devoid of life. Bud felt the points of Ethan's mace pressing into the small of his back, directing him toward a pair of winged reptilian figures. Their handler grinned devilishly through his long wispy blonde hair when he looked toward the specimens, their blue and purple scales shimmering like waves in the sunlight. The miniature dragons were eerily similar to Tsarina's tattoo, and Bud wondered if they had perhaps come to her in a vision. Tuffs of tan hair grew thick around their underbellies, and their muscular hind legs allowed them to stand upright like giant birds. Long thin wings, aligned with six joints, produced curved razor-sharp bones, a foot long, that jutted toward the sky. Flickering tongues slithered in and out of their lips with alarming frequency, and four razor sharp toes on each foot planted their stout legs firmly into the road. Two stained bones at the ends of their tails protruded, forming a *V*. The flail-like appendages were double the length of their bodies, and both creatures were fitted with ornate leather saddles, bathed in sapphires, large enough for two riders.

"Beautiful aren't they?" asked Ethan.

Bud remained silent, concentrating solely on finding the perfect moment to kill the handler, or at least bludgeon him enough to make an escape and find Tsarina. Ethan muttered something in response to the unanswered question and then pulled out a thin black rope from his leather saddlebag. Brilliant speckles of tiny gemstones glistened inside the rope as he bound Bud's hands behind his back, and with each attempt to wriggle free, Bud felt the rope cinch, coiling tighter around his wrists like a snake. Eventually, the rope began to cut into his skin, forcing him to cease his struggle. Ethan sniggered, as if he had seen the futile attempt a hundred times before, and then he shoved Bud onto the back of female wyvern. When Bud landed in the saddle, the mount stomped, hissing a blast of grey steam out of her nose, and turned her head to examine her new rider.

"Settle yourself Hildegard. We're in for a long ride. You don't see Bingen stomping and snorting around here like some wild steed now do you?" he asked rhetorically, referring to the slightly larger wyvern. Obstinate as the creatures seemed, Ethan had a gentle rapport with them, similar to that of a seasoned horse trainer, and Bud assumed this was the man's primary occupation, as he didn't look, or sound, like much of a fighter. His legs and chest were clothed with simple tan breeches and a modest woven shirt. The only semblance of armor on his body was a set of leather bracers, covering his arms from the elbow to wrist. Even so, the thin man was going to be hard to best with Bud's ever tightening handicap. His hopes sunk into the emptiness of his predicament as the gigantic red sun burned low behind the white conifers at the far end of the town. Defeated for the time being, he watched the sinewy man pull a purple and green, gourd-shaped fruit from his saddlebag and bite into it with a smile.

∞∞∞Cavern of Doubt

Water dripped off the walls of the cavern into an unseen stream, muffling Tsarina's voice when she asked, "Where are we going? We gotta to go back for Bud."

"Do not fret thyself. The waterway that lies ahead 'twill lead us to safety. 'Round the bend, 'tis a flatboat that will lead us to—" Indimiril cut his words short and glanced behind. "Come child, the dwarf approaches. We must hurry."

Sprinting around the bend, Tsarina ducked through a low antechamber into a spacious cavern to catch up with Indimiril. Black stalactites littered the roof, dripping water into a midnight blue stream that meandered silently in the darkness. A lone, azure flame with an auburn tip sang an eerie, crackling song, burning atop a perfectly level obsidian rock. It illuminated a flat-bottomed boat that was tied to two wooden posts.

"Is that it?" asked Tsarina.

"Yes, here we shall depart for the Cairn."

"For what?"

"Cairn Rose, 'tis where the Eminent Archon of Adytum resides along with his students and faculty."

"We can't just leave Bud!" she demanded.

"His fate is beyond our control. At best, he is captured and on his way to Viduata's Peak. At worst—" Indimiril paused and continued ushering her with frantic flicks of his hands in the direction he wanted her to move. "No, we must make it to the Cairn."

"Where is the Cairn?"

"In the mountains, past the fields of Jasmine," he explained as he stepped onto the dory. "Now hurry onto the boat."

"No! Bud could still be up there. We've gotta try to help him!" She stood her ground on the bank.

"My dear, Halcyon and the council only can help us now. The grand wisdom and power of the archons 'twill, no doubt, provide the best course of action," he explained, rushing to untie the flatboat from its soggy moorings. Before Tsarina could inquire further, Sükh unleashed a battle cry and rounded the corner, silver boots clanging the ground like tin buckets.

"Come, child!" Indimiril urged, as the dwarf passed through the archway. Rushing, he cast the small wooden boat from the shore with his bone staff, and Tsarina begrudgingly hopped aboard.

When they approached the middle of the underground river, Indimiril began swirling his arms over his head, paddling the air, chanting, *"Porro in ventus,"* and an unnatural wind swept through the tunnel to blow them down the river.

Accelerating with each paddling hand gesture, the dory proceeded against the slight current, while Sükh pursued from the bank. Once in range, the dwarf launched a flat silver blade at Indimiril's head with desperate precision. As the knife hissed through the air, Tsarina swallowed her scream and grabbed the warlock's sleeve, jerking him into the center of the dory. The projectile zipped through the tips of his peppered hair, splashing harmlessly into the chilly water.

"Gruhks!" Sükh barked, stomping into the stream until the waterline overtook his boots. The dwarf launched another knife that fell short, and he howled as the small boat slipped into the darkness.

Tsarina slumped inside the hull and propped her head over the front of the wooden flatboat. Peering into the watery abyss, she sat exhausted, her mind conjuring visions of Bud trapped in a stone cell. *What could I have done?* she questioned her decision to flee and tumbled into despair, searching for the answer. At the height of her dismay, a brilliant blue light appeared over the front of the boat, momentarily freeing her from her self-inflicted torment. She welcomed the newfound visibility and turned to locate its source. Indimiril sat at the stern with his eyes half-closed and his bone staff pointing toward the ceiling, the sapphire on top aglow.

"How are you doing that?" Her voice careened off the water onto the obsidian walls and back around.

"'Tis a continuum of energy." He cracked his squinty eyes. Then he waved his arm, steering the boat slightly to the left and said, "I believe thou hast much to learn regarding this world and our energies, milady. I would say, first, thou must prepare thyself by releasing the ties that bind your perception to reality. Reality 'tis merely perception."

"Yeah, people keep saying that," she muttered. "So what? Are you trying to give me advice over here, or are you just talking to hear yourself speak?"

"I—"

"Whose reality are you talking about anyway? Nothing here is real to me."

"That is precisely the idea. 'Tis an excellent beginning." He smiled vaingloriously. "Sounds as if thou art ready to open thy mind."

"To what?" she asked.

"To the energy that lies within."

"Energy? What energy? And if you know so much about energy, then why couldn't you stop that dwarf and save Bud and Althea?"

The corners of the warlock's mouth drooped. "I fully understand thy concerns for the boy, and for Madam Althea. Alas, we were, and still are, completely outmatched by the warrior and his wyvern, and if thou art truly a descendant of Istia, then thou art far too precious to risk."

"Who told you that?" Tsarina questioned.

"After the dwarf came looking for you, Madam Althea sensed a powerful energy inside your aura. She begged me to save you at all costs and escort you to the Cairn just before she—"

"How could she know?"

"Madam Althea is—" Indimiril paused to gather himself. "was one of our most accomplished mentalists on all of Adytum. She had an uncanny ability to enter the minds of others and search deep within their thoughts. She finds things in others, even they could not see in themselves." His eye convulsed, fighting emotion. "She whispered her findings in my mind before Sükh—" Indimiril fell silent and peered into the water, the muscles in his neck tense.

"There's nothing you could've done?" Tsarina asked.

"Some of us are warriors and some of us are scholars. I, myself, possess a great many abilities, however none that would have bested the dwarf and his cohorts. First and foremost, dwarves have an innately high resistance to magic, and if you were to notice, Sükh was wearing mirror armor, a blocker of mentalist magic. Hence, he did not flee when Madam Althea employed her terror spell upon their minds. She did quite well to frighten the Noctiss, and her courage most certainly saved our lives. Furthermore, 'tis not to mention of the danger of the wyvern I heard snorting fire and prancing about outside. They are what surely blew down Althea's door and would have shredded us to pieces on a whim."

"So basically, you're a coward?"

Indimiril's frail back stiffened. "Hardly. I am invariably a man of practicality," he contended with a scowl. "'Tis of no consequence now. Whatever thou art wont to believe, we are extremely fortunate to be alive and on our way toward the Cairn."

Tsarina glared at him, searching for a better answer, which he did not provide. His cowardice irked her, but before she could unleash her poison laced thoughts, he responded, "Our only option was to flee. Undoubtedly, the dwarf would have thee in chains at this very moment, and I would most certainly be lying on the floor right alongside Madam Althea and thy friend, Bud. The very reason he may still be alive is to serve as a bargaining piece for you. No, my dear, we shall have to find another way to save him—if, in fact, he still lives."

"Don't say that!" she growled.

"I am truly sorry, but thou must weigh facts. No matter the cost, we must press on to Cairn Rose—'tis our only hope for thy safety. The archons will be able to protect you far better than I, and hopefully, answer all thy questions. 'Tis even possible they might be able to save thy friend, but whatever they decide, now is certainly not the time to stand and fight these mercenaries, assuredly."

Tsarina refused to accept his reasoning. The thought of Bud held hostage in ransom tortured her. She faced the front of the boat and grabbed her backpack then buried her head into it, hiding her tears. The sounds of the waves slapping against the wooden hull of the flatboat gradually drowned her anguish, allowing sleep to overwhelm her.

∞∞∞*Simply Magic*

When Tsarina awoke, a throbbing pain in her lower ribcage forced her to wince as she lifted her body upright with her arms. Swaying inside the tiny vessel, she gently rubbed the bruise with her palm. The pressure forced upon her thigh sent a surge of pain into her hips and she moaned, remembering she had no antibiotic to treat the wound.

"Good morning, Madam Tsarina," Indimiril said.

"Yeah," she replied, still harboring the ill feelings from their last conversation. She ran her fingers through her knotted hair and tossed it around a bit, securing it with a hair tie from her pocket. "Where are we?"

"By my estimation, we should be near the fields of Jasmine."

"Is that good?"

"Quite, we are moving at a steady pace, despite the current."

She peered into the water, measuring the speed with her fingertips.

"Madam Tsarina, forgive me, but I feel the necessity to apologize for our misunderstanding yesterday. I did not trust thy words from the onset, and I fear my hesitation caused our tragedy, but thou must understand, Earth 'tis a fool's subject here on Adytum. Nothing for the able minded to trifle with, or so we are taught."

"Why?"

"Earth 'tis is nothing more than a fairy tale told to children at bedtime—a fantastical story of Adytum's creation. A myth so unbelievable, no one questions how mythical it is."

"How about you give it a shot?"

"A what?" he questioned.

"I wanna hear this fantastical tale of Earth," she answered with a touch of sarcasm.

"Well, I suppose—" His eyes drifted upward. "Where to begin?" He sighed, scratching his long peppered beard. "'Tis been so long since I've spoke on't—"

"Ah yes," he recalled, clearing his throat and straightening his back. "I have it now. Many ages ago, on another world—'tis Earth I speak of." He nodded for her understanding, as if explaining to a toddler. "A nomadic group of hunters traveled with their priestess, Istia, and in their travels, they happened upon a great sea surrounded by land. 'Twas known as the Sea of Baikal. Inside this great sea, sat a small island, which housed a Dwarven clan known as the Olkhon. The Olkhon were high masters of forging magic into weapons and armor."

"They were dwarves, like Sükh?" Tsarina asked.

"Dwarves yes, but 'tis doubtful they are of any relation. This particular clan could craft magic energies into objects, and their most prized possession 'twas an orange-rose sunstone which could harness a thousand times more energy than any gemstone they had ever known." Indimiril sat forward, the passion of the tale flowing inside his rosy cheeks. "This ancient gemstone could harness the power of the sun and store it to do thy bidding. Whoever possessed this sunstone could weave grand spells of untold power, so the legend goes. It was also told to grant visions of the past, and of the present, and of a great many things unknown."

"Sounds pretty awesome."

"Quite. But alas, one day the sunstone was stolen from the Olkhon's shaman by a giant bear and taken deep into his cave in the center of the island."

"A giant bear stole it?" Tsarina raised an eyebrow.

"'Tis how the story goes. At any rate, upon hearing of this magical gemstone, the leader of the nomads, Hartha, proposed a deal with the Olkhon. Hartha vowed his men would retrieve the sunstone from the bear, if Istia would be allowed to study its power. The Olkhon reluctantly agreed to the terms and led them to the bear's cave. Upon approaching the cave, Hartha's warriors were inexplicably stricken with fear and dared not enter. No doubt a glyph of fear was set around the entrance. Istia had a stronger mind than the warriors, and she was able to disregard and move past the guardian spell.

"For several days, Hartha's clan waited outside the cave with the Olkhon, until finally, they assumed all was lost. On the third day, as the men were preparing to leave, Istia emerged with several bears trailing her like docile pets. She then spoke to the men of a winged horse who lived inside the cave, ruling the bears as their king."

"A horse, with wings?" Tsarina tittered. "I'm starting to see why you guys don't believe this."

"Yes, well, the horse was said to be a god from another planet, and seldom would he ever venture into the world for fear of capture. I believe Istia referred to him as Pegasus."

"Oh. Okay, I get it now."

"Yes, 'twas Pegasus who illuminated the stars in his image. He scribed them as a map for Istia and her vision. He also foretold of a world, much like theirs, and placed the alternate world within his mane. This planet was, of course, Adytum."

"Quite." Tsarina smirked.

"Soon after, the nomadic priestess bore dreams of an alabaster altar set in the middle of a vast field covered in head high grasses with a bright orange sun shining overhead. Istia used her vision, along with the sunstone to weave a spell, creating a bridge to Adytum."

"When was this?" Tsarina asked.

"Supposedly five or more centuries, I believe. And so, the spell was passed down to the descendants of Istia, and each year, on the day of the Summer Solstice, when the power of the sun was at its pinnacle, the gatekeepers would pass between the worlds and help their brothers and sisters of magic flee from Earth, until one day, a young gatekeeper, whose name I forget, was killed by her own townspeople for practicing necromancy. She was accused of gathering the energies of dying souls to feed her power, and the gatekeeper was drowned in a drinking well, along with the Eye of Istia."

"Do you know the name of the town, and who was the gatekeeper?"

Indimiril's eyes shifted. "I'm sorry, I do not recall those details. You must forgive me, 'tis been quite a while since I've recited this tale. At any rate, the eye was lost for a time, but resurfaced again by some miracle of fate." Indimiril squinted. "Some texts speak of a secret group of watchers, calling themselves vigils, who hide in the shadows and follow the eye and the daughters of Istia, keeping them safe, but have never allowed their identities to be known."

"The vigils protect the gatekeepers?" Tsarina asked, remembering the inscription on the albino's chain.

"Yes. I believe so, but I am certainly no expert. Tales of this sort never warranted my time as a youth, therefore I never allowed them much of my time. And so, that is the myth of Earth, as I recall it. Now, as thou can see, 'tis quite a far-fetched tale, no?

"Yeah, I guess it would have sounded pretty unbelievable to me too, until yesterday," Tsarina agreed.

"So, thou dost understand?" he asked.

"Yeah, a little bit. I've had people telling me all this magic stuff was real from day one, but I never believed them either. My mother told me about Istia, and—" She lifted her blood stained pant leg, revealing the anklet and the sunstone. " I have this."

Upon sight, Indimiril's eyes beamed with an excited stupor. He bent forward to gain a better look. "Ah, so this is what Sükh was after." Lifting the stone with his finger, flipping it once, he concluded, "Well, 'tis certainly a sunstone, a brilliant gemstone as the histories suggest. 'Twas thy mother's?"

"Yeah."

"Then Althea was correct. Thou art from the line of Istia, dear girl, and now you have come to Adytum, thou hast fallen into a world of grave danger."

"Tell me about it." Tsarina muttered.

"Well, I suppose—"

"No, it's just an expression," she explained, puffing a laugh. "You don't really have to explain it."

"Oh, quite." His face scrunched into a frown.

An awkward pause developed, and Tsarina lowered her pant leg. "Is the water ok to drink?" she asked. "I'm dying of thirst, and I need to wash this wound."

"Yes, but be careful, there could be grinders and all types of nastiness in these waters."

"Grinders?"

"Yes, a fish 'twill shred the flesh from your bones. They swarm to gnaw on flesh."

"Awesome."

Tsarina pulled an empty plastic bottle from her pack and dipped it in the river, watching closely for any movement as it swallowed the cool water. Once the bottle filled, she finished half and offered Indimiril a drink.

"Thank you." He nodded and took a sip.

"Go ahead. Finish it. I gotta fill it back up to clean out this wound."

Indimiril took the last swig and handed the bottle to her. As she dipped the bottle again, he started, "Once thou art finished, I believe that in order to prove Althea's theory regarding your namesake, we should test thine ability and focus on the presentable future."

"Ability?" she questioned, removing the bloodied scrap of cloth covering her wound.

"But of course. Madam Althea spoke of a grand magical aura deep within you, and it seems as though she was correct. Therefore, the construct of a rudimentary spell should come to thee with relative ease—one should imagine. Wouldst thou care to have a go?"

"So what, you gonna teach me how to read minds or something?"

"Well…no, actually. Mentalism 'tis not exactly my area of expertise. I am more of a Materialist. My mastery resides within the realms of water and light," he explained. "You see, there are two distinctly different subjects of magic: Mentalist teachings, which focus on perception and control over the minds of all living creatures, and Materialist teachings, which focus on the manipulation of physical elements like earth and water."

"Hmm…kinda like inorganic verses organic," Tsarina suggested, pouring the cool water over the gash in her thigh.

"I am not familiar with those terms," Indimiril admitted, recoiling a bit at the sight of the wound.

"Don't worry, it's just basic science. Please, continue."

"Quite. At any rate, Mentalists, like Madam Althea, probe the mind and are able to create illusions from within the mind—'tis quite troublesome and perplexing if you ask me. I much prefer the precise art of Materialism. There are far less variables."

Indimiril's bony fingers curled around the base of his staff. "Observe." He thrust it forward, commanding, "*Amplio.*" Suddenly, the azure light, swirling inside the gemstone, doubled its intensity, casting brilliance over the rippling water below. "Control over the elements, 'tis a far more consistent art." He smiled. "Light always reacts in the same fashion—'tis not so easy with the mind of a living creature. Each living subject is unique, like a—.

"Snowflake," Tsarina finished his thought, wincing as she reapplied the bloodied bandage. The image simply popped into her mind before he spoke.

"Quite," he said cautiously, "but—"

"I don't know, I just saw the image in my mind. Sorry for interrupting."

"No. 'Tis no worry, but thou showst signs of mentalism with that observation. Does this happen often?"

"All the time," she explained, pulling her pant leg down to give him her full attention.

"Interesting. I wasn't trying to conceal my thoughts, necessarily, but I was not expressing them directly either. You see, generally, 'tis quite tedious, entering minds. Some creatures are strong-minded and some are weak; some are sane and some are insane; some have control over magic; and some do not. The variations are endless"

"Some people definitely are not as smart as others. I feel you on that," Tsarina joked.

"Quite. There are many dim-witted creatures in the world. For example, 'tis easy to control the mind of a Bog Rat or a Fellbird. Conversely, invading the mind of a powerful warlock, 'twould be near impossible. Powerful Mentalists learn to glean unchecked thoughts from their targets then they calculate the appropriate amounts of energy in order to affect a specific reaction. Generally speaking, it takes countless years of study, and undoubtedly a great deal of patience to become competent in this art of magic—neither of which, I feel, are in my repertoire."

"Sounds like it was an easy choice for you," Tsarina commented.

"Quite, Materialism appeared early in life for me. As a youth, I found 'twas easy to harness water and air and bend light with my thoughts. When I was of a certain age, my mother and father petitioned me to enter the school of Materialism in Splinter with Archon Jindon. 'Twas quite an accomplishment to gain acceptance at that time," He boasted. "Archon Jindon was considered to be the most knowledgeable Materialist in all the realms. Needless to say, I was quite distraught when I lost him as a mentor."

"What happened to him?" Tsarina asked.

"Archon Jindon was offered a position on the High Council, and now, unfortunately for the remainder of his flock, he rarely imparts his knowledge with anyone."

"He gave up teaching altogether?"

Jindon's face soured. "Oh, I suppose he stops into Splinter now and again to check up on our more gifted students and to give oration. However, yes, for the most part, we have lost a great teacher to political affairs, but I digress. If thou wouldst like, I could teach thee several spells within mine own art, however if you wish to learn Mentalism, then you will have to consult with one of the other great teachers like Archon Halcyon or Archon Joan."

"Who are they again?"

"Archon Halcyon is our Eminent Supreme Archon. He presides as Archon over the entire realm, and Archon Joan is the protector of the Fields of Jasmine. She has quite a way with animals and all things wild. We shall pass through the northern section of her realm in order to reach the Cairn."

"The grasslands?" Tsarina asked.

"Precisely. Her realm stretches from the edge of the Splinter woodlands to the fields of Jasmine near the Dormeer Mountains. I am quite certain the Cairn will summon her upon knowledge of thy presence. All of the Archons will most likely be summoned by Halcyon for such a monumental discovery, I would assume."

"So what's Halcyon's deal? Is he cool? You think he'll be able to help us find Bud?"

"There will be no deal. Furthermore, I fail to see how his body temperature would weigh on the situation. Suffice it to say, Archon Halcyon has more resources at his disposal than any other being on Adytum. He has sat as the head of the council for one hundred and eight years and is widely regarded as the most powerful mentalist in all the realms—although some say his powers wane with age. Personally, I rather like him, however, from what I hear, Jindon seems to think him too old and stubborn for our future. 'Tis as if they are constantly bickering like school children from the tales beginning to circulate." Indimiril paused suddenly and then lowered his head, shaking it in shame. "Forgive me. I should not gossip so," he apologized. "Truly, 'twould be quite a great honor to benefit from either archon."

"Sounds like a lot of pressure," Tsarina thought aloud.

Indimiril took a patriarchal tone. "Do not stress thyself child. I assure thee, they will treat you with the utmost dignity and reverence. Archons are a cultured folk. We value respect and honor. Simply allow these men and women what thou knowst in all honesty, and the rest will tame itself." He gave a fading smile. "But enough with all these droll politics and gossip. Art thou ready to begin crafting?"

"Sure, but I have one more question."

"Certainly."

"Can anyone learn magic?"

Indimiril paused and turned his nose to the sky. "To my knowledge, 'tis only certain people who art blessed with the divine ability."

"So it's a genetics thing?"

"Hmm…I…well…what…what is a *genetics thing?*" he probed, skimming the water with his hand, as if gauging the temperature.

"You know, genetics." She shrugged and waited for a response, which never came.

The warlock's face remained expressionless.

"Ok, quick science lesson. Genetics is a science devoted to heredity—your heritage. It's like this: There are patterns of inheritance from parent to child—it's the qualities you get from your mother and your father.

"And how do we get these qualities?" asked Indimiril.

"Exactly. Now you're thinking scientifically. There's a little macromolecule called DNA that makes us who we are. For example, your nose probably looks like your mother's or your father's, right?"

Indimiril thought about it for a moment then smiled. "Yes, I suppose I do have my mother's nose. My father's was quite a bit shorter and fatter."

"Okay, right. Well, that's genetics, and there's probably some gene that granted you the ability for magic. Were your parents able to use magic?"

"But of course."

"So yeah, in theory, it all makes sense. It's probably some kind of mental gene that allows us to open our minds to the possibilities of alternate thinking—a.k.a. magic."

Indimiril sniffed, pursing his lips, then commented, "Your world, 'tis translated in such a different fashion from ours. I believe there can be much wisdom shared between our worlds—for the good, of course. My only hope is that the other archons will share in this conclusion as well."

"Why wouldn't they?"

The wizard squinted, as if making a life or death decision. "I fear that, for as much good can be gained, I imagine there is an equal amount of evil, and I know the Archons are quite cautious when it comes to powerful matters such as this. I have simply found it to be a taboo subject whenever I have heard it voiced in the council, and I am uncertain of their exact views on the subject. I, more often than not, leave those debates to the wisdom of the elders. I also find their debates quite tedious to tell the truth. Come now, let us put this discussion away for the moment and focus on a more lighthearted subject shall we? A spell for thee to practice, yes?"

"Sure," Tsarina agreed.

"Splendid. Then let us begin with a simple illumination spell. Dost thou remember how I enhanced the energy inside the gemstone to light our path?" He asked then stabbed his staff into the bottom of the boat.

Tsarina nodded.

"Good. 'Twas simply a manipulation of the sun's energy stored within this gemstone."

"Like photosynthesis for rocks," she chuckled.

"I assume, 'tis more of your science?" he questioned.

"Yeah."

"Then I imagine, yes. The words form a bond with the caster and the energy. These bonds allow the caster to release the energy. The caster is simply the medium. You will be the medium, and you will feel the energy flowing within the stone. Simply associate the words with the energy—allowing it to grow, manipulating it as you wish." He closed his eyes and instructed, "And this is thy first word, *lumen*."

The light in the staff flickered to life then went out.

"Latin," she muttered spiritlessly.

"Excellent. So, thou art familiar with the ancient language of the Archons?"

"Not really."

"Oh." He frowned. "Nevertheless, 'tis what most Archons use for instruction. If thou wouldst study from any of the great masters, 'tis a prerequisite."

"Awesome," she groaned. "So, you gonna teach me that spell or what?"

"But, of course. 'Tis my turn to enlighten thee," he offered with a gentle smile. "Take my staff and place your hand over the sapphire."

Tsarina did as instructed and looked to the archon for further instruction.

Indimiril pressed two fingers against his mouth. "Now focus on the energy contained within the sapphire. See if thou canst feel it."

Tsarina closed her eyes and tried to sense heat, or vibrations, or sounds, or anything inside the gemstone. After several attempts, she thought she felt a slight sensation, like coals warming the gemstone, but she wasn't completely convinced. The warming sensation came and went, fading in and out in subtle waves, and she asked, "I think I kind of felt something, like it was warm."

"Good! Yes, now place your hand directly under the stone and try to channel your energy. Let it flow into the bottom of the sapphire. Focus on the word *lumen* and connect it to the energy. Nothing else."

Tsarina followed his instruction and began chanting the word, but she struggled to find quiet focus. Every sense in her body seemed magnified. She noticed the drops of water falling off the stalactites into the calm stream. She noticed their echoes, bouncing off the black cavern walls, and the cool draft as it wafted under her hair. The gentle motion of the boat swaying back and forth disrupted her balance, and after several minutes of trying to tame all the sensations, her will faded.

"Balls!" she brayed, choking the staff with her fingers. "Is it supposed to be this friggin' hard?"

"Quite, 'tis to be expected, actually. Sometimes it even requires a shock to the system, like a surge of anger, or fear to activate the caster's energy for the first time, and in most cases, it requires several weeks, or even longer, for the feeling of the energy to enter one's mind, and then thou must learn to control it. Incidentally, in thy case, thou art quite beyond the years when most begin their training. At this age, your mind undoubtedly has deep rooted barriers that have grown like weeds, choking your mind. As long as there is an inkling of doubt in thy mind, the spell will never take root and grow."

"So how do I get past that?"

"'Tis an answer for you alone." He grinned. "Thou must learn to clear thy mind of all doubt and open the door to your faith in magic—as when thou performed the portal spell in thine sleep. Dreams are wonderful. When we dream, there are no barriers to prevent you from belief. Conscious crafting, like anything else, merely takes practice—once you believe."

Tsarina returned the insubordinate staff to Indimiril. He tapped it gently on the bottom of the boat, and the light flashed, accentuating his point. "Rally on—'twill come in time, as will your endurance and control. For now, you should allow yourself a respite and have a go again when thy mind is refreshed."

∞∞∞*A Dalton's Duty*

Tsarina gazed over the bow of the flatboat, wondering if she would ever learn to calm her overactive mind into the focus required for casting a spell. A million thoughts, like wild children running in every direction, crowded the space in her mind. She needed a technique: yoga, tai chi, vodka—something.

Three iridescent shafts of sunlight radiated down from the roof of the cavern into the water as the dory slowly passed under the arch. The warm air calmed Tsarina. Outside, under the brilliance of the auburn sun, head-high, yellow and green grasses swayed aimlessly along the riverbank while patches of white and violet trees loomed over the river. A flock of alabaster birds soared above in a *V* formation, cawing intermittently in the indigo sky. She envied their freedom.

"Where are we now?" she turned and asked.

"'Tis the edge of Archon Joan's territory. Those are the Fields of Jasmine. Three exits emerge from Splinter's Cavern. Apparently fortune smiles upon us. We seem to have chosen the one least expected. Sükh might very well have been waiting for us, but it seems we are safe for now."

"So, that's good." Tsarina commented.

"Quite. From here, we shall travel upstream through the marshes, using the cover of the reeds and trees to hide us. Only a small stretch of land remains uncovered before we get to the Rose Mountains."

"We're gonna have to climb them?"

"Hopefully not without aid," he answered. "Once we reach the base, I will petition Master Jasper to allow us the use of his mounts. From there, we shall ascend Jasper's path up to the towers of the Cairn." Indimiril took a worried tone. "We can only hope his mood is agreeable. Master Jasper tends to be much like his goats at times."

"Goats?" Tsarina questioned.

"Quite," the warlock stated flatly. "Master Jasper breeds the ancient Burmese mountain goats and offers them as a service to traveling merchants on their way up to the Cairn. I am in hopes he will lend us a couple without too much of a fuss, due to the urgent nature of our journey."

"So, right. You got animals here from Earth."

"What dost thou mean? Animals from Earth?"

"Well, there was the cat, and goats are animals we have on Earth too—and Burma's a place with big mountains where they raise goats, so—"

"Interesting. Yes, I suppose I am unable to recall the exact origin of these animals, so that may be a worthy estimation," he surmised.

"Yeah well, when I see this goat, I'll let you know if it's the same stubborn ass we have on Earth."

"From that description, it sounds as if they are quite possibly one in the same. Jasper's goats are certainly not amicable creatures by any stretch of the imagination."

Tsarina chuckled and lounged against the frame of the dory as it drifted deeper into the interior of the prairie. The afternoon sun invigorated her hands and face and she closed her eyes allowing it to consume her, thankful to be out of the darkness of the damp cave. When she opened her eyes, she noticed sporadic clusters of slender trees, beginning to line the edge of the riverbank. Green and orange rings surrounded the purple interior of their leaves, and their bright colors beamed in the sepia of the orange sunlight. She wondered if the sun was the source of their brilliant colors, if it affected their pigmentation. Curious, she turned to ask about the power of the Adytum sun, but her words stalled upon sight of an alabaster bird resting in the palm of Indimiril's hand. Gently, he placed the fowl close to his mouth then whispered several indiscernible phases into its ear. The bird's metallic blue eyes darted chaotically, and its long blue tassels, dangling from its golden ears, swung from side to side. It seemed to be ingesting Indimiril's words, and when the wizard finished, the bird's eyes settled on Tsarina. Indimiril released the envoy into the air with a pronounced breath, and then he closed his eyes as if whispering a silent prayer.

"What was up with the bird?" she asked.

Indimiril's eyes popped open. "Oh, 'twas Silus, my carrier. I hath sent word of our dilemma to Archon Halcyon in hopes he shall send assistance."

"You mean with the bird? Were you…talking to it?" she asked.

"Quite, Daltons are quick studies of language, due to their intrinsic musical nature. It makes them perfect messengers."

"Cool. You gotta teach me that one."

Indimiril puffed a chuckle. "There is nothing to teach. I am certainly no mentalist, however, most can enter the porous mind of a Dalton. They are extremely transparent creatures, which sing wonderful songs. Once one learns to feel their vibrations—well, 'tis truly more about the animal than the person."

"What do you mean, feel the vibrations?"

"'Tis merely a language of sound, similar to that of music. Let's see, I assume thou hast bards or minstrels on Earth?"

"Bards?" she giggled. "Yeah, we call them musicians."

"Do their songs produce magical results?" he asked.

"If you call getting your groove on in the club, magical, then yeah, I guess."

Indimiril's brow furled and his lips pursed as if he had just tasted a sour lemon. "No, the vibrations in music stem from energy—vibrational energy which allows one to enter the mind of their subject—'tis a language unto itself."

"Like radio waves," Tsarina mused.

"I suppose. Anyhow, most animals can learn quickly, given the right sponsor. You see, when a bird sings, it sends vibrations into the air. Thou canst simply associate words with these vibrations and listen for the response. Animals oft use these feelings and actions to communicate with each other. As with all things, the younger, the easier to train of course—fewer barriers in the mind."

"So, where did you find Silus?"

Indimiril smiled in reflection. "On the contrary, madam. 'Twas Silus who found me."

"How so?"

"Once I was appointed Archon of Splinter, Halcyon awarded me my own Dalton. It is customary, each Archon receives an envoy as a means of communication with the council—'tis quite an honor, and 'twas perhaps my greatest day of joy, but 'twas not without distress."

"Why?"

"Before my graduation ceremony, I was called to meditate in the Hollow Trees, a chamber of sorts, filled with Daltons and Matriarch trees. The final step on the path of the Archon is to receive your Dalton from the Hollow Trees. Pride overwhelmed me, as the grand birds soared in the purple treetops. They looked down upon me when I entered—'twas quite intimidating, once inside," he sighed. "After several hours of meditation, and listening. I shuddered, wondering if I'd ever be chosen by one of them. I fell into despair. What might I become, if that were to be my fate? What would become of my status? Would the council shun me into the forest like a leper? All I had worked for seemed to be slipping through my hands like grains of sand in an hourglass. Then, at the pinnacle of my anxiety, Silus must've felt my anguish. For just as I was to lose hope, he soared down from his perch and drifted to rest upon my shoulder. I honor him everyday for his kindness."

"That's pretty cool." Tsarina looked to the sky. "You think he'll make it?" she asked, watching the Dalton disappear into the clouds.

Indimiril covered her hand with his. "Let us hope so, madam."

∞∞∞*Nox Noctis*

Tsarina listened to Indimiril offering tidbits of the history of Adytum as night fell on the prairie. He spoke of the Tamara River and how it was once a great trade route from the Cairn to Splinter. Over the years, the river had diminished, and the water levels had sunk so low that only flatboats, like the one they were on, could navigate the shallow waters. The two moons of Adytum,

Lunis and Aquius, were directly in line with one another on this night, both in crescent form. Lunis' radiance cast a frothy white aura around Aquius, blurring the two together as Tsarina rubbed her eyes. This anomaly occurred once every twenty-seven years, according to Indimiril, and the creatures of the dark would be celebrating due to the veil of darkness.

"This night is known as *Nox Noctis*, The Night of Darkness," Indimiril explained. "The darkness will aid us, conceal our position,"

"From what?" asked Tsarina.

"Foul creatures that walk the night."

"Come on, quit clowning."

His expression remained stoic.

"Ok, so what is it we got to worry about?" she asked.

"Countless evils walk Adytum at night. Fortunately, Archon Jasmine has kept her plains free from most terrors over the years." His eyes turned toward the surface of the water under the stern. "However, for some reason, recently, we've noticed creatures seem to be growing quite a bit more dangerous in the valley. I must admit, even I have seen several Noctiss, lately, and even a Likho on the fringes of Splinter—And then there was the episode with you and the mercenaries yesterday.

"*Likho*? That means bad luck in Russian," Tsarina recalled.

"Undoubtedly. One-eyed goblins, which live in hollowed out trees, mostly in the darker forests of Splinter. They were cursed by a spurned witch with their hideous shape. One eye—quite foul, a portrait of evil. I have only come across one in all my travels, and the encounter was not a pleasant one to say the least. I highly recommend flight if we are unfortunate enough to encounter one."

"When do you not?" she jabbed.

"Usually, I find it to be the best course of action—that is, if one wants to survive."

"You think we'll be safe in this raft?" she asked, scanning the dark fields stretching beyond the water.

"Certainly, if we stay on the water, then all we have to avoid are the vodyanoy."

Tsarina pressed him with her eyes. She felt her mind slipping into his.

"Knowledge powers strength, milady. Not to worry, I will tell you, vodyanoy are quite rare. They are worth mentioning, however, because they are certainly the most dangerous of swamp and stream creatures. Tales of their existence surface from time to time. Fishermen who sell their catches in Splinter speak of them. Apparently, the creatures are not stealthy, which is good for us. They are said to slink along the river on a half-sunk log and make loud, splashing paddles. Most of the time, they sit and wait, and when frightened or angered, the vodyanoy are said to drag their victims underwater, to lairs where they serve as slaves."

"Lovely." Tsarina cringed.

"Quite. 'Tis a tall tale most likely—as I'm not sure how they would keep their victims alive without drowning them." He tugged on his beard, "unless 'twould be some sort of air spell."

"What do they look like?"

"From the descriptions, these creatures have the body of a wrinkled old man, a greenish beard, presumably colored from water scum, and long whiskers. Black fish scales where their skin should be and webbed paws for hands. Imagine them with a stout fish's tail and eyes burning like red coals. The fishermen call them, *grandfather*, as a joke I suppose."

"Hilarious."

"Ha. When a drowning occurs, tales surface about the *grandfathers*. Imaginations run wild in Splinter—all the young, excitable minds."

"I don't blame them. I'll be up all night."

"Fret not, madam. I shall keep watch tonight. Along with the vodyanoy, I venture to say that we do not even know half the evils lurking in the darkness."

"Not helping."

"Sorry, you should rest. You will need strength in the days to come," Indimiril warned.

"Yeah. Thanks."

Tsarina turned her back and pressed to see the future. Now, when she needed the light, darkness came. She slumped against the rail and closed her eyes. The gentle waves rocked her. Drifting in and out of a light sleep, she awoke to the sound of Indimiril's ragged snoring. A splash echoed under the stern, discordant to the droning waves. Darkness melded into the edges of the boat. She rubbed the corners of her eyes and peered into the darkness. Splashes penetrated the fog.

Tsarina crabbed toward Indimiril and reached to wake him. A slimy, webbed hand pierced the surface of the water, and attached itself to her forearm, tugging her toward the edge of the boat. As she lurched backward, she shrieked and wrestled from the wet claw. Stumbling portside, she stared across the boat. A mossy face lifted out of the water. Webbed, fungus-ridden claws anchored the creature to the side of the dory. Its crimson eyes glimmered at her. She lunged forward and snatched Indimiril's staff from his lap, whirling it overhead. A solid blow landed across the monster's forehead, sending it crashing backward. Grabbing the side of the boat, it tipped the edge of the dory below the waterline. Tsarina continued pummeling the monster with the head of the staff as the water poured over the rail. The creature snarled, clawing for Tsarina's leg, and with a flip of its tail, it spilled into the boat.

She leaned against Indimiril and elbowed him in the stomach. "Wake up, dude!"

With a raspy cough, the warlock sputtered to life, groggily searching for his staff with his hand. "Who? What? What is the meaning of this?" he groaned.

"Wake up! It's here!" Tsarina shrieked.

"W-What?" Indimiril stuttered. "Vodyanoy?" His eyes popped as the vodyanoy dove forward. "The light! Use the light!"

Tsarina quickly pointed the crystal at the vodyanoy's eyes, as it wrapped its yellow claws around Indimiril's leg and began towing him off the dory. A cold rush of adrenaline surged through her chest, and she gripped the staff tighter. Energy flowed from her chest into her arm as her heart pounded the blood. With Indimiril howling, slipping into the water, she aimed the gemstone at the creature's head and commanded, "*Lumen!*"

To her surprise, a huge blast of indigo light beamed from the crystal tip, blinding the vodyanoy. It released its grasp and slithered into the water.

"Magnificent!" Indimiril exclaimed as he pulled himself into the dory.

Tsarina leaned against the rail, choking the staff.

Indimiril began waving his arms in circles, paddling the boat forward with currents of air. As the boat surged forward, a wave bounced the dory out of the water by several feet, and it came splashing down against the surface, dislodging the staff from Tsarina's hand.

"What the hell was that?" she demanded, rolling to gather the staff.

Before Indimiril could answer, the boat surged out of the water again. He grabbed the side of the boat, and screeched, "Oh my!"

"Do something." Tsarina commanded. "It's gonna flip us over."

Indimiril waved his hands faster, propelling the boat forward, while the vodyanoy continued battering the bottom of the boat with its hardened back. Tsarina wrapped her fingers around the staff, trying to recall the energy. She plunged the crystal below the surface of the water and bellowed, "*Lumen!*"

The gemstone did not react, and another blow from the vodyanoy launched the dory several feet out of the water. Tsarina screamed, "*Lumen!*" Electricity shot through her body and a brilliant flash sparked under the boat. "*Lumen! Lumen! Lumen!*" she chanted. Blue light echoed her words, growing brighter with each utterance, saturating the murky water.

Indimiril continued flapping his arms, and the boat lunged forward. They sped into the darkness, and the battering dissipated. Tsarina scanned the surface, searching for the vodyanoy.

"Rare, huh?' she grumbled.

"Yes, well, I can assure thee t'was my first encounter with a vodyanoy," Indimiril stated.

"And hopefully the last." She grimaced. "What happened to you keeping watch?"

"Apologies. The darkness and the water must've taken my senses. I'm truly sorry."

"Whatever. Sleep all you want now. I'll be awake forever after that."

∞∞∞∞*Riders On The Storm*

In and out of consciousness, Tsarina drifted, afraid to close her eyes. She watched an auburn sun poke its head over the crest of green and purple trees and listened to the lilting coos, echoing across the plain. She brushed a clump of dewy curls from her face, and noticed Indimiril, snoring softly, his pointed chin propped firmly upon his chest.

With a breath of disgust, she scanned the field and spied three rose-colored mountain peaks glowing faintly in the morning light. The trio seemed much larger now, and Tsarina wondered how far they had traveled during her intermittent slumber. Her stomach growled a rough interruption, and she realized it had been days since she had eaten anything. A can of tuna fish remained in her pack, however Bud had the opener. "I wonder if there is a spell of opening for that," she muttered.

While searching the shoreline for anything edible, she noticed a fork in the river, looming several hundred yards ahead. For a moment, she stewed over which direction to steer the boat then decided to wake her snoring guide. "Hey, Indy. Hey. Wake up, man." She pressed her forefinger into his belly until his eyes cracked open.

"Huh? Oh my! Not again! My staff! he exclaimed, lurching forward, grasping for his staff.

"Whoa, chill out. It's cool." She touched his sleeve. "The sun's out. There's no monsters, but there's a fork in the river. Which way do we go?"

Indimiril exhaled, "Oh dear, thank goodness. I was afraid we might be under attack again." He quickly assessed their position and said, "'Tis a right thing thou hast knocked me up," "We must bear left." With a quick wave of his hand, he steered the dory to port.

"So, are you hungry?" Tsarina asked, unable to ignore her growling stomach.

Indimiril cocked his head and placed a hand on his stomach as if he had forgotten it was there. "Why yes. I suppose I am. We have expended a great deal of energy. We should stop and pluck dangleberries and solgrass from the field. They grow wild in this region and are quite tasty. I believe thou willst find them rather satisfying."

"Sweet."

"Quite."

Indimiril directed the boat toward the southern shore with a wave of his hand and moored it with a word, *Ligare*. The muddy bank housed sporadic patches of high reeds interlaced with tall blue-green mushrooms. The pungent grasses retained moisture from the night air. Tsarina hopped onto the shore, and the mushy soil squirmed beneath her shoes. She trailed Indimiril into the grasses, tiptoeing deeper into the field, waving her arms for balance. After the perpetual swaying motion of the water, the ground felt as if it were moving underneath her feet.

"Come, we must gather the berries quickly," Indimiril urged.

Tsarina crouched and watched the wizard brush the tops of the grasses from their bases. The thin strands of the thorny vines moved with his touch, and he demonstrated how to uproot them from the ground without getting pricked by grabbing them around the top and plucking them from the soil. As he shook them vigorously, clusters of yellowish-green berries fell into his hand.

Tsarina prodded the bright yellow-green grasses and began harvesting the bluish berries before Indimiril was able to finish his explanation. Tossing them into her mouth, she relished succor, and in the midst of her gathering, she happened upon a patch of the same colorful bugs that had reminded her of flying Skittles. Patrolling the long shafts of the grasses, the metallic insects scattered into the air when she brushed them away, their wings clicking in flight. She shied away from the noise and stashed the berries into her shirt.

Several yards away, Indimiril seemed anxious, chewing a piece of solgrass. As he began walking swiftly toward the dory, he called to Tsarina, "Come we mustn't tarry any longer. The dark of night hath protected thus far, but I fear the dwarf will soon find us if we stay in one position too long."

Tsarina glanced at the sky then asked, "How far we gotta go?"

"We are quite close," Indimiril answered. "Dost thou see those mountains to the southwest?" He pointed toward the endless line of mountains, looming like a great wall of crystal across the pasture. In the center, a set of three rose colored peaks shone above all the others. "At the pinnacle of those mountains rests Cairn Rose."

Upon seeing the magnitude of the massif, Tsarina began dreading the inevitable climb up to the peaks on the back of a goat. Her eyes slid down the sheer-faced mountainside, and she spotted a cloud of dust billowing against the backdrop of the horizon. "Do you see that?" She pointed.

"Bless you Halcyon!" Indimiril exclaimed. "It appears to be riders from the Cairn. They must've ridden all through the night to approach us so expeditiously."

"Are you sure?" she asked.

"'Tis most likely, given their direction of approach. However, as a mild precaution, 'tis best we should conceal ourselves, until we can spot them in full view. Let's move the boat a bit."

"Gotcha," Tsarina agreed and hopped onto the dory.

Indimiril plunged his staff into the water and manually directed the flatboat behind a thicket of head-high, tan reeds growing next to the shore. "The riders will be upon us momentarily," he said. "Hopefully, I will recognize them."

Tsarina buried her head between her arms, ducking low in the boat.

Moments later, pounding hooves shook the trail, and a wave of anxiety froze Tsarina. As the faces of the riders came into full view, she studied Indimiril's reaction, suppressing fear until he called out, "Anton! Thank the Archons!"

Both riders tugged their reigns, halting their horses in the middle of the trail. Indimiril waved as he stepped onto the shore in plain view.

Upon sight, the first rider called, "Ah, there you are Indimiril. I was beginning to doubt myself. I sensed your aura, but could not see you. It was quite disturbing."

"I see!" Indimiril joked. Then, with an outstretched hand, he beckoned Tsarina to emerge from the dory. Clumsily, she stepped onto the muddy riverbank and stood at his side.

"We are safe for now," he assured.

A breath of wind fluttered around the lead rider's scrawny shoulders, tossing his platinum hair to the side as he dismounted his black stallion. When he approached, the young man placed two fingers over his heart in a *V* and nodded in an apparent sign of respect. Indimiril returned the gesture in an almost religious fashion without expression.

"So, this must be the priestess from Earth," the blonde rider stated with a hint of excitement in his tone.

Indimiril nodded. "Yes, 'tis Madam Tsarina."

Anton bowed slightly toward Tsarina and reissued the sign of the *V*. "Anton Van Arden," he relayed. Blushing, she politely returned the greeting with a similar bow and an ameliorated sign. The dark rider behind Anton remained seated, silent in his saddle, examining her with his recessed, coal-like eyes. Tsarina felt a slight chill from his gaze.

Anton gave a quizzical look at his peer before his introduction. "Madam Tsarina, this is Yarrow. He is not much for words, but is an excellent tracker and a good friend to the Archons of Cairn Rose."

Yarrow remained silent, scanning the plains like a falcon from under his olive hood. His finely woven garment was trimmed with tiny black birds linked together at the wings. The intricacy of the patterns mesmerized Tsarina until Indimiril interrupted, "Well gentlemen and lady, I do apologize for the abbreviated introductions, however I fear 'tis only a matter of time before we are spotted by Sükh and his wyvern—if they are not already aware of our presence."

"Yes," Anton agreed. "In our haste, we wasted no energy cloaking our arrival. I am sorry for that oversight, but we—"

"On the contrary," Indimiril severed the apology, "'tis we who are grateful for thy extreme haste. We were quite fortunate to have eluded the dwarf in Althea's cavern, and we drifted back and forth somewhat in the marshes under the cover of night, but if I know anything of those persistent Dvergar, this mercenary will not give up so easily, and I believe there is ample coin fueling his resolve. 'Tis safe to wager, if he is any sort of tracker, he has deduced our path from here to the Cairn by now, and we will be highly visible, as there is no longer cover along the Tamara river from here. He shall surely find us if we do not make haste. How fresh be thy horses?"

Anton glanced at the two steeds. "They have several hours if we allow a comfortable pace. With a short rest, we should be able to reach Jasper's cabin by nightfall and hopefully evade the storm that was on our heels.

"Very well then, let us be off at once," Indimiril said.

Anton glanced at Yarrow as if communicating telepathically, and the dark-skinned warlock dismounted and positioned himself next to the dory.

Tsarina caught a notion of his intention to sink the boat and called out, "Wait." She grabbed her backpack out of the dory and nodded to Yarrow. "Ok, go for it."

Yarrow nodded, then closed his eyes and raised his hands, stretching forward as if corralling a sphere of air in front of him. "*Occulto per unda*," he chanted in a low monotone voice, and after a few seconds, water flooded over the edges of the flatboat as if a giant vacuum were hidden somewhere inside. When the last plank disappeared below the surface of the water, Yarrow hopped onto his stallion and returned to gazing into the sky.

Anton nodded approvingly at Yarrow and then mounted his steed, extending a gloved hand for Tsarina. "This fine stallion's name is Barrak, and that is his little lover, Missina."

Tsarina gave an appreciative smile as she settled onto the horse, and the instant her arms wrapped around Anton's waist, he spurred his heels into the steed. They lurched forward, galloping in the direction of the rose-colored mountain range with Yarrow and Indimiril close on their heels.

For several hours, Tsarina bounced around on the back of Barrak, and a stinging pain developed underneath her tailbone. Fleeting, illogical thoughts of dismounting and running into the wilderness of Splinter to search for Bud confused her. Eventually, she realized that even if she were to abandon the troupe, Bud was assuredly no longer in the forest, and she had little idea where he had been taken, assuming he was still alive. The realization of his fate crushed her spirit, and the blistering midday sun, along with the whipping winds, scalded her body into submission. She pulled the last fresh t-shirt from her pack and tied it around her head like a turban to cover her face. Swaying back and forth, she absorbed the slowing pace of he horse's hips. Near the final quarter-mile of grassland, before the ground became barren and rocky, both horses whinnied, pleading for rest.

"We have covered quite a bit of ground. The horses must drink," Anton informed, as he steered Barrak toward the riverbank. The mounts rushed to the edge of the river and dropped their heads into the crawling water.

"Are we close to Jasper's?" Tsarina asked.

"Almost halfway. If we keep a steady pace, we should arrive before nightfall," Anton answered.

Yarrow grunted, and Tsarina watched as the warlock looked to the darkening sky above the Cairn. His deep voice surprised her when he spoke. "A storm approaches from the West." Then, as if he had willed it so, the winds increased ruffling the crests of the waves on the shallow river. Violet clouds hung low to the northwest, threatening to head in their direction, and deep rumblings of thunder sounded like an orchestra of timpanists off in the distance. Tsarina looked to the Cairn, and without warning, a loud whooshing sound cracked from behind.

"Wyvern!" Yarrow bellowed a tardy warning.

Between flaps, the scaly beast shrieked, diving toward Tsarina, talons fully extended. Barrak rose on his hind legs, snorting and whinnying, and inadvertently tossed Anton into the wyvern's thrusting grasp. Sükh tugged at the reigns of his flying mount, attempting to alter their course, but the effort was an instant too late, and the beast's talons ripped into Anton's shoulder, plucking him from the saddle like a field mouse.

As Barrak exploded forward, heavy drops of Anton's blood splattered across Tsarina's face. Pulling herself tight to Barrak's shoulders, she gathered the flailing reigns, and the leather straps cut into her palms as the stallion continued accelerating. She held tight, rattling around, bouncing higher and higher until they rounded a sharp bend and she lost her center. Barrak's powerful strides ejected her sideways into the deep grass. Her wrists absorbed the brunt of the fall, and she rolled, head over toes, settling to rest in a cluster of giant, withered, yellow flowers. Flat on her back, covered in dirt and blood, she searched overhead for the wyvern and its master. She heard its wings then she saw it flying in the sky to her left, plummeting toward the fleeing stallion. After two powerful flaps from his wings, Bingen was upon the horse, and his talons pierced Barrak's hindquarters and plucked him from the ground. With the stallion's legs still racing over the air, Bingen flung the horse into the grass, and with another flap, he changed direction, turning his violet gaze upon Tsarina.

The wyvern's scaly webbed feet touched the ground with powerful grace allowing Sükh to dismount. The dwarf approached

Tsarina with a calm sense of purpose and drew a long shimmering dagger from his belt. His eyes glinted of victory in the fading sunlight. Crabbing backward, deeper into the tall grass, Tsarina pressed her throbbing hands into the ground, and a smug grin widened inside Sükh's beard as he stalked her.

"Ah there, little witch, there be no more places for you to hide, unless ya can make yourself invisible," he chuckled. "Go on then, poofity poofius." His face turned cold. "Ah, guess you got no ancient words for invisibility then, do ya? No burning fire coming from your hands either. Don't see what's the big deal with you. Just a common thief is all I see." He continued forward, planting his boot into her ankle before she could rise. Tsarina howled as the sharp pain shocked her leg, and she stabbed the ground with her hands.

"Well, that's too bad for ya then. So it seems if ya should be givin' me that anklet and coming with me to Viduata."

"Is Bud is alive?" she moaned, gritting her teeth.

"Concern from a snarling thief," Sükh huffed as he removed his silver gauntlet. "Touching. Now hand over tha' anklet 'fore I rip it off ya." He stabbed at the Eye of Istia with his stubby hand, and the orange sunstone glistened in the sunlight as the dwarf pinched it between his fingers. He seemed to lose himself for a moment in its majesty. Tsarina slapped his face when he ripped it from her ankle. The pointed tips of the stars pricked her skin as they left her for the first time in thirteen years, and tiny drops of blood leaked from the wounds.

A staunch voice suddenly rang out from behind the dwarf, "*Estus quod no,*" causing him to remove his foot from Tsarina's ankle. She scuttled backward on her hands and knees, and rolled up into a wobbly stance. Sükh remained focused on her, refusing to acknowledge the warlock approaching from behind. Then, as if in an anti-gravity chamber, every rock and pebble within ten feet of the dwarf ascended from the trail and shot into the joints of his armor like heat-seeking missiles, burying themselves beneath his chain mail cuirass and boots. The Eye of Istia hissed as well, searing his palm, and smoke billowed from all parts of his body.

The dwarf pranced about like a cat tossed into a boiling pool of water, howling, "Kill! Kill the damned bastard!"

Bingen spun and snorted a tiny puff of flame from his nose, while the warlock quickly redirected his mare toward the mountains, spurring her just as the wyvern hissed a blast of orange and blue fire. The expanding flame singed Missina's tail and most of Yarrow's back as she launched forward into a full sprint, narrowly avoiding incineration.

The wyvern leapt twenty feet into the air and unfolded its massive wings, surging toward Yarrow and his mare. With four air-blasting flaps, Bingen descended upon the horse and rider. His talon slashed at Yarrow's head, but with a deft bob, the warlock ducked the attack and dismounted with a slap to Missina's hindquarter sending her racing in the direction of the Cairn. Stumbling to a stop in the middle of the trail, Yarrow pivoted and ran toward Tsarina. He grabbed her hand and she sprang forward, challenging her legs to match his speed.

As they sprinted across the road into the field, the chest high grasses whipped her face. She glanced behind and thought to turn around and retrieve the Eye of Istia. Sükh was stripping out of his sizzling cuirass and would have been easy prey, but Yarrow had a firm grip on her wrist and forcefully yanked her from the notion.

"Damned sherkats!" Sükh howled. "Bingen, find 'em! They be somewhere in the field."

The wyvern was several hundred yards down the path, chasing his prey, too far in the distance to heed the call. Yarrow slowed his pace, and then abruptly stopped and squatted underneath the canopy of swaying grasses. Tsarina mimicked him.

"*Solvo tempestas…Solvo tempestas…*" the warlock began chanting, eyelids fluttering like hummingbird wings. After a moment, a soothing wind flitted across the tops of the stalks, and the intensity of the current increased proportionately with the opening of his hands. Off in the distance, a small crackle of thunder murmured in their direction, and a blustery wind began whipping through the valley, swirling the tops of the grasses into wispy, green and yellow flails.

Bingen returned to his master, riding the currents while the storm gained momentum. The wyvern cawed a desperate plea for retreat, but his obstinate master simply mounted him with a look of sheer determination on his face. The dwarf whipped the wyvern forward into the howling winds, and the duo continued circling overhead, searching for their prey, until the tempest eventually overpowered Bingen's wings, forcing their retreat.

"Now! This way!" Yarrow shouted under the howling wind as he staggered to his feet. For a moment, he remained upright then collapsed to one knee, placing his palm to his temple.

"Are you alright?" Tsarina offered her hand.

"Yes," he replied and wobbled to his feet with her help, unable to look away from the ground. "We must go."

"You don't look alright," she said.

"The crafting drain me. We must go."

"Where are we going?" she asked.

"Safety of the knoll."

"The knoll?"

"Yes. Will be safe from the storm."

"What about Indimiril and Anton?" she said, dodging flowered stalks like a prizefighter as they threw punches at her face from Yarrow's wake.

He glanced back and answered, " We can only hope they will find shelter as well."

∞∞∞Safety Of The Knoll

Tsarina looked into Yarrow's dulled eyes and asked, "So, how'd you do that?"

"What?" he replied.

"Make that storm."

"Wind convergence," he stated flatly, stumbling forward in the tall grass.

"What?"

"Heat and cold energy come together," he explained, clasping his hands, illustrating the bond. "Direct those forces—create a storm."

"Oh," she shouted through the roaring winds, pretending to grasp the concept.

After a half-hour of battling the wind and rain, Tsarina wondered if they would ever reach the safety of the knoll, then Yarrow stopped and bent over at the waist. She waited, expecting him to collapse. Instead, he brushed aside a cluster of head-high, tan and green grasses, revealing a small adit.

"The knoll," he explained, and then crawled into the earthen hole on all fours. Tsarina noticed the worn soles on his leather wrapped feet as she reluctantly followed him inside. Yarrow spoke a spell, similar to the one Indimiril had used in Althea's cave, and a topaz light sprouted from the crystal inset in the handle of his silver dagger. The dark tunnel shimmered in a greyish-yellow, and outside the boundaries of the light, a low howling sound reverberated off the walls like a disheartened specter. The quaking sensation rattled Tsarina's bones.

After several twists and turns, the muddy passageway opened into a small cavern that was wider but with a lower ceiling.

Yellow and green roots dangled down and tickled the top of her head as she sloshed on her hands and knees through the muck. The foul smell from the velvety roots suffocated her. She began crawling on her hands and knees. She found it hard to decide whether it was easier to crawl, as Yarrow was doing, or to walk, bent over at the waist, sacrificing her back. She alternated between the two modes when one became too painful. Proceeding for what seemed like an eternity without conversation, she finally quipped, "I feel like friggin' Harriet Tubman down here."

Dumbfounded by the Earth-born historical reference, Yarrow remained stone-faced, continuing to slosh forward on his hands and knees without a response.

His stoic demeanor grated her patience. "Are you sure we made the right turn back there?" she questioned.

Yarrow paused to wipe his brow with his muddy sleeve and answered, "We have several hours until we reach the other side."

"Great," she moaned. "Whose path is it anyway? Looks like it was made by a frickin' hobbit or something."

"These were the mines of the of the Listermen. Now, they are the trails of the Osedax," he answered stolidly.

"Do I even want to know what that is?"

"I don't know."

"Yeah, ok, who the hell are the Osedax?"

"Not who." He crawled forward. "What. Osedax is the *bone-eater*.

"The what?"

"A giant worm with bristles that hiss gas. The gas disintegrates solids into another gas, which they breathe. That is how they feed."

"What? Are you serious? Do these things still creep around down here?" she grimaced.

"Yes."

"Well, shouldn't we be worried about that?"

"Yes."

Tsarina frowned at his lack of concern. The decision to take the knoll to *safety* had suddenly become an absurd solution, however she deemed it useless to continue discussing the subject and fell in line, muttering obscenities. Sloshing forward in the murky water, Yarrow remained silent while rain from above continued flooding the bottom of the mine.

Water dripped from the ceiling, harboring fluorescent green worms, the size of small snakes, with sharp ridges like dorsal fins that landed on Tsarina's hair and shoulders. As she plucked the soggy, wiggling creatures from her curls and back, their fins pricked her fingers, producing tiny droplets of blood. She longed for a clean, warm bed; a cup of Earl Grey Tea with some cream; a horrible romance novel; and the noises of the bustling city to lull her to sleep. *Where are my dirty little pigeons?* she languished. *A sewer rat. Something fricking normal!*

Once the water rose above her waist, she began to question their safety on a different level. "Hey, is this tunnel going to flood?" she asked.

"Would you like gills?" Yarrow responded, chuckling slightly at his words. Tsarina scowled at his first attempt at humor and focused her burning eyes into the back of his head, in and attempt to ignite a sense of urgency through sheer will. She almost believed it worked when he reverted to his banal tone. "We should reach the surface soon. The tunnel turns upward here. The water flows stronger against us now."

His logical response pacified her for the moment, and she waded forward, imagining what she would look like with gills. *He was kidding, right?* Then, a great rumble grated off the walls, disrupting the water.

"What the hell was that?" she yawped, pressing her hands against the tunnel.

Yarrow glanced behind, "Not good."

"Care to elaborate?"

"It comes for us."

"The bone-eater?"

His averted look spoke volumes. "Hurry," he urged.

"Look it, I know you're trying to be all cool and shit, but what are we going to do when that thing swims down this tunnel?"

"It approaches from behind," he corrected.

The opaque water quivered into stillness. A second rumble shook the walls with doubled intensity, and giant waves spread out across the water, forcing Tsarina to hold her breath. When the surface settled, she shoved Yarrow's hindquarters and commanded, "Move it!"

Yarrow lurched forward, slightly off balance, and began thrashing against the rushing water. As the current continued surging underneath their waists, chunks of brown and red clay showered from the ceiling with each successive tremor, and a phosphorus-like stench crept into Tsarina's nose.

"Holy crap, That smell!"

"It approaches!" Yarrow alerted.

Tsarina's back began to burn, as the putrid fog thickened, and she let out a small yelp. Her hands sizzled, struggling to remove her backpack in order to salvage her mother's grimoire. As she tired to pull the pack into her body, the nylon straps disintegrated between her fingers, and a powerful wave ripped it from her grasp. She fell backward into the hissing current, and when she surfaced, water poured down her face. She opened her eyes to watch the remains of her backpack floating downstream; deeper into the acidic fog, a thin piece of the shredded strap remained in her hand.

The swift current sucked at her legs, straining the muscles around her shins, and the yellow fumes smothered her lungs as she fought to stay above the waterline. She drew just enough oxygen to keep from drowning then plunged below the surface. Swimming with the current, she opened her eyes. The warm water diluted the effects of the worm's acidic breath, allowing her a split second of sight. Through the murky water she caught a glimpse of her backpack, an arm's length ahead. With a swift scissor kick, she surged forward and wrapped her fingers around the frayed strap fluttering in front of her. As she drew the pack closer, the Osedax emerged, snatching the backpack from her grasp with its maw. Thrusting backward, Tsarina released the strap and stabbed her heels into the muddy bottom of the tunnel. Whirling, she thrust her thighs and surged forward.

Boiling water stung her back as the Osedax wormed closer, and she imagined the horror of what it would be like to survive its bite and to live the rest of her life without legs. Struggling against the current, she surfaced and heard a snapping splash. She pressed the balls of her feet into the ground, lunging forward, narrowly avoiding the reach of the Osedax's stench. As the calamitous waves thrashed her face, she gasped a breath of air before submerging again. The rushing undercurrent ripped her legs from the ground, and she became a prisoner to its grasp. She peered up through the cloudy water and glimpsed a shaft of light penetrating the tunnel from above. Thrusting her legs and arms toward it, she fought the current pressing her backward into the snapping maw of the Osedax. As it moved closer, the giant worm unhinged its jaws, and then a solid current of pressurized water vacuumed Tsarina from above. She shot out through the muddy opening with the head of the Osedax close behind. A vibrating roar shook the ground and gaseous fumes sprayed over the earth as water spouted from the hole like a geyser. The Osedax was sucked down into the tunnel while Tsarina crashed into the bubbling pool of mud and clay face down. She heard Yarrow chanting, "*Propinquus…Propinquus…*"

Wiping the muck from her eyes, she saw the warlock near the opening. He seemed to be directing his thoughts toward the cloud of yellowish-green gas that was pouring out of the hole, contaminating the air around them. Chanting monotonously, he directed the handle of his dagger at the opening. The yellow gas shot clumps of mud high into the air, spewing sizzling chunks over them like tiny meteors. The ground below suddenly collapsed, creating a large sinkhole. Each chunk of the gooey substance charred their clothes, hissing upon impact. Tsarina crabbed outside the perimeter of the acidic rain. Yarrow remained beside the hole, chanting, "*Propinquus…Propinquus.*"

"Come on! Forget about it. We're good!" she urged, but her words had no effect on the spell weaver. "Is that the Rose?" she shouted through the deafening sounds of the falling rocks and fizzing gas, pointing at the tallest peak in the colossal mountain range—still, no answer. She grabbed him by the collar and towed him from the collapsing earth against his weakened will. Once they were safely outside the perimeter of the debris, he answered in shallow tone, "Yes. Cairn. Base of mountain…Jasper."

∞∞∞*Soft Goods*

A salmon fire flickered behind a frosted window. The mahogany exterior and mossy roof camouflaged the log cabin from any would be travelers not looking for Jasper. The little house blended so well with the surrounding foliage, only the grey puffs of smoke billowing out of a stone smoke stack betrayed the organic structure's position. Tsarina watched three puffs of smoke coalesce into light grey clouds for a moment before she asked, "Is that Jasper's house?"

Yarrow nodded weakly under his hood. "Yes. We'll find safety there."

"That's what you said about the knoll," she groaned.

Yarrow gave a subtle look of indifference and then muttered something indecipherable before pressing forward. While searching for the entrance, Tsarina marveled at the ingenuity of the cabin's design. Whole tree trunks, buried deep into the ground, framed the tiny structure. Hunter green and maroon mosses trimmed the bottom, making it hard to discern where the ground met the base of the building. Rounded shafts of mahogany, sawed at the joints, rested on black triangular iron hinges and served as the front door. A small recession in the last plank appeared to be the handle.

When Yarrow approached the door, he gave it a couple of swift taps with the butt of his dagger, and after a moment of silence, a creaky voice rattled from inside, "Who the hell's rappin' at this hour of the night?"

"Yarrow, from the Cairn," the warlock announced.

"Huh?"

Yarrow struggled to raise his voice. "YARROW SIR, from the CAIRN."

The tiny iron plate, centered in the upper portion of the door, slid down revealing a set of yellowish-white eyeballs that rolled around behind a thick pair of rectangular glasses. Once Jasper determined it was truly Yarrow, he questioned, "Us?"

"Yes, I travel with Madam Tsarina," Yarrow explained, lighting her mud streaked face and hair in a grotesque yellowish-green hue with the glowing topaz from the handle of his dagger. "She has been summoned by Halcyon to the Cairn."

"What by Hothar's blade he be wantin' with that?"

"She is a visionary—"

"Huh?"

Yarrow spoke again, louder. "SHE IS A VISIONARY. AGNI'S MINIONS PURSUE HER—a dwarf named Sükh along with many Noctiss. I witnessed it myself. Sükh's wyvern almost decapitated Anton, attempting to capture her."

"Where be Anton then, huh?"

"We left him with Indimiril in the fields of Jasmine. We can only hope they are alive and they found shelter. We narrowly escaped ourselves—through the knoll."

The old man scrunched his eyes and stood motionless.

"Master Jasper, please pardon the intrusion, but may we continue this discussion inside? I have expended a great deal of energy today."

"Well, seems you be 'bout as straight as a blind yassar's tail, but I suppose you can come in anyways," Jasper determined, then turned to Tsarina and warned, "Mind your way around here Medusa or Sir William will be making a full dinner outta you."

Moments later, the heavy door grated over the ground, and the gaunt, grey haired man with a bald spot on top of his head, pressed against the door with all his might. Jasper was modestly dressed in a feldgrau shirt and trousers that looked like comfortable old pajamas. His only display of vanity was a large emerald ring on his right ring finger. Using a knotted shepherd's axe as a lever, he continued driving his frail legs and body into the door with little success. Tsarina alleviated his struggle by grabbing the depressed handle and pulling the door open. Jasper looked up with an exasperated frown and ushered her inside with a tap and a point of his axe.

The thick walls of corded wood magnified the echo of the crackling fire inside. Flames danced in a rust-colored fireplace made of stone located in the corner of the room. The dry timber produced a clean smoke that hinted of dried sage and careened up and out of the house through a small smoke stack. Next to the fireplace, a black and grey wolf rested motionless on the floor save for his sagging eyes, which followed Tsarina's every move. The beast was slightly larger than its owner, and Tsarina presumed this was the aforementioned "Sir William."

Jasper answered her unasked question with an arctic eye. "Don't let Sir William fool ya. He's a pure killer, that one," the codger informed and pounded his cane on the hardwood floor as a warning.

Tsarina forced a wary smile, wondering if he had listened to her thoughts, and sat down on the small wooden chair by the table that had the head of a Billy goat carved into the backrest. As she looked to the floor, she noticed Jasper's carpet revealed their crossing. She lowered her head—ashamed at the mud they had tracked into his tidy home.

Yarrow noticed the floor as well and apologized. "Master Jasper, sorry to intrude at such an hour, but we have no one to shelter us, and you *are* the unofficial gatekeeper to the Cairn."

The calumnious reference did not seem to bother Jasper, as he shuffled across the creaky wooden planks with a uniform pace. Upon reaching the mahogany armoire, he paused and asked, "So slice it straight off the bone. You be sneakin' this girl in for your own purposes. You know, I usually only trade in the hard goods not *soft*."

"Oh...no," Yarrow blushed, his tone a slightly higher pitch. "This is Madam Tsarina. I was sent by the order of Halcyon to return her to the Cairn."

"She some kinda thief then—a wicked killer?"

"No. There is nothing wicked about her."

Tsarina felt an awkward tension, as the two men spoke in front of her as if she were not present.

"What be so special about this—Medusa then? What does Agni want her for?"

Yarrow looked at Tsarina, issuing a subtle warning with his eyes, then turned to Jasper and said, "I'm not certain. Halcyon did not say."

"Must be quite a little trickster then, if all these folks be scavenging for her. What'd you do lassie? Kill Viduata?" He grumbled a chuckle.

Tsarina contemplated how to explain her journey and started, "No, I just—"

Yarrow interrupted, "She is a visionary, and we must keep her ability hidden. As you know, many desire this gift."

"I see, so you be a knowing witch then, huh? Haven't heard of one of them 'round here for a long time. Probably, old Gracie was the last of 'em, as I recall. You say you be riding with Anton? Strange, I didn't see you pass through on the way out, and where be your horses, and Anton?"

"As I said, we lost our horses to the storm, and now we travel by foot to the Cairn. Anton and I passed through yesterday, but you were not here."

"Hmm...Is that so?" Jasper continued staring at Tsarina. "Yep. Probably was out fishing the stream for golbus. They's supposed to be running upstream these days, seen 'em going down, though. Don't make much sense. Didn't catch a one either. Had to cut up another damned slogger," the old man recalled as he pulled out two pairs of pants and two long sleeved shirts from inside the armoire. "Getting tired of eating slogger," he finished before shuffling over to Tsarina and Yarrow. Once in range, the old man tossed the fresh garments into their laps, then asked again, "So where Anton be? Huh?"

Yarrow lowered his head, frustrated, and began explaining the journey from the beginning.

Tsarina interrupted politely, "Sorry, is there some place I can change?"

Abandoning his attempt to sit, Jasper squinted and turned up his nose. "You can use that screen over there, but mind yourself missy. William's a watching."

A cold, electric spark tapped her spine after the old man spoke. She wasn't certain, but the chill seemed to emit from his stare. Acknowledging the caveat, Tsarina shouldered her new outfit and carried it behind the silkscreen wall. The colorful barrier, illustrated with green, purple, and red birds flying over a marsh of tan reeds allowed her a bit of privacy. Unexpected windfalls of emotion showered her body as she undressed, and her thoughts sank to Bud's predicament. She realized she was getting farther from him with each moment and worried that the longer she was away from him, the more time his captors would have for torture or worse. She couldn't bear the thought for more than a moment and quickly pressed it away. Bending an ear to the old man's movements out in the living room, she heard a pot clank against brick and peeked around the screen.

Jasper took an iron pail off the top of the fireplace with a furry towel, and waves of steam rose out of the pot as he walked over and placed it on the wooden stool sitting next to the silkscreen. "Use this to wash the grime off," he instructed.

"Thank you," Tsarina answered then dragged the knee-high stool behind the screen. While the pot simmered, she quickly examined her body for bumps, bruises, scratches, and strange worms swimming in her hair or ears. Nothing pained her too terribly, except the newest gash in her thigh. She ran her finger over the three-inch scab and suffered a bout of vanity. She was certain it would scar, which in turn reminded her again of her all-too-brief time with Bud and if he would find it repulsive. She had now spent more time on Adytum without him than with him.

Lamenting the realization, she splashed her face with the hot water then rubbed the heat from the cloth into her knotted muscles. Chunks of caked mud filled the bowl when she submerged her hair in the water, and after a thorough rinse, she dried her mangled curls with the soft towel and buried her face in its lingering warmth.

Refreshed, she emerged from the silkscreen in her new attire, and Jasper inquired, "Feelin' better, missy?"

"Yeah, thanks." She smiled.

"Huh?"

"YES, THANK YOU," she repeated, doubling her volume. "Sorry about the mud, and I didn't know what to do with the old clothes, so I just left them on the stool over there. They're pretty trashed. I can just toss them—"

The wrinkles on the old man's face cinched together as he pulled a mahogany pipe from his pocket. "At's fine. I'll burn 'em at the forge tomorrow," he related, then lit the bulbous pipe and looked her over in the awkward silence. "So you be hungry, the two of you?"

Yarrow quickly stood and answered, "Oh, no. Thank you, but do not trouble over us. We rest and depart at first light."

"Nonsense. You're gonna need food to make it up that mountain and get outta my hair. I got some stew here needs be reheated and eated. Sit yourself down, you look hollow as a dead Filler tree."

Tsarina responded, "Sure, if it's not too much trouble, I could definitely eat."

Yarrow accepted the old man's offer with a nod and returned to his seat while Jasper moved a pot from the counter onto the stovetop and began reheating some sort of stew that smelled of bacon and potatoes. He hummed a tune soft and low through a mild smile, stirring the pot with a wooden spoon.

Tsarina welcomed the dry clothes and the warmth of the fire as she pulled up a chair next to the table where a steaming cup of green tea was waiting for her. The sweet and sour aromas from the tea, the pipe, and the stew, all blended together as she took a deep inhale before her first sip.

"So where you be from again, missy?" Jasper questioned, puffing his pipe.

"Earth," she answered.

Yarrow choked a laugh and shot a chastising look at Tsarina. The bubble of tension wavered in the air until the codger inexplicably burst into a smoky cackle, "Ha! I like this one, she's a real wagger!" Still chuckling through a rasp, he raised his wooden cup to salute her and then took a giant swig, drooling the dark liquid down his scraggly white beard.

Yarrow produced a contrived laugh. "Ha, yes. She's a jester."

After determining Yarrow wanted to keep her identity a secret, for whatever reason, Tsarina played along with his rouse—even though she had a sense Jasper was aware. If he was, however, he played the fool to perfection.

Once she finished her stew, Tsarina took one last sip of tea and excused herself to the bedroll Jasper had prepared. Rolling onto her side, she closed her eyes and allowed her fatigue to overwhelm her anxious mind. Her last thought was a wish—a wish for the morning light to wake her and whisk her away from the unending nightmare of Adytum, even though she knew her dream of returning home was now the fairy tale.

∞∞∞*Up The Goat*

Early the next morning, the sound of a cast iron skillet clanging against the stovetop shattered a disturbing dream Tsarina was having of Agni and Tasha arguing in Tasha's Greenwich Village apartment. Tsarina slowly opened her eyes, blinking the vision from her mind as she uncurled her body. Before she could focus, a globule of snot landed on her cheek, and William's cold nose brushed across her face. Still half-asleep, she wiped the wet tickle from her dimple and opened her eyes wide. The massive, black and grey wolf hovered over her, panting, staring at her face, begging for attention with bright, aquamarine eyes.

"William!" She heard Jasper shout. "Leave that girl be!"

For all their might, his words changed nothing. William remained enamored, licking her face while she rose to her feet. Jasper was too busy setting out the breakfast to realize the ineffectiveness of his words. The old hermit placed three plates on the table, and asked, "Slogger 'n eggs will do ya? Huh?"

"How'd you guess?" Tsarina quipped, as she made her way to the table with William loping at her heels.

Jasper shook his wooden spoon at William. "Alright you damned, mangy animal, get outta here so she can eat in peace. Why don't you go and kill something—earn your bleedin' keep," he ranted and pointed toward the door with his spoon.

William took one last look at Tsarina before bowing his head and sulking over to the exit. As the beast pressed the latch down with his paw, in walked Yarrow, wiping his soiled hands on his trousers.

"Thank you William," said Yarrow.

William looked behind then huffed a sigh and walked out the door.

Yarrow's eyelids looked dark and weighted when he turned his attention to Jasper and said, "I saddled the goats. I will send them home once we are up the mountain. Again, many thanks."

"Alright. Now go and wash up and get you some messings here before you take off this morning."

Yarrow nodded and walked over to the water bowl next to the stove.

Tsarina took a breath between bites and said, "Wow, this is pretty good."

"Huh?" asked Jasper.

She choked down the morsel then shouted, "PRETTY GOOD."

"Ah. Yep, them be eggs from my chickens and meat from the sloggers."

"What's a slogger?"

"Huh?"

"SLOGGER. What is it?"

"Oh! Good for nothin' creatures—'cept getting eat. I keeps 'em just for that," he snickered.

"Sounds like a pig? Do they squeal a lot?"

"Huh?"

"Do they SQUEAL A LOT?"

"Oh yeah. Squealin' and snortin and messin'," he bellowed, his belly rolling.

After hearing about the goats and chickens and sloggers, Tsarina wondered how many animals had made the trip from Earth as she continued to devour her breakfast. The hearty meal gave her a strange sense of home and reminded her of Jana's greasy southern cooking, but it also brought a sinking feeling of isolation. She questioned if she would ever get to taste Jana's biscuits and gravy again.

When she finished her last bite of slogger, she thanked Jasper and placed her dishes in the water basin then walked outside where Yarrow had secured two large goats to a post with a rope. The giant animals were almost twice the size of a normal goat, and their silvery white coats hung down past their knees, contrasting starkly with their wispy black manes.

"That thing's a friggin' horse," Tsarina blurted, while the goats bleated disapproval.

"That one's Mary," Jasper informed, pointing his shepherd's axe at the shorter one on the right. "Watch out for her. She bites."

"Great," Tsarina muttered.

"Huh?"

"Don't worry," Yarrow offered, "I'll ride her. You mount Richard."

Tsarina looked at the other goat, which seemed just as contentious, and placed one foot in the leather stirrup. With a step up and over, she bounced onto Richard's back and settled into the saddle. Once she and Yarrow were secure, Jasper loosened the lead ropes from the mahogany post and prodded Mary's backside with the tip of his axe.

"Go on you damned beasts! Get your bleedin' arses up the mountain!" Jasper howled.

Reluctantly, Mary plodded forward and Richard followed with an equal lack of enthusiasm. Tsarina waved goodbye to the old hermit, who returned the gesture. William followed the crew as they sauntered toward the narrow trail that would eventually lead them to Cairn Rose. After awhile, Tsarina began wondering if the wolf was going to follow them all the way up the mountain. A few hundred yards later, he stopped and let out a long howl then returned down the hill to his master.

Shiny pebbles littered the steep slope, crunching under the goat's hooves. As the slope snaked its way up the jagged path, the surface shimmered in the morning sunlight, and the harsh glare from the crystal mountainside stunted Tsarina's sight. She longed for a cheap pair of sunglasses a she squinted to see the top of the mountain. Each crag reflected rose-colored sunrays like giant mirrors. The spectacle resembled the inside of a giant kaleidoscope, showering the three peaks with light.

Mary and Richard continued loping along at a snail's pace, allowing Tsarina to absorb the sunlight and the scenery, and she giggled to herself, wondering if she would have made better time on her own two feet. The leather saddle wiggled under her tailbone with each step, and she could feel blisters forming on her thighs. After awhile, the acute pain in her derrière and inner thighs began throbbing incessantly, and she found it hard maintain one position for any length of time. Yarrow rode behind, providing horrible company as usual, saying nothing to take her mind off the pain. At times, she even wondered if he had fallen asleep, and occasionally looked back to check his status. For hours, they meandered up the path without a word until Tsarina couldn't endure the boredom any longer.

"So," she started, "I noticed you were trying keep the whole Earth thing a secret with Jasper, right? That's why you were acting all weird?"

"Yes. The fewer who know of your origin, the safer you will be."

"You don't trust Jasper?" she asked.

"Jasper is old and has many dealings with merchants and couriers. A loose tongue, for any reason, would betray you."

"Right," Tsarina acknowledged.

Plodding along, the goats walked stride for stride, occasionally snapping at one another's whiskers and bleating their annoyance. On either side of the central mountain peak, waterfalls bubbled and splashed, while the misty air ruffled Tsarina's hair. She considered the spell Yarrow had constructed in the field and wondered if she could use it.

"Hey, you know that wind convergence stuff you were doing the other day? You think you could you teach me that? I was just thinking we could do something constructive, since we got all this time on our hands." Tsarina gave a pleading smile. "When I was on the boat with Indimiril, he taught me how to make the crystal in his staff glow."

"I am no teacher. Instruction is best left to elders. It is dangerous."

"Dangerous? Indimiril's spell saved our lives, and besides it's just a little wind, and I suck at this stuff. I probably couldn't get a puff out of it anyway," she contended.

"Wind energy is volatile."

"I'm not talking about creating a hurricane over here. I just want to see if I can make a little breeze float through my hair—you know, to take some of this heat off. That can't be too dangerous, right?"

Yarrow remained stoic, looking forward.

"Look it, I promise, I'll take it easy. Come on, what could it hurt?" she pleaded.

"Us both," he replied.

"Please?" She attempted to soften his resolve with her eyes.

"No."

Tsarina gave a stern look to the warlock, seething on the inside. She tugged the reigns on goat and stopped in the middle of the path. Yarrow's goat stopped as well, and he looked at Tsarina. "Come. We must go."

"I'm not going anywhere unless you teach me that spell," she replied.

"What? There is no time for this. We must get you to the Cairn."

"Then you should start teaching me that spell because I'm not moving. Maybe Jasper will teach me some shit."

The warlock's tanned brow furled, and he turned to face her and huffed, "You must do exactly as I say. It is easy to over-weave, and if that happens, you will become too weary for travel, or worse, die." He turned his gaze toward the sky. "The sun is strong today. It will provide you with energy. Do not press hard. Now, come. Let's keep moving."

"Cool. Thanks."

"I will try wind collection with you," he groaned, "but when you feel sluggish, you must stop. Agreed?"

"Yeah, of course." Tsarina's eyes widened with anticipation.

"Did Indimiril teach you to clear your mind?"

"Yeah, but that's the part I'm not so good at."

"Find the darkness," he instructed.

"What does that mean?"

"Find the black," he stated with a blank stare.

"You're right, you suck as a teacher."

Yarrow scowled, " it is a darkness that captures all and lets nothing out."

"A black hole," Tsarina mused. "Ok, that helps, then what?"

"Feel only what you wish to control."

"Ok, and how do I do that?"

"Most connect the spell with a word. For this spell, I use *ventus*."

"What if I don't want to connect it to a word?"

"You must," he answered.

"Why?"

"Because"

"Because why?"

"Because that is the way it is done."

"I don't see how a word helps," she explained.

"Then I cannot help you." Yarrow folded his arms over the horn of his saddle and prodded Mary forward.

"No, look it, I'm just saying there's gotta be something more to it. Why do you have to connect the spell to the word, what are doing with that?" she asked.

"When you speak the word, you connect it with your thoughts to the air. This allows you to become one with the energy of the air. It helps your mind make the connection."

"There you go. That's what I'm talking about. That makes sense. So, you gotta merge your thoughts with the energy in the air."

"I suppose…yes." He blinked.

"Got it. Then what?" she asked.

"Once you feel the wind's energy, you will notice its chaos. Air is a difficult element to master. You must bend it to your will." He pressed his hands together in a semicircle.

"Ok, how do I start?"

"I chant the word until I find the darkness and became one with the air."

"Ok, I'll give it a shot."

Tsarina closed her eyes and concentrated on the darkness, excitement tingling the tips of her fingers. Blocking out the light was easy, she simply had to close her eyes, but the outside noises weren't so simple. They grew louder in her ears when she closed her eyes. Instead of trying to shut them out, however, she allowed them to blend together. She imagined how the sounds of New York would blend together, creating a hum that eventually diluted everything into nothing. She absorbed the calls of the birds, the hooves of the goats, the winds sifting through in the trees and mashed them all together to create a similar hum of nothing.

"*Ventus...Ventus...Ventus*" she chanted.

She spoke the ancient word in a constant stream of consciousness until she felt only the air touching her hands and her face inside the darkness. Gradually, the mantra became as natural as breathing, and she began to understand how the word acted as a bridge between her and the air. It was a rhythmic tool like music. She felt the chaotic energy of the air pushing and pulling in the darkness, flowing through the valley. She glanced with one eye at Yarrow and said, "I think I got it. Now what?"

"Control it," Yarrow answered in a slight tone of awe.

Tsarina continued the chant inside deep concentration. She imagined the gentle waves of air, brushing the hair from her face, but they refused to oblige. With each second, frustration frayed the edges of her concentration, and she began questioning her sanity for even trying to control the stupid wind. Her focus wavered like a sputtering propeller. She pursed her lips, trying to hold the connection, and Yarrow gave a supportive look of determination. She gleaned his non-verbal command and refocused.

The air, however, wasn't listening. It seemed to have it's own agenda. Tsarina felt a tiny puff of air ruffle the bottom of her hair, and she latched on to it, following with her mind. She felt the current's connection to the others and then began to feel them all before they passed. She continued chanting *ventus*, and with each utterance, she felt the wind gradually increasing.

"Yes," Yarrow acknowledged softly with a tinge of concern. "Now focus on the intensity and direction."

Tsarina fell deeper into the trance, and the path opened wider for her thoughts to flow. She felt the seemingly infinite power of her energy, and as it expanded, a strong gust of wind pounded her body like a wave of invisible force, tossing her off the goat. She landed on her back, and her head bounced off the ground, dizzying her.

Yarrow bellowed a grunt and leapt from his mount, staring at her with concern.

"Whoa! Holy crap! That was awesome! Did I just do that?" Tsarina marveled.

"Yes, but you used too much."

Tsarina nodded, trying to harness a somewhat serious expression through her wide grin. Yarrow offered his hand, and she wobbled upright. She gathered her balance and dusted her butt, disregarding the throbbing pain in her tailbone and at the back of her head. The blast had shocked her, but more so, it was exhilarating. She had felt the untapped power of her mind opening like a vortex to control the wind, and it did not seem outlandish. It felt natural. She began to accept what her mother had always touted—she had a gift.

"How do you feel?" Yarrow asked, helping Tsarina climb onto Richard's shoulders.

"Pretty amazing" she said. "Actually, I felt a little nauseous when that big gust hit me, but the adrenaline rush took care of that."

"Adrenaline—"

"Yeah, the rush. It's straight up biology. I keep forgetting you guys aren't down with science."

"Please explain, Adrenaline," he said.

"Adrenaline is a hormone in your body that kicks in when you're traumatized. People have been known to pick up cars and do all kinds crazy shit on adrenaline."

"Cars?"

"Yeah, cars. We have these machines with four wheels that move without us having to do anything but press the pedal with our foot—like a carriage without a horse."

"I do not understand. Is it propelled by magic?"

"No, but to you it would probably seem that way. It's fueled by gas or even electric. Don't worry about it, just know that we have some pretty cool stuff on Earth, we invented with science, but hey, I could say the same about some of the magical things I've seen here, so it's al the same really."

Yarrow nodded, still obviously confused, and turned his gaze toward the Cairn. Tsarina smiled and continued playing with the wind until Yarrow noticed and advised her, "If you do not stop, you will not make it up the mountain, and I will have to tie you to the goat."

She could feel the effort draining her energy, but the exhilaration was addictive, pressing her to continue. She yearned to play with the feeling. Every so often, she would quickly try to connect with the wind, without the word, and Yarrow gave a look of concern when he noticed. By the end of the day, as the sun was plummeting behind the mountain, the ensuing darkness and the elevation change brought cold winds. Tsarina's eyes grew heavy in the darkness. She tucked her legs tighter into Richard's wool and rested her head on his mane, absorbing his heat.

"Keep alert. We are almost there," Yarrow informed.

"Good, I hope you guys have a heater," she joked.

Yarrow's eyes narrowed. "The fires inside the Cairn are warm—"

∞∞∞∞Warm Crystals

When the path took its final turn, a blue light from an indiscernible source illuminated two, fifty-foot statues, marking the entrance to a set of fortified towers carved out of the three adjacent mountaintops. The menacing crystal warlocks stood watch with their stone staves raised halfway over their heads, as if ready to unleash a furious spell at any would be intruder. Their cyan eyes seemed to follow Tsarina as she rode underneath and into the courtyard.

Inside the area, blue shrubs and crystallized plants, resembling vines with ice plant fingers, littered the ground, providing the base for six spectacular sculptures of men and women, all dressed in flowing tunics. Off to the right, two female sculptures pointed with limp wrists at a man kneeling between them, his head lowered. The women were covering their mouths with their hands, as if whispering a secret. Tsarina puffed a smile, wondering the context of the joke as she drew near. On the left, two sculptures of hooded men with daggers in their hands, were standing behind a warlock who was pointing his staff toward the night sky, as if angry with the gods.

Yarrow dismounted, several yards inside the courtyard, and motioned for Tsarina to do the same. Sliding off Richard, she felt her feet accept the hard ground and she stroked his long mane. With each removal of her hand, he bayed, prodding his nose into her hand, begging for more attention. Then, after several heartfelt strokes, she ended the long goodbye, and Yarrow sent both Mary and Richard down the trail with several clucks on their leads.

"Shouldn't we feed them or something?" Tsarina asked.

"They will feed off the land."

After a final glance at Richard, Tsarina returned her attention to the jagged crystal towers, and a touch of nerves shivered through her body. She wondered who she would find inside, and if they were to be trusted. Yarrow had saved her from the dwarf and made good on his word to bring her to the Cairn, but in this strange land, she believed it foolish to trust anyone completely. She followed Yarrow to the base of the first tower, where a set of arched double doors, five-feet thick and forty-feet high, made from solid blocks of sheer quartz, beckoned them inside. An iridescent oak tree, etched in the middle of the doors, with cyan branches hanging down symmetrically on both sides, split in half as the doors grated open with a wave of Yarrow's hand. As they crossed the threshold, Tsarina felt the air gradually growing warmer. She marveled how they could keep a structure of this enormity climate controlled.

Glowing, diamond shaped tiles of azure crystal extended from the floor onto the walls, giving the massive foyer a honeycomb-like appearance. A tile beneath Tsarina's feet morphed from the face of a beautiful woman into that of a little girl with similar features. Most of the tiles seemed to be alive with similar motion. An astounding array of shapes and images continued weaving in and out of them like magical picture frames. Questions raged in her mind as she followed Yarrow into a large antechamber, but before she could ask, he instructed her to rest on a bench cut of azure crystal, seemingly chiseled directly from the mountain.

"Please, wait here. I will alert Halcyon of your arrival."

"No need," a white-haired man announced from inside the hall. His words faded into silence as he rounded the corner. The lower half of his silk tunic fluttered when he approached, and he extended his withered hand—bony, white fingernails poking through the baggy, cobalt blue sleeve of his tunic. Tsarina accepted his offering, and the old wizard released his ornate staff, crafted of bone, to Yarrow.

He then relaxed his hand against hers and smiled. "Ah, just in time Demetrius," he said, switching his gaze in the direction of a slender young man who followed. The boy's feathery blonde hair wisped around his bronze, hexagonal framed glasses as he removed his focus from a thick brown book in his hands. He closed the book and removed his glasses then asked, "Where are Anton and Indimiril?"

Yarrow lowered his head. "Caught in a storm."

"You left them there?" the boy challenged.

"Tsarina was in danger. A Dwarven mercenary flew on a wyvern. Caught Anton off guard then struck him to the ground with the beast's talon. Indimiril dismounted to aid, and the dwarf attacked Tsarina. I was able to distract them with a storm, and we took shelter inside the knoll. I am not certain of what became of them after."

"I see. We will send for them at once," Halcyon stated.

"I shall go master," Demetrius offered, arching his back as if to show off his chest, of which there was very little.

"Very well, Demetrius. Saddle your horse and take Aurora with you. If Anton is injured, you will need her healing prowess. Ride with several others, as well, for safety, and ride swiftly. The threat of this dwarf and his wyvern may still be neighboring."

"Yes magister. Thank you. I will summon Aurora and the others at once. But who is this mercenary?"

"I do not know," Halcyon frowned, "Indimiril's Dalton did not speak on their pursuers." The Archon turned to Tsarina and asked, "Madam Tsarina, did the dwarf indicate anything to you of his intentions or of his origin?"

"Yeah. His name was Sükh, and he said he was working for this dude Agni, and that he was hired to grab me because I stole the Eye of Istia from some witch named Viduata. He came into Splinter with a bunch of those Noctiss creatures."

"Viduata?" Halcyon mused. "Interesting."

"You know her?" Tsarina asked.

"Ages ago, I thought I knew her, but that time has long since past." Halcyon turned to Demetrius and said, "Godspeed."

The tall boy nodded then scrambled down the hallway. Halcyon's eyes sharpened as he shook his head, and a frown lurked inside his long white beard when he settled his gaze upon Tsarina. "This is most disturbing," he stated.

His somber expression lightened as the moment of doubt seemed to pass, and a small curve appeared in the corner of his mouth. "Well now, Madam Tsarina, I understand that you must have more than a few questions for me, however I am also sure that your journey has been long and arduous and that you might need a bit of rest and a solid meal to boost your strength. Shall I show you to your quarters before we tax you any further?"

"That would be good. I'd love to chill out for a minute."

"I do apologize. Is it too warm for you inside the Cairn?"

"What? Oh…no," she giggled. "I just meant—I'd love to get some rest. That sounds wonderful. Thank you very much, sir."

"Certainly." The Archon's cheeks relaxed. "Well then, we have prepared a room for you, and a feast that should pacify your hunger. Come. Let us to your chamber straightaway. There will be plenty of time for tales later, as I believe we have all had our trials for today. Until we know the full extent of Agni's grasp, and Viduata's role in his plans, I'm afraid we are mostly in the dark. I believe you shall find that I have as many questions, if not more, than you," he informed with a calculated smile.

The Eminent Supreme Archon turned to Yarrow and said, "Thank you for your service Yarrow. Go now and rest. For in the days to come, you will surely be called upon again." He then dismissed the haggard warlock with a nod, and Tsarina waived a faint goodbye. Yarrow responded with the two-fingered *V* sign across his heart, and she mirrored the gesture with an appreciative smile.

"Please, come this way," Halcyon entreated.

Tsarina followed the old wizard under the high, fan-vaulted ceilings. Warm currents of air floated above, brushing against the long tapestries of gold and rose crests hanging from the webbed ceiling, causing them to flutter in the light. When Halcyon stopped at the end of the hall, he and Tsarina stood before of a set of double doors, fifteen feet high, whereupon he motioned her to enter with a wave of his hand. As she approached the opaque crystal doors, they swung wide, revealing a grand suite with a large domed ceiling. From the center of the room, a solitary vase, filled with purple lilies, greeted her as if to say, *welcome home*. Beyond, a curved white couch beckoned her weary body. She took a step down into the circular azure floor, sliding past two overstuffed white chairs and plopped down on the couch. She thanked Halcyon with a faint smile as her back melted into the soft cushion.

Graciously, he accepted her valediction with a nod, placing two fingers over his heart, and then he exited without another word. When the crystal doors closed, the room grew silent. Tsarina felt odd. She was alone. It was a feeling she hadn't experienced for days, and seemed like years. It was unnerving for a moment, but the luxurious surroundings began absorbing her anxiety like quicksand, and her eyelids paid the toll from the long stretch of days.

∞∞∞Cairn Comforts

In the quiet hour that followed, Tsarina catnapped on the velveteen couch, her dreams as vivid and real as any she had ever experienced:

Slivers of white moonlight dripped through the rust coated iron bars into the stone well that imprisoned her. She did not feel like herself as she gazed up the long shaft in search of a way out. The physical body she inhabited was frail, weakened by starvation, and a strange woman's memories chattered despondent thoughts inside her head. As she struggled to fine-tune the vision, she listened for any sights or sounds that might provide clues as to her whereabouts, and why she was trapped in a well. A vague memory of a rangy preacher, dressed in puritanical black garb, shoving her into the murky hole floated through her mind. The vision shocked her as she gazed the firmament. Hunger pangs gnawed upon her host's innards like virulent maggots, and the solitary confinement wove a cruel maze for her disoriented mind to traverse. Hallucinations of puritanical strangers morphed in and out of her consciousness with distressing frequency, and her head ached from the chaos.

As she peered into the stagnant water around her pruned feet, reflections of moonlight bounced off the surface, representing a pattern—a constellation—Pegasus. Nine points of light delineated the pattern of the winged horse, and near his neck, an auburn haze burned below. When Tsarina reached down to touch it, the ensuing ripples destroyed the astrological template. As the pattern faded, Tsarina envisioned memories of her host's friends—most likely, peers who had been burned at the stake or drowned by neighbors. She felt the paranoia of the villagers, and it grew worse with each vision. The woman's imprisonment in this well was apparently due to her simply mentioning an herbal tea as a remedy—a potion concocted to help her best friend, Mary Watson, gain favor with her new beau.

I must survive. I must survive this night until the Solstice comes. Then I will use the Eye to escape. The woman affirmed in her head, battling her fears.

"Katrina," a low voice called from above, disrupting the thoughts. "Katrina, I have come to rescue thee. Grab onto this rope as I lower it." Suddenly, the sound of a pole prying open the grate above jolted the woman's heart like a defibrillator. Tsarina felt her body tighten. Seconds later, a cold rope slapped against her chest, and she reached out with both hands and put a firm grasp upon the rope, coiling it around her wrists.

"I have it," she confirmed.

"Hold tight. I will pull you up."

As the rope began towing her out of the well, she placed her bare feet on the cold stone blocks, pressing her spine against the opposite side. Water rained off her soiled dress, splashing the pool below, creating tiny circular waves as she inched her way toward the top. When she reached the opening, a wiry man dressed in a black cloak was at the end of the rope. His smiled over his chiseled jaw and on his last heave, beckoned, "Come, we must hurry and get thee far away from here."

"Yes, but who art thou?" Katrina asked.

"Thomas Goodman, a believer in thy good magic."

Beads of cold sweat dripped down Tsarina's forehead and chest as she awoke, her lungs short to expand and exhale. Gradually, the serenity of the azure, crystal room quelled the hyperventilation, and she came to realize she was no longer inside the dream. She rose from the couch, intoxicated from the excess oxygen, and staggered into the marble bathing area.

Inside the room, a shimmering crystal tub, three feet deep, sizeable enough to hold several people was masoned into the azure floor and invited her to approach with promises of warm water. She knelt beside the cold frame and searched the edges for a faucet and handles. A cone-shaped hole resting at the bottom of the basin appeared to be the drain, but she could not determine where the water was supposed to flow. Gazing overhead for divine inspiration, she spied hundreds of tiny holes punched into the polished tiles above. Then, she noticed a golden tassel, intricately weaved from velvet, hanging from the ceiling down to the floor. Curiously, she gave a gentle tug. A moment later, lines of steamy water, smelling like mulberry rain, shot through the holes with flawless precision.

    Tsarina's eyes bounced around the room in search of anything resembling soap or shampoo. Several, funny-shaped, multicolored vials sparkled under the blue flame lamps, resting on the edge of the basin. Scurrying over, she opened them like a curious raccoon, sniffing each to ascertain their sundry properties. One, in particular, contained a mild liquid that smelled like eucalyptus and immediately became her favorite. She placed the vial of soap on the front lip of the crystal basin and quickly slipped out of her robe. As she hopped into the middle of the downpour, her body tingled when the hot water splashed off her skin. She poured the thick soap into her palm and rubbed her hands together, inhaling the fresh scent with a deep breath. Rich lather foamed over her pores as she scrubbed away the caked mud that had collected on her body like crusty barnacles on the bottom of a neglected ship.

    Reluctantly, she pulled the cord to end the shower and stepped out of the basin feeling refreshed and civilized. Tossing her wet hair, she made her way over to the crystal shelves in the far corner of the room and grabbed two fluffy white towels from a neatly folded pile. The soft fabric caressed her skin as it absorbed the excess water. She wrapped a towel around her curls and another around her chest. With fluffy bursts of energy, she dried the hair around her ears and then tied the towel around her head. The luxurious towels reminded her of the fine organic hemp towels she had once used in a posh Russian hotel on the Upper East Side. A fond memory, when her sister had treated her for her sixteenth birthday. Unexpectedly, the images of home haunted her once more. New York, the world she once knew, was slowly becoming the dream, and now, Adytum was the reality.

Tsarina wrapped the towel around her chest tighter and searched the crystal countertop for a hairbrush to detangle the rat's nest that had formed upon her head over the past week. On the corner of the vanity, she found a shiny silver brush encrusted with brilliant red gemstones. As she ripped the stiff bristles through her tangled black ringlets, hoping to brush aside her debilitating thoughts of home, the reality of the physical pain helped draw her into the present, and once the last knot was obliterated, she rested the jeweled brush onto the countertop. She then made her way across the room to a tall crystal closet marked with the iconic, cyan oak tree. She determined it must be the official crest for the Cairn and pondered its significance.

Inside the thinly framed door, a rainbow assortment of tunics, sorted in the order of the spectrum, hung down like bodiless fairies. Sifting through the lustrous garments with her fingers, she found a silky, rose-colored tunic and removed it from its wooden hanger. The breast of the tunic had the same aquamarine oak tree stitched over it, and as she slipped into the satiny robe, the sheer opacity of the fabric gave her goose bumps. The fabric was unlike any other she had ever felt—thin and soft to the touch, but warm and firm.

Her mind wandered chaotically as she looked to the steps ahead and tried to formulate the questions she would ask Halcyon. She needed to squeeze every ounce of knowledge from him about Adytum if she had any hope of returning to Earth. The biggest obstacles at the moment were that she had lost her mother's grimoire and the Eye of Istia and she hadn't memorized the portal spell.

A crystal bookcase, situated at the far corner of the living room, captured her attention when she scanned the room. She scurried over and sifted through the various titles. Many of the books seemed like histories, however it was difficult to tell if they were fiction or non-fiction. The titles read names like: *Arteist the Sculptor*, *Leeanoor of Dustmoor*, *Tavaras the Tyrant*, and *The*

Eight Tribes of the Valley. On the second shelf, however, a leather-bound book sparked her curiosity, *The Summer Solstice*. She slid the thick brown book into her hands and walked it over to the massive bay window at the back of the room. Nestling into a lounging position amongst dozens of white pillows that were also etched with the Cairn's cyan emblem of the tree, she turned the first page.

  Adytum's two bright moons, Lunis and Aquius, cast their auras off the snowcapped mountains outside, sending beams of blue and white light through the crystal windows onto the cream-colored pages. A warm feeling of security enveloped her body as she began deciphering the calligraphic text written in what seemed to be fifteenth century English.

  The first chapter offered exact dates of Adytum's solar and lunar occurrences, like an almanac of sorts, and she wondered if they corresponded directly to the timeline of Earth. As she flipped the page to begin chapter two, a slight rap came at the door. She placed the book on a pillow and shuffled across the room to greet her visitor.

  When she neared the doors, they swung open and Halcyon stood in the hallway, dressed in a formal white tunic, outlined with gold stitching around the neck and cuffs. "My, my, you are a ravishing priestess by all accounts," he admired. "I trust your rest was adequate, and your attire is suitable?"

  "Oh yes," she answered, then lowered her tone as if to utter a secret for only Halcyon to hear, "And that shower was awesome. Thank you."

  "Not to worry. It is our humble pleasure to serve you, *awesomely*, milady."

  Tsarina giggled at his acknowledgment of her vernacular. Everyone else on the planet had let it pass over their heads or failed to even try to decipher her words, but Halcyon seemed to recognize her meanings were a bit different, even if he didn't fully comprehend.

  Halcyon smiled a knowing smile and continued, "My only desire is to see that your every wish is granted in your time here. If there is anything you require, anything at all, please, do not hesitate to ask."

"Thank you. That's sweet." She narrowed her eyes. "So, are we gonna have that talk now?"

"In good time, my child. We mustn't press ourselves without succor, at my age, there is only so much I can do without food and a bit of wine." The Archon winked. "First, I propose we honor your presence, and provide you with proper introductions to the members of the Cairn. I would like for you to meet all who reside here at the Cairn—the ones I hold prisoner to their studies," he joked. "Now, would you honor us by dining in the Hall of Spirits? That is, of course, if you are hungry."

"Are you kidding? I'm friggin' starving."

"Well then, let us proceed, and I will introduce you to the members of the Cairn straightaway," he announced, taking her by the hand.

As they strolled the long hall, the human images fluctuating inside crystal frames on the walls and floor engrossed Tsarina.

Halcyon illuminated, "I see our history has taken you."

"What?" she asked. "Oh yeah, the walls. They're amazing. How do they do that?"

"The images you see are memories of those who have inhabited the Cairn and their families. Once you become a member of the Cairn your mind is forever linked to this place. We draw strength from our collective knowledge. As a member of the Cairn, one shares their thoughts and memories in order to preserve our history."

"But, that's crazy, how do you put a thought into a rock?"

A tittle of amusement leaked from Halcyon as he tried to explain. "My dear, this *rock* is similar to your mother's sunstone. Certain objects have the ability to absorb all types of energy, and as a result, we can direct these energies as we so choose. That is what makes the Cairn so magnificent. It is a mountain of pure energy."

"So, I could think of someone and place their image in the halls of the Cairn?"

"When you are ready, yes." His gaze grew serious. "Which brings me to a delicate matter. I have begun to accept the reality that you are a daughter of Istia, and that Earth is your home world; nonetheless, there are those here who would not be so accepting of this reality. Especially since we have no Eye for proof. This is why I would like to introduce you to the members of the Cairn as a visionary, and a dream weaver—my newest pupil. You see, until I am certain that you are truly safe here, and that the portal is secure, I wish to keep your secret hidden. I hope that is agreeable."

"Yeah, okay. Yarrow said the same thing, but what about Anton, and Indimiril, and Yarrow? They know."

"Precisely, I trust them with all my being."

"Ok." Tsarina began to think of all the people who were aware of her true history and then the thought of Viduata sparked a different question. "So, who is this Viduata person, is she a witch? And how does she know about me and the Eye of Istia?" asked Tsarina.

"That is quite the mystery, yes. All these things, we shall explore in time. For now, let us forget where we are for the moment and simply enjoy being. Put away these puzzles and fill our bodies with sustenance."

Halcyon's lack of candor and the threat of potential spies troubled Tsarina, but she understood how it might be better to be safe and silent for the time being. Then she suddenly realized she might have to lie. "Okay, but what if someone asks where I'm from?" she asked.

"I believe you came to us from just outside of Splinter. Isn't that correct?"

"I suppose...*technically*."

"Excellent. Do not worry, I am very good at directing conversations," he informed as they approached the Hall of Spirits.

The members of the Cairn were seated around a large crystal table in the center of the room and rose collectively from their places when Tsarina entered with Halcyon. A crowding sensation squeezed her mind, as the azure light dripped off the crystal shards that were hanging from the chandeliers overhead.

The domed ceiling bore a mural of a grand feast with men and women of all shapes and sizes, draped in colored tunics, much like the congregation amassed below. On the baronial table, a cornucopia of meats, vegetables, breads, cheeses, fruits, and spices were overflowing in their crystal dishes and bowls, and a blue light dressed everything in the room, giving it a magical aura.

Halcyon stopped before the congregation to introduce Tsarina. "Esteemed scholars and Archons of Cairn Rose, thank you for your attendance. We have a very special guest this evening. She is a visionary and a dream weaver, the likes I have never seen in all my years. It is with great pride and honor I present to you our newest pupil, Madam Tsarina."

All the members pressed the customary backward *V* sign with their fingers to their chests and nodded. Embarrassed, she returned the gesture with a little more confidence than her previous attempts and fashioned a humble smile.

Halcyon continued, "All that I ask, is for you treat her as one of our own and make her feel welcome here in her new home. As with you all, I wish to cater to her every need, and for now, she is *friggin' starving*." His queer remark sent a chain reaction of confused glances around the room, and Tsarina snickered at his little inside joke.

"Now, let us feast," he urged, followed by a faint clap of his withered hands. Then, like trained seals, the disciples tumbled into their seats and started loading their plates.

Struggling to ward off the stares from prying eyes, Tsarina took her place alongside Halcyon with as much grace as she could muster. She felt a barrage of probing sensations, as if thirty mosquitoes were stabbing at her mind. The uneasy feeling clipped her hunger, and she turned to Halcyon for support. The Archon nodded knowingly, and the feeling subsided, as if he had placed a warm blanket around her thoughts. She relaxed and placed her napkin in her lap before settling into the high back chair.

Halcyon smiled and turned to the young man seated next to him and asked, "Would you be so kind as to pass the wine, Garrard?" The grace of the Archon's movements and the gentle tone in his voice weighed like gravity on her soul, and everyone else's, or so it seemed.

The youth broke his gaze from Tsarina and responded, "Oh…Yes, certainly Magister." The boy, slightly older than Tsarina, handed the crystal carafe to Halcyon, who then filled her gold trimmed glass half full, turning the last drop like a seasoned waiter and then did the same for himself. Timing the toast, after a polite smile, the Supreme Archon raised his goblet and pronounced, "Let us feast tonight and thank the stars for our newest gift."

The congregation raised their respective goblets, sharing in the toast, and after the glasses clinked and settled, everyone began feasting on the food. Amidst the muffled voices, Halcyon snared a huge breast of some type of cooked fowl with his fork and placed the juicy piece of white meat on Tsarina's plate. "This is one my favorites," he confided.

With the rest of the congregation's attention on the food before them, Tsarina was able to settle into her meal. First, she sipped from her goblet, and the red wine tasted of wild fruit with a hint of ginger. Next, she tasted the succulent, cream-colored breast of some bird that reminded her of tarragon-roasted duck, and she wondered if someone at the table had prepared it. Glancing over the faces, she tried to open her mind to ferret out the chef, then, just as she noticed the large man seated at the end of the table, Halcyon inquired, "Do you find it suitable?"

"Yes, it's wonderful. What is it?"

"Eysty," he said, then pointed with his eyes at the wide-faced man, grinning through a wiry brown moustache, sitting at the end of the table. "Gordy is our master chef."

Gordy was, by far, the largest person at the table, at well over three hundred pounds, and he blushed at the mention of his name.

Tsarina smiled at him. "It's really good. This is better than most of the—" She stopped before mentioning the restaurants in Manhattan. "I mean, it's better than anything in most of the places I've been to outside the Cairn."

Gordy bowed his head, revealing the balding spot on top, and his thick jowls rolled over his neck as he responded with a childish voice, "Glad you like it Madam."

From the end of the table, an eager voice popped out of a lanky boy's mouth. "They live up in the crags of the mountains. Big old nasty thieves they are. They'll take anything shiny that isn't tied down. So we eat 'em!" Tsarina chuckled along with several others and watched the fair-haired youth take a sip of his water before he asked, "Madam Tsarina?" He cleared his throat. "Is everyone from your village as beautiful as you?"

Blushing, amidst the collective laughter, she wasn't quite sure how to respond. "I guess, I'm about average," she answered.

The boy looked down, his face glowing like a bright tomato on the verge of exploding, and proclaimed, "Then I hope to travel there one day. Where—" His voice simply stopped, as if he had lost his train of thought, and another set of hearty laughter erupted from the congregation. Tsarina suspected this was Halcyon's doing—the *direction of conversation*, he had previously mentioned.

When the mirth subsided into quiet banter, a young woman dressed in a yellow tunic with a lime green hood that melded with her golden hair, interjected, "Madam Tsarina, please do not mind Timothy. From where do you hail, and are the boys there so cute?" Tsarina felt the mosquito sensation stabbing her mind again. This girl had apparently caught Halcyon off guard or had tremendous control over her thoughts.

"Let us not glean, Melinda," Halcyon interrupted. "It is not polite."

"My apologies, Archon, terribly sorry."

"Madam Tsarina is from a small farm outside of Splinter and wishes to keep her family and her origin untied to the Cairn."

"Again, my apologies, Madam Tsarina," Melinda lamented. "I have a family that would not approve of my studies here as well."

"Melinda." Halcyon chastised.

"It's okay," chimed Tsarina, "and to answer your question, the few boys there are really cute—most of them." The innocent, girlish conversation led to thoughts of Bud and his predicament. Tsarina took a deep breath and looked away.

"Oh my. Was I impolite again? I did not mean to—" the young woman grimaced, ashamed.

"No, I was just reminded of someone at home."

"I sense him in you, but he is out of reach."

Halcyon scowled and shot Melinda a look. "I do apologize for Melinda, she is quite a gifted mentalist, who sometimes has trouble controlling her gleaning."

"It's okay, really. He's my—" Tsarina realized she didn't quite know how to describe her relationship with Bud. "—friend." They had certainly been intimate in the brief time they were allowed together, but that was just it—brief. "He was taken by mercenaries when we were on the way to market in Splinter." Tsarina grasped onto the hope that he was still alive and fought a tear with another sip of wine.

"Oh my. I'm terribly sorry. I had no idea," Melinda apologized.

"It's not your fault." Tsarina shook her head, as if she could somehow physically toss the misery.

Halcyon wiped his mouth with his napkin and placed it on the table. "Let us not fear for your friend. What is his name?"

"Bud," Tsarina answered.

"Yes, have faith you will see Bud again. Faith protects us and strengthens our convictions," he comforted. With a gentle smile, he turned to the young girl, who was holding her head low, and said, "And thank you, Melinda, for broaching such an important, yet delicate subject. We shall deem Bud our highest priority, and I would ask that you personally head the search for him."

"Me?" Melinda questioned, with a startled glance toward Tsarina.

"Of course, who better than such a gifted mentalist to scan the minds of Splinter for a trail of answers?" Halcyon responded.

"Certainly magister, I am most grateful for the opportunity." She bowed her head. An enthusiastic sparkle beamed in Melinda's eye when she turned Tsarina and asked, "Milady, do you have any thoughts on who might have seen him last, and where he might have been taken?"

"There were women and children hiding in the buildings across the street from Althea's shop. Those were the last people I saw outside. They might have seen him after—" She paused, and all eyes turned on her.

"After?" asked Melinda.

"After the dwarf, Sükh…killed Althea."

Thunderstruck gasps vacuumed the remaining blithe spirit from the air.

Halcyon's eyes widened with solemn intensity. "You mean to say that Madam Althea is dead?" His stare tumbled over the shocked faces of the congregation, deepening the fervor, as several forks clattered to the table. After a moment of silence, Halcyon found his voice. "I am sorry to you all. I was unaware of this devilry. This news is quite disturbing. Althea was a valued teacher, a healer, and more importantly, a friend to us all."

Tsarina felt his pain cutting his voice short, and she placed her hand on his. Confusion from the awed stares around the table clouded her mind and a dull pain mauled her temples.

The creases of Halcyon's wrinkles deepened, and his lips stiffened before he formally addressed the members of the Cairn. "Ladies and gentlemen, given this news, there is much to be done. I am sorry to cut my presence short, but for now, you must excuse me. This old Archon has grown extremely weary and needs to examine the path we shall tread next. I will visit with all of you and explain your duties in detail, but for now, know that evil acts such as these will not be tolerated and justice will be served. Melinda, please come with me. I will see you at once."

"Yes magister." Melinda nodded.

When Halcyon pushed his chair away and pressed his staff into the ground, Tsarina stood along with him and said, "I would like to be excused as well."

"Of course," Halcyon agreed, "let us walk together then. Go forth Melinda. I will escort Madam Tsarina to her chambers, and then I will meet you in my study."

"Yes, magister," Melinda responded and exited swiftly.

Halcyon scanned the concerned eyes of his congregation and bid them a good night, flashing their customary sign, which was returned by all. Tsarina quickly issued the same gesture and followed the Archon out of the dining hall.

She felt comfortable walking alongside Halcyon, something she had not expected. *Maybe it was the wine,* she mused.

Yes, I sense it as you do. Your place is here with us. His inaudible voice invaded her mind, as if he were thinking with her.

"What?" she questioned aloud and stopped in the middle of the corridor.

His voice sounded in her head again. *Your acceptance of the Cairn is a blessing. I would enjoy enlightening you to all its wonders, in time, if you would allow me such an honor.*

"Okay, but—"

Do not be afraid, child. In time, these unimaginable ideas shall become second nature to you, he comforted, continuing to stroll at his normal pace. She hurried to catch up, solicitous of his power, and waited for his thoughts to enter her mind again.

Relax your mind. Conversation through mentalism is as natural as speech—if not more. These are ancient ways, tried and true. Ways apparently lost to you on Earth—quite a shame. It is obvious, however, you possess a natural ability for the arcane. You simply must allow it to flow without restriction. Hear my voice in your mind and answer with yours along the same path. Send your voice for me, alone.

Tsarina gazed into his wrinkled brow and focused on their connection. His icy blue eyes housed great energy, and she connected to it easily. Absorbing it, she voiced her thought along the path. *I do feel safe here. But there are so many things I don't understand, and I'm still worried about Bud and the Eye of Istia.*

I understand your fears. And they are valid; however, there is nothing you can do to alter them this evening. I suggest you put them to rest tonight, so that we may attack them fresh tomorrow morn. Then, we shall solve these puzzles together. As for your friend, do trust in Melinda. I will illuminate her on the image of Bud. May I have a picture of him from your mind?"

"How—"

"Create an image of him in your mind."

Tsarina closed her eyes and recalled the last time she saw Bud, trapped under Sükh's boot.

That is enough. Thank you. I will relate this to Melinda. She is impulsive, yet trustworthy. Despite her youth, she is one of my most gifted disciples. I have no doubt she will uncover the clues to his whereabouts. So for now, try and rest your mind and body. Tomorrow we will begin anew.

Thank you, I'll try.

As they approached Tsarina's chambers, Halcyon opened the door with a swipe of his hand and then bid her a warm goodnight with the customary *V* gesture. She returned the greeting and stepped into the dimly lit suite. The crystal walls inside wrapped her in a chilly vapor that ran down the length of her spine. As the double doors rumbled shut, she felt a touch of claustrophobia, even though the space was larger than any she had ever slept in before. She slithered into bed and wrapped the covers around her shoulders, embracing the warmth that followed. When she finally laid her head to rest on the padded pillow under the laced canopy, she worried for Bud and gave way to a dream from the past:

Tsarina envisioned herself as another woman dressed in a white summer dress, and a tall gaunt preacher was dragging her along a dirt road. His oversized hand clamped around her wrist, she felt pain coursing through the woman's wrist as if it were her own. The preacher held a torch above his head, casting an eerie light over his ashen face, accentuating his angular features. Tsarina's foreign body was not struggling against the preacher, as he led her into the town square of a small colonial village.

The smell of lamp oil thickened in the center of town, and an angry mob had gathered around a frail man tied to a large wooden cross. Underneath his soiled feet, large fire logs glistened like auburn gold in the fading sunlight. The townsman writhed, pleading for his life, struggling with the thick ropes that bound his wrists and ankles. When Tsarina's host body approached, the man raised his head and warned, "Katrina! I am sorry. Hell's fury hath found me!" He looked to the crowd. "You must forgive her. She knows not what I am. I am the devil that tricked her."

Katrina fell to her knees in the middle of the crowd and began weeping. Tsarina felt a strong connection between the two lovers, possibly husband and wife. She sensed Katrina wanted to run to Thomas and free him from his bonds, but something akin to fear, prevented the woman from acting, and then Tsarina realized Katrina was pregnant with his child.

"Burn him! Burn him now!" the puritanical villagers rioted, paying her no attention. They pressed forward around her kneeling body, as if she were a vision only for him to see.

From the middle of the crowd, the preacher parted the mob by raising the torch above his head then declared, "You will burn in the depths Hell for all eternity, warlock!"

Tsarina watched from inside Katrina's body, helpless, as the embers floated to the ground like dying fireflies on a cold night. Then the clergyman struck the base of the kindling, setting it ablaze with the torch, and as the flames rose up around the pole, the bound man's screams grated Tsarina's ears. She suffered with every breath, watching as his pale skin charred to his bones. The black flames crackled around his face, transforming it into Bud's likeness.

"I love you Thomas!" Katrina howled.

∞∞∞∞ Who's Got The Herb

Bud suckled the last drop of tepid water from the wooden bucket. The pail had provided his only source of nourishment over the past several days, and he wondered if his captors would eventually refill it, or if they would let him die of dehydration. A thin strand of light beamed down from the barred window, looming thirty feet above. It had come and gone three times by his recollection. Hunger consumed every waking moment. Moist, black stone surrounded him. Putrid vapors of feces and urine wafted up from a square hole in the corner of the floor, and the only exit was a short wooden door, fashioned with a window of black iron bars. The view past the bars was darkness.

Bud rubbed the golf ball-sized knot on the back of his head, and it throbbed at the touch. In his state of delirium, thoughts of the future fluctuated between slow death and suicide. Then a sedated voice hissed from the antechamber above, echoing down into Bud's cell. "Whats iss itss? Smellss ofs guts ofs seas fowlers."

"Some kind of herb," a garbled mouth grumbled, followed by an outburst of robust laughter. "Try it!"

Several minutes passed, and then the sound of a chair clacking to the ground awoke Bud from his daze. He heard hissing gasps for air and exaggerated coughing. His nose filtered the unmistakable scent of burning cannabis.

I've gone mad, he thought, and crabbed away from the door.

"Is wes goings tos kills strangess mans?"

"No. We don't have the girl yet. Sükh says we wait. We can kill him when we have her."

"Cans wees tortures hims?"

"Ha! At's fine. Poke out his eyes for all I care, just don't kill him 'till we have the girl."

"Wheres is shess?"

"How should I bloody know? They're all off somewhere looking for her. Viduata might be knowin'. You wanna go and ask her?"

A burst of hissing laughter stung Bud's ears, reminding him of his previous encounter with the Noctiss in the forest, and then the blurred memory was interrupted by the sound of footsteps, slopping closer.

"Littless mans. Heys littless manses yous awakes?" Bud heard the intoxicated Noctiss ask, as its slimy fist banged on the wooden door. Torchlight flickered outside the small, barred, iron window, burning Bud's eyes like the midday sun, as he searched for its holder.

"Yeah," Bud growled, squinting away from the flame.

Another loud hiss of laughter erupted from the opposite side of the door. "Whatts thiss weeds ins yas bagss?"

Bud vaguely recalled a small bag of pot he had been given by his roommate at a festival and assumed they had gotten a hold of the stash. "It's sativa," he explained.

"Strangess. Wheres yas gets itss?

"I'll tell you, if you bring me a leg of that turkey I been smellin'," he bargained.

"Whatss turkeess?"

"The damn meat! Whatever it is you got up there. Bring me some of that food, and I swear I'll tell you all about the little herb and where you can get all you want."

The torchlight faded from the window, and Bud heard the Noctiss slopping up the stairs.

"Damn it!" he croaked, as he slid down onto the floor. Pondering his next move, he waited for a several minutes until the shuffling sounds of sticky feet returned. When the Noctiss approached the door, Bud struggled to stand. Rattling keys echoed in the corridor, as the creature fumbled them back and forth, but before it could insert the key, the keychain fell to the ground with a loud clink, and a disgruntled hiss spit from its mouth. The Noctiss bent over to recover the tangled mass of iron and wobbled a bit. The second attempt with the lock brought success, and the heavy door creaked open. Through the thin space between the door and the wall, a mouthwatering leg of some type of smoked fowl emerged. Bud snared the appendage from the bumbling jailer, and in an instant, he devoured the meat off the bone, sucking it clean and biting off the rounded joint.

"Nows, wheres yous gets this herbs?" the Noctiss interrogated, gawking at Bud's rapacity with its shiny, purple eyes.

"From Hell motherfucker!" Bud whispered a soft battle cry and drove the bone shard into the eye of the unsuspecting Noctiss. Sliding his hand over the creature's mouth, he prevented a howl and jerked it into the cell. Once inside, he grabbed the back of its head and corkscrewed the fresh shiv deeper into its skull, and the mashed eyeball popped out of its socket. Fiery, purplish-red blood began streaming down the creature's face, and as the Noctiss attempted to wriggle free, Bud covered its venomous mouth with his free hand, suppressing its hissing screams. Acidic saliva gurgled out the creature's mouth, singeing Bud's palm, forcing him to retract. Spastically, he ripped the bone shard out of the eye socket and plunged the shiv deep into the creature's ear, twisting the final blow. He released the creature's limp body onto the cold stone floor.

Backing away, Bud listened, panting and chanting:
No one heard. The bastard's dead.
No one heard. It's in my head...

A low, maniacal laugh bellowed from somewhere deep inside his diaphragm—somewhere he wasn't aware even existed, and he wondered if this was the beginning of irreversible madness. Murder seemed to be getting easier with each kill and taking less of a toll on his soul. Mindlessly, he collected the rapier attached to the creature's waist and waved it around, feeling the weight. He gave it a few slashes through the cold air, testing its balance and enjoyed the power of being armed. It was invigorating. The crude instrument had minimal padding on the handle, but its pointed tip was certainly sharp enough to puncture any man or beast unlucky enough to cross its path.

Outside the cell, two torches crackled along the far wall, providing light for the staircase, but little else. Bud crept into the sparse light and several seconds elapsed before his pupils adjusted. The damp onyx staircase rose into the faint torchlight and was seemingly the only exit. As he ascended the steps, the aroma of seared meat, marinating with the distinct flavor of sativa, overwhelmed his nose, and his mouth began to water.

Poking his head over the top step, he spied a portly man with a trimmed beard, sitting at a small wooden table with his belt undone. The apparent warden for this dungeon was busy gorging himself on several fist-sized pieces of grey meat and flushing them down his throat with gourmandizing swigs from a tarnished goblet.

Using the man's gluttony and intoxication as an ally, Bud exploded from the shadows—rapier protruding like a bowsprit and plunged it deep into the jailer's heart. Awestruck, the felled man deflated in his chair, and his silver goblet clanked to the floor. Blue liquid splattered across Bud's feet and ankles. Inexplicably, he felt no sympathy for the warden. He felt inhuman, like a machine built for the sole purpose of killing.

Toppling the overstuffed corpse out of the chair, Bud grabbed the wooden carafe from the table and slammed the blue fluid against the back of his throat. He regurgitated the crisp, bold alcohol, and it spilled out of the corners of his mouth. As the fluid continued flowing down around his jugular veins, he choked, swilling between coughs. The libation tasted like blueberry-flavored vodka and mercifully began settling his haggard nerves with each gulp.

As the Dionysian spirit invaded his body, he stabbed across the table and ripped a leg from the cooked bird. He consumed the remainder of the carcass with aggressive bites like a wild dog. Once satiated, he sank into the large wooden chair, rubbing his belly, sipping the wine. Wiping his mouth clean, he pondered escape. He glanced around the room and spotted a thick wooden door opposite the stairwell that appeared to be the only exit.

Rolling out of the hard chair with a belch, he slogged over to the door, but when he tried to force the handle, it didn't oblige. A black iron keyhole located underneath the handle seemed to be the source of the mulishness. Bud grunted at the fixture then returned to the blood-soaked warden in search of a key. As expected, a black iron keychain with dozens of keys, all shapes and sizes, rested on the dead man's belt. Bud took the mass of keys then ransacked the pockets of the warden's trousers and found ten silver coins the size of half-dollars, each with a symbol of an oak tree printed on both sides. He then decided it would be easier and more beneficial to leave everything in the pockets and simply switch outfits with the warden. Hopefully, the dull grey garments would cloak his appearance enough to slip out unnoticed.

    The sleeves of the shirt were short, so he rolled them up to his elbows. The collar was baggy, and the pants were short by several inches. He cinched the leather belt low around his hips, extending the length of the inseam. Jostling around, he attached the scabbard to the belt and attempted to slip into the warden's leather boots. They were too wide and too short and cramped his toes, so he left them unlaced. After he adjusted the outfit as best he could, Bud returned to the lock, fully armed with the arsenal of keys and began systematically firing each one into the iron hole. Several attempts later, a rather large black key with a cloverleaf handle turned inside the lock with a pronounced click.

    Bud slipped through the heavy door and made his way past another torch lit stairwell that led into a grand hall carved out of polished black rock. Red torchlight flickered off the reflective stones like fiery ghosts pacing inside the walls, and along the high arched ceilings, maroon banners, embroidered with crests of stitched vultures, wavered gently in the rafters. The black birds had six orange tentacles for legs and were depicted rising out of the fiery sheets. Their incendiary eyes seemed to stalk his every move as he scurried across the black and red checkerboard floor.

    A cool flow of air, brushed against his face and he turned toward its direction. The flow led him to a massive iron portcullis that seemed to be the main entrance for the tower. Beyond, he could see a dark path of flat obsidian rocks, stretching into darkness. Two large Noctiss, holding partisans, fitted to their size, stood between him and freedom. Gold ceremonial blades, flat and wide, fastened at the end of the dark wooden shafts, gleamed with each turn of the slimy creatures' shoulders. The guardians stood at attention in front of an enormous iron lever located along the far wall, and they were not showing any signs of abandoning their position save for the occasional head turn. Bud guessed the lever was the catalyst for opening the gate, and he began to look for a subtle option rather than attacking the Noctiss directly.

Scanning the room, he spied a small corridor along the opposing wall and decided to explore. The staircase spiraled down, and as he descended, the stench of rancorous meat crept into his nose. Wide patches of darkness dotted the walls where water seeping through the black stones, running down the walls like tiny streams, had intermittently snuffed the torches.

Farther down the corridor, a series of iron doors lined the left side of the passageway, each with a series of red rivets set in symmetrical patterns. The first door bore the crude etching of a broom; the second, a ball of fire; and the third, a horse. The *ball of fire* door seemed the most intriguing, but when he tugged on the handle, it was locked.

"Figures," Bud groaned and pulled the keychain off his belt loop. A small key with a ruby carved like a flame, inset at the head, seemed the logical choice. The key slid into the lock with ease and opened the door, revealing a five-foot by five-foot storeroom filled with six wooden crates, stacked three high along the back wall. The lids were nailed shut. Using the tip of the rapier, he pried the lid off the top crate and sat it aside. Yellow and orange straw, thick and soft, lined the inside. Bud slid his fingertips deep into the packaging. Toward the bottom, he felt an uneven row of smooth orbs and palmed one. Extracting it, he held it up to the light and shook it vigorously like a snow globe. After a moment, the bluish liquid inside began bubbling and hissing with increasing fervor as the color quickly changed from blue to purple. Backing away, he stumbled over the lid of the crate and searched for a safe place to put the volatile orb. He scrambled into the hall and pressed down on the iron handle to the broom closet, which opened without a struggle and he quickly tossed the vibrating orb inside. Glowing red and roaring with effervescence, it hissed as he slammed the door shut and stepped away. Just as the latch caught, a powerful burst of red light exploded from inside the room, unhinging the door, launching it into Bud's chest. The door spun, slamming him against the wall, knocking the wind out of lungs as he rolled out from under the door. As he struggled to sit, a large cloud of black smoke billowed from the closet clogging his lungs. Inhaling and coughing, he rolled over and struggled to his feet, wiping the soot from his forehead with the back of his hand.

"Cool," he coughed, as he crept into the fire closet to gather more of the bombs. Wrapping four of the orbs inside his extra clothes, he carefully placed into his backpack. While packing the last, he heard the familiar sounds of slimy footsteps shuffling down the corridor and hissed words. Turning from the sounds of the approaching Noctiss, he pulled the drawstrings on his backpack tight and tossed it over his shoulder.

When he stepped forward, a tall woman with long, braided, silky blonde hair blocked his exit. Her transparent image faded in and out like a ghost as she peered at him with sky blue eyes. Bud blinked at the apparition. Her Norse features clashed with her black gown, which had red lace hanging from every angle, accentuating the tiny streaks of red in her hair. A string of crimson beads, stacked four high, layered around the bottom of her neck, jangled, as she looked him over. Her lips curved into a devious smile when she spoke. "You are quite resourceful. That will serve you well here."

"Thanks," he stammered, clutching the hilt of his sword.

"However, you will need more than a few fire orbs and an dull rapier to escape Viduata's Peak alive."

"Is that where I am?" he asked.

"Yes, and you must leave at once."

"Thanks for the tip. And who are you?"

"I am Freydis, of the Pequot clan, and I serve as Viduata's vigil."

A lump formed in Bud's throat as he imagined she would turn him into a frog, or worse.

"Noctiss!" hissed the woman under her breath.

Bud sank into his quads and drew his rapier.

"Put that away," she scowled. "They come soon. Follow me."

Frozen with indecision, Bud watched Freydis swiftly drift down the hall, flowing away from the oncoming sounds of the Noctiss. He sheathed his weapon and followed, asking, "Why are you helping me escape? Isn't Viduata the one who wants me here?"

"No, that is Agni's will. Viduata is no longer in control of her thoughts, and she grows worse everyday. Listen to me—Tsarina is the only one who can reach her now."

"How do you know about Tsarina?"

"Viduata has visions of the priestess. You must bring her to this place. Tell her the Eye is here, and she must use it to open the portal and save us."

"Save us from what?"

"Agni." Her face turned hard. "He means to harness the powers of Earth. Now hurry, the guards will be upon us soon," she advised.

Bud sprinted, trailing the floating apparition into the darkness. The torchlight decreased with each footstep as they circled down and around. Freydis led him to a solitary torch that charred the wall with its soot in the shape of a raven.

"Toss an orb down the stairs," she instructed.

Bud recognized the diversionary tactic and removed one of the smooth orbs from his pack and rolled it down the staircase like a bocce ball. With a clink and a ting, the crystal orb followed gravity down into the abyss, changing hues with every third bounce. Freydis's body gradually became solid, and she grasped the base of the lone torch, unhinging it from the wall. The black stones framing the torch made a low grating sound as they depressed into the wall, and a tiny ingress opened just wide enough for Bud to squeeze through.

"Hurry inside," she whispered. "This passage will lead you outside of these walls. From there, make your way down the mountainside, but you must stay off the road."

"Ok, thanks, but what about you?"

"My place is with Viduata for now. Go, you must hurry."

Slinking into the dark passage, Bud felt along the cold rock wall with his hands. The narrow corridor was no more than three feet wide and five feet tall, and as he squeezed forward, the grating sound of stone rubbing against stone behind spawned an ominous feeling of entrapment, and the corridor lost its last speck of light.

The knot inside Bud's stomach intensified, almost crippling him, as he inched forward in the darkness. The stone floor was smooth with a gradual, slippery decline. The walls angled in, and he was forced to tuck his elbows, in order to squeeze through the cramped space. With each step, he gained confidence and accelerated his pace until a void in the wall forced him to pause. Waving his hand inside the empty space, he felt nothing except a cold pocket of air and took a cautious step forward into the space.

Awesome. This feels like another passage. Which way do I go? Freydis didn't say anything about a turn or another passage. He took another step forward. *I guess I can always come back. I've only made one turn. I just have to remember to take a right out of this passage on the way back.*

Even though he felt he was headed in the wrong direction, curiosity goaded him forward like a hound following a fresh scent, and after several minutes of creeping up the corridor, a stench began burning his nose. Pale light drained down from the ceiling, and as he looked around, he noticed he was standing, ankle high, in a giant pile of dung.

Glancing overhead, he spotted a large iron grate, thirty feet above, lit by moonlight, droppings crusted onto the bars. A horse snorted from above, and Bud wondered if he could somehow ascend the shaft and steal the horse to make a cinematic escape like Errol Flynn. Even if he were able to make it to the top, there was no assurance the grate would be easy to remove, if at all, and surely, the horses would have some sort of security or handlers. Discarding the swashbuckling plan, he decided to return to the previous tunnel, assuming it would lead him out of the tower, as long as there weren't any other unforeseen forks in the corridor.

As he made his way back to the main passage, Bud shuffled the decline for several minutes, and soon after the turn, he felt a cool draft flutter his hair. Strange clicking sounds, as if made by metal crickets echoed inside the walls, growing louder with each step, and he anticipated the exit.

After another sharp turn, Bud found a blanched ray of moonlight, lighting an arched exit to the passage. The opening was a foot smaller in every dimension and blocked by a black thorny bush covered in red berries. Mindful of the thorns, he carefully pressed the rigid limbs aside and slipped past the bush. In his wake, dozens of fist-sized bugs, with silver wings and long mandibles that clicked, erupted into the night air, and he followed the alien bugs as they zipped off into the midnight blue sky. He stumbled over a craggy rock, forcing him to pay more attention to his footing. As he stuck his arms out for balance, a blistery wind blew down from the peak of the mountain, carrying unruly hisses from a far off horde of Noctiss. The excited grumblings emanated from the hill where the horses were stationed, and he staggered away from the noise. Traipsing down the slippery terrain, he welcomed the pitch-black night that would help him disappear.

Dozens of narrow trails led down the jagged onyx scarps and made choosing the right path a tedious labor of trial and error. Several times throughout the night, he was forced to backtrack in order to avoid severe elevation changes, and after countless hours of crisscrossing down the mountainside, cursing every wrong decision, Bud came across a small terrace resting below a giant rock face. Blinking his zoo of fears aside, he determined it would be a reasonably safe place to rest until morning's first light. He used his backpack for a pillow and quickly fell into a sound sleep.

When he awoke, he found himself lying in a grassy field, Tsarina sleeping at his side. The edges of his vision were hazy, and crowing sounds came in and out of his ears like crashing waves. The warm, hard ground pressed into his back as he sat up to gather his bearings. Peering into the dark sky, he wiped his eyes with his knuckles, producing sparkly stars that floated through his view.

Monstrous blackbirds circled overhead, moonlight sheening their feathers. Without warning, they descended from the nebulous clouds at an alarming rate of speed and struck out, stinging Bud's arms with orange tentacles. Yellow-orange beaks pecked his face, and he managed to bash the birds away with his fists, striking their heads with wild swings, sending the flock crowing away in all directions. The sight of fresh blood oozing from his forearms sparked a frenzied reaction from the birds, and they quickly returned to the feast like ravenous mosquitoes. Wide-awake and throbbing with pain from every extremity, Bud drew his sword and sliced their long thin necks, one by one, as they mindlessly approached. When the last black feather hit the ground, he turned, searching for Tsarina, but only a heap of mutilated birds surrounded him, and he realized her presence had only been a dream.

For the rest of the evening, Bud tossed and turned until the first auburn rays of sunlight began casting faint shadows over the flat, steep face of the crevasse. They warmed his tattered body, and he found the strength to affect a slight smile. As he looked below, a sparkling mist loomed over the crags, supporting a rainbow, preventing him from gaining a true sense of his elevation. He searched for an easy way down the mountain and settled on the route with the widest path.

As he descended the sheer rock face, he recalled his first semester at Fordham, which was mostly spent as a blocking dummy, and as a climbing partner for his hyperactive roommate, Cole. At all hours of the night, Cole would pull him out of bed and coerce him into sparring, and as a result, Bud had unintentionally learned Wing Chun, purely out of a desire to not get smacked in the face, or kicked in the shin at three in the morning. The Navy specialist in training would also drag him down to a small rock-climbing gym in Hell's Kitchen every Saturday morning, and at the time, it seemed like a fun thing to do, but now, Bud realized it was probably going to save his life. Gazing down the face of the mountain, he hoped some of his training would reemerge through sheer muscle memory. Carefully positioning his hands and feet on the tiny protrusions of rock, he began his descent, foot by treacherous foot.

With each new hold, his confidence in his technique grew and his pace quickened accordingly. After several hundred feet, he spied a ledge, half the size of a basketball court, covered with thatched straw and littered with oily feathers and large bits of shed tentacle skin. The nest looked padded enough for a fall, so he tossed his backpack down and waited to see if the orbs would explode. When they didn't, he let go his grip and fell the twenty feet, landing toes first into the soft thick straw. His ankles and knees buckled upon impact, absorbing the preliminary shock, as he tumbled onto his backside in a roll.

When he pressed his hands into the hay to stand up, the straw spread apart, and a sparkle of crimson flashed below the surface. The smooth edge of a red gemstone brushed against his palm. Reaching deeper into the silage, he uncovered what appeared to be a ruby, the size of his fist. The stone sparkled as he rolled it around in his palm, and he wondered its value before quickly stashing it in his backpack. Overwhelmed by greed, he dug around in the straw for more of the gemstones, but after a thorough search with no success, he abandoned his prospecting and decided to continue the descent down the face of the mountain.

The tips of his fingers throbbed, and after several hours of descent, he began doubting his chances of making it to the bottom. He clung onto a tree branch to rest, and when he looked down he saw a dense growth of trees dominating the mountainside and a path wedged between them. With his fingers numb, Bud scaled the last hundred feet of black rock and hopped off the ledge onto a pebbled path.

As he walked, black dust puffed under his boots each time they patted the earth, and the angles of the rock face decreased and flattened. The density of the surrounding foliage created a vacuum, capturing every sound like an organic amphitheater. Vibrations of extraterrestrial life reverberated throughout the thick corridors of wood with clicking and scraping tones leading the orchestra. The noises served as a prelude to the sound of hooves that began battering the trail like strident war drums, announcing three tanned warriors wearing loincloths and beaded necklaces.

Bud slipped deeper into the forest, out of sight, and aped up a wide tree filled with gnarled black footholds that resembled faces of wailing ghosts. The giant warriors rode into view on oversized Palominos, forcefully cracking the reigns, steering their horses up the mountain trail. The powerful steeds responded, kicking up black rocks and leaving a sooty haze in their wake. Bud remained hidden until the thunderous sounds faded to dull rumblings. As he dropped from his perch, he listened for more riders. *This road has to lead somewhere. Should I follow those dudes or head the other way? Other way's good.*

∞∞∞∞*Student Teacher*

Beneath silk covers, Tsarina slept soundly in her crystal-framed canopy bed. When her eyes finally struggled open, she saw a rose hue of sunlight bathing the quartz walls surrounding her.

Ah, this is Cairn Rose, she realized.

The shimmering rose-colored walls draped her in the thick aura of a dream, but she knew this was no dream. These walls and this fortress in the mountains were her reality, perception or not. She sat up, refreshed from her slumber, and slithered around inside her silk pajamas as she wiggled out of bed. Wrapping a matching silk robe around her shoulders, she stepped into a pair of fur-lined slippers, taking pleasure in the delicacy of her new garments. Strolling to the bay window, she cinched the sash tighter around her waist and stretched under a giant yawn. She gazed out of the window at the snowcapped mountains slathered in the rosy morning light, and the intense glare forced her to squint. She thought of Bud knowing his accommodations were not as glorious. An interrupting knock came at the door, and a timid voice asked, "Madam Tsarina? Pardon me, but are you awake?"

"Yeah, what's up?" she answered.

"Um…yes. Well, Master Halcyon would like to offer you breakfast, and he has asked to speak with you this morn at your leisure, of course."

"Oh yeah, sure. Come in," she called, adjusting the top of her robe.

As the door gently swung open, a short rawboned boy dressed in an aquamarine tunic sauntered into the room. His angular hands balanced two glasses atop a slim crystal tray, and an assortment of colorful fruits and pastries circled the glasses. Their sweet aromas filled the air as the boy shuffled with a turbulent gait over to the coffee table and placed the tray next to a vase of freshly cut purple lilies.

Tsarina hadn't noticed the lilies. *Was someone here last night?* she wondered, then immediately discarded the thought, in case the boy was gleaning. A burning sensation warmed her head, and she caught a flash of his thoughts—his admiration of her body. She looked to the ground for a moment, like a schoolgirl caught peeking at something she shouldn't have.

"Well, madam, is there anything else you require at this time?" The boy bowed after he spoke.

"No thanks. It looks delicious," she replied. *Was he the courier who had delivered and arranged the flowers during the night? Do I have a secret admirer?*

The youth bowed again politely, but his eyes stayed with hers as he turned to exit.

"Where does Halcyon want to meet when I finish?" Tsarina asked, as he strode away with his chin tucked into his chest.

The youth glanced over his shoulder and stated, "You must only think of him, and he will answer," and then the door closed without a sound.

"O...kay..."

Mental conversations were still awkward, and she wondered if the youth had gleaned any of her thoughts. The invasive feeling left her wondering if she would have to learn to guard her thoughts at every moment, along with her words. Whatever the case, she decided to improve on both.

After catching a whiff of the fresh fruit, she turned her attention to the meal sitting in front of her, and her mouth began to water. She took a sip of the red juice. It fizzled inside her mouth, tingling her tongue. The liquid was a blend of grapefruit and cherry flavors. A surge of pure energy shot through her skull when she swallowed, instantly clearing the morning fog from her mind. She picked up the oval fruit next and bit into its neon green skin. Sweet juice burst inside her mouth and ran down her throat. She felt the organic purity of the fruit, stripping away years of fast food, pizza, and Shelby's greasy southern cooking. *Shelby would be miserable here,* she giggled to herself, but as she did, bittersweet memories of her roommate frying bacon, scrambling eggs over scattered hash browns, and covering biscuits with sausage gravy filled her mind. Those wonderfully sinful meals had been their Sunday tradition for the past year. "A good old southern breakfast will set you right!" Shelby would boast whenever she would use it to cure a hangover. Her memories of college seemed like another life as she sat eating the chilled fruit inside her crystal room.

When She finished her meal, she took a giant swig of the red juice then focused on Halcyon's request. Reticent, she begged for an audience with the Archon through her thoughts by speaking his name in her mind, as well as conjuring an image of his face.

Hello my dear, the old magister answered, almost immediately per her request. *Good morning to you. When you are ready, please proceed to my study. There, we shall begin today's lesson. Follow this path,* he instructed.

When his words faded from her thoughts, a detailed map of the Cairn's corridors posted in her mind, revealing an exact route to his study. Tsarina took a few minutes to absorb the thought by brushing out the knots in her hair and changing into an emerald tunic. It was going to be a long day, and at the very least, she wanted to be comfortable.

In the hall outside her quarters, the crystal walls were no longer coated in the bluish-purple hue, as they had been during the evening. Now, the entire structure was bathed in the same rose-colored hue as her room. It felt like an exalted monastery, rich with history and pageantry. Murals of the members of the Cairn, past and present, hung between twenty-foot tall, stained glass windows, their eyes casting knowing gazes upon her. The living members of the Cairn, who were strolling about, welcomed her with subtle glances and reassuring nods as she passed them on her way to the study.

After several minutes of twisting and turning through the halls, Tsarina stood in front of a double door, marked with three open scrolls scattered under the Cairn's iconic turquoise oak tree. Halcyon sat behind an onyx desk and seemed to be lost in a piece of parchment when she entered.

"Ah, wonderful, you have found me," he chimed, lifting his head to smile at her. The archon propped himself on his bone cane and stood to greet her. "Please, do have a seat. I wish to show you something of interest." When Tsarina sat down next him, he asked, "Would you be so kind as to read this and tell me if it means anything to you?"

The small note quivered in her hands as she scanned the blotched calligraphy. After a quick read, she recounted, "Well, it seems like this guy, Thomas—Hey, Thomas Goodman? No, that's crazy. I had a couple of dreams about this guy." His face flashed through her mind again.

"Interesting! And what were these dreams?" Halcyon lifted an eyebrow.

"This Thomas guy pulled me out of a well in Salem, but it wasn't me. It wasn't my body. I was a puritan lady in the dream—a witch. Anyway, this woman, me—whatever, was thrown into the well and left to die—at least, that's what it felt like, being in her place, and this Thomas guy said he was a 'believer in her magic,' and that was it. I woke up after that. The other one was he was burned at the stake."

Halcyon gave an understated frown. "Yes, I believe he was. I also believe he, along with this woman, Katrina, were the last two to enter Istia's portal from Earth—that is until you came along, of course."

"You think she was one of my ancestors?"

"Yes, I believe Katrina must have been a daughter of Istia, and she was providing safe passage for those persecuted, like her, into this world. I also believe Katrina remained here on Adytum for a time in order to promote and continue the vision of Istia, while Thomas remained on Earth until his demise. It seems he was the one who prepared her followers for the journey from Earth to Adytum. From the few letters I have been able to collect, Katrina and Thomas were truly star-crossed lovers.

"In his letters, Thomas speaks of a secret coven—a coven on Adytum organized to protect the Eye of Istia and the daughters of Istia. The letters tell us Istia was the original constructor of this particular portal spell—the one you seem to have stumbled upon. From the writings, it appears Madam Istia was a priestess from millennia past. She unearthed the sunstone and used it to harness the power of the sun, which in turn magnified her own unique abilities. There is a story of her finding the gemstone in a cave."

"Yeah, Indimiril told me about it."

"Excellent. Then you are familiar with the myth—or rather, should I say, the history." Halcyon shook his head. "I believe it will take quite a bit of time to get used to speaking of Earth in these terms of reality."

"Tell me about it," Tsarina muttered.

Halcyon smiled. "Nevertheless, with the stored energy, Istia was able to create her portal from Earth to Adytum. It seems her wish was for Adytum to become a sanctuary for the arcane arts, and so she passed down the sunstone to her offspring. The daughters of Istia continued with her dream over the course of many centuries. According to her writings, I believe she somehow was able to weave into her spell, the stipulation that only a descendant of her bloodline may wield the power of the stone. That is why you, as her descendant, became the recipient of the gemstone, and of its power. So you see, you are quite a rare gemstone yourself my dear lady. Undoubtedly, there will be many who will want to possess or destroy you—as well as the Eye, by any means possible."

"Why would anyone want to destroy it? What's to gain from destroying the portal?"

"I am certain most people here, especially the uninformed, would fear anyone from Earth, due to the tales of horror surrounding the subject. Granted, most, if not all of the inhabitants of Adytum, have no belief in Earth; however, many have heard the stories—which I assure you are not favorable by any means. They are stories of persecution and death. Earth, even as a myth, is not a place the people of Adytum would desire to know."

"Wow." Tsarina grimaced. "It's not so bad, really."

"I'm certain this might be the case for people without magic at their disposal. However, imagine if the people of Earth discovered a warlock living amongst their midst? Have you evolved to the point where he would not be persecuted as before? Even worse, could you imagine if someone of power from our world would enter yours and use their abilities for evil?"

"I see your point. They would have a bunch of mad scientists, trying to figure out how to harness the power." The albino's face flashed in her mind. "Oh my god!"

"What is it my child?" Halcyon asked.

"I just thought of the guy who was chasing us in my dorm."

"What do you mean?"

"When Bud and I first woke up that morning, we were trapped inside our dormitory, and this pale guy with red eyes and blonde dreads had a bunch of Noctiss with him. He was leading them, and he was the one looking for me and the stone."

"Hmm. Most likely Agni," Halcyon informed.

"You know him?"

"Yes, quite well, in fact. Many years ago, Agni was one of our brightest students. He trained with Jindon in Splinter in the ways of Materialism. Sadly, he lost his way with our order when his father mysteriously disappeared one night. Agni tried to convince us that a portal had swallowed his father, however we did not believe him. It seemed at the time that the shock of the loss had taken his senses, as there was no evidence of any portal. It seemed more likely that his father had perhaps been eaten by some creature or had suffered some other horrific death in the fields. Nicholas, his father, his abilities were limited, and Agni was quite vague in his report. Several days later, Agni's mother was found dead, and Agni had disappeared."

"Do you think he killed her?" Tsarina asked.

"We do not believe so. It was an apparent suicide, by poison. She was found in her bed with a bottle of nightshade. We assumed the loss of her husband was too much for her to bear, and that she wanted to fade silently into the void."

"Agni just disappeared?"

"Yes. We caught wind from traveling merchants alluding to the fact that Agni had a strange obsession with finding the witch, Viduata. Merchants claimed they had seen him near the Narlwaka Mountains. It seemed so, as that is where she lives among the Noctiss, ruling them as their queen. By all accounts, it was a drunken bard's tale, what sent him there, and it has been many years since we last heard any mention of his whereabouts."

Tsarina questioned aloud, "Was his father an albino too?"

"Yes," Halcyon confirmed. "That is the trait of their family. Why do you ask?"

"When you said he lost his father thirteen years ago—I had a dream thirteen years ago—which, I guess, wasn't a dream after all. Nicholas was there. He must've been the man who was with us when my mother opened the portal that night. But, I can't remember what happened to him. I just remember ma screaming in the darkness of the field, and I think he helped us escape."

"Ah, so it seems this may not be your first trip to Adytum after all," Halcyon remarked.

"I guess not. But I have a question. Why would Agni stay on Earth if he was after me? He didn't try to follow us when the portal was closing. He just stayed inside the building. He must've known he would be trapped there."

"That is curious." Halcyon gazed out the window. "I suppose if Agni believes his father still lives, trapped on Earth, then one can only assume he would want to search for Nicholas no matter the cost. His father was not a powerful crafter by any means and would certainly have made no large intrusion on your world. He was a gentle man—one of serenity. Unfortunately, Agni did not inherit his father's temperament."

"Yeah, he didn't seem very chill. He lit this one lurker up like a match just for arguing."

"Yes, chaos suits him."

"Great. So how worried should we be about Agni on Earth? He seems capable of a lot of chaos."

Halcyon turned to Tsarina with a concerned look. "His powers over the material world were unmatched at his age. By the age of ten, he was quite a terror. He would often practice his mastery of fire by destroying bails of hay in the fields with giant fireballs just to watch them burn and spook the animals. He was also gifted, in the fact that he needed no words for casting. His ability to perform, *unspoken*, as we refer to it was remarkable.

"Unspoken?" Tsarina asked.

"Yes, generally, one must find a chant or a word that suits their needs, and then create a spell like the one you used to open the portal—often times, using a device such as the sunstone to amplify their power. Agni could simply think of the action and perform it. Unspoken. It is a rare and powerful method of crafting."

"I see," Tsarina observed.

"At any rate, Agni was Jindon's prized student, and Jindon did well to rein him in on many an occasion. He once kept the lad from destroying the entire forest of Splinter."

The endgame within his statements strangled Tsarina, and a hot wave of guilt flushed her cheeks—anyone she cared about would be a target of Agni's cruelties. On Earth, Tasha and Shelby were in grave danger, and she had no way to warn them.

"Yes, that is another matter altogether," Halcyon acknowledged her thoughts, again to her surprise. "Which brings us to Madam Katrina and the ways of your world. Her history is relevant to your ancestry. She apparently formed a coven to help transport the persecuted witches from a village called Salem to the fields of Jasmine here on Adytum. Does this village, Salem, still exist on Earth? I believe I heard you speak of it earlier. Was it in your dream?"

"Yeah, but Salem is just another city like any other city these days—nothing special, except for its history with the witch trials."

"Witch trials?"

"Yeah, anyone considered a witch in those days was subject to a *trial*. Not very judicial though. It consisted of the accusers drowning the accused, or throwing them off a cliff. If they survived being drowned, or flew when they threw them off the cliff, they were obviously witches, and were burned at the stake. If they drowned, or fell to their death, then they were cleared of all charges, and their family's honor was salvaged. Obviously, you can see the problem with that system."

"Deathberries or nightshade for dinner, yes. So you see, our fears here on Adytum about Earth seem unmistakably valid. Do these trials still occur?"

"No. At least, not with witches." She frowned. "Most of us stopped believing in magic and witches a long time ago."

"I see. I suppose it is easy to comprehend the loss of such an idea. Who of sound mind would want to openly practice magic and thereby subject themselves to such barbaric atrocities?"

"People like Shelby and my mother," Tsarina stated flatly.

"Yes, there will always be those who are wont to oppose their oppressors, no matter the cost."

"You make it sound it sound like they were heroes."

"Weren't they? Does it not take great bravery to rally against an unjust system, such as the one they faced on Earth?"

"I guess, but it just isn't that serious on Earth anymore."

"Because there is no magic left?" he questioned.

"Yeah, it looks like it all ended up over here."

"I suppose, except for the few artifacts like your mother and the Eye of Istia. I am curious as to how she recovered the Eye. The last report of its existence was during the time of Tavaras."

"When was that? I saw a book about him in my room," she asked.

"Tavaras—" Halcyon took a deep breath and adjusted his spectacles. "It is wonderful read. I highly recommend it."

"Yeah, I'll check it out, but can you just give me the Cliff notes for now?"

"Who is Cliff and where would I find his notes?" he asked with a disturbed look on his face.

"He's nobody," she chuckled. "I just meant, can you give me the summary."

Halcyon squinted as if trying to refrain from gleaning more information about Cliff, and then continued, "Certainly. Tavaras was a tyrant vying for power around the time of Katrina. During this time, her coven transformed the region of Jasmine into an agricultural masterpiece with their unique methods of farming. I can only assume, now, that they brought this knowledge with them from Earth."

"Indians," Tsarina mentioned.

"Indians?" Halcyon squinted.

"Yeah, the native people in the Americas were really good at farming and living off the land," Tsarina informed. "They look a lot like Yarrow, actually—but anyway, keep going—what about Tavaras and the Eye?"

"Yes, Tavaras. For many years, the fertile land supplied the valley with food. Then, as all things are meant to do, the world changed. Around that time, there were several diplomatic problems brewing on Adytum, and without a true form of government, a ruthless baron named Tavaras arose to power with the idea of *cleansing* the land. A powerful materialist, Tavaras, usurped Katrina's lands in order to feed his ever-growing kingdom. Even today, the fields and streams of the Jasmine Valley provide the richest source for food and are sought after by many clans. But those times are changing as well. We have seen a steady decline in the fertility of the land. At any rate, Tavaras burned most of the settlements on the outskirts of Jasmine, near where Katrina had taken residence. During the coup, she was taken captive and made to bed with the baron. Their union produced a daughter, presumably continuing the line of Istia. It is said that Tavaras kept the child and Katrina under lock and key, and that is the only story we have of how your ancestry and the Eye of Istia were lost."

"Wait. So, what happened to the Katrina, and her child, and the Eye?" Tsarina asked.

"Time and complacency eventually took their toll on Tavaras's mind, and he became weak and foolish, as old men do," he tickled his chest with a finger, "foolish enough for a high mentalist from Katrina's coven to gain his confidence. After several years of lying in wait under his service, the mentalist inserted herself into his bed. It was a night during *Solemnitas of Lux Lucisa*, the festival of light—a time of heavy drinking and mirth," He grumbled. "The mistress, armed with a vial of nettle poison, fed Tavaras his death during their lascivious behavior."

"So, how was the Eye lost, if she recovered it?"

"Tabitha, for some unknown reason, made off with the Eye of Istia that evening and was never heard from again. I assume this to be true, because the sunstone was never spoke of again in any of the annuls of our history."

"Then how did I end up with it?"

"That, my dear, is the question for the ages. More importantly, how did your mother come across it? And how could she possibly know how to use it?"

Astounded by the lack of information, Tsarina pressed, "With stories like this, why was Earth is considered a myth? How could no one believe it was real?"

Halcyon chewed gently on his bottom lip and glanced at the numerous shelves of books surrounding them. "Do you see all of these tomes around us?"

"Yeah."

"Each one tells a story, some are composed from fact, some from fantasy. Now, if you were to open any one of them, would you be able to tell the difference?"

Tsarina thought for a moment then realized that she had wondered the same thing about the books in her room earlier and came to understand his point. "I guess I wouldn't."

"Precisely. You see, without a scholar or a historian to testify to the authenticity of these stories, they become myth, or history. It is true, we are all believers in the arcane here, however one must consider this: would you have believed a portal could be opened between Earth and Adytum, if you had never seen such a thing, or been able to create one on any level for that matter?"

"No way."

"Neither would I. And I have seen a great many things beyond the realm of what is considered *possible*. Many generations have passed since the portal has been opened or spoken on. Adytum has evolved, in and of itself, without the presence of Earth, and people have simply stopped believing in the notion of Earth—much like magic on your world. With no one remaining from the old world, the reality of these ideas has vanished like a phantom into the void, and when there is no need for the phantom, he simply becomes a burden on the minds of the people, like a religion, lost in time."

"The extinction of an idea," Tsarina mused.

"Exactly."

"But, don't you ever wonder where you came from?" she asked.

"I am certain we all question the beginnings of our existence, but there are limitless answers to that design, are there not?"

"Not really. We kinda figured it out, scientifically. It's called evolution."

"Evolution, from what?"

"Single celled organisms. Humans evolved from microscopic organisms in the sea, into the species we are today."

"Interesting, and where did these organisms come from?"

Tsarina thought for a moment. She scavenged her mind for the theories of abiogenesis then realized he was essentially right. "Well, the short answer is: you're right, we don't really know how life actually went from nonliving material to living. I mean, there have been a lot of experiments that give us some possible theories, but we can't really prove them."

"I see."

Stymied, Tsarina decided to refocus the conversation. "So now you know Earth is real, what do you think is going to happen when other people here find out about it?"

Halcyon grimaced. "I cannot be certain. I presume no one will believe in its existence, at first, that is, unless the portal is reopened for all to see, and at this moment, that prospect seems very fragile. For now, I believe we must focus our efforts on finding the Eye of Istia and more importantly, keeping you out of harm's way."

"Ok. I like that plan, but how do we get the Eye? Sükh is taking it to Viduata, and those mountains you were talking about don't seem like an easy place to invade."

"Certainly not. However, it is obvious she needs you to open the portal. Otherwise, Sükh would have simply killed you and your friend, and taken the sunstone. Without you, the Eye is useless. That is our strength, and we must not allow her to know Agni's presence on Earth disturbs us."

"I think she's counting on that."

"What do you mean?"

"I have a sister on Earth, and if Agni finds her, they will have another bargaining chip to hold over my head. Or maybe, they could use Tasha to open the portal. I mean, if I'm a descendent of Istia, so is she, right?"

"That is true, however she may not hold the power to open the portal as of yet, if ever. Make no mistake—the spell you wove was no small incantation. Do not underestimate your gift. For now, I believe the advantage lies with those who wait. If Viduata sends mercenaries to find you here, then we shall be ready."

"What if they don't ever come? We can't just let Agni run free on Earth, and no offense to you and this wonderful place, but I don't want to be here any longer than I have to. I just want to find Bud and go home."

"We will most certainly search for the Eye to get you home—"

"And Bud?"

"Yes, of course. However, for now, I think it best you remain here, in the safety of the Cairn, and allow us to nurture your gift. I'm afraid you will certainly need strong magic in the days to come, and if we were to lose you to Viduata, finding the Eye will matter little."

"Ok. I get it, but Bud is still out there, gripping, in a world he knows nothing about. We need some kind of plan is all I'm saying."

"Agreed, but I suggest we wait to see what Melinda uncovers in Splinter then we can make appropriate decisions regarding how to proceed. I have no doubt she will find Bud to be held deep within the walls of Viduata's peak, along with the Eye. However, until these issues are solidified, there is truly nothing we can do to further our cause. In the meantime, I would be most interested to hear more about life on Earth, that is, if you wouldn't mind entertaining an old man."

The conversation going forth was decidedly one-sided as Tsarina fielded question after question regarding her family and Earth's history. Midway through the conversation, Halcyon insisted they communicate without words, and after an hour of giving a nonverbal history lesson, Tsarina was mentally drained and longed to return to her chambers.

Halcyon allowed a respite for lunch, but made it clear he was still curious about a great many things and wanted to hear more of her tales once she was rested. When she returned to her room, a small meal of fresh vegetables and fruits, presented neatly on a bouquet of green leaves, was laid out on a crystal tray. A blue dipping sauce, which tasted of honey and lemon laced with a hot spice, accompanied the vegetables. While she grazed, Tsarina dreamed of escape, and tried to recall the chant of the Solstice spell. The words didn't come, and she feared the spell might be lost forever. *Someone has to know it*, she hoped. *It's gotta be written somewhere.* If she could not find answers with the Archons here, she would have to set out to find someone else who knew the history of the spell. With those thoughts, she composed a list of questions for her next meeting with the Halcyon—questions that would hopefully help her navigate the alien world if it came to that extreme measure. Keeping her secret of not knowing the spell was going to be difficult, given the Archon's mental prowess. She grimaced at her lack of confidence in hiding her thoughts as she placed the core of her purple fruit on the tray.

∞∞∞*I Thought I Saw A Pequot*

After a solid day of pounding the black-pebbled road, Bud stumbled upon an encampment of wigwams and yurts nestled behind a twenty-foot high wall. Built out of severed trees, the walls hid the interior, except for the angled tops of the residences. A clear stream, hinging the borders of the encampment like a tuning fork, reflected red sparkles off white-capped crests that were glistening with the auburn glow of the afternoon sun. The massive wall of timber, lined atop with spiked logs gave Bud an uneasy feeling as he searched the encampment for activity. He discovered a tall tree with vines wrapping around it like snakes, and he perched on a thick branch midway to the top to observe the movement inside the village. After his previous encounters with the locals, he wanted to get a sense of the village and its inhabitants before storming in like a drunken soldier.

Bud edged out on the branch to get a better look. Over the wall, a large grass field played host to a form of Lacrosse. A female warrior with fiery red hair was chasing a hulking male opponent across the field, and when she caught up with him, she whipped the rounded butt of her webbed stick across the back of his head. A cloud of blood sprayed from the man's neck, splattering crimson droplets across the blue sash covering the girl's firm breasts. As he collapsed in a heap, the young woman, paying no regard for her opponent's well being, adroitly scooped up the red skull that had dribbled out of his webbed stick and sprinted toward the opposite goal.

The black goal posts were webbed with a thick tan rope. Howls from the girl's teammates accelerated her gait as her opponents converged upon her like a swarm of killer bees. Then, as if she had eyes in the back of her head, she cocked her stick and hurled the red skull diagonally across the field to a teammate who was built like a linebacker. He snared the tumbling skull out of the air with his webbed stick and dashed toward the goal, separating from the pack with an impressive burst of speed. Like a flock of spooked quail, all the participants changed direction in pursuit of the red skull.

During the interchange, two competitors, several yards away from the main action, stopped in the middle of the field for no apparent reason other than to attack each other with their sticks. A fierce battle ensued, and both warriors slashed wildly with their webbed staves. Ultimately, the man in the green loincloth struck a gruesome blow to his opponent's head, rendering him unconscious or possibly dead.

Damn. I thought football and hockey were rough, but this shit is ridiculous, Bud observed as he continued spectating the fracas from the shade of the tree.

Meanwhile, farther down the field, the man toting the red skull raced toward the open goal with his ornate stick cocked over his shoulder in a shooting position. A lone defenseman protected the goal, twirling his slightly larger stick like a propeller, waiting to block the oncoming shot. When the skull carrier came into range, the goalie hurled the blunt tip of his stick at the carrier's chest, and as the pole flew toward its target, the man quickly whipped the skull to his streaking forward, just as the oncoming pole bounced off his chest, sending him tumbling to the ground.

The girl secured the skull with one fluid swipe of her stick, and then with a flick of her wrist, she launched the skull into the goal. Riotous cheers erupted from the remaining members of the blue team as the skull rolled around in the webbing, and her teammates surrounded her, raising her up onto their shoulders, chanting *Astrid! Astrid*!

This was obviously not as civilized a community as Splinter, which by comparison now looked like the height of society on Adytum. *These barbarians are crazy. Is a meal and a bed worth it?* Bud questioned, mulling the possibilities of death by barbarian. After several moments of deliberation, he finally left his perch against better judgment.

As he approached the gate, the distinct sound of bowstrings stretching taught creaked from atop the towers and a lump formed in his throat.

"Halt!" A gruff voice resounded down the weathered log wall. Dozens of hatchet marks lined the logs, and several hatchets remained lodged in the bark, some still trapping bones into the structure. A head-sized window in the gate slid open, and a tan, tattooed face poked through, looking down. "What is your business here, Officer of Agni?"

Officer of Agni? Bud almost questioned the man then realized he was wearing the jailer's garments. Then he replied in a stale, haughty voice, attempting to hide his southern drawl with clear enunciation. "Greetings. Allow me to introduce myself, I am the first officer of Agni, and I am on an important mission from Master Agni. A vile assassin hath escaped, and he is to be considered armed and extremely dangerous, and furthermore, if anyone here is caught harboring such a felon, they are to be sent to Agni's tower directly."

"No assassins here," the tanned face grumbled.

"Excellent! Then I won't have to involve Master Agni. Notwithstanding, I must inspect the grounds. He's always watching, you know," Bud informed, pointing to his eye.

The face, framed in the window, glowered. "Wait there. Must find Sassacus." And with that, the small window slammed shut.

Bud stood in the middle of the road, not knowing exactly what to do. He gave a faint smile and glanced overhead. A dozen archers, poised to fire, flashed the silver tips of their arrows in his direction. He glanced at the forest, contemplating retreat.

Atop the tallest tower, a green flag wavered in the wind. The crest was an image of a brown deciduous tree perched on top of a hill. Inside the base of the hill, a white wolf sat on top of a burning fire log. Bud pondered its significance as he fidgeted in the waning sunlight.

Eventually, the surly guard returned with the aforementioned Sassacus. The massive barbarian stood well over seven feet tall, and his coal eyes glared down from atop the fortified tower. Dark green tattoos, representing fanged animals and warfare, covered his broad neck and shoulders and weaved their way up to his sun wrinkled face with sharp, curved lines like the markings of a Bengal tiger. Those lines spread from his nose down to the back of his neck where a necklace, comprised of miniature skulls and curved teeth, dangled over his hairless chest. High, chiseled cheekbones and silky black hair suggested he was of Native American Indian heritage.

"So this is our officer?" the chieftain asked.

The guard nodded then backed away.

"Agni has sent you to shadow Sassacus?" he questioned.

Bud shuddered at the goliath's deep tone, and inhaled through his nose as he measured his words. "Well, actually, he's more concerned with the reports of a deadly assassin in the area."

Sassacus squinted. "I have heard of no such man. Nor of you! What is your name officer?"

"Really?" Bud scoffed, skating the accusation, then he blurted the first name that came to mind. "Name's Bond, James Bond. And if an assassin had made it thus far, then we would have a great cause for concern, am I right?" he winked. "I'm simply here to ease Agni's paranoia—we just want to keep him as happy as possible, right?" He offered a smile.

Sassacus stood stoic.

"Right. So I made the journey from the tower to..." Bud paused, realizing he had no idea where he was, then continued, "...here. And, well...obviously there 'tis nothing noteworthy here. So, but honestly, all this walking has created quite an appetite for me." He smiled. "You know, I could be on my way with a solid meal and a good night's rest. For that small courtesy, I shall bring-ith good news back to Agni, and all will be right with the world." Bud choked as he listened to the false words dribbling out of his mouth.

After a moment of dead air, to his surprise, the large spiked gate swung wide from a command of the giant's hand to someone below. Bud half-heartedly paraded under the walkway, feeling much like a lamb walking toward a curious pack of wolves.

Inside the massive gates, children the size of full-grown men chased each other around the wigwams and yurts, whacking one another with pointed lacrosse sticks and laughing at the sight of blood. Hardened women, Amazonian in stature, some topless, wore beaded bone necklaces, bracelets, and anklets. Colorful tattoos with flowing lines of animalistic designs shaded their tanned bodies and accentuated their curves. The villagers, male and female, were all at least six or seven feet tall, muscular, and with shoulder length hair or longer. As the gates closed with a bang, Bud immediately regretted his decision to dupe them.

Sassacus emerged from the crowd with a wide smile. The titan wore no shirt, only a pair of tanned leggings that fit loosely around his thighs and tightly around his ankles. Fine red stitching ran down the sides of the garment along with bunches of tassels and a rather ordinary looking war axe, save for its glistening edges. The stone-faced leader's veins popped out of his neck when he spoke. "Welcome officer Bond. You are Agni's personal sniffer, eh?"

"I guess you could say that," Bud answered.

"I just did." Sassacus bellowed a deep guffaw and slapped Bud on the shoulder, thrusting him off balance. "Ha! If all you need is a full belly to give good word for our small village of Idlewylde, then let us step into Sassacus's tent and feast this night." Then he glanced over at several women who were wrapped in ornamented skirts. "Prepare the meat!" he commanded with a thunderous clap. Instantly, the half-naked maidens darted off in different directions. "Gertumah," he called over the crowd. At the sound of her name, a middle-aged woman wearing a tan sundress with tiny brass bells hanging off her shoulder straps stepped forward. Her emerald eyes captured Bud's attention as she approached.

"Show officer Bond a wigwam. Come to me when it is done," Sassacus ordered.

The leathery woman nodded then motioned for Bud to follow with a swift turn of her back. As she strode away, her pace challenged Bud, and he pressed through the prying eyes and the whispers of the crowd, jogging to catch up with her. The gathering of giants parted as she paraded through the middle, and he used her like a blocker, chasing her across the village to a wigwam painted with images of a red, fox-like creature that had two heads biting each other. Gertumah opened the animal skin curtain serving as a door, her eyes distant, and ushered him inside with a wave of her hand. Bud immediately noticed the lack of amenities, as there was only a wood-framed bed sitting along the wall and a matching nightstand, which held a clay bowl filled with fresh water.

"Wait inside until I come for you," she advised. "It will be safer."

Bud nodded, swallowing the knot in his throat, as she exited. *What in the hell am I doing?*

As soon a the cloth door blocked the open frame, he began developing his back-story and decided upon the rouse that he was a spineless loafer from a small farm outside of Splinter, only interested in flowing through life along the path of least resistance. Agni's work seemed like easy pay and promised security, so he took the job. After settling on the masquerade, he slumped onto the feathered bed and closed his eyes, praying to find a bit of rest.

∞∞∞Dubious Minds

Strolling the long hall on the way to Halcyon's study, Tsarina rolled her eyes. "Yeah, I get it," "But what if I don't want to stay here? What would happen if I just left?" she asked Timothy, the young student assigned to cater to her every wish.

Timothy fumbled, "I…well, I am sure you would be asked to return, for your own safety, of course."

"Of course…*asked*?" she mocked. "Sounds like a friggin' Nazi answer if you ask me."

"What is a friggin' Nazi?"

Tsarina did not feel like explaining the history of World War II and the Third Reich, so she made the remainder of the trip to the study in silence. As they entered the study, the door closed behind Timothy, and Halcyon shuffled over to the desk and pulled up a chair across from Tsarina.

"I am sorry for Timothy's brusque grumblings. He means well, but his tact is sometimes less than desirable. Your safety—"

"I know, and I sorta understand—I'm the only one who can open the portal. I get it. But it doesn't make me feel any better about being held prisoner here, while Bud is still out there alone. I don't see the point of doing nothing."

"My dear, by no means are you a prisoner. I am truly remorseful if you have been made to feel as such. I feel that I have failed you." He frowned. "You are most certainly free to leave anytime you like. However, I am of the opinion your safety is the utmost priority to both our worlds, and I was under the impression that you were of the same mind. Know that I understand your concern—"

"Frankly, I don't think you do," she complained. "Everyone keeps saying that, as if it will make everything ok, but my friend is still out there, probably getting tortured, or maimed, or worse, and we're up here doing nothing."

Halcyon took a moment to ingest her words before he spoke. "I see, very well then. What would you suggest we do, madam?"

"I'd like to go to Splinter and talk to the people there. Somebody has to know something."

"To that end, I would ask you place your trust in Melinda. She is more than capable of gleaning information from the residents there. It is likely we should receive her Dalton within the next few days. I suggest, at least, we should wait for her response before we make a rash decision upon our course of action. If you were to venture outside these walls, we would not be able to guarantee your safety."

"Yeah, I guess," Tsarina muttered. Unhappy with his logical plan of action, she refocused. "Then, if that's the case, I'd like to know more about Viduata and Agni, and how they found me."

"Unfortunately, that is quite a mystery to me as well. My only conjecture is: She is a powerful mentalist, and somehow she felt the power of your aura across the stars. I'm almost certain it was not Agni's doing. He is more of a Materialist weaver than a Mentalist, and if she is strong in the ways he is not, therein lies the strength of their union."

"I still don't get it. Who else knows about the portal here on Adytum? I thought you said nobody believes it ever existed."

"There are those who continue to recite and record the stories of Earth, however those people are likely regarded as fools, no matter where they reside, and like anything else, I am sure there are a few who took it as their quest. This may be the reason Agni sought after Viduata. She obviously is a believer in Earth and knows of the Eye."

"Like Area 51," Tsarina mused.

"Pardon?" Halcyon queried.

"Nothing. I think I got it."

"Excellent, then with your permission, I would like to explore your magical aura."

"That sounds a little creepy," Tsarina cocked an eye.

"Certainly not. It is simply a series of examinations that will allow me to assess your abilities. I am quite excited by your potential, actually."

"Because I opened the portal?"

"Precisely. I have known only one other in my life to have successfully weaved a whorl, and that was only a small hole in a cave from one side to the other. Even then, I was amazed."

"Cool. So what do you want me to do?" she asked.

"First, we shall start with a simple spell like—"

"*Lumen,*" she finished his thought and then pointed to a crystal fixed on the wall. As the rose glow beamed inside the crystal, Halcyon's jaw quivered, as though he had forgotten how to speak. "I've been practicing that one," she boasted.

"So I see. It seems I have been beaten to the weave. Archon Indimiril's doing, I assume?"

"Yeah. We had some spare time on the boat. It's cool. I like to play with the feeling. It's fun."

"Precisely. The feeling. You are beginning to understand the energies around you."

"I guess. It's weird though, sometimes the feeling is stronger than others."

"Quite, familiarity breeds consistency and strength. Well now, since you obviously understand the basics of Materialism—*and Mentalism,*" his voice finished in her mind. *Then I suggest we converse within our minds going forth for practice. Agreed?*

She formed the word in her mind. *Okay.*

Excellent! Now that you are becoming familiar with this form of communication, the first, and most important, task you must learn is to protect your thoughts from prying minds. Inevitably, there will be thoughts that you will not want to disclose, even to your closest ally, or to your magister, as the case may be. Thoughts are a great deal more fluid than words, and you must learn to control them, protect them from prying minds. Never allow them to leak out of your control, inside of emotion. Even under duress.

I got you.

You must. Now, if you had wanted to protect that thought, what could you have done?

Besides not think it? she asked.

Yes, that would certainly work; however there are other ways you can conceal your thoughts. Think of throwing a black cloak over them. Learn to protect them with darkness. Let us try it now. Create an image. Imagine only you can see the image. Conceal it from the rest of the world and find a place in your mind to hide it. Try this now and alert me once you believe you have the image cloaked somewhere deep in the corner of your mind. I will focus my attention away until it is done; then I will attempt to remove the veil you have created.

Tsarina thought for a moment then created an image of Jasper's wolf, William. Placing the image in the back of her mind, she wrapped him in a black plastic bag, and buried it in a dark corner. Once it was done, she spoke aloud. "Okay, I got it. You can pry, or whatever."

Halcyon's icy blue eyes turned on her, his pupils piercing hers like tiny drills. *Yes, that's the idea. William was fairly well hidden.*

"Obviously not," she groaned.

Rest assured. Unless a mentalist was looking for him, he would not have been found easily. The use of the strange material was your downfall. It was quite easy to spot, given I have never seen anything of the like. It stood out like a burning tree in the middle of a desert. But you are correct: a mentalist would have recognized your cover and removed it easily. Another trick is to keep the thought moving, flowing to and from different veils. Displace it under the different cloths of darkness in your mind as quickly as possible, as if it were jumping from place to place inside the maze that is your consciousness. Now, let us try it again. This time, try moving the image as fast as you can from one cover to the next. Again, let me know when you are ready.

Okay. This time, Tsarina thought of the white altar of Istia in the field of Jasmine. She draped a black cloth over it and tucked it away. She alerted Halcyon without words. *I'm ready.*

Reflexively, she moved the heavy altar like a giant chess piece in her mind to another cloth in a different place.

Halcyon focused his gaze upon her again. *Yes, that's the idea, but faster. Do not feel the weight of the altar; imagine it, light as a feather.*

The altar felt like an ivory anchor as she dragged it around inside the imaginary spaces in her mind, and she sensed Halcyon was tracking it with ease. *This is friggin' hard,* she complained.

Certainly, yet well worth the effort in the end. There is nothing more important than a well-executed mental defense. Continue increasing the speed of your movements, now that you have the basic idea. You should practice, experimenting with different covers until the transitions become quick and crisp. Trade one cover for another. Soon, you will find the subjects that are easiest for you manipulate.

After several attempts, her energy waned, and she reverted to audible speech. "I feel a little bit dizzy. Can we take a break?" she asked, the room spinning slightly, as she placed both hands on her forehead.

Yes, of course, Halcyon allowed. *You covered quite well. That was an impressive first display of Mentalism.*

The sound of the door opening broke the silence. Then, as if summoned, which he probably was, Timothy entered with a crystal carafe of water and two crystal goblets. He placed the goblets in front of Halcyon and poured the clear liquid into the glasses until it covered the string of Daltons chiseled around the rim. Halcyon grabbed both glasses and offered her one. The water, clean and chilled to perfection, slipped down her throat, washing away the pressure behind her temples. *Thanks.* She spoke without voice, unintentionally to Timothy.

The young man stood upright, thrusting his shoulders backward, and answered hesitantly with a thought. *You are quite welcome.*

Yeah, you gotta watch out for me now, she cautioned.

A gurgling chuckle spluttered from Halcyon's lips as Timothy turned to leave, and Tsarina felt as if she had missed something, perhaps a mini-conversation between the master and the student. She rolled the thought back and forth, up and down, under a black cloak in her mind. *Think of something else,* she cautioned herself and immediately created a beagle puppy with floppy ears as her primary thought. She moved it around under cotton covers, and the intense headache resurfaced. She fell back into her chair, placing her hands on the armrests and asked, "May I be excused?"

Halcyon's face came as a blur when he answered with voice. "Of course, I will summon Timothy for you."

"Oh, no. It's okay. I can manage."

"Nonsense, it is no trouble at all." He rose with her, as she struggled out of her chair.

"No offense, but I kind of want to be alone right now," she said.

"Ah, I see…certainly, my dear. By all means, take your leave. Simply alert someone if you lose your way."

"Don't worry. I'm cool."

Halcyon's consternated expression belied his apparent kindness, and Tsarina wished she could descramble his thoughts, but when she probed his psyche, an intense feeling of fear squashed her desire. She was forced to stop. She wobbled out into the expansive hallway where the walls seemed to be breathing in rhythm with her accelerated pulse, and she quickly inhaled oxygen through short breaths as she staggered forward. In an effort to control the rhythm of her lungs, she paused and took an exaggerated breath, to the count of four, then released it to the count of four, and again. She repeated the exercise several times until she wobbled, and then she grasped a downward-sloped section of the crystal windowsill and sat.

Images erupted in her mind's eye, like lightening bolts shaping the night sky: Her mother draped in a black and red cloak; Bud surrounded by darkness; her sister dropping cans of soda over a linoleum kitchen floor. When she let go the frame and stood on her own, calm washed over her. First, the walls stopped breathing, and then the haze lifted, her temples throbbing in the aftermath. She stumbled forward as if attempting to walk in high heels for the first time with ankles made of softened butter. The sounds of footsteps from the Cairn's residents reverberated off the walls with alarming volume. She covered her ears and staggered forward, anticipating an unwanted encounter.

Upon reaching her room, she wrestled with the idea of running away. *Can I find my way out,* she wondered. The long cold walk down the mountain, as well as the distance to Splinter and what would come after, buried her desire. She slumped onto the couch, allowing her impatience a respite. She followed the cracks in the crystal walls with her eyes to a central point above, where a mural of star-like glitter covered the ceiling.

∞∞∞*Out On The Town*

Agni stood transfixed in the middle of Tsarina's dorm room, holding his father's necklace, staring through the fuchsia colored Venetian blinds at the montage of electric lights, blaring horns, aggressive humans, and skyscrapers that give Midtown Manhattan its life. The city was full of people and places. Without a guide, he had no starting point in the search for his father. The local guards had reopened the building, and he wondered if anyone, other than these *police,* would return.

After scouring the apartment from one end to the other, he cursed the fact that there weren't any clues specific to the location of his father. He had found the Sentinel necklace given to his father as a symbol marking his duty to watch and protect a daughter of Istia, but nothing explaining how it ended up in Tsarina's room. An image of Tsarina, smiling alongside what appeared to be her mother and sister, inside a wood frame mocked him and his ignorance of Earth. Tsarina's tongue was sticking out of her agape mouth, and her sister looked disgusted by her antics. Anastasia was posed elegantly between them, wearing purple sunglasses and a purple scarf tied around her head.

In the midst of his frustration, the front door flew open and a portly girl sauntered into the living room. Her brown purse banged against the wall as she came to an abrupt halt in the middle of the common room. Hazel eyes radiated through her auburn hair, locking onto Agni's with a lurid stare.

He greeted the freckled girl with a curt smile. "Hello, my dear."

"Uh…hi," she responded, aloof. "And who are you?"

"Pardon me," he apologized, "I am Agni. Nice to meet you…" He questioned for her name with his eyes.

"Lacey," she answered.

"Yes, Lacey. Perhaps you could help me. Do you know where I might find this woman?" he asked politely, holding up the photo for her to examine.

"Which one?" she asked, placing one foot inside the beaded doorway.

"This one," he conveyed, and pointed to Tsarina's sister, Tasha.

"Are you a cop or something?" Lacey interrogated with her brash Long Island accent.

"Yes, and I must to find her at once."

"Whatever, you aren't a cop. What do you want with Tasha?"

"I simply wish to speak with her."

"Ok. So who let you in here?"

"Tsarina, of course. Her sister had something for us, however she went out to find her and never returned. I assume she is still with Tasha."

"I'm sorry man, but I don't know you, and if you don't leave, right now, I'm calling security—"

"You will alert no one." His sinister undertone forced her backward.

Lacey clacked through the bead curtain, grabbing at the handle on the front door. "*Zakryvat*," he uttered, stalking her from behind, enunciating the spell, simply as a measure of instilling fear.

Lacey tugged on the door with both hands. "How did you—" Her head whipped around. "Let me out," she pleaded. "Please, don't hurt me. I don't know where she lives! I swear!"

"Someone here must know," he hissed.

"Maybe Shelby. Are you one of her friends?" She threw her back against the door. "But she won't be back for a couple of days."

"Then it is settled, we shall wait for Shelby to return."

"Okay. Well, you don't need me for that. So, can I just go?"

"Unfortunately not. We shall wait here, together. This Shelby might find herself lost and not able to return. Then where would I be? Stuck here with no guide. Meanwhile, you shall help me inspect this domicile for clues to this *village*."

"Look it, sir—"

"Please, call me Agni."

"Ok, sir. I know where *The Village* is, but there are like a million apartments down there. You're gonna need her address."

"And how do we acquire this address?" he asked.

"I don't know," Lacey whimpered.

"Strange. Unfortunate, but I do not believe you." Agni pressed closer, backing her against the door with his stature.

"Tsarina might have an address book or something, but I don't know—"

"Excellent, then let us try and recover this."

"Okay, but if we find it, will you let me go?" she begged, tears welling in her eyes.

"Certainly, I have no need for you, my dear. My only wish is to find Tasha and to ask her for assistance regarding a matter with my father."

A tiny drop of salty water trickled down Lacey's cheek as she agreed, "Okay, fine. I'll help you look for Tasha's address."

"You see how easy that was? Now we are making progress."

Lacey nodded then cowered past Agni into Tsarina's bedroom where she began rummaging through several small spiral bound notebooks that were scattered on top of the computer table. Agni noticed her becoming increasingly flustered as she ripped the books from their perches and tossed them onto the floor. When the last book hit the ground, Lacey lowered her head, tears streaming from her eyes, and she muttered a final gasp, "The computer." She reached her hand behind the strange silver box and pressed with her forefinger.

Agni watched from behind, confused, as a light flickered inside the mirrored screen and then filled the box. "What is this?" he asked, pointing at the luminescent glass.

Lacey cocked her head to the side and replied as if he were an imbecile, "A computer?"

"And how can this computer help us?"

"She might have the address in here."

"Inside this box? This box of light contains information?" he questioned, peering deeper into the monitor, wondering how it would convey the information.

"Uh, yeah…a lot."

Once the computer finished blinking and making noises, Lacey began touching the screen and said, "Got it."

"Excellent, then you will take me there."

"But you said if I found the address—"

"My dear, I know nothing of this village. I will certainly need your assistance finding it."

"Then you'll let me go, right?" she asked with a dejected look.

"But of course, fret not. Remember, it is you who are doing me a great service," he reminded. "Now, let us be off."

The corners of her mouth eked a skeptical smile, and she reluctantly escorted him out of the apartment. Upon reaching the end of the hall, she pressed a small silver button on the wall, and a circle of yellow light surrounded the button. "What is this device?" Agni asked.

"The elevator?" she asked, seemingly puzzled by his question.

Wary of a trap, Agni frowned as the metal doors emitted squeaking and grinding noises. Then, after a brief wait, a bell dinged, and the steel fuchsia doors slid open. Lacey quickly stepped inside and motioned for him to follow. He entered what now seemed to be an obvious pinfold. Truly, this child was not capable of such cunning, he thought, but as the steel jaws clanged shut, encasing them in the metal tomb, he scanned the device for ulterior exits, as a precaution.

Lacey's pudgy finger pressed another lighted button inside the elevator, and with a lurch, the mechanical device began its descent. Agni secured his hands against the wide steel rails, bracing for a fall or some type of impact. Within seconds of the elevator slowly lurching downward, he understood the purpose of the machine and mused, *Ah, these people of Earth are quite clever after all.*

"What drives this moving room?" he asked.

Lacey paused for a moment before responding with an upward inflection, "Electricity."

"Electricity?" he echoed. The notion that these idiots had harnessed the shocking power of the skies for such a simple device was astounding. He thought to inquire further, however before he could proceed with the line of questioning, the elevator grinded to a halt, and the doors opened as before. Several disheveled students filtered into the middle of the space, and Agni remained positioned like a statue along the back corner. Two young girls, each in baggy cotton attire, waded into the elevator with electronic tablets tucked under their arms, whispering to each other as they slid toward the wall, paying him no attention. Immediately after, two pimply-faced boys swaggered inside and turned their backs to him.

One of the boys was continuing a conversation. "Are you kidding me? The Yankees are gonna be fucking awesome this year! Look at their pitching staff, bro! Same as last year," the taller one proclaimed.

"Yeah but my Sox got the fucking bats," his short, wide, baldheaded friend argued.

Scoffing at the debase language, the young girls continued whispering about their overbearing teacher, while the short boy continued his rant. "Yankees can't hit shit neither. It's gonna be rough for them this year."

"Rough? I'll bet they win fuckin' the division."

"I don't know about that," the short one groaned.

"What? Ok. How's about you give me five to one odds on the Sox to win the division?" the tall boy crowed, grinning like a pompous lord.

"Are you friggin' stupid?" The other glared, awaiting a response. When the boy in the navy cap gave no offer other than a steely glare, he said, "Sure! How much you wanna put on it?"

"I don't know…twenty bucks."

"Garbage. Go a hundred on that shit, bro!"

His tall friend paused for a second. "All right, a hundred to win five, but no paying with your friggin' meal card this year bro. This shit is for cold hard cash."

"Deal."

The boys confirmed their wager with a firm handshake as the elevator bell sounded and the metal doors slid open. Agni wondered, *who are these Yankees and Red Sox, and why are they so important to these boys?*

As the students shuffled out of the elevator and began loping down the hall, Lacey followed, leading Agni toward the guard stand. An older couple was chatting in front of the counter. Agni noticed the blood had been wiped clean from the walls and the floor, and a new guard was stationed at the post, as if nothing had ever happened.

A tall, middle-aged, blonde woman was busy explaining something to the dark guard stationed behind the counter. She clamored, "Oh yes! Oscar, we just came back from the big library in midtown, you know. It was just so…" She searched for the right word. "…Grand. I mean, it was so amazing, all of those books, and all that wonderful architecture. What a stunning wealth of knowledge. Of course, Clark fell asleep in the lobby as usual," she tittered, rubbing her husband on the shoulder, "but I was just absolutely fascinated."

"Yeah, I never been, but I heard it was real nice," Oscar replied with an unfamiliar accent.

"Well, you'll just have to go down there and see it for yourself. It truly is marvelous," the lady contended then grabbed her husband by the arm. "Come on, Clark, let's go see Jenny. "A—dios, Oscar." She waved goodbye.

Stopping in front of the desk, Agni asked, "Where is this wealth of knowledge she spoke of?"

The guard glared through his black-framed glasses and replied suspiciously, "What? You mean the library?"

Several awkward seconds ticked away while Agni waited without answering.

The guard continued, "Well, if you're looking for the library, the one she was talking about is on the corner of fortieth and fifth."

"Yes, thank you." Agni bowed his head with a forced smile and then prodded Lacey toward the exit with a look.

As they began trudging toward the glass doors, Oscar stopped them. "Hey…Lacey. How's it going? Everything alright with you?"

"Yeah," she mumbled without looking at him directly.

"Who's your friend here? I ain't seen him around before."

Pausing for a millisecond, she smiled half-heartedly. "Yeah…he's my…uncle."

"Oh, okay." The guard returned his attention to Agni and asked, "So what, you from Russia or something?"

Agni replied steadfast, "Yes."

Oscar closed one eye as they marched away, and Agni overheard the guard mumble under his breath, "Friggin' Euros man."

Outside the building, putrid smells of urine and garbage filled Agni's nose as he made his way behind Lacey. Wandering along the grimy concrete, he gagged, suffocated a bit by the humidity and stench. He felt his weight more than ever before and noticed his energy draining rapidly. He wiped his brow with the back of his hand.

Walking a giant step ahead, striding deliberately, Lacey swerved in and out of the congested mass of humans, and Agni struggled to keep pace. There was so much to observe. Earth had only been a strange vision through the prognosticative eyes of Viduata, and although she had explained this world to him many times, and shown him visions in the pool of Istia, it never actually seemed real. Now, perceiving it with his own sight, he reveled in his accomplishment.

Mechanical wonders of all different colors, shapes, and sizes whizzed past, weaving in and out in an endless stream of audacity. Horns blared under the control of their angry commanders who shouted obscenities through open windows, while other humans rode small, two wheeled vehicles powered by their legs and glided down the avenues, narrowly avoiding death with each calculated turn. The constant flow of all these mechanical carriages overwhelmed him. *These people may not bend so easily*, he surmised.

The enormous architecture was, unequivocally, the true spectacle, and as he continued to glance upward, he almost lost Lacey. She plowed ahead, maintaining a quick and steady pace, her eyes locked forward, as she guided him through the corridor of tall buildings down a street she called Broadway. The signs marking the streets were quite helpful, once she explained their meaning.

After several blocks, they came upon an underground tunnel, and Lacey shuffled down the stairwell until several, waist high, metal gates blocked their way. She dug into her pocket with a sigh and pulled out a thin object then instructed him to pass through the turnstile. When she swiped the object through the reader, she hesitated, and Agni sensed her desire to escape. With a stern glare, he discouraged the notion. She slumped and obediently passed through the heavy turnstile behind him.

Out on the dingy platform, Agni leaned forward, anticipating the next transport. An acrid wind swept through the underground tunnel as he peered deeper into the darkness, and after a loud screech, a light pierced the black scrim. Unsure of what to expect, he inched backward, watching the transport speed into the station. The tail of his cloak whipped around his ankles, and when the train stopped, the doors slammed open. Suddenly, an animated mob exited, and the people on the platform pressed their way inside the train car. Agni felt the grip of claustrophobia wrap around his neck as he stepped inside behind Lacey's thick figure. Elbows and shoulders pressed against him. He resisted the temptation to incinerate everyone with a blast of Taurit's Breath and thought, *What a horrific method of travel.* The train accelerated, and with each bump and turn, he readjusted trying to create a little space.

After several excruciating stops and starts, the train howled into to the Washington St. Station where Lacey quickly darted out and made her way up the stairs onto the street level.

"Is this the village?" Agni asked, grateful to be back on the surface, even though he was still inhaling the hot, foul air into his nostrils.

"Yeah. You see the buildings are smaller here—kinda."

"And how far is it to Tasha's home?"

"Like, three or four blocks. We're almost there."

"Excellent, then let us be there quickly."

Along the way, they walked past a caged area where men were bouncing an orange ball and tossing it into a rusty cylinder draped with a chain net and backed by a metal board. A sign on the corner of the fence read, *West Fourth Street*. A small crowd was gathered outside, watching the event, and several women howled excitement when the ball passed through the cylinder.

When they rounded the corner, Lacey stopped and informed, "Well, this is it. This is as far as I can take you." She nodded then began creeping away, hands firmly planted on her thighs.

"Not quite. How can I be certain this is Tasha's home? No. You must escort me inside and introduce us. Then you may be off."

"Okay, fine, but she'll have to buzz us in," Lacey griped, and poked the buzzer. After several frantic attempts, she sighed, "I don't think she's home. Do you wanna wait here all day?"

"Hardly," he replied, and brushed her aside to examine the lock. After a brief assessment of the mechanism, he felt the innards with a touch from his hand then he thought of the bolt unhinging, and the lock clicked. With a smirk, he opened the door.

"Whoa!" Lacey exclaimed. "How'd you do that?"

"It was open," he lied, ushering her inside with a flick of his hand.

Inside the dilapidated building, two sets of thick brown doors faced them, and Agni reached out to open the first door, but Lacey stopped him. "That's not her apartment."

"I thought you said she lives here?"

"She does, but she doesn't own the entire building. She's in 1B. I think it's the back unit." She pointed toward the last door in the hall.

Agni touched the lock and moved the inner-workings. Inside, the apartment was tiny but tidy. *This shouldn't take long,* he speculated.

"So, can I go now?" Lacey pleaded from behind.

"*Tisina,*" he mumbled under his breath, stifling her vocal cords, then continued scanning the small room for signs of his father.

On top of the mahogany mantelpiece, several pictures of Tasha, posing with her mother and Tsarina, sat as frozen moments in time. Agni lost his hold on Lacey's throat when he grabbed the smallest picture and placed it inside the inner pocket of his cloak.

"Ok…so, I'm gonna take off," she murmured then moved toward the door.

He ignored her, and with his hesitation, she fled out of the warm room like a mouse released into an open field. Agni reached for another picture: Anastasia in a black dress, standing alone in a vast field.

"Viduata?" he whispered.

∞∞∞ *Warm Welcome*

After several hours of waiting for Tasha to arrive, Agni grew restless. He shuffled around the apartment, rummaging through every drawer and closet for the second time. As the dimming orange sun began sinking behind the buildings, he heard the jingling of keys outside. With a click, the door flew open. Tasha stumbled inside holding a white bag in her arm. An instinctual, bloodcurdling scream erupted from her mouth when she noticed Agni seated at her kitchen table. She released the bag, and the cylindrical containers inside smashed into the hardwood floor with a thud and burst. Bubbling liquid sprayed all over the room as the cans spun around like pinwheels. Tasha continued screaming, pausing only to inhale.

"*Tisina!*" Agni commanded, directing his finger toward her mouth. She grabbed her throat with both hands and lunged for the front door.

"*Zakryvat,*" he uttered, slamming the door shut, locking the deadbolt.

Tasha pressed her weight upon the door, and after several violent jerks, she surrendered and turned to face him.

"Are you quite finished?" he asked.

With a flustered sigh, she nodded and mouthed without voice, "Yes."

"Good. Now, shall we hear your beautiful voice?"

She nodded agreement.

"Excellent," he said, relieving the pressure from her lungs. "It is Tasha, yes?" he asked, pulling out a rolled paper filled with Tyzing herb from his pocket.

She nodded, massaging her throat, then rasped, "Who are you? What do you want from me? I don't have any money."

"I do not desire your currency milady. I am no common thief," he touted. "I desire—"

"Oh, fuck that!" she cried.

"Ah, do not flatter yourself. It is not your body I desire, either. Rather, it is your mind. I simply wish to ask you questions about my father."

"Your father? Who the hell is your father?"

"His name is Nicholas, and he is a mentalist from Adytum."

"Never heard of him."

"You met him thirteen years ago when your mother tried to escape this world into ours."

Her eyes widened. "Okay. Look mister—"

"Please, pardon my manners. Call me Agni." He sparked the rolled herb with his mind and took a puff.

"Okay, Agni." Tasha started with a look of disbelief. "I'm sorry, but I don't know what the hell you're talking about. I never heard of nobody named Nicholas."

"I believe the contrary," he suggested. "On the night your mother was lost, you fled with your sister into the portal. You can be honest with me. I know of your family's power—of your lineage. I will not think you ill for it. It is quite impressive actually."

Her eye pressed him. "I don't know how you know all this, but that night was just a dream for Tsarina, and she's never recovered from it. I've worked hard to keep her away from that insanity."

"Obviously you have failed," he sneered. "She has reopened the portal, like her mother years ago, and now she is on Adytum."

"You're a liar. Tsarina is at school. I know, because I took her there," she charged.

"When did you see her last?"

"Three days ago."

"Yes, before the Solstice."

"Whatever. So?"

Agni remained stoic, puffing on his smoke.

"Let me call her then," Tasha petitioned.

"Do as you must."

As she reached into her bag, Agni cautioned, "Careful, what are you doing?"

"Grabbing my phone, I'm gonna call her right now."

With a thin eye, Agni watched Tasha pull a small black device from her bag. She pressed on it with her finger several times then held it up to her ear.

"If this is some sort of trick—" he warned.

She shook her head and waved off his concern. Seconds later, she pressed on it again and stashed the phone in her purse. "Okay, so it went straight to voicemail. What the hell have you done with my sister? Is this some kind of ransom or something?"

"Fool!" he raged, tossing his rolled herb to the ground as he stood to face her. "I am tired of these games. Where is my father?"

"Where is Tsarina?"

"Dead, if you do not start answering my questions."

"I told you, I don't know anything about your father. I never met anyone named Nicholas," she shouted.

"The man in your sister's dream. What do you remember of him?"

"Nothing!"

"Liar!" Agni howled and grabbed her by the throat.

Her back stiffened and she wrapped her hands around his wrists.

"You will tell me what happened that night!" He squeezed harder.

"I can't remember!"

"You will remember, or you and your sister will die!"

"No, you can't—"

"First, you will watch her burn!" He pressed harder, singeing her neck with his touch. He felt her hands losing strength.

"Okay," she choked. "I'll tell you. Just don't hurt her."

He maintained his grip and glared into her dimming, blue eyes.

She gasped, "All I remember is ma running into that field. A man in a black cloak was running after her." Agni lightened his grip, allowing her to continue. "I was holding Tsarina's hand. We were following them then Ma disappeared into a patch of tall grass. She was screaming. The man turned around. He told me to take Tsarina into the apartment. He said he would go after ma. That's the last I saw of them. I swear."

"Nothing more?" Agni pressed, releasing her from his grip. "Where did he go after?"

Tasha staggered over to the table and fell into one of her chairs. "I don't know, but..."

"But what? Speak!"

"I didn't believe it, but I think he spoke to me in my mind," Tasha whimpered.

"What did he say?"

"He said he was her vigil. But I don't know what that means."

∞∞∞∞Tall Tales

When Bud awoke, light from the oil lamp allowed him to scan the inside of the dark wigwam for unwanted guests. He wondered how long he had slept, and who lit the lamp. It illuminated a freshly placed, cream towel and a red clay bowl filled with clean water, but the edges of the tent remained shadowed beyond the flickering light. Dipping his hands in the cool water, he splashed it upon his face and thought, *Gertumah must've done all this*. Then, as if she had supernatural hearing, she appeared through the curtain door. He grabbed the towel and said, "Hey. How's it going?"

Looking him over, expressionless, she answered, "Come. It is time. The Sachem waits," signaling him to follow with a curl of her pointer finger.

"Sachem?" Bud repeated the phrase, trying to recall why it sounded so familiar. Then he recalled his great-aunt speaking of a Sachem in a story about his great-great grandmother. The word was an old Native American term for chief. On a visit with his great-aunt, when he was nine years old, Bud listened to a story of his great-great grandmother, a medicine woman, known as Nahatima. She had been a healer for over a hundred years, and everyone in the neighboring tribes around Mount Mitchell knew her. When anyone in the area was sick or dying, Nahatima would be called upon to work miracles, and more often than not, she was successful. She was the personal healer their Sachem. Bud smiled and rubbed his neck, remembering the night in New Orleans when he solidified his respect of his heritage with a tattoo of a Cherokee star, inked across the back of his neck.

Tossing the towel on the nightstand, he readjusted his ponytail and followed the woman out of the tent. She led him past dozens of smaller tents in the village to a tent triple the size of the others. It stood alone at the south end, next to a small locked gate. The gate blended with the ivy-covered wall, so much so, that Bud only noticed it after a thin warrior hustled through, a silver longbow in hand. The Pequot slipped through the torchlight like a shadow and disappeared behind one of the smaller wigwams.

An olive flag, marked with the *wolf-under-the-tree* crest, flapped overhead in the warm night breeze, and as he poked his head through the animal skin curtain, he inhaled the aroma of smoked meat and noticed several large plates of food beckoning from a long wooden table. Inside, Sassacus sat in a high-backed, wooden chair at the far end of the table, eyeing Bud as he entered.

The leader wore a blue, flowing, long-sleeved shirt and a pair of navy trousers trimmed with skeletal wolf patterns that ran along the seams. His skull necklace had been replaced by another made of white vertebrae. When Gertumah crept away, the giant extended his massive hand and offered Bud a seat.

"Sit, Officer Bond."

"Thank you, Sassacus." Bud replied, cringing at the sound of his assumed name, and slid onto the oversized chair. The tips of his toes dangled as they scraped the floor, and he felt like a child, sitting at the grownups' table. He inched his spine toward the back of the chair, crossing his legs in the wide seat.

With a forced smile, he glanced across at the giant, waiting for the interrogation to begin. The barbarian's leathery hands snared several pieces of meat off the nearest platter and slopped them onto his plate. Then, he then recklessly slid the platter across the table, and it clanked into Bud's plate.

"Do not be shy. Take what you like. We are proud to have such a noble member of Agni's clan here in Idlewylde," Sassacus explained as he bit into a giant leg of meat, juice flowing down his chin.

Bud nodded appreciation and surveyed the spread. Several types of seared animal carcasses and steaming vegetables were presented on large wooden platters. They all called to his growling stomach, and his mouth began to water. After a moment of indecision, he took one of each. He searched the table for a fork or some kind of utensil and noticed Sassacus eating with his hands. Following suit, he grabbed the red, oval-shaped vegetable off his plate with his hands and took a bite.

Sassacus grunted.

Bud nodded, chewing with a closed mouth. As he savored the foreign taste, his eyes shifted, and he wondered if the giant was inclined to ask questions. He thought it best to continue eating and wait for Sassacus to initiate the conversation. He didn't want to break any social rules, if there were any, and the less he would have to say, the better. He licked his fingers after he finished the red vegetable and began gnawing on the alabaster meat, which tasted sweet, like pork. He figured it to be some type of reptile or amphibian from its texture, which was chewy like alligator meat. A smile grew upon his face as the food calmed his weary body.

"Ah, I see you like the Yassar!" Sassacus ended the silence.

"Of course. This is good. Which type is it?" he asked, exhibiting a chunk of the white meat between his fingers.

"Yassar," Sassacus answered.

"Oh Yassar? Yeah, which yassar?"

"Yassar," the barbarian responded, a curious look on his face. "Slithery, hisser." The giant took a large sip from his goblet, then, with crimson wine dripping from the corners of his mouth, asked, "Are you not from this region?"

Bud blinked. "Uh, no. I actually hail from the fields past the forest of Splinter," he answered.

"And you never had yassar?"

"Not this one. We mainly ate vegetables in my village."

"Ah, had a bunch of witches cooking for you then?" he laughed and bit into another piece of meat. "How long have you searched for this *assassin*, Officer Bond?"

"Oh, about a week," Bud responded, intentionally focusing on his plate, wiping his mouth with the back of his hand.

"Tell me more about him. What are his features?" Sassacus pried, as he casually chewed on the piece of meat, seemingly unconcerned with the answer.

Bud grabbed his glass and took a long swill, allowing a moment to conjure a fictitious image in his head. "From all reports, we think he is about my height, however, he is lighter skinned, with a thick moustache."

"Moustache? Ha! No man with face hair here. Good for us," he crowed.

"Yep," Bud nodded, picking at a grilled, red and green, oblong vegetable that had been sliced into strips.

Looking toward the back of the tent, Sassacus raised his empty goblet and swirled it in the air then gave a short whistle. Within seconds, a voluptuous young woman, covered in tribal markings, emerged from a dark corner to fill their wine glasses. Her skirt banged against her thick ankles. It was slightly open in the front, revealing her inner thigh, which bore a colorful tattoo of the tribe's crest—the lone wolf resting under the tree. The crest seemed to be etched on everyone and everything: the doors of the wigwams, the skirts of the women, even the backs of the children. The marking seemed vaguely familiar, however Bud couldn't quite put his finger it. The entire encampment reminded him of a Native American settlement, the glaring difference being the oversized stature of the inhabitants.

Bud and Sassacus continued eating in awkward silence, and by the end of the gorging, Bud's stomach felt like an overstuffed vacuum bag. As he pushed away from the table with a small groan, the well-endowed maiden bent in front of him to remove his plate, while another woman, thin as a bird, entered carrying a wooden box. Carvings of green and red herbs decorated the dark cedar lid and ran down the sides. The server placed the chest in front of Bud then backed away, motioning for him to open it with a wave of her hand.

"Take your pick," Sassacus directed.

The airtight box contained a dozen cigars of various colors and sizes. The darker ones were the size of his thumb, and the lighter ones were almost ten inches long. Sitting in a bed of crushed red velvet, they all looked of high quality, and Bud mulled over each one, sniffing their unique aromas.

"Choose one for now and one for later," Sassacus suggested.

"Thank you," Bud replied, plucking one small and one large from the box. He placed the dark cherry scented cigar in his shirt pocket, and stuck the almond scented one in his mouth.

Sassacus waved for a third maiden to approach from the corner of the room. She held the lines and grace of a ballet dancer as she stalked toward Bud with a slow burning cedar stick in her hand. The glowing red tip produced a stream of smoke, and he watched it glide up over her perky breasts. Pressing the cigar deeper into his mouth, he nervously chomped on the end as she singed the tip. Methodically, he puffed the pungent herb to life, rolling the thick smoke around inside his mouth, savoring the hints of almond and caramel. Vaporous clouds swirled down the back of his throat, and a warm rush of blood flooded his body as they entered his lungs. He felt his lips loosen, and his mind relaxed. "This stuff is nice," he said to Sassacus. "What do you call it?"

"Skullcloud," answered Sassacus. The maiden glanced at the giant with a smile and rushed to light his cigar. "Ah," Sassacus puffed, "finest herb in the valley. You have a good nose Officer Bond," he hinted with a prying tone. Then his eyes deepened, corresponding to his voice. "Tell me, Officer Bond, how you came to service Agni? You seem young for a guard of such importance. Finding an assassin is a worthy task. You must be good tracker."

The giant's sudden change in demeanor and tactful line of questioning disrupted Bud's enjoyment of the Skullcloud. He puffed harder on the cigar, trying to shove down the lump welling in his throat. "Oh, I'm not that important." He spit a little cough. "Personally, I think Agni's sent me on a wild goose chase. I know I'd never be able to catch a real assassin, but I guess Agni figured I might stumble across his tracks and flush him out like a bad bird dog. As for the work, I ran into some guy who worked for him couple of years ago. He signed me up, no questions asked. It seemed like a good deal at the time. I needed the coin, you know."

"Ah. Strange. Do you enjoy your service?"

"It's a job," Bud replied, fighting the strange urge to reveal the truth about his recent incarceration.

Sassacus interrupted, "So you trade easily. What if I had a job for you?"

"What do you mean?"

"Coin. For the right amount, I ask information about the warlock and his tower."

"What kind of information?"

Sassacus rested both arms on the table, leaning forward as he spoke. "Things you might know about the tower, and the witch inside."

Bud inhaled a deep breath. The decision to come clean was squarely looking him in the face, burning through the coal eyes of the giant sitting across the table. A wistful haze of smoke lingered in the air, swirling around his eyes as he exhaled. He felt the effects of the unfamiliar narcotic pressing him closer toward disclosing the truth about his stay in Agni's dungeon, but he resisted. "I can tell you what I know, but I don't think it'll be worth much."

The giant's eyes widened. "Much can be useful."

Bud felt his mind slipping. "Okay, here's the deal—I'm not one of Agni's officers," Bud blurted to his own surprise, unable to fight the overwhelming effects of the Skullcloud.

Sassacus's brow folded over his eyes, and he slammed his fist into the table, knocking over several glasses and a tall candelabra. "A spy!"

Bud scraped the ground with his toes when Sassacus stood from his chair and stomped across the room.

"No? What—" Bud started, his body shaking from the vibrations coursing through the table. "That's the last thing I am. I probably hate the bastard more than you do."

The giant's gait slowed.

Bud repositioned himself on the chair and continued, speaking faster. "Those damned Noctiss things have been chasing me and my girl ever since we got here, and then Agni's guards locked me up in that dungeon. Think about it man, if I were trying to spy on you, then pretending to be one of his guards would be pretty stupid, right? I mean, what would you tell a guard? Honestly, I don't know who you are, or why he would even want to spy on you."

"Liar!" Sassacus bayed, hovering like a lion. The giant placed his hands on the table, inching his face closer. "How did you make it down the black road unnoticed?"

Bud backed away from the barbarian's nauseating breath. "Road? What road?"

"There's only one entrance to Viduata's peak, and it is through the black road in the crags. There are many patrols. You would have never made it past them unless he allowed you."

Bud surprised himself with a small laugh. "I didn't see anything remotely resembling a black road until I got all the way down the mountain. Wish I did though. That would have been a heck of a lot easier than the way I came. I climbed down the side of a sheer rock face to get here."

Sassacus probed Bud with frozen eyes, obviously trying to accept the explanation as truth. "If you are playing me the fool, I swear by the edge of Galetaer, I will slice you, piece by piece, until your bloody eyes are the only things left to watch you die."

"Hey man, I promise, the last thing I want to do right now is lie to you and piss you off any more. Sorry I lied to you from the beginning, but I was just starving and obviously delirious. When your guard called me officer, I just went with it without thinking. I guess I figured I'd try and play it out for a free meal and a good night's rest. But I swear on my grandmother's grave, I hate Agni, and I have no problem telling you everything I know about his tower. Seriously brother, I hope you mop the floor with all their slimy asses. Just tell me what you want to know, and I'll do my best to answer."

Sassacus looked up at the angled rafters and inhaled, as if to separate his thoughts from his rage, then he returned to his chair and said, "First, let us start with—who you are, and why you are of such value to Agni."

"Ok. No problem. My friends call me Bud, and to be honest, I don't know what Agni wants me for. I'm kind of surprised I'm still alive, actually. My guess is he's using me as bait to get to my girlfriend, Tsarina, and God only knows what happened to her. Last I saw, she was being pulled down into a trap door by some wizard named Indimiril—that was in Splinter—you ever heard of him?"

"No." Sassacus shook his head negatively and grunted, "Why do they seek your woman?"

"She's got some special ability, apparently, and she has this weird stone on her ankle. It's a family heirloom called the Eye of Istia, and Agni wants it, and her."

"What is this stone's value?" Sassacus asked.

"Tsarina believed it had something to do with us coming to this planet." Bud cringed at the sound of his statement.

"This planet?" The giant's eyes became small slits as he peered into Buds face.

"Yeah, to Adytum. That's what you call this planet, right?"

"Adytum, yes, but I think the Skullcloud has taken you. You make no sense."

"Probably not," Bud agreed. "Now I know this part is gonna sound super crazy, but I'm not from around here. Have you ever heard of a planet called Earth?"

Sassacus puffed a single snort from his nose and looked incredulously at Bud. "Yes—a fairy tale told to me as a sprout."

"Well, hate to break it to you man, but Earth ain't no fairy tale. That's where I'm from," he explained then waited for the barbarian to behead him on the spot.

To his surprise, Sassacus bellowed a deep laugh, filling the tent like a hot air balloon. Then the giant took a wild puff of his cigar, inhaling a fraction of the smoke then rolled the tiny hit around in his mouth. Bud surmised Sassacus was trying to trick him into recanting his statement with calculated silence, or he was trying to figure out how he was going to behead him. He remained stone-faced, forcing Sassacus to exhale a grumble. "I thought we were done with lies?"

"We are, man. Believe me, I think all this shit is crazy as hell. Just sitting here with you is blowing my mind. One minute I'm in bed with the girl of my dreams, and the next we're on this wild ass planet with frogmen chasing us into a giant forest of purple trees where Lincoln Center should have been. It's all been a load of horse-bullshit ever since then."

Sassacus's hand hovered across his furled brow, wiping nonexistent beads of sweat and then his fingers crept behind the back of his neck like a tentative spider searching for its web. Finally, his fist came to rest upon his chin, giving the impression he was mired in thought. He remained silent for several seconds, which seemed much longer to Bud. The implausible Americanized discourse had obviously confused the barbarian into silence, and he snorted before he asked, "How did this happen?"

Bud chuckled, "Like I said, I don't know. I think Tsarina cast some kind of spell that opened up a portal from Earth to here." The words sounded so unbelievable to Bud as they dribbled from his mouth. He bit his lip and waited for another outburst from the giant.

To his surprise, Sassacus's face absorbed the explanation like a tincture of truth. "I have heard such tales from bards who sing of witches traveling between worlds. Stories of olden days, using a stone of power." He squinted. "You are a strange boy, but strange tales from strange boys are not enough to trust you are no spy. Why shouldn't I behead you where you sit?" The giant pressed him with cold silence.

Bud took a moment to formulate his case. He needed hard evidence to support his claim—something simple enough for the giant to understand—something tangible. He fidgeted in his oversized chair, and felt the answer, resting snug in his pocket. "You ever seen one of these?" he asked, brandishing the lighter like a magic wand between his thumb and forefinger.

"No," Sassacus responded with a downturned twitch of his nose. "What is it?"

Expecting a wowed reaction, Bud sparked the lighter, and the flame burned steady from the metal tip.

As predicted, Sassacus's eyes widened with astonishment. The giant braced his hands on the table and asked, "What magic is this, warlock?"

"That's just it man. I ain't no warlock, and this ain't magic. It's basic chemistry—lighter fluid and a little flint inside this plastic case spark the flame," Bud explained, tapping the dark blue shell with his finger. "I'll bet you probably never seen plastic before either. Here—" He tossed the lighter to Sassacus. "You see that little silver wheel with the ridges?" Bud asked.

Sassacus examined the lighter with a perplexed look and answered, "Yes."

"Roll your thumb over the metal part real quick then press down on the red button under it."

Sassacus's oversized thumb bobbed up and down over the button.

"Go ahead, try it," Bud urged.

Methodically, the giant rolled his thumb over the flint wheel, creating a faint spark, but he failed to press and hold the red tab, and the lighter didn't flame. A small groan of frustration gurgled from his mouth.

"Almost," Bud encouraged. "But you have to press down on the red button, and then keep holding it down. Don't let off it. That's what shoots the lighter fluid out and keeps the flame going. It's fuel, like the oil in your lamps."

The second attempt was a success. Sassacus beamed with pride as he watched the flame burning steady in his hand.

With the Sachem gratified, Bud relaxed in his chair and puffed his cigar. "You see? No magic. Now take a look at the material on the case. That's plastic. We use it to make all kinds of stuff on Earth. Pretty much everything is made out of plastic nowadays.

Sassacus remained intent on the lighter and released the red tab then thumped the metal atop of the lighter. He stroked the plastic shell with his finger, and after a pregnant pause, he chuckled, flicking the lighter on and off repeatedly. "Magic fire with no magic. We have much to discuss."

"Go ahead, keep it," Bud offered. "I got another one."

The giant smiled appreciatively then said, "If what you say is true, the Grey Wolf smiles on me, but I will need more than this trickish flame as proof—could still be an illusion."

"Well ok, if that ain't enough, then what do you propose?"

Sassacus reclined and puffed his cigar, blowing a giant cloud around his head. "You seek your woman, as I do. My Freydis was lost several weeks ago, and I believe Agni and Viduata are responsible for her disappearance. I want their heads on pikes atop our walls. If they are the ones who have taken her—"

"Wait," Bud stopped him. "Freydis?"

The giant froze with the mention of her name. "Yes? Do you know of her?"

"I think I saw her in the tower—she looked more like a ghost at first—but she helped me escape, and she said she was Viduata's vigil—whatever that means."

Sassacus sat silent for a moment, as if paralyzed by the words. The tension in the room grew thicker with each passing second until the giant said, "I do not know of what you speak. The witch must have her mind, but if she still lives, I must find her. This is where your knowledge will help."

"What knowledge?"

"Of the path up the mountain. I have been searching how to enter the tower, but the road is well guarded with many patrols. We are not a catlike people, and I am certain we do not have the numbers for war."

"Yeah, getting in there sounds impossible," Bud agreed.

"If we travel the road, war is certain, but you have traveled a different path and have knowledge of what lies beyond those walls."

"Yeah, I know another path, but it's a royal pain in the ass."

The candles on the table fluttered from a slight draft as Sassacus spoke. "No matter the cost. We must make the journey. If they have my Freydis, then they also have the chalice. I must retrieve them. Without the chalice and Freydis, my people will lose their strength."

"Wait, what chalice?" Bud questioned.

Sassacus grinned, puffing his cigar, as if he were getting something off his chest for the first time in years. "The Chalice of Zosimus. It is the key to our strength."

"That sounds pretty serious," Bud said.

"Ha!" The Sachem clapped his hands together. Then, as if a thundercloud rolled into his mind, his expression darkened. He sat back in his chair and took a long pull off his cigar. "I want to tell you something I should not, but the Skullcloud works inside me now, and I feel it will help you understand why we must go to the tower."

"Ok," Bud puffed his cigar in anticipation.

"Bud, from Earth, we will be bonded after this night, and if not, you will die."

Bud coughed up a bit of smoke, the words setting him on edge.

"I wish you to know the truth of my Freydis. The mother of my child is not of Pequot blood," he confessed. "She is Vikingr—blonde hair, supple face—a beauty to behold, and easy to spot as different here. My tribe in the North did not welcome her as one of our own. As Sachem of the Pequot, I was only to mate with another Pequot—a female from our tribe with gifts of magic. This way we are to keep the line pure. By this union, the female is made high priestess, and the Chalice of Zosimus is given to her care. For me to wed an outsider was not accepted."

"But ya'll don't practice magic?" Bud questioned.

"There are a few in the tribes, but yes, the choices are few. Freydis as an outsider was not recognized as a Pequot after I chose her. I trusted Freydis with the fate of our people. My passion for her is uncontrolled."

"I know the feeling," Bud remarked.

Sassacus smiled. "I could not see why they could not trust her, as I did. I was their Sachem. To the north, I am known as Sassacus, son of Suggayoh and Grand Sachem of the Pequot. So, to protect my tribe and our honor, I left our village in the Mountains of Groton and my position as Grand Sachem. I took a handful of my finest warriors and their families—my true brothers, and made a life here. Now, I travel to Groton only for the festival of Zosimus."

"Festival?"

"It is when our young ones become old enough to drink *Nequt's Blood* from The Chalice of Zosimus and become strong."

Bud nodded, as he took a hit off his cigar. The Skullcloud continued to fray his focus, and brought visions of his own rites of passage. He recalled shooting his first deer with a bow at age fifteen and then washing his hands in the animal's blood, tasting it while it was still warm—supposedly a ritual performed by the shamans of his grandmother's tribe. It was intended to connect him with the animal and thank it for surrendering its life, so that he may survive. The memory reminded him of his father. He wanted the chance to return home and thank him for that lesson, which had given a greater appreciation for the value of life.

Sassacus's voice wafted through Bud's drifting memories. "Each year, at the time of the first harvest, the high priestess performs the rite of passage for those born into the tribe. The chalice is filled with Nequt's Blood. Children drink it to become strong."

"And Freydis was preparing for that when she disappeared?" Bud asked.

"Yes, Freydis left to gather Whitestem, an herb used in the potion of Nequt's Blood. After many hours, dusk settled on our village. When she did not return in time to prepare for the ceremony, I searched for her. The sun was close behind the trees when I found her tracks at the base of the mountain and smelled her scent."

"So, why would the Noctiss—or, I guess, Agni want the chalice?"

"Nequt's Blood. When the potion is sipped from the chalice, it makes things grow big, strong. I believe he means to use it to create giant Noctiss."

"Yeah, that would be not be good."

The Sachem puffed his cigar harder.

Bud continued, "It sounds like Nuppe was practicing magic though. I thought your people hated magic, and why would ya'll need to use potions anyway?"

"Nuppe did not practice magic. He was our first Grand Sachem. His advisor, Zosimus, made potions for Nuppe. In the beginning, Nuppe traveled with Zosimus to find a new home for our people—a home away from those who would try and steal Zosimus's creations. Nuppe was a wise leader. He settled our people away from all others. Merchants had to travel great distances to our lands to gather the power of these creations. Distance from others gave our potions great value."

"Good business plan," Bud muttered.

"In the days of the beginning, Nuppe searched the lands and found the purple mountains to north. He made these lands his homestead, away from the settlements in the plains. The early Pequot carved a village into the rock, and called it Groton. Groton sat high in the middle of the northernmost range of Deepst mountains and became one of the richest villages on Adytum."

"That is pretty clever," Bud acknowledged.

"Ah, but it was not easy for our people in the beginning. We troubled to grow food in the cold mountains. And the Dwarves were no help." Sassacus glowered. "Even with Zosimus's knowledge of farming, food was scarce and hard to manage—too many mouths to feed—the burden of their success. Too many mounds of ice and snow took away good harvests. The village came to the mercy of the travelling merchants, and when merchants were away for too long, the chill of winter cut deep into their profits and bellies. For many years, Zosimus worked on new potions, trying to grow bigger and stronger plants, and because of this, we now stir healing salves, mind potions, fire potions—too many to name in a night," the giant chuckled and took a sip from his chalice.

"So why didn't your tribe just pack up and move? There had to be another remote spot where you could grow food."

"Nuppe enjoyed the mountain. It was his home, and he was a stubborn leader. They battled winter, and our people were almost destroyed because of his pride. It took many years of suffering, until one day Zosimus stirred a potion that changed our people's way of life forever. Nequt's Blood, a potion of growing. An elixir so powerful that after several small doses, goroms and yewers grew to three and four times their normal size. They grow from the rocky mountainside even today. It was Nequt's Blood, saved our people."

"So why is it called Nequt's Blood?" Bud asked.

"Because the legend wasn't made of crops. It was made from Nuppe's use of it on his son. Nequt, could not walk or play, like the others after five summers of life. The boy lacked strength. Nuppe called medicine men from many tribes. All looked at him and said his bones would crack at any touch—said he was cursed, that he would never leave his bed, destroying his right to become Sachem. Nuppe's line would be lost without an heir and another would inherit the line of Sachem."

The intensity in the giant's voice grew as he continued spinning the yarn.

"Nuppe wondered if Zosimus's new potion could strengthen his child, as it did plants. He worried of the effects, but in the end, he could not watch his child suffer. That is not the fate of a Pequot. Fortunately, for little Nequt, Zosimus was loyal to Nuppe without question, and he agreed to do whatever necessary to save the child. He and Nuppe knew the tribe would not approve, but they decided to give the potion to Nequt. They told no one of their plan, and in two harvests' time, Nequt grew to be a full head above his father—became strong as a Wiegert."

"Wiegert?" Bud shook his head and took a puff, not recognizing the reference. The room spun accordingly on a rolling river of wine and Skullcloud smoke.

"Ha!" the Sachem bellowed, "Wiegerts are hairy four-legged beasts who live in the caves below the mountains of Deepst. They are foul creatures with giant bellies, and they sit on their wide asses all day, farting, and belching, and eating slogger. The fat bastards hoard weapons stolen from dwarves, who are constantly at war with them. Devils stand about ye high and are impossible to move." He illustrated by lowering his hand a little below the height of the table.

"The dwarves or the wiegerts?"

"Huh?" Sassacus stammered, placing his cigar in his mouth, then let out a grand laugh, "Ah! The wiegerts!" Raising his hand only a fraction of an inch, he japed, "Dwarves be about this tall." The giant bellowed another deep guffaw, and Bud laughed along with him, easing into his chair, trying to picture the creatures in his mind.

After the amusement settled, the Sachem slurred, "Yes, wiegerts. Their fur is wiry, spiny, tough as steel. But we were speaking of—"

"Nequt," Bud reminded.

"Ah yes, Nequt. After little Nequt drank the potion from Zosimus's chalice, he became solid as stone. Nuppe could not hide his son's strength. The tribe feared him as a product of dark magic, and Nuppe lost the trust and respect of the tribe. The tribe feared the magic, but soon they realized they could be stronger and faster without harm from the potion. On the day of the first Festival of Nequt, our people drank from the cup, and Groton became a village of giant Pequot warriors. That is how my ancestors became who we are today. Nequt's Blood, and its recipe, remain our fruit alone. No one born outside the tribe is allowed to drink from Zosimus's Chalice, and now, I fear Agni shall gain the recipe from Freydis and use it on the Noctiss—a strong force that would be."

"Yeah, a giant Noctiss would be a serious problem."

Sassacus frowned. "I am glad you understand. As a sign of your trust, I ask you show loyalty to the Pequot. Will you help us recover the chalice and my Freydis?" he asked.

"Do I have a choice?"

"It will be that…or die."

"You drive a hard bargain Sachem. I guess you got a deal—with one stipulation—I will help you, but I have to find Tsarina after we're done, and I'm gonna need some supplies and a horse. If you can provide those things for me, you got yourself a deal—seeing as it would benefit you as well. When I find Tsarina, and she opens the portal to Earth, Agni will probably want to come back through. That's what Freydis seemed worried about the most, and Tsarina is the only one who can open the portal."

The Sachem's eyes sparkled. "And grant me my revenge. Yes, then it is settled. We make the pact: You help us retrieve the chalice, and you will have all you need from our village and my support in finding your woman."

"And a horse?"

"And a horse." The Sachem grinned.

"If I survive, I guess I can live with that."

Sassacus raised his glass and affirmed, "My people will be in your debt after your help, and your loyalty will not be questioned after."

Bud raised his glass and nodded as he took a sip. His eyelids weighed heavy, and he felt his legs sliding down the chair.

Sassacus noticed his fading energy and offered, "You look like skunked meat. We rest now and plan tomorrow."

"Yeah, that's cool. This skullcloud has me pretty messed up. A bed sounds pretty good."

"Your speech is strange. I must learn your tongue," Sassacus laughed then looked around the room with sloppy eyes. "Where's our priestess?"

As if conjured by the hovering layer of Skullcloud smoke, a raspy voice blew through the door, "You request, Sachem?" Trailing the swirling cloud, a gaunt woman with more wrinkles than hair wafted into the tent. Large beaded necklaces made from bleached bones clattered about her collarbone as she shuffled over the maroon and yellow carpet covering the dirt floor. Small skulls from various critters dangled off the chains around her ankles, and she held a pink rose with flaming petals. The flames did not consume the petals. They seemed to be an extension, burning smooth from inside. The priestess waved the fiery perennial over Bud's goblet while she chanted several phrases that sounded vaguely like Native American tongue. When she finished the chant, she produced a bat-like creature with four eyes and spiked wings from her pocket. The rodent's iridescent green wings flapped in her palm as she pricked through its silver scales, deep into its breast with her stiletto-shaped fingernail. Squealing, the orange-eyed bat flopped spasmodically in her hand, and the puncture produced two large drops of orange blood. The witch then squeezed the drops into Bud's goblet, and she held her hands high, motioning for him to drink from the cup. As he sipped the sour drink, she performed a similar ritual over the Sachem's wine, and Bud tipped his last drop along with Sassacus. The priestess exited, humming a soft, eerie tune in a minor key.

Inadvertently slamming his goblet on the table, trying to balance, Bud croaked, "What the hell was that? I thought you didn't like witches?"

"I do not."

"That looked a hell of lot like a witch to me."

"Sometimes they are necessary. She provided our blessing for the days to come. Now we put this night to rest," Sassacus informed dryly. He clapped his hands together once more and shouted, "Astrid!"

∞∞∞*A Walk In The Dark*

In the time it took Bud to stand up from his chair onto his wobbly legs, an athletic young woman with flowing auburn hair strode into the room on sprinter's legs. A lighter shade of tan than the rest of the villagers, and slightly smaller in stature, she was by far the most beautiful girl he had seen amongst their ranks. Blinking several times, he cleared the film from his eyes and then recognized her as the skull carrier from the Lacrosse game who had scored the final goal. Gold streaks ran down the front and the back of her blouse like dyed rays of sunlight, accentuating her chiseled frame. Wrapped inside a tight silken skirt, her thin hips and muscular thighs darted from side to side as she strode across the room toward him. Bud remained speechless when she took him by the hand and led him toward the door. Wondering how to react, he looked to Sassacus for a sign. The giant simply gave a nod of approval, then grinned knowingly as he bid goodnight. "Astrid will take you from here."

Bud widened his eyes, trying to focus on his path. He followed the young woman, who escorted him out of the tent with his hand in hers. Stumbling through the dark village, he heard chirping sounds of mating bugs, resonating in the cool night air, and he slurred, "So how long have you worked for Sassacus?"

The long legged maiden giggled smugly, sustaining her pressing gait.

"What?" he croaked, dumbfounded by her amusement.

"Since birth," she responded. "I am his daughter, Astrid, and tonight, whether I like it or not, he has asked I look after you—keep you out of trouble and inside the walls."

"What?" Bud tripped forward, struggling to keep up with her long strides. "Oh shit. Well…cool. So, I guess, that makes you my bodyguard?"

"I suppose, if you mean, am I to guard your body from harm, then yes. I am your bodyguard. Do not do anything stupid and no harm will come to you."

An intoxicated laugh hissed from his nose. "No offense honey, but you are the smallest person I've seen around here. What if one of these big dudes tries to jump me, or something? You gonna wrestle them to the ground?"

She whipped her head around, eyeing him sternly, and her honeyed face soured. "I'll have you know, I am the best warrior with a pole-arm in all of Idlewylde. Man or woman."

"Damn, really? So you think you can take me?" he mocked.

"I would have you disarmed and pissing yourself in an instant," she boasted.

"No shit? Really?"

"There is no doubt."

"You ever Indian wrestle?" he asked.

She looked at him sideways, tossing her auburn hair over her shoulder, then answered, "Not that I am aware."

"Well, Miss Bonnie Badass, it's a type of wrestling, and just so you know, I'm pretty good at it. Wanna give it a shot?"

"I really don't think—"

"Aw, come on. You're the warrior here, but I can understand you being all scared and whatnot—"

A hiss puffed from her thin nose. "What are we to do?"

"Cool. Here, you just take my hand, like this," he instructed, cupping her hand in his. "Now put your foot up against mine, like this." He felt the soles of her moccasins against his, as she mimicked his crouch, then he lowered himself into an athletic position for leverage.

"Yes…now what?" she groused.

"Patience Pocahontas," Bud stammered, trying to stabilize himself. "Now we just try to knock each other off balance—like this!" he shouted then shoved her shoulder quickly in an attempt to catch her off guard. She stood firm, like a deep-rooted oak tree, and violently countered. Her retaliatory strike sent him toppling, ass over head, to the ground, and he landed flat on his back.

"Like that?" she jeered, wiping her hands together, as if she had somehow soiled them.

"Yeah…like that," he echoed, shaking his head side to side, trying to stop the world from spinning. Punchy, he attempted to stand, but the ground was rotating out of control and he collapsed to one knee. Astrid pulled him upright with a snarky grin then led him into his tent with her arm wrapped firmly around his waist.

∞∞∞*Be Our Guest*

Anxious for news regarding Bud, Tsarina occupied her time strolling the herb garden where the alchemists grew various and sundry plants for their potions and salves. The tranquility of the expansive garden calmed her nerves, and she began spending more and more time there with each passing day. Refusing to accept her role as guest and student at the Cairn, she found herself more often than not dreaming of escape. Archon Halcyon's teachings were developing her powers and mental focus and adding confidence that she could survive outside the walls. Her desire to begin the search for Bud was becoming unmanageable.

As she turned through the outer corridor of the garden toward the main exit, several students broke quietly from their meditation and began following. Tsarina smiled politely and altered her course toward her chambers, covering her desire to flee deep within the reaches of her mind.

She entered her chambers, opening the crystal doors with her mind, and determined, *if there is no news from Melinda today, something must be done.* She couldn't stand the uncertainty of Bud's fate any longer. Meandering to her armoire, she picked out a rose tunic and slipped into the satiny fabric then returned to her living room. She wished she could become invisible and float through the walls like a ghost. She also thought it seemed more than coincidental invisibility spells were the lessons Halcyon kept denying her when she would ask to learn something new. Each time she would inquire about disappearing, he would inform her that *it was a hard lesson, and she was not ready for it quite yet.* She was coming to believe he wasn't going to allow her to leave, even though he claimed otherwise. She also knew her inability to hide her thoughts of flight betrayed her with each lesson. Halcyon's practiced mind was too powerful and alert, and no thought was safe from his prying. It felt like a burning needle poking her forehead when she tried to block him, but at least she could sense of his probing.

The intricacies of Mentalism were slowly settling into her mind, even as the distraction of Bud's fate weighed heavy on her concentration. Strangely, she found no preference between the Mentalist lessons from Halcyon and the Materialist lessons from Madam Veronica. She didn't find it odd as everyone else; both simply came natural to her.

Plucking a book with a red spine from the bookstand, she returned to the bay window to practice a bit of telekinesis. Telekinesis was by far the most challenging of her lessons as well as the most stimulating. Sitting in the bay window, she bathed in the rose light and attempted to lift the crimson book into the air without using the word *orior*, which meant lift in Latin. Tsarina wished to stay away from using words to project her spells—especially Latin words. The process of connecting energy with a word or phrase seemed like a waste of mental focus and time, and she felt more powerful and free when she could simply think of the spell and have it take effect rather than chant it like a parrot. *Unspoken*, as Halcyon had called it, was relatively easy for the first set of basic spells she was learning, but the second batch, required more energy and were quite a bit more elusive – telekinesis was one such spell. Through careful focus, she elevated the book and began dragging it in her direction. A gentle knock came at the door, breaking her concentration, and the thick manuscript fell with a thud onto the ground, giving the virginal corners dents. It came to rest like a teepee, binding up, mocking her effort.

"Who is it?" she called.

"It is Timothy, milady."

"Come in," she instructed, opening the door with a wave of her hand, anxious to see if he brought news. "Any word on Bud?" she asked, as the young apprentice shuffled into the room.

"No, milady." Timothy frowned, wringing his hands together. "I am sorry to say, Jayson has not seen Melinda's messenger this morning."

Tsarina puffed through her nose, "Wasn't the bird supposed to arrive this morning?"

"Yes milady, however the winds are blowing strong from the west, and that is surely the reason for the delay. I predict we shall see her Dalton before nightfall. Do not worry, as soon as the tower guards see the bird, I will be here posthaste to inform you. I do, however, have news from Demetrius, but I'm afraid it is marred with horror. He arrived late last night with Anton and Indimiril. But—"

"But what?"

"I'm sorry to say that Anton was—he wasn't alive."

"Oh." Tsarina inhaled a breath that burned the inside of her nose and fought the tears welling in her eyes. She had watched the fatal blow, a blow meant for her.

The lad lowered his head then took a deep breath and asked, "Madam Tsarina?"

"Yes?" She gritted her teeth and wiped the corner of her eye.

Timothy hesitated and looked at the floor when he spoke. "Do you mind if I ask you a question."

"Yeah what?"

"Well, I often wonder why you are so anxious to leave the Cairn? Do we not serve you satisfactorily? Is there anything more I can do to make you stay more pleasurable?"

"What?" She frowned. "No, Timothy. It has nothing to do with you, or anybody else here. I just miss my family and friends. I'm worried for them." She affected a disheartened smile. "And I don't belong here. I'm supposed to be studying normal things like Biology, and Russian history, and how to use an EKG machine—not the histories of Adytum, or how to speak to birds, or how to move books around the room with my mind and hide my thoughts from people."

"I understand, milady. Truly, I do. I do know what it is like to be away from one's family. I, myself, was sent here at the early age of five to study with Archon Halcyon. The program here is quite intense. I am only allowed to see my family three times a year, or when they come to visit me, which they never do." He grimaced. "They are old, and it is too hard for them to make the journey up the mountain."

"Then why do you do it if you miss them so much? Couldn't you learn magic from someone closer to your home?"

"I suppose, however my mother wishes me to study with Archon Halcyon. She says I could be a powerful Archon someday, and that would bring honor and prestige to our family, where now, there is none. I suppose that is my desire as well."

"That's cool. At least you have a purpose for being here, but me, I just wanna find Bud and go home and eat a greasy slice in the park."

"But you have a gift. They say you are the only one who can open the portal between our worlds. You are—" His eyes darted away.

"What?"

"I do not know..."

"Timothy?" she interrogated with a scolding, motherly tone and focused inside his mind. His errant thoughts radiated into hers like a dream, and she listened to his pent up aggression shouting at his mentors. She noticed his desire for her and felt his reluctance to divulge what he knew regarding her fate. She worried the intrusion would embarrass him, but he did not seem to care. She realized she wasn't disguising herself very well and felt a warm feeling of comfort inside his thoughts, as if he were allowing her access. Then, a slight stinging sensation blossomed in her forehead, as Timothy quelled any further invasion and smiled.

I'm sorry, I—she started.

Do not worry. These things happen. I could have hidden myself better. But—

When she shut down the connection, he looked behind and whispered, "I haven't heard them say anything, however, as the keeper of the portal, they want you protected at all costs—of that I am certain. Your children must survive as well. Without the line of Istia, there can never be a portal to Earth. From what I have been witness to over these past few days, I believe the council does not desire to return to Earth, or for the portal to ever be used again, however I imagine they should wish to keep the option available, as it would seem unwise to let such a magnificent power simply slip away."

"I get it." She turned and looked out the window. "I just don't know if I can handle the pressure. I don't want to be treated like some kind of freak, and I certainly don't want my kids to be burdened with that kind of crap. I haven't even thought about kids yet. I just want to live a normal life on my world."

"I am afraid it is too late for that. That was never your destiny."

His words lingered in an awkward silence, taxing Tsarina's desire for a simple future and she turned to face him.

"I must go now," he said. "However, I promise I will inform you the very moment Melinda's Dalton arrives, and I will keep your desire to leave locked away from prying minds." He flashed the two finger sign and quickly shuffled out the door, closing it with a thought on his way out.

Wondering if she would ever see Bud, Tasha, Shelby, or Earth ever again, Tsarina returned to the windowsill and gazed out into the massive courtyard framed by the crystal mountain walls. Rose hues lit the underbelly of a Dalton opening its wings to land, and her eyes sparked with excitement. She bolted out of her chambers and dashed down the hall to Halcyon's study. As she pressed through the door, cooing sounds echoed inside the room, and Halcyon stood holding Melinda's Dalton up to his ear. He gave a smile and nodded. When she questioned him with her eyes, he nodded again and placed the bird on the table, stroking its back. It cooed and pranced, flapping its wings then took flight and exited out of the open window.

"What'd it say?" asked Tsarina, bouncing anxiously on the balls of her feet.

"I'm afraid there is little word," Halcyon answered flatly. "Melinda was only able to gather the tiniest bit of information from one child in the village, who simply stated that Bud was taken away on a wyvern, which means he surely is under Agni's control."

"And Viduata," she stated.

"Yes, if they are together, as we suspect."

"We gotta to go to him now."

"It isn't that simple I'm afraid."

"What do you mean? You know where her tower is, right?"

"Yes, we know of her tower, but—"

"But what?" Tsarina spat. "Let's go."

"My dear, I must suggest patience. If we were to try and force our way into Viduata's tower without any knowledge of what is inside, then we would waste our efforts and perish doing so."

"You've got a gang of warlocks and witches here, don't you have some spells you can use when we get there? Like, just go invisible and sneak him out—"

"There are powerful mages here, of course, but we would be foolish to underestimate the powers lurking in Viduata's tower.

We must gather knowledge on what lies inside before we attempt a rescue of any sort."

"Well, I'm leaving, with or without your help."

Halcyon gave a cold stare. "I'm afraid I cannot allow that Madam Tsarina."

"I don't care what you will allow! My friend is out there, and I'm going to get him," she blasted.

"Madam Tsarina, would you allow your entire world, and ours, to be destroyed to save this one boy? Your sister and your family on Earth would surely fall to Agni if you could not open the portal because of your rash death. The portal would be closed forever and the line of Istia broken. You must realize your sole importance to these worlds. Consider the greater good. If Bud is alive, he will be so, whether you go to him now or later."

Tsarina felt the weight of his words grounding her in logic. If Agni and Viduata were holding Bud, it was only to get to her. As much as she wanted to burst out of the room and run down the mountain, she realized her efforts would ultimately be in vain. "So what can we do? I can't sit here and do nothing anymore," she murmured.

"We must focus our attention on your studies until we devise a plan to recover the Eye of Istia. Until we find a way to breach the mountain without great losses, we must remain patient. We need more information on the mountain and where the Eye is being held. Without it you will never be able to open the portal and return home."

What if I can't remember the spell? She leaked the transparent thought without a filter.

Oh. Halcyon paused and focused on her eyes. In that moment, Tsarina detected a faint, shimmering light sparkle inside his mind—almost as if he had leaked a smile. He turned and gazed out the window into the sea of rose light. *That would be quite unfortunate.*

∞∞∞Hammer It Out

As the first rays of morning sunlight bled through the tanned hide roof, Bud felt a sharp, throbbing pain inside his head. He rubbed it gently then rolled onto his side. His hand brushed against a smooth, toned thigh and he felt the warm sensation of human touch. A young girl with light auburn hair and a chiseled body was lying next to him, sitting upright in the bed, fast asleep. She seemed vaguely familiar. He tried to recall her name, but the thick fog lingering from the Skullcloud and the wine, created an impenetrable roadblock.

As he tried to piece together the events of the evening, her long muscular legs stretched out beside him, and he wondered, *Where am I?* When his hand slid off her thigh, her bright aquamarine eyes opened.

She leapt out of the oversized bed, adjusting her silk skirt around her waist. "Oh! Sorry, I must have fallen asleep," she apologized, with a stern look, as if she had disobeyed a direct order from a drill sergeant.

"Yeah…uh…" Bud struggled.

"Astrid," she reminded.

"Right." He pointed to his chest. "Bud."

"Yes, I remember. You were the one, pickled."

The chiseled angles of her shape were a rhapsodic sight after being trapped in Agni's musty dungeon. Sensual thoughts brought guilt, and a sheepish smile smuggled its way onto his face without his consent. He wondered if anything of an adult nature had taken place. *Plausible deniability?* he postulated, rubbing the back of his neck.

"It appears we made it safely through the night, and you are still alive. My duty here is finished. I will wait outside until you are ready to see my father," she informed, struggling to sound proper through her crackling voice.

    The pressing need to ask about their night together consumed Bud. He sat up and watched Astrid quickly duck beneath the cloth door of the wigwam out into the early morning sunlight. After several minutes of slipping in and out of a dreamlike state, he eventually summoned the will to tear through the web of crapulence pinning him to the rough-hewn, sweat soaked sheets. He lifted his poisoned body off the bed with shaky arms then stood for a moment to feel his weight against the soft floor. A pair of tanned moccasins rested beside the bed, and the smell of the fresh leather sifted into his nose as he slipped on the footwear. In a moment of clarity, he noticed his backpack resting against the foot of the bed and checked for the globes of fire and the ruby. They were still safely wrapped inside his clothing.

    He brushed his hair into ponytail, then pulled the weathered curtain door and poked his head out of the wigwam. When the sunlight touched his face, the fleeting hangover seemed a small price to pay for the glorious night of conversation and intoxication with the Sachem. The epicurean night had restored a bit of his humanity.

    When he stepped into the light, Astrid was standing outside, conversing with a middle-aged woman holding a toddler in her arms. The discussion seemed to be warm and light until the woman spotted Bud emerging from the tent. She pointed a finger at him and marched away.

    Astrid spun with a frown and asked, "If you have your senses, Sassacus is ready."

    "Yeah, sorry. That Skullcloud worked me over pretty good last night."

    "Hmm. I thought it was me," she jabbed flatly.

    A faint vision of the Indian wrestling match zipped through his head, and he wondered if that was their only romp. Quietly, he followed her, fighting to keep his focus away from her hips as they swayed back and forth.

When they came to the Sachem's tent, Astrid pulled the curtain and ushered Bud inside. Sassacus sat hunched behind a wooden desk, sharpening a small hatchet. The wrinkles on his forehead flattened when he noticed Bud, then with a wave, the giant dispersed the half-naked woman standing next to him then casually motioned Bud to have a seat. Astrid nodded at her father, expressionless, and then disappeared into the glaring sunlight.

"How's your head?" Sassacus asked.

"Not a hundred percent. Feel like I've been run over by a Mack truck."

"Mack truck?" he smiled.

"Yeah, like a wyvern."

"Ah," hummed the giant.

"So, do we have a plan?" Bud asked. "Last night is a little hazy, but I do seem to recall us talking some crazy shit about climbing up the side of that black mountain and recovering a magical chalice. That was all just drunk talk, right?"

"Ha! Good plans made from Skullcloud. I spoke with my two finest warriors, Tatoben and Meatoc. They will be ready."

"So, I wasn't dreaming." Bud grimaced. "Great. How long before we leave?"

"We prepare today and leave tomorrow at first light. We can waste no more time."

Bud wafted through a moment of incertitude then remembered how he had been given no choice in the matter. "If we're leaving tomorrow morning, we got a lot to do. There's a bunch of supplies we're going to need just to get up that mountain."

"Ha! You steal my questions like a knowing witch. I have sent for Gertumah, she will get any items needed for our journey. "Gertumah!" Sassacus bellowed, shocking Bud's ears like a thunderclap. Instantly, the hard-faced woman entered the tent and awaited instruction. The Sachem turned to Bud and said, "Tell her what we need."

Calculating in his head, Bud relayed in a stream of consciousness, "Let's see—We'll probably need four ropes, about two hundred feet long, strong enough to hold two men. I don't know if you have any kind of hooks, but we'll need something to loop the ropes through—to tie them together, if possible. We call them carabineers back on Earth. They're made out of aluminum usually, but—"

"Harron is our smithy," Sassacus interjected, "he can forge any metal we need. After we finish, I will take you to his forge, and you can explain these things to him."

"Sounds good. What about those pointed staves I saw the kids playing with the other day? Those would be perfect for staking into the ground and tying off the ropes."

"Gertumah, four swackers."

"Yes, Sachem." She nodded.

"More?" Sassacus asked Bud.

Bud squinted. "Yeah, we'll need water and food. About six days worth, I imagine, and each of us will need a pack. If you have something like my backpack, that would be perfect."

Sassacus interjected again, "Less food. Six grain crackers each. We can kill or harvest for the rest."

Gertumah nodded, "Yes, Sachem." She informed Bud, "I remember your pack. We have similar ones made."

"Thanks. Also, do you have gloves with the fingers cut out?"

"What type of glove?"

"Something light and durable, like leather, but without the fingers. We'll need them to keep our palms from getting torn up by the ropes and the rocks." He rubbed the calluses inside his palms together, squeezing his hands into a ball to illustrate.

"I will have them woven for you from tanned Fossic hide with extra padding inside the palm."

"Cool. Let's get a pair of those for me, and Sassacus, and—" Bud had already forgotten the names of the crew, and he looked to Sassacus to finish the thought.

"Tatoben and Meatoc," Sassacus reminded.

"Right, Tatoben and Meatoc," Bud repeated.

"I will fit them today," Gertumah informed, then she took Bud's hand and turned it over, measuring it against hers. She apparently made a mental note of its size and did the same for Sassacus. "Will that be all?" she asked.

Bud thought for a moment. "I think that's about it." He looked to Sassacus for any further suggestions.

Sassacus gave the woman a nod and said, "Thank you Gertumah. That is all. Bring the items when ready."

"Yes Sachem," she replied, then exited the tent.

Following her out the leather door, Bud strolled with Sassacus to the archery range located at the front of the village near the gate where he had first entered. Gertumah strode far ahead and grabbed the hand of a beast of a man standing without a bow. She matched his hand to hers and took a measurement. The giant was the only man Bud had seen in the village who was bigger than Sassacus. As Gertumah began taking measurements for the thinner archer, the two men started arguing, and Bud felt Sassacus's arm bar across his chest.

"Let us wait here. I wish to see this," informed Sassacus.

Both warriors wore leather loincloths secured around their waists, and belts of animal skulls hung low over their thighs. The thin heads with long snouts had fangs protruding from the bottom jaws, and Bud wondered what animal had lost its life to these men. Beyond that, they were naked, save for several tattoos and dull-colored pieces of jewelry made out of beads and shells that adorned their necks, wrists, and ankles. He overheard the larger man say, "You can't split three arrows in wolf's head."

"How much coin if I can?" the archer asked, seemingly unphased by his looming companion.

"A belt of sixty white and forty black."

"No one trades in wampum. What else?"

"20 Hinson fletched arrows," he countered.

"Straight ones this time."

"Always, straight ones," the giant grumbled.

"Not always. And if I miss?" asked the archer.

"Five bloomish pies."

"Pies again, Meatoc? If you keep winning these bets, you will be big as a Warpund Ox."

"He already is," Gertumah jabbed then walked away.

"Your sister's pies." Meatoc looked up to the sky with a grin.

"You should learn to master your cravings for my sister and her pies. However, today not to worry," the sinewy archer boasted.

In one fluid motion, he drew his bow to his ear and released the silver-tipped arrow. In an instant, it zipped fifty yards across the field and pierced the canvas target with a sharp thump, directly through the wolf's red eye.

"Lucky shot," Meatoc rumbled in Tatoben's ear.

The archer let two more arrows fly, one on top of the other, splitting the top of the first. "Amazing. I must be very lucky to have hit all three, and now my luck has turned into 20 straight arrows."

Sassacus began clapping as he stepped forward. "I should have warned you not to make such a bet Meatoc. Sorry I arrived too late." The Sachem glanced at Bud and smiled.

Both warriors stood erect at the sound of his voice and turned to face their leader.

"You make sure and pay later," Sassacus said. "Now, meet Bud. He is to help us recover Zosimus's Chalice."

Meatoc examined Bud with a frown and said, "Scrawny Ruzzer. Half a meal for a Noctiss."

Bud assumed the brute's tactless statement was just his way of getting to the point, and replied, "I appreciate the concern, Meat, but I've only been here a week, and I've already killed 5 of those slimy bastards. How many have you killed this week?"

The Pequot looked at one another and shook their heads decisively, as if the response was exactly the one to garner their respect.

Bud continued, "Good, then if you're done being a horse's ass, I'd like to get down to planning our trip up the mountain. We got a lot of work to do before I drag ya'll up there."

"Ha! Yes," Sassacus agreed. "Come, let us find Harron and make our plans on the way."

During the short walk through the village, Bud explained the treacherous parts of the climb and warned the warriors of the sheer-faced cliff walls looming in the shadows of the peaks. Meatoc seemed undaunted, grunting at the end of each explanation.

Tatoben, however, expressed his concern. "How are we to climb these cliffs if they are sheer rock as you say?"

"We're going to use ropes to pull each other up, one at a time."

Tatoben looked uncertain. "How long must these ropes be, and what if they are not fit? How are we to secure them?"

"The ropes only need to be long enough to get us from one landing to the next. One of us goes up first and secures one of the ropes to something—a stake or a tree. Then we put the ropes through iron hooks to make the climb easier for the other two. You just alternate people all the way up, and nobody gets worn out."

"And these hooks, what are they for?"

"They make pulling easier, and they allow a secure connection between the ropes if we have to tie them together to make them longer. It's cool. Don't worry, I'll show you how it all works when Gertumah brings us the gear."

Behind a large black tent, clangs of iron, banging against iron, grew louder with each step. The droning sounds hypnotized Bud as he walked toward the tall blacksmith. Harron's massive forearms were steadily pounding a silver hammer into the black blade of what would eventually be a double-edged great axe. Incandescent coals flamed inside a soot-stained stone pit, lighting the blacksmith with orange heat. He wiped a bit of perspiration from his brow with his forearm and continued pounding the hammer into the anvil.

Sassacus addressed the blacksmith, "Looks like another masterpiece Harron!"

Harron stopped hammering and acknowledged Sassacus, "Yes Sachem, but this new metal is harder to fold. Takin' me twice as long to beat it to shape."

"This new metal, is it worth the price?" Sassacus asked.

"Should be, it's stronger than Hillert's old metal—that's for certain." Harron's eyes flickered with the spark of the anvil as he struck his hammer into the blade a final time.

"Good, we will need them for more than chopping fire logs," Sassacus informed. Then he unfolded his arms and touched Bud on the shoulder. "Harron, this is Bud. He has agreed to show us a path to Viduata's peak, but he says we need something from you."

The charred wrinkles around the old smithy's eyes cinched together as he scrutinized Bud's face. "Well?"

Bud cleared his throat. "Well…we are going to need stakes with rings on the top."

"What be the sizes?"

"The stakes need to be about a foot and a half long with the rings large enough to fit a rope through, and the lighter the better, but they have to be strong enough to support our combined body weight, if that's possible."

"How many?"

"About twelve."

Harron grumbled, "About twelve, or twelve?"

"Twelve. Sorry."

"Twelve it is." Harron rested his hammer on the anvil and then turned to Sassacus. "When you need 'em by Sach?"

"Tomorrow, before first light."

"Günter's red ass. I'll have to start now and finish these damned axes later—"

"So be it. Stakes first. Thank you, Harron. We will leave you to your work."

"It'll be done." The blacksmith nodded and placed the smoking axe on the ground.

After a short walk to the Sachem's tent, Bud doubted if he could lead the expedition. When he entered the tent, he saw the four ropes positioned on the center of Sassacus's table, neatly coiled and ready for inspection, and the task of instruction settled his nerves. Bud took the end of the nearest rope and felt the general weight of the fiber, snapping it between his hands to test the strength. The static rope was extremely light, belying its strength.

"Will these do?" Sassacus asked.

"Only one way to find out," replied Bud.

"Ha!" The giant laughed. "Then I will test them from the tower later. Gertumah can pack them with the other supplies."

Tatoben grabbed one of the ropes and examined it. "Before we put them away, I would ask Bud how we are to use them."

Bud agreed and began schooling the men on the knots he had learned from his days with Cole—the ones that would hopefully make their lives easier around the eight thousand-foot elevation mark, when their bodies were dangling over a hundred foot drop. He decided on the clove hitch first, because it was the easiest to master, and the one he knew best. Early in the lesson, Bud concluded that Tatoben was the most receptive to his instruction and gave him the most attention, so he could help train the others. Meatoc kept looping the second loop over the rope on the same side as the first, which kept coming undone, prompting low growls from the goliath. When Sassacus completed his knot, he wondered aloud why it was upside down, and Bud explained that it didn't matter.

When Tatoben finished, he attempted to help Meatoc. The archer grabbed his peer's fingers and forced them into the right positions. Bud chuckled.

After deeming everyone was well versed on the clove hitch, Bud moved on to the figure eight and finished with the bowline. Concluding the lesson, he informed, "I think ya'll just about got it. Keep practicing those knots until they become second nature, and we should be all good. Remember, if they don't work properly, we'll fall to our deaths." He smirked. "Any questions?"

"What happens if we do not have enough rope?" asked Tatoben with a frown.

"Then I guess we'll just have to wing it?"

Tatoben cocked an eye. "Wing it? I am no warlock. I can not sprout wings and take flight."

"I don't expect you to." Bud smirked. "Wing it means—to make do, or to figure out another way to get something done."

Sassacus chortled, "I am sure we will manage, Tatoben. Let us finish now. We gather here at first light. Go, prepare yourselves for the journey."

Both men nodded, leaving Bud alone with Sassacus.

Sassacus turned and said, "We feast as a tribe after dusk in the center of the village tonight. All are welcome. Join us."

"Thanks. I wouldn't mind having some more of that grilled snake. Ya'll gonna have some of that, right? What was it called again? yessir?"

Sassacus chuckled, "Ha! Yassar. There will be plenty!"

"Yeah, the yassar, and actually, there is something I would like to do today, if Tatoben has the time."

"Tatoben?"

"Yeah. I'm a pretty good with a bow, but after seeing him on the range earlier, I think he could teach me a thing or two. I figure it'll come in handy in a fight, and from what I've seen already, I'm pretty sure I'm gonna have to do plenty more fighting."

Sassacus's eyes caught fire. "You have a good eye. Tatoben is our best bowman. I will have you train with him, then after midday meal, you train with Meatoc. He is our master of arms."

"Alright, sounds good. I'll head over to see Tatoben now."

∞∞∞∞*Training A Ruzzer*

On his way to the archery range, Bud recalled the hissing screams of the Noctiss when he butchered them in the forest. He had become desensitized. More so, he had stabbed a man while eating without a second thought. It was only now, long after the fact, he felt a speck of remorse for what he had done.

When Bud approached the archery range, Tatoben stood in a large circle of arrows and moved around inside, steadily firing arrows into different targets with deadly precision. The archer held his bow low and pivoted when he heard Bud's footsteps. "Hello Bud. Care to fire a bow?"

"Yeah, actually."

"Ah. Are you practiced?"

"Yeah, I grew up bow hunting with my dad, but after watching you shoot I figured you could probably give me some pointers. That is, if you don't mind."

A humble smile, sprouted on the warrior's tattooed face. "I would be honored to show you what I know. But first, let's see what you know," he said, and picked a short flatbow from the rack. After stretching the drawstring, which seemed more like a reaction than a testing of the tension, he handed the bow to Bud. "Pull an arrow and pick a target. I will study your form."

Bud accepted the bow with a nod and plucked an arrow from the ground. He nocked the arrow and placed the bowstring between the first joint of his forefinger and middle finger, the way his father had instructed, then drew the string to his eye. Once he had the center of his target in focus, he released the string and his attempt just caught the bottom of the wooden wolf's head.

"Not bad, but you shoot low—too much tension. I would alter your grip."

"Ok," Bud agreed.

Tatoben restructured Bud's grip, placing the tips of his fingers directly on the strings, creating a looser feel.

"With this grip, you must learn the smooth draw," Tatoben instructed then turned, plucked an arrow from the ground and fired.

It was the same fluid motion Bud had witnessed Tatoben employ earlier that morning and had wondered why it was so effective. It seemed as if the constant motion of the draw would cause too much movement to be accurate, but he quickly found it to be quite the contrary.

Tatoben explained, "Aiming is the goal throughout the entire motion. When the bowstring becomes level with the target, the aim is already set. This way you are fast and accurate."

The fluidity of the draw allowed for the muscles in Bud's back to do most of the work, thusly keeping his grip loose and his aim steady. He struggled at first firing high and then low. After a dozen awkward attempts with the new technique, he finally split the wolf's head.

"Excellent," Tatoben encouraged.

The Pequot flatbow felt smooth and light, lighter than any compound bow Bud had ever used. It was thick in the middle with tips about two feet long, and the depth of the pull was effortless.

"Who made this bow?" asked Bud. "It's awesome."

"Thank you. I make them."

"Nice." Bud smiled. "Yours looks like silver though. Is it special?"

"Very. However, I cannot take credit for its life. *Stau* was crafted long ago." At the mention of its name, the bow glimmered a hint of auburn around its edges, and Bud imagined it had caught the light of the sun just so. "It is unknown," Tatoben continued. "Many believe Hobomock, the god of fire, crafted it from the flames of his own breath. The bow has been passed down to Pequot archers for many centuries."

"Damn. How'd you end up with it?"

Tatoben gave a puzzled look.

"I mean—not to say that you're not worthy—I just want to get a little bit of history on it. Like, who gave it to you?" Bud asked.

"My brother, Kerin, passed the bow to me when he slipped from this world."

"Oh, sorry. I didn't mean to—"

"I have made peace with his passing and honor him by making use of his gift everyday."

Bud understood, and now he realized what fueled Tatoben's passion for archery. It was an honorable passion. He spent the next several hours beside Tatoben, developing his form with the smooth draw. By the end of the session, he felt comfortable with his new grip and thanked Tatoben for showing him the technique. When he placed the practice bow on the rack, Tatoben said, "You have done well today."

"Thanks." Bud offered his hand. Tatoben took it in his and then pressed them both toward the sky, wrapping his forearm around Bud's and squeezing them together. "That is the Pequot way," he stated.

Honored by the handshake, Bud smiled and hurried to his tent where a light lunch consisting of several strange fruits and vegetables and a piece of uncooked fish was waiting for him on the bedside table. The fish head had three eyes, the odd one on top a yellowish-green.

Licking the last bit of lemon juice from his fingers, he strapped the guard's dull sword around his waist and made his way to the sparring circle behind the lacrosse field—A circle with arced wooden trestles, spaced five feet apart, allowed for multiple entry points. Meatoc was standing in the center of the arena, maintaining an athletic stance—an eerily calm expression.

Surrounded by five warriors armed with wooden staves, the giant slipped their attacks effortlessly. Countering, he swung his wooden, double-edged battle-axe, like a helicopter blade, striking the warriors' training staves in succession, knocking the youngsters off balance. With a sweep of his leg, he downed the two warriors in front of him and then blindly slammed the butt of his axe into the stomach of the warrior behind. Pivoting, he faced the last two combatants who were still upright and took a calculated swing. The staggered warrior's stave absorbed the force of the blow. Upon impact it flew out of his hand, careening outside the ring. With his opponent disarmed, Meatoc drove the butt of his axe into the warrior's forehead, knocking him to the ground—his axe positioned perfectly to block the oncoming blow from the remaining combatant's stave. As the pole bounced off the shaft of Meat's axe, he twirled it, stopping the blunt edge of the wooden blade just short of the man's temple.

"Enough!" Meatoc commanded and rested his axe upon his shoulder. He turned to face Bud and said, "Welcome, Noctiss killer. Have you come to teach us to fight?"

"No, I have come to see what you got. Sassacus sent me."

"Ha! And what will you fight with?"

"This is all I got." Bud pulled the dull rapier from its scabbard and held it in front of his face.

"Hmm. Toss it over." Meatoc scowled.

Bud flipped the blade and lofted the hilt through the air to Meatoc.

The giant caught the tiny blade and examined it, waving it in front of his belt. "Worthless," he grunted and tossed it outside the circle at Bud's feet. "Go to the rack and grab a wooden axe."

"Okay." Bud nodded and began searching for an axe that would fit his relatively small hand. A myriad of training weapons, crafted entirely of wood, sat before him. He decided on an axe with a single blade, three feet long with a rounded pommel. It appeared to be the lightest and easiest to wield—worst case, he would be able to recover from a mistake quickly.

When he brought it into the circle, Meatoc stood alone inside, scowling.

"Good axe for a ruzzer," Meatoc confirmed.

Instantly, wild, unannounced slashing from Meatoc sent Bud leaping backward until he felt his back pressing against the wooden trestle. Meatoc raised his great-axe above his head, and

Bud dodged, rolling along the rail just before the blunt head of the axe came crashing down upon the supporting log. Splinters flew and several of the men outside the ring snickered and howled as the wooden weapon reverberated in Meatoc's hands. The battle master shot them a vile look and grunted.

"Good! You're quick as a ruzzer rat. Now, let's see if you can strike as fast." Meatoc positioned his axe in front of his chest, and shuffled toward the center of the ring. Bud followed slowly, creeping toward the giant, raising his axe. He took a calculated swing at Meatoc's chest, but the giant easily blocked the awkward blow with the shaft of his axe then hooked the underside of Bud's blade, jerking it from his grasp, sending it spinning like a propeller across the arena.

"First lesson ruzzer—disarm your opponent, if you can. Without a weapon, most will fall."

"Brilliant," Bud muttered.

"Now pick up your blade and try again."

Bud walked over to the axe and gripped it tighter. He took a wild swing at Meatoc's feet and the giant sent the head of the axe into the dirt with a parry and slid his axe up to Bud's throat.

"That's how you take off the head," Meat laughed. "You have much to learn, we better get started."

For the next hour, Bud continued hacking and slashing with Meatoc, and after his initial lesson, Bud was allowed to spar with the other Pequot warriors. Eventually, he began finding the balance points for the axe, and by the end of the day, he felt a bit more comfortable with the weapon. It seemed manageable, and certainly capable of massive damage, given the correct blows. It was also quite useful at blocking and hooking. At the end of the day, he thanked Meatoc and his sparring partners for their instruction and returned the training axe to the rack.

On his way out, he gathered the sword Meatoc had discarded and began to sheath it.

"What are you doing ruzzer?" Meatoc growled. "Toss that into dung into the forest. I'll bring you a real weapon in the morning."

"Oh. Okay, thanks," Bud said and heaved the blade into the trees surrounding the field.

"Good toss ruzzer!" Meatoc howled, "Maybe we get you a sling instead."

"I definitely feel like David," he muttered under his breath.

∞∞∞*Last Supper*

After a much needed nap, Bud sat up and noticed darkness had fallen over the village. He worried he had missed the meal as he pulled himself out of bed and quickly slipped on his moccasins. Rushing out of the tent, he spotted the fires burning on the other side of the village. When he drew near, he saw Pequot villagers filtering around the three long wooden tables situated in a triangle around the crackling fire. Flames reached above the heads of the mingling Pequot, casting an orange glow over their faces as they took their seats.

Sassacus sat at the head of the center table and greeted Bud when he approached. "Good to see you survived your training with Meatoc and Tatoben."

"Barely," he replied, rubbing the bruises on his forearms. Tatoben and Meatoc echoed amusement, smiling at one another and Bud puffed a laugh with them. Looking over the spread, he reminded himself to take it easy at dinner with the wine and the Skullcloud in order to prepare for the quest ahead.

"Come, sit with us," Tatoben offered.

"Thanks." Bud nodded and sat quietly with the eyes of the village following him. He settled into his seat and waited for the Sachem to speak.

Sassacus raised a silver goblet and pronounced, "This night we honor our newest brother."

Grumblings of anxious agreement rolled over the table as Sassacus looked at Bud and took a long swill of the potent wine.

Bud followed suit and felt his nose burning as the harsh liquid rushed down the back of his throat.

"To honor your service to the Pequot, we would like to present you with gifts to aid in your quest," the Sachem said.

Bud flashed wide eyes, wondering what he was about to receive.

"Don't worry, these gifts are to protect us as well." The Sachem joked and looked toward hi axe-man. "Meatoc."

Meatoc rose from his seat, holding a well-polished, silver battle-axe in his hand. A three-foot haft was crafted into the blade, shaped in the image of a bird's head, similar to that of an eagle. It was shaped like a flat, backward *S*, thick at the crown and pointed at the bottom with serrated ridges along the backside. A sharp hook extended, serving as its beak, and intricate lines flowed down the shaft, seamlessly flowing into the contoured handle, which looked like a curved silver talon.

Bud humbly accepted the masterpiece, feeling a sense of awe, pride, and guilt all in the same moment. Words of appreciation percolated in his mouth, but he held them in as he examined the lines of the weapon and measured its weight. Finally, he stuttered, "I...this is magnificent." He shook it over the table. "Thank you."

Meatoc gave a firm stare. "She is Falchion. She was my mother's sister's axe—a good size for you. If you prove your worth, and we come home with the chalice, she is yours."

Sassacus stared at Meatoc for a moment. "You honor our tribe with such generosity, Meatoc. I am certain Bud will earn every ounce of your faith."

"I won't let you down," Bud avowed with a sincere nod.

Then it was Tatoben's turn. The thin giant rose from his seat with a flatbow made of dark cherry wood. "I saw your skill with a bow, but today was practice. In battle, it will be harder. This weapon will aid you under pressure. It is made of Chertee wood and crafted in the same mold as Stau."

"It's beautiful," Bud said. As he took the bow into his hands, he noticed the pointed tips were razor sharp and tipped with silver, so that the bow could be used as a spear, or staff inside close quarters. He plucked the string a bit to feel the draw weight and raised the bow to his cheek, looking down the handle. It had just enough weight to feel solid in his hands, but it was also light enough to not be a burden. He had the urge to take it directly to the range and fire it at once, but nodded his appreciation and cradled it in his arms.

    He looked across the faces the Pequot with admiration. "Thank you. I don't know what to say. I can only promise I will do my best to help find Freydis and recover the chalice. I know when I first showed up here, most of you saw me in the enemy's clothing, but I aim to prove nothing could be farther from the truth. I also have a quest of my own—to find my woman, and return with her to my home. Agni stands in the way of that. We have a mutual enemy, but even if that weren't the case, I would still be honored to call you all friends. I want you all to know, I have a great respect for the Pequot and I am honored to help you."

    "Well said, brother!" Sassacus raised his glass. "Now if the eye watering is done, let us feast!"

∞∞∞*Emergency On Planet Earth*

    The six regional wizards of the Grand Council sat across from each other around the long, crystal, meeting table. Halcyon sat at the head of the table referred to as the *Table of Wisdom*. Polished, clear as a diamond mirror, it reflected the fading, rose-colored sunlight as if the table itself were burning from inside. After Melinda's Dalton returned, Halcyon had called the emergency gathering to discuss the apparent threat to Earth and to Adytum, summoning each ruling Archon from the six civilized provinces of Adytum. Tsarina felt the weight of their stares as she sat back in her chair and pressed her forearms into the armrests.

She closed her mind and focused on listening and absorbing their personalities.

At the end of the table sat Scythian Deepst, King of the Northern Dwarves. Scythian was clearly a dwarf, but one of the few with innate magical prowess. He was a descendant of the original Deepst clan, who, according to legend, came directly through Istia's original portal from Earth. His magic was not limited solely to the fashioning of spells to objects; the materialist ways flowed freely through his veins, and his skills of manipulation with earthen elements were widely known throughout the land.

To his left, sat Joan Temptura, the soft-spoken leader of the valley people, a tanned race of rangers and herdsmen, druids known for their mentalist powers over the beasts of the lands. Her long, chiseled body was draped in a satiny green gown embroidered with different types of flowers indigenous to her province. Tsarina watched her fidget in her chair, twisting an emerald ring on her finger as everyone waited for Halcyon to explain his mysterious, impromptu meeting.

Loassan Dustmoor's eyes also watched Madam Temptura, and Tsarina noticed he was admiring the druid in more than just a professional fashion. Her smooth, dark olive skin and strikingly sharp features made her a magnet for alluring glances. Tsarina recognized the lady was uncomfortable most of the time because of it.

Joan casually glanced at Dustmoor, forcing him to look away toward the center of the table. His leathery black skin and thick build camouflaged the brandings etched into his face and arms, tribal symbols of snakes and birds. Little was known about the dark warrior or his clan, due to their nomadic nature. Halcyon had mentioned it was rare to find him at the Cairn, or anywhere for that matter. *Maybe that's why Balin's staring at him*, Tsarina thought, attempting to keep her thoughts hidden from the others. When several glances shot her way, she feared she was not succeeding.

Balin was by far the youngest of the Archons and was having a hard time keeping his focus from Joan's rapturous features as well. Tsarina caught him sneaking peeks when Joan would play with her ring, and she wondered his age. As the Archon of the ocean province to the south, Balin was, despite his lack of experience, a very important man. Most of the trade goods on Adytum passed through the city of Water Knorr due to its southernmost location on the water. Because of its location his province one of the most populated and sought after.

As a port town, Water Knorr received ships and tradesmen from all over Adytum, providing the Archon with numerous headaches on a daily basis. Balin was thrust into the role of the merchant king at a very young age. Tsarina had read one of the manuscripts detailing how Altas, Balin's mentor, had perished several winters past while sailing the Salinus Sea to the south in search of Tasmariel, a lost island of purported untold treasures. Atlas' entire crew was lost on the voyage and rumors surfaced of an Astridal sea creature. It seemed a fitting way for Atlas to die, consumed by the sea he loved so much.

Jindon Tremate, watcher of the forest, sat next to Halcyon. He was the elder teacher of the materialist's ways, and his schools in Splinter and Latchen were the most revered in the land. As the mage scanned the table with calculating eyes, she recalled Indimiril's gossip and waited for a reaction from Halcyon. Jindon pressed the Supreme Archon to begin with a raise of his eyebrow. Taking the hint, or more likely, reading everyone's mind, Halcyon stood and addressed the table.

"Welcome, Archons of Adytum, and thank you all for attending on such short notice. As you have already heard, I have received word of a transgression against the sacred pact of our forefathers, beyond the loss of Agni's father—A pact buried into oblivion by the tales of sages and bards.

"In the great histories, there is mention of a grimoire and a gemstone used to create the first portal from Earth to Adytum. The grimoire is known to hold the spell of *Istia's Escape* and as we know, Earth has been drowned in these myths and otherwise protected from all that would seek to destroy or conquer her. I, myself, was uncertain of her existence until now. Many convoluted stories I have heard over the years, and they have performed their duty well. They have led us to believe Earth was merely a fantasy world, and that we were true children of Adytum—not bastards from a far off planet. But this myth, it would seem, is reality.

"A planet that cannot be seen by the naked eye, inhabited by our ancestors? Who would believe in such absurdity?" Halcyon squinted. "But today, we have to look through a different eyeglass—a vision that illuminates us with facts. I am certain these stories are true. Our clerical misrepresentations of Earth and our lack of belief have allowed us to let down our guard, and now, it seems Agni's father excavated her like some forgotten treasure.

I believe he along with Tsarina's mother opened the portal thirteen years ago, and we all are aware his son's mind has never been the same since that day. Halcyon paused for a moment to heighten the effect of his words. "I say this with extreme certainty—through some unknown magic, he has summoned Tsarina and used her as a medium to open the portal."

Lossan turned a curious eye to Halcyon and asked, "What proof do you have of these wild stories?"

"The proof sits before you." Halcyon smiled at Tsarina.

Jindon grimaced. "So, my child, how is it exactly that you have traveled to our lands?"

"You mean, how did I open the portal?" Tsarina responded timidly. The pressure of the strange, intense faces suffocated her like summer humidity.

Jindon nodded, asking her to continue.

"Well, I had a dream about a week ago. I saw my mother looking at me in a pool of water, and she told me where to find her grimoire and when to chant the spell. After I performed the spell on the summer solstice, I had another dream, and I started chanting the spell in my sleep. I was wearing the anklet with the Eye of Istia, but I had this strange feeling my mother was controlling my mind in the dream, but—"

"And where is the Eye of Istia now, child?" Joan asked.

"Sükh took it from me in the field."

"The dwarf? So, you do not have it now?" Jindon continued the line of questioning.

"No," Tsarina answered.

"Curious." He turned to the table with a frown. "And what of the grimoire? Do you still have it or have you lost it as well?"

"I don't—"

"So you have no evidence of the sunstone or the grimoire?" He looked around the room. "We are to simply assume a girl we have never seen or heard of speaks the truth about an ancient myth of our origins. Pardon my objectivity, but why should we believe in this fantastic tale?"

"I don't know." She squirmed in her seat.

"Hmm." Jindon frowned.

The following second felt like an eternity and she bit her tongue.

Halcyon interjected, "Jindon, Indimiril validated she was pursued by Agni's mercenaries, and that at one time, she possessed these items. In addition, I discovered a town on Earth in the journals of Thomas called Salem. This child not only knew of the town, but she was able to provide an accurate description of it without ever seeing the journals. And, as you know, the only copy of these journals is located here in the Cairn."

"I see." Jindon stroked his beard. "Then, I propose to the council no action be taken until we have secured the Eye of Istia and the grimoire questioned Madam Tsarina further."

The crowd grumbled, and one by one agreed to the proposal with nodding and rumbling.

Before Tsarina could react, Halcyon looked toward her and offered, "I will take responsibility for the girl and chat with her further. She will stay as our guest in the Cairn for now." Halcyon summoned, *Timothy, please escort Madam Tsarina to her chambers and attend to her needs.*

"*Yes magister.*"

Halcyon spoke directly to Tsarina. "I will visit you a once we resolve our final issues here and then explain our decisions to you my dear. Do not be afraid. You will find safety here."

"Sure." Tsarina glared at the other members of the council, feeling strangely like a convicted felon, as Timothy escorted out of the hall.

∞∞∞*Zosimus's Chalice*

A ray of golden sunlight spotted Bud's forehead when he awoke, and he rolled over to avoid the blinding shaft. His body ached from the training sessions, but apart from that, he felt amazingly alert. He had abstained from the wine and skullcloud at dinner and was reaping the benefits of his wise decision.

Strapping his backpack over his shoulder, along with his new bow and quiver, he gathered his axe and ducked out of the wigwam into the quiet village. As he made his way through the occasional running children to Sassacus's tent, he noticed the eyes of the Pequot offering looks of respect and gratitude. He felt as if he belonged with the Pequot, and he knew he would soon be a part of their history, for better or for worse.

When he entered the Sachem's tent, Sassacus asked, "Sleep well?"

"Morning. Yeah, I'm good to go."

"Good. When Meatoc and Tatoben—"

"Our ears burn," Tatoben announced, as he and Meatoc entered the tent, both dressed in black breechcloths and leggings, matching those of Bud and Sassacus. Gertumah had outfitted them like a team of giant cat burglars. Bud chuckled when he thought of the troupe as stealthy.

"I was beginning to think we were going to have to fight the Noctiss without you," Sassacus japed.

"Ha! We would not let you have all the fun," Meatoc replied.

The men shared a laugh of determination and then gathered their gear. As they paraded out of the village, cheers and well wishes from the Pequot villagers filled the air. Women ran up to the warriors and gave hard slaps to their butts and planted firm kisses on their faces. Bud imagined this was how rock stars felt when walking on stage.

Within the span of a half hour, Bud found himself trampling into the black forest, looking up through the orange and green leaves at the base of Viduata's peak. His eyes scanned the thick timberland, searching for a landmark to provide him a sense of the trail he had used. With each step forward, his anxiety grew. He soon heard grunts of incertitude from Meatoc.

Bud continued plodding along, projecting false confidence while searching for the path, hoping the men wouldn't become aware of his growing uncertainty. He kept silent and steady, but shot his eyes everywhere, scanning for a marker.

"Are we on the right path?" Tatoben asked.

"Yeah, man," Bud replied. "I'm just looking for a tree."

"I see lots of trees," Meatoc said.

"This one is black and gnarly. It stood out like a sore thumb. It was around here somewhere—"

"Then we will help you look for this tree," Tatoben said.

"Yeah, we just need to keep heading up the hill and we'll find it. It was right off the path."

Just as he finished, Bud spotted the gnarled tree. "There," he pointed, suppressing a sigh of relief.

The next several hours the troupe spent slipping up the pebbled trail, eventually reaching the jagged cliff, and Bud gazed up into the crags. "This is where the fun begins," he joked. "Time to break out the climbing gear. Who wants to go first?"

"You will go first to show us the way," Sassacus said.

"Right."

Bud dug his fingers into the black rock. Once he found a hold, the pull was easy. He felt light and remembered the lack of gravity, and for the first time he welcomed the fact that he was on Adytum and not Earth. Hold by hold, he inched his way up the sheer rock face, slipping in and out of positions, using his fingers and toes like spikes. He found a ledge, thirty feet above, and tapped the first anchor into the rock then secured his rope around a fat dome rock and hammered a second stake into it, fashioning the rope through the eye. After testing the security of the stakes, he dropped the rope to the men and shouted, "Come on up! Weather's fine!"

    Tatoben took the rope first and began walking up the side of the mountain. When he reached the edge, Bud pulled him up, and called for Meat next. "Meat. You're next! That'll let us know if the rope is strong enough for Sach."

    "Ha!" Sassacus bellowed. "Good idea!"

    Meat groaned and adjusted his backpack then grabbed the rope with both hands. As he put his full weight on the line, it creaked, tightening around the base of the rock. Inching upward, Meatoc apprehensively placed one foot ahead of the other, working in conjunction with his hands. Slowly, he pulled himself toward the ledge. When he approached, Bud and Tatoben offered their hands and hauled him onto the ledge.

    "Ok, that's all there is to it." Bud wiped his hands together. "I'm going to head up to the next ledge. Send Sassacus up, and we'll just keep going like this until we get to the top."

    He secured another rope to the same rock and slid it through the carabiner on his belt, tying a thick knot on the end.

    "What is this rope for?" asked Tatoben, as Bud took his first hold.

    "That's in case I slip. At least, I'll only fall thirty feet." He gave a wry smile.

    "Ah yes. Wise."

    Bud scaled the bulging, hexagon-shaped rocks and heard Tatoben call down to Sassacus. "We are ready. Begin your climb."

    Bud shifted his weight and crawled to his next hold, foraging his ascent with relative ease. The men ascended quickly after the initial section, and by the time darkness began blanketing the mountainside, they had climbed several thousand feet. Bud's shoulders burned, and his fingertips stung. His hands were starting to cramp at regular intervals, and he fought the urge to relax his grip as he scanned the jagged cliff for a flat spot to rest.

When he reached for the ledge, several rocks crumbled, and his hand found no purchase. The sudden shift in weight caused his foot to slip, and he clung to the slick face with one hand. A cramp flared in his palm, and he made the mistake of looking down. Fear marred his vision and shot a charge of pain down his spine. He felt his grip weakening.

"Hold tight!" he shouted down at the men. Scraping wildly at the wall, he lost his grip and slid downward with increasing speed, bouncing in a direct line toward Tatoben below. The archer pulled a stake from his belt and thrust it into the hold on his ledge as Bud fell past. Tatoben reached out to grab Bud's arm but missed. Bud struggled to keep his weight pressed against the face of the rock, but he bounced outward and tumbled into a free-fall. As he crashed toward Meatoc, the rope attaching the men snapped tight, jerking Tatoben from his hold, ripping his stake from its perch. Tatoben and Bud flipped down the mountainside, overshooting Meatoc. Bud caromed off the side of the mountain, away from the giant's outstretched arm, continuing in a free-fall past the Sachem. Sassacus was in the process of finding a grip when his rope snapped taut, cracking like a whip against the rock face. Seconds later, Tatoben slammed against the side of the mountain near Sassacus, and Bud's line stretched to its length, tossing him into the rock face. Breathless, he looked overhead and saw Meatoc smiling down, the muscles in the giant's arms bulging.

"Good knot!" Meatoc belted.

Bud labored to catch his breath and his nerves burned with the fire of adrenaline. It took several moments of taxed breathing for him to replenish his strength, and after curbing his heart rate, he continued the ascent to the ledge.

Crawling into the Varrow's nest, he flopped onto his stomach and shut his eyes, allowing his burning muscles to relax. After a moment, he removed his backpack and rolled upright, examining the fresh cuts and bruises on his arms and legs. "So what do you think, should we stop here? There isn't really another ledge like this one for a while?" he asked.

"Yes, we have done enough damage today. We stop here tonight," the Sachem answered. "We will need strength tomorrow to reach the tower. How much more of this mountain?"

"It'll take the better part of tomorrow to get up there. Early evening, even if we start first thing."

"Good. We will take our time and be rested and ready by nightfall when we arrive. Darkness is our best chance for passage unnoticed."

Tatoben and Meatoc agreed and dropped their packs to the ground to secure their piece of the nest. The temperature had dropped at least thirty degrees due to the elevation, and Bud pulled several shirts from his pack and layered himself.

"Too cold for you, ruzzer?" Meatoc asked.

"Yeah, I don't have all those bloomish pies insulating me," he replied.

Sassacus let out a laugh and said, "Yes. We will all have bloomish pie when we return with the chalice."

Once the men settled in their spots, Sassacus passed a small cigar to Bud. "Light this and pass it around. It will help us sleep tonight," he prescribed.

The skullcloud, as expected, initially sparked conversation, and Bud found himself spinning the tale of his battle with the Varrow. He cautioned the men to keep one eye open during the night in case of their return.

"Yes, they are smart." Meatoc agreed, speaking of the birds. "Once a Varrow swooped down and stole a mirror off my belt when I was not looking. They love shiny things—much like women," he gobbled. I hear stories of treasures found in their nests. We should search this one!"

"I already did," Bud confessed. "I found a ruby colored stone, about the size of my fist when I came down through here before."

"The size of your fist?" Tatoben gawped.

"Yep."

The archer looked to Sassacus with a questioning eye and asked, "A Devil's Rose?"

Sassacus turned his gaze upon Bud and asked, "Still have this stone?"

"Yeah." Bud blinked.

"Let us see."

Bud dug around in his pack and extracted the red gemstone from the bottom. When he gave it to Tatoben, the archer took it in both hands and rolled it around, examining it, holding it close to his eye.

"You should have told us of this before, brother. Our priestess could have examined it for magic. It may be great power," Tatoben said.

"Sorry, I didn't know what it was."

The archer shook it a little. He blew gently over it. He sat it on the ground and waved his hands over it. Then, after a brief pause, he picked it up and determined, "I see nothing special with the stone, but I am obviously no warlock. Keep it tucked away until we find someone who knows of these things."

Bud nodded and accepted the stone. "So, is it valuable, even without magic?"

"Yes. The Devil's Rose is a rare and valuable stone, especially to those who practice magic. Even without a spell attached, they are a powerful stone of holding. Any warlock would pay a good price," Sassacus informed.

As Bud repackaged the stone in his backpack, he felt one of the orbs brush against his fingertips. "Hey, check it out, I also have these balls I found in the tower." Bud replied, and pulled one out for them to see.

"What is this?" Sassacus asked.

"It's pretty much a bomb from what I saw. When you shake them up, they change colors for about 20 seconds then explode."

"Useful," remarked Tatoben.

With the cigar smoke flowing, Bud asked, "So Sassacus, what's the story with your axe? Not to sound rude or anything, but it doesn't look like all that much. I mean, this axe Meat gave me is pretty spectacular looking, and well, you're the Sachem running around with that?"

Sassacus sat up in the straw, and laughed. "It is not the axe that is dangerous, but the one wielding it."

"Yeah, but shouldn't people fear your weapon? Or at least think it was the weapon fit for a Sachem?"

"Ah, but she is. This is Galetaer. Her steel may be old but she bites with bitter cold. She can freeze a man solid if she chooses."

"What do you mean, if she chooses?"

"Like many women who are to be feared, Galetaer has a mind of her own," he chuckled. "I do not know when she will bite hardest, but I have seen her turn men's blood to ice with a single blow."

"I don't understand. Is it magic?"

"Yes. A Dwarven blacksmith from the north blessed this blade with a frost spell when she was forged ages ago. I don't how she works, and don't care."

Bud snickered, "How did you get her?"

"Freydis." Sassacus smiled. "Galetaer was the greatest weapon of the Eiriksdottir Clan. When Freydis's father died, he passed it to her. She is the last of her clan, man or woman. Her brothers were killed in battle for their land. She is all that remains of their line. When we find her, I will allow her to tell the tale," Sassacus said with confidence in his voice.

"I look forward to hearing it." Bud rested his head upon his pack, looking up at the stars. Darkness brought a chill, and he buried his body underneath the deep straw.

∞∞∞She's A Little Runaway

As Tsarina entered her parlor, she looked to see if Timothy was still trailing.

"Madam Tsarina," he asked, "is there anything you require, while you wait?"

"No, thank you, Timothy. I'd just like to be alone if you don't mind."

"As you wish, Madam." He nodded. "But before I go, and pardon me for saying this, but I don't agree with the council's treatment of you."

"Thank you."

Timothy nodded and turned to leave.

"Wait," she called, stopping him. "So, you heard they're keeping me here, right?"

With a smile, he faced her. "Yes. It seems as if you are trapped, as you have feared."

She walked toward him and whispered, "I gotta get out of here. Would you help me?"

"I…I don't know," he stammered.

"It's ok if you won't," she said. "At least, can I trust you not to tell anybody I'm planning on leaving?"

"Certainly, my faith in the council has been damaged. The more I think about you losing your freedom—it is not a mindset I agree upon. You should be able to make your own mistakes or successes."

"Then will you help?"

He put his hand to his forehead. "I suppose, but what can I do?"

"I don't know." She frowned. "I guess I was hoping you might be able to give me some ideas. You know this place better than me—And these people. I know, even if I get out, they're going to try and track me down."

"Yes." He nodded, closing his eyes. "You will need to lead them in the wrong direction."

"So, how do I do that?"

He thought for a moment. "Halcyon believes your first concern would be for Bud, would you agree?"

"Yeah, I made that pretty clear."

"In that case, Halcyon should assume you would seek the quickest route to Viduata's tower if you were to leave. And the quickest route would be south toward Celeste Isle. There, you could take a ship along the coast to Water Knorr then north to the tower. You would most likely receive this advise from Jasper with whom you are already familiar."

"Ok, if that's the easiest way, then what's my other option?"

"Horseback. I know a breeder to the North with champion stallions."

"Awesome," Tsarina muttered.

"My brother works for him. I believe we could borrow two of them to trek across the plains."

"We?"

"Well, yes. If this plan is to work, you will need me to convince my brother to loan us the horses."

"And you'd do that?"

He hesitated for a moment and answered with a smile, "Yes. I am."

"But what'll happen with your studies? If they find out it was you, then they won't let you back, right?"

"That is most likely, however I believe your safety is worth the risk."

"Thanks, but I don't want you to lose your future just to help me."

"After hearing the council tonight, it seems all I have worked for may be corrupt, and besides, if you do not succeed in opening the portal, I will have no future, Archons or no. Ultimately, none of us will have a future."

"I suppose that's true." She frowned.

"It is simply logical," he stated. "But we must hurry, the Archons may finish their discussion at any moment, hopefully it will take hours as it normally would, but in either case we should leave promptly."

"You wanna leave now?"

"This is our best window to leave before more watchful eyes are placed upon you. After the meeting, Halcyon will have watchers on you at all times. As of now, I alone have that duty."

"Right. We should go," she agreed.

"Good, follow me."

Timothy rushed toward the door and extended his hand, stopping Tsarina as he opened the door. He stepped outside and scanned the halls, then closed his eyes as if he were listening for something or someone. With a convinced look, he motioned Tsarina to follow.

As they headed down the slope toward the stables, Tsarina asked, "Are we gonna grab a couple of horses on the way out?"

"Yes, we can take the horses to Jasper. After we convince him we are headed south, we will ride a tad more in that direction, then send them on without us. The archons and disciples following from the Cairn will track our horses south, but we will alter our course, north, toward my brother."

"Got it. Solid plan." She smirked. "You're pretty good at this."

"I excelled in strategy," he boasted softly.

"Oh, cool. You guys study more than just magic?"

"Certainly, most of us are interested in becoming archons, and take studies in leadership and strategy," he explained as he opened the door to the courtyard where the horses were stabled. "Come, stay close to me. Can you cloak yourself?"

"You mean, become invisible?" she asked.

"Yes."

"No. Halcyon refuses to teach me that."

"I see. Well then, Torrence will be working the stables tonight, and he is a stickler for the rules. Without a decree from Halcyon, I will not be able to acquire the horses. We will have to find a way to distract him and steal the horses without him noticing, otherwise he will sound the alarm."

"Can you do something to his mind?"

"I could try to persuade him, but he is quite powerful. I fear I would fail. With a distraction, however—if you were to engage him in a mentalist conversation and confuse him, preoccupy his thoughts. I might be able to weave a sleep spell."

"Ok, what do I need to do?"

"You must engage his mind with something he would invest all of his thoughts in. Something of passion."

"You want me to seduce him?"

"Yes, but—no that is perfect. No offense, but it is not you he desires. It is Melinda. I know he pines for her greatly. You could perhaps mention that she was talking to you about him, and asking your advice on how to approach him. Make him think she desires him."

"Does she?"

"I do not know. I suppose it is possible, but that is no matter. Do you think you can engage him in such a conversation, mentally, while I focus on putting him to sleep?"

"Yeah, I can do that. But how do they know each other? I need details."

"I know she comes to the stables to practice her animal mentalism on the horses, and they have polite conversations when she is here. I once overheard him asking her if she would like to ride into the fields of Jasmine with him one day."

"Oh yeah, that is perfect," Tsarina smiled.

"Good, then this is our plan. Are you ready?"

"Yeah."

Timothy nodded and led her into the stables through back passages out of the Cairn. When they arrived, Torrence was sitting behind a small wooden desk reading a book. The rough looking man looked up and placed it on the table as they entered.

"Timothy. What are you doing here at this hour?" Torrence asked.

"Hello Torrence, Madam Tsarina wanted to get some fresh air after the council meeting, and I have a trip planned next month to see my family. I wanted to show her the horses and look for a good steed for when I put in my request."

"Ha, you are always the planner."

"Yes, I suppose. So may I have a look?" Timothy asked.

"Of course, pick you out a good one. Century, down at the end, is in great shape. Take a look at her."

"Excellent. Thank you." Timothy nodded to Tsarina and began walking into the center of the stable.

As he loped down the row of stalls, Tsarina entered Torrence's mind. *So, you are Torrence? You must be the one Melinda is always talking about.*

She felt a shock like a small electric charge in her mind when he asked, *She mentioned me?*

Tsarina felt a glow with his answer. *Oh yes,* she smiled. *What did she say?*

Well, I believe she has a little crush on you.

Really, Are you sure?

Yeah, she was very excited one day, talking about how she was going to go on this ride with you into the fields of Jasmine, but she didn't want to seem overanxious, so she was going to wait for you to ask again.

Oh no, I thought she was simply not interested.

Tsarina giggled. *No way, we girls are just tricky to get to know. We like to be pursued. You gotta keep after her and show her that you are really interested. She'll let you in once she's ready and feels safe with you.*

I see. Thank you for your advice, Madam Tsarina! This is wonderful news. His thoughts began to quiet, and Tsarina could barely hear him whisper, *I think I will sleep on it and seek her out in the morning.* With the last word, his head fell and he slumped in his chair. A tapestry of electric darkness was all Tsarina was left with as she crawled out of his mind. The transition from conscious to sleep was gradual and serene.

After she broke free, she looked down the row of stalls for Timothy. Emerging from one of the stalls with a brown horse in tow by the reigns, he quietly walked the gelding toward her, and she whispered, "Wow, that was cool. How long is he gonna be out?"

Timothy answered in her mind as they walked out into the courtyard. *He should sleep through the night. At least several hours, long enough for us to put a good bit of distance from here.*

Good. I bet he has some nice dreams of Melinda, she smiled. *You're right, he really digs her.*

I suppose digging her is good?

Yeah, digging her is very good, unless she doesn't dig him.

Interesting saying, he mentioned as he mounted the gelding and took the reigns. *This is Ezekiel. He is a calm soul. He should be easy to ride.* He stroked the horse's golden mane. *How are you on horses? Can you ride?* He asked.

I'm getting used to it, but I'm still not very good.

Here, let me help you. He offered his hand and pulled her up into the saddle made for two riders.

∞∞∞*Ascension*

The next morning, Bud woke before the others and munched on the cracker Gertumah had provided the men as the sun rose over the tip of the mountain. When the Pequot awoke, not many words were spoken while they prepared for the final ascent. The first hour of the climb was painful, but eventually Bud's muscles warmed to the task. Thankfully, the day brought a strenuous but uneventful climb. As Bud approached the last section of craggy nooks, the overhanging tips of the giant black cones made the final push almost unbearable. With each finger hold, he thanked Petuluma, Gertumah's daughter, for sewing the leather gloves for the men. Fur lined the outer edges of the wrists, and the fingers were cut out just as Bud had requested. The gloves fit snug and felt like a second skin. Without them, he was certain that he wouldn't have been able to complete the climb.

When Bud clawed over the top of the last rock, he spotted motion against the black, pebbled road out of the corner of his eye. Frozen, he waited for the Pequot to draw closer then raised his hand slowly, motioning them to crouch behind a large boulder. After several seconds of lying in wait, he saw the silhouette of a lone Noctiss marching into view, travelling toward the black spire.

"I will kill him," said Meatoc.

Tatoben shot a perturbed look and said, "If you would like to take on the entire tower, we will watch from here."

"I'll stalk him like a wussarn and kill him quietly."

"You are nothing like a wussarn," Tatoben countered.

"What's a wussarn?" asked Bud.

"A large black feline," Meatoc responded, his eyes floating back and forth with anticipation.

"Enough!" Sassacus halted the argument with a forceful whisper. "There could be many guards unseen, and we did not come to fight them all. We will wait until this one leaves."

Meatoc squinted, frustrated, and took his hand off his axe.

"Where is the hidden entrance?" asked Tatoben.

Bud pointed past the stables, following the base of the mountain with his finger. "There's a crack in the mountain, below the stables, that leads into the tower."

After the leather clad Noctiss changed direction and began marching toward the large portcullis, Bud crouched low and led the men across the road toward the thorny bush that hid the opening to the tunnel. When he pressed the branches aside with the head of his axe, he found the crevasse filled with obsidian rock. It was as if the opening had never existed at all.

"What the hell?" he mewled. "They must've covered it up?"

"Are you sure it was here?" asked Sassacus. "These rocks look the same."

"Yeah, I remember this bush."

"The guards discovered your escape and covered their weakness," Tatoben surmised.

"Is there another entrance?" asked Sassacus.

"The only other I know of is that big gate—" Bud started, then the smell of horse dung wafted into his nose, jarring his memory. "Except—there is a grate in the stables, but it's about a thirty foot drop to the bottom, and the shaft ain't that big." He cast an unsure glance at Meatoc, wondering if the massive Pequot would fit.

"Lead us to the shaft," said Sassacus.

Several hundred yards across the road, Bud spied the row of covered stalls and pointed them out to the men. Above, Maroon and black crests with Agni's vultures looming in the pattern fluttered in the light wind. Stationed on either side of the entrance to the stables, two men dressed in black and red, leather armor were glaring at two Noctiss with black and red sashes tied around their waists. The antsy creatures held metal polearms and hissed and croaked toward a horse that was easing its nose out of the stable to catch a whiff of the fresh air. The stallion snorted and stomped at their taunts and stepped into his stall with nervous flicks of its tail. Inside the stable, a bearded human handler stroked the stud's chocolate mane and gave an admonishing look toward the Noctiss. They hissed a chuckle, revealing their curved fangs, then returned to their conversation of strange hisses and croaks.

"Right, so how do we take out the guards?" Bud asked, noting their numbers.

"Simple," said Sassacus. "When Meatoc and I get behind the guards, you and Tatoben shoot the Noctiss and we will take out the guards. Come Meat, we will use the rocks to hide."

"I thought we weren't killing?" asked Bud.

"Without an entrance, this must be done. It is quieter than storming the front door, agreed?" answered Sassacus.

"Yeah, I guess," Bud acknowledged.

"We must hide the bodies and move quickly after." Sassacus said. He waited until the Noctiss began teasing the horses again then snuck behind the stables, using the large black rocks and the dark shadows for cover with Meatoc following.

Tatoben twisted an arrow from his quiver and Bud mimicked the move. Once Meat and Sassacus were settled behind the set of barrels, Tatoben tapped Bud on the shoulder, then nodded and raised his bow. A split second later, Bud loosed his arrow, which lodged itself in the target's chest. The Noctiss staggered backward into the wall, but the wooden planks braced the creature, and it remained upright, clutching and tugging at the arrow with both hands. Hissing frantically, it looked for its assailant, while Tatoben's target lay dead on the ground, an arrow positioned perfectly between its eyes. Realizing his mistake, Bud quickly drew at his mark again, but before he could inhale a steady breath, an arrow from Tatoben's bow pierced the Noctiss's skull, pinning it to the wall. Bud turned and offered an apology with a dejected glance toward the ground.

"No noise. Split the head—like we practiced." Tatoben reminded.

Bud gave a single nod.

As the Noctiss took its last breath, Sassacus and Meatoc erupted from their crouched positions, grabbed their respective marks from behind, and slit their throats in synchronized choreography with long curved daggers. The handler erupted from the stable entrance with a thin riding sword and thrust the blade toward Meatoc's back, but Sassacus whirled and blocked the blow, disarming the handler. A swift arrow pierced the man's forehead, and Sassacus and Meatoc reacted with smiles as they looked to Tatoben.

Tatoben shouldered his bow, sprinting toward the fallen guards and called softly, "Come, let us clear them from sight."

Plucking the Noctiss from the wall, Bud began dragging the body into the stables, leaving a trail of purple blood while Tatoben followed with his own corpse in tow. Two horses whinnied and pranced in their stalls at the commotion and Bud rubbed their cheeks, calming them.

Once the bodies were stashed in the last stall, Bud tossed several layers of hay over them and turned to face Sassacus who had entered from the side.

"Where is this grate?" Sassacus asked.

"It must be under the hay somewhere in one of these stalls," Bud said. "I'll look in this one. You guys take the others." He kicked tufts of hay to the side, and after several attempts, his foot made contact with the grate. The iron bars, crusted over with bits of feces, looked firmly set into the stone floor. "Hey, I found it," he called with a harsh whisper.

Tatoben entered the stall first, followed by Sassacus and Meatoc, and as they peered into the shaft with twisted faces, Bud asked, "Do you think we can lift it?"

"Stand back," Meatoc boasted and stepped forward, cracking his knuckles. The behemoth squatted over the wide grate, wrenching his hands around the outer bars. With one clean pull, he jerked the bars from the stone, lifting them up to his expanding chest. Huge veins popped in his arms and neck as he sat the mass of iron and rock to the side.

"Good, Meat," applauded Sassacus. "Now, let's hope you haven't had one too many pies fit down this hole."

Meat brushed his hands and gave a small, unappreciative huff, while the Sachem spit a little chuckle.

Gathering the rope from his pack, Bud knotted it to a post and dropped the loose end into the hole. "Guess I'll go first," he said, removing his backpack and tying it to his leg to create a slender profile. He instructed the others to do the same then lowered himself into the cold shaft and began walking down the wall. Tatoben slid after, followed by Sassacus and finally Meatoc. As Sassacus stretched toward the floor, Meat howled a low grunt.

Sassacus jabbed, "Too many bloomish pies, Meat? Suck 'em in!"

Meatoc grunted heavier, thrashing violently with his legs as if he were running in place. "Yassars!" he howled. "I'm stuck. Pull me out of here!"

Tatoben stood beside Bud at the bottom of the shaft, fighting a chortle. "Maybe we should leave him. If we come back in a week, surely he will have lost enough weight and dropped by then."

Bud laughed, but Sassacus was no longer amused. "Hold steady, I'm coming to get you."

The muscles in the giant's arms expanded as he reeled his body up the rope and positioned himself underneath Meat, jamming his legs against the shaft for support. With a firm hold, he grabbed Meat by the ankles and then released his legs, allowing his weight to pull them toward the floor. Several particles of loose rock caromed down the shaft, forcing Bud and Tatoben to look away. The two giants above wriggled down several inches, but remained dangling over the shaft. "Suck in you fat slogger. You're almost free," bellowed Sassacus as he kicked his legs toward the ground.

With a deep inhale, Meatoc's belly pressed firmly into his ribs, and Sassacus pushed down with his legs. The duo continued rhythmically in that pattern as hundreds of pebbles rained down over Bud and Tatoben, followed by the two Pequot. Sassacus spread his legs and arms wide, using them as brakes to slow their descent. Below, Bud and Tatoben dodged, avoiding the avalanche of flesh and rock as Meat landed on Sassacus.

"Günther's giant ass, you're heavy." Sassacus grunted, shoving him to the side.

Meat moaned and rolled over on his back.

As the Sachem stood, he looked into the black corridor and asked, "How will we find our way in darkness?"

Bud flicked his lighter. "Follow me."

"Ah, the lighter." Sassacus smiled. "You must show us how to make these when we return. They are better than magic."

"Uh, yeah. We'll work on that," Bud mumbled with a hint of sarcasm.

Tatoben chuckled at the request and nocked an arrow. "*Stau*," he uttered, and instantly a brilliant auburn flame appeared at the tip of his arrow, lighting the tunnel, washing out Bud's faint light.

"Holy crap! What is that?" Bud asked.

"Stau has magic inside. It lights fire once an arrow is nocked and its name is spoken. Sometimes magic is better."

"Damn." Bud stashed the lighter in his pocket. "By all means, after you."

Bud directed Tatoben toward the door where he had originally entered the passage, but upon reaching the end of the corridor, he found the door blocking the exit and realized Freydis had opened it from the other side.

"There's got to be a lever, or a handle, or something to open this door from this side," he speculated. "On the other side, it was a torch. She just pulled it and it opened." Bud scanned the walls. Several indentations and bumps looked promising, but nothing stuck out as an actual door handle. He continued poking and prodding each anomaly in the wall, but nothing produced any sign of hope. "Anybody got any bright ideas?" he asked.

"Hold the flame," Tatoben said, then handed the bow to Bud. "Where was the torch?"

"To the left."

Nodding, Tatoben measured a crease with his finger then pulled an arrow from his quiver. "Hold the light there," he instructed and jammed the arrow into the gap. Twisting it, he continued until there was a noticeable click. "There," he said and pressed the arrow deeper with his weight. Something caught inside, and he carefully pulled the arrow from the hole, and the wall grated open.

"A hidden talent, yassar?" Sassacus joked then turned to Bud. "Where now?"

"Up the stairs," Bud answered.

As they entered the circular corridor of stairs, Bud held his hand low, cautioning them to listen for the presence of guards. "I'm not sure what's down those stairs," he whispered, pointing to his left, "but up there, leads to the main entrance with the portcullis and another set of stairs."

Sassacus calculated for a moment, surveying the stairwell. "We move quick—out of sight. Tatoben and Meat, take the stairs down. If you find Freydis or the chalice, take them to Idlewylde and do not look back. If you find nothing, head to the Varrows' nest and wait there. If we do not return by nightfall, get to the village. Take our people to Gorom. Satoucth will know what to do."

Tatoben and Meatoc frowned at one another.

Tatoben argued, "But Sassacus, we should not leave you here if we find nothing. We should stay and help you search."

Meatoc agreed, nodding with a grunt.

Sassacus scowled at the two warriors. "If we fail, you must alert Satoucth. The chalice cannot be lost. We cannot all die here and lose the knowledge of this entrance."

"Yes, Sassacus," Tatoben responded. "You are wise."

"If you make it back without the chalice, find Satoucth. Have him gather our warriors and find another way to retrieve it if we fail. If Bud and I find nothing, we will wait for you at the bird's nest until nightfall. Understood?"

"Understood," Tatoben replied.

"Good. Now, let us find the chalice and return it to our people," Sassacus whispered.

Tatoben and Meatoc nodded then turned and marched down the stairwell into the cool mist.

"Do you think they will listen?" Bud asked, watching them go.

"If they do not, I will have their hides on a belt. Now, lead us to the chalice."

∞∞∞∞ *Viduata*

Bud strode over the cold black steps toward the main hall. When he reached the corner, he peaked around toward the portcullis. Two human sentries, stationed next to the large gate, were slouching and fidgeting a bit, trying to maintain a ready position. Dressed in black leather armor with a maroon vulture crest spread upon their chests, they held shiny pikes a foot taller than their heads.

"There's two guards across the hall," Bud reported. "You think we can sneak past them and up those stairs?"

Sassacus growled softly with a frown. "We will try."

"If the chalice is here, I bet it's up that way. The other door leads to the dungeon," Bud said.

"Yes, then we follow the shadows. I will stay behind. If they detect us, I will kill the one on the left first."

"Ok." Bud responded, assuming the one on the right was his responsibility.

Waiting, he timed his first dash when the guards turned to speak to one another and kept his body inline with the nearest post, out of the guards' vision. He secured a position behind the last black stone support and turned to monitor Sassacus's progress. Between the third and fourth post, the giant's body swayed ever so slightly and his shoulder came into view of the sentry. Bud heard the guard shout, "Intruder! Sound the alarm!"

With shocking acceleration, Sassacus broke from his intended path and made a straight line toward the guard. Bud nocked an arrow and coiled around the pillar, firing upon the preoccupied guard. The serrated tip pierced the man's mouth just below the nose guard, and blood gurgled from his lips, painting the black stone as he slid down the wall. His counterpart raised his pike in time to deflect a mighty blow from Sassacus's axe, but the violent impact dislodged the pike from the guard's hands. Sassacus pounced, wrapping his thick arms around the man's shoulders, crushing him like a python.

"Hold your tongue yassar, or this breath will be your last," Sassacus threatened.

The man held still, glaring at the Sachem with contempt.

"What do you know of a woman named Freydis, and the chalice she carries?" Sassacus interrogated.

The man cleared his throat and spit in the Sachem's face.

Infuriated, Sassacus knocked skulls with the guard and wrenched tighter, squeezing the air from his lungs. "Speak!"

"I know nothing," the man huffed, a spot of blood dribbling from his forehead.

"Then you are of no use to me!" Sassacus grabbed the man's throat and began crushing his windpipe.

"Wait," Bud shouted, appealing to the guard. "How about Viduata? Do you know where she is? Just give us that, and I'll try to convince this brute not to crush your windpipe."

The guard remained silent.

"Come on man, don't waste your life for this," Bud pleaded.

When the man looked at Bud, Sassacus loosened his grip, allowing him to speak.

"You'll get nothing out of me boy," he choked.

"Dude—" Bud shook his head. "Alright, have it your way." Raising his eyebrows, he said to Sassacus, "Let's take this fine gentleman to the dungeon and find out what he knows. I'll drag the other one out of sight."

Sassacus snapped the sentry's arms behind his back and shoved him forward. The man winced in pain, and the Sachem warned, "We must kill him. He knows nothing."

"Not yet," Bud said, as he gathered the dead guard by the ankles and dragged him over to the large wooden door leading down into the dungeon. The bloodstain trail on the ground marred his effort to conceal the murder, but he continued, hoping it might at least buy a fraction of time if someone were to follow the trail to the body before sounding an alarm.

Pulling the keys from his backpack, he said, "There will probably be a jailer in there, and maybe some guards, so let me have this dude. You should go in first and clear the room."

Sassacus nodded, stoic to the inevitable wave of death he was about to unleash. Bud handed him the keys then unsheathed his knife and placed it up to the guard's throat. With a short inhale, Sassacus opened the door and launched into the room with Galetaer at the ready. After several slashing sounds and a thud, the giant appeared at the door, blood dripping off the blade of his axe. "It is done. Bring him inside."

Although the sentry made no visible or audible signs of fear, Bud felt the blood coursing through the man's jugular with increasing turgor. He shoved the guard into the middle of the room, passing him to Sassacus then quickly returned to gather the corpse. After dragging it inside, he locked the door behind and asked of Sassacus, "Hold his hand down on the table, and spread his fingers wide."

As if they had rehearsed the play to perfection, Sassacus nodded and grabbed the guard's wrist, slamming it onto the wooden table, flattening his fingers over the surface. Bud rubbed the honed blade of his knife across the guard's knuckles, slicing his skin like a deep paper cut. The man's body tensed, but he made no noise.

"This blade is a little dull, so I might not get all the way through on the first cut. Which one of these would you like to keep?" Bud asked.

"Take them all," the guard snarled.

"Oh, I will. I'm going to chop them off, one at a time, until you don't have any left. And then, if you're still all Billy badass after that, then I'm gonna work my way down to the more precious parts of your anatomy," he explained, pointing the tip of his blade at the guard's crotch. "Now, do you really think this bit of information is worth all that bloody mess?" He repositioned the blade over the guard's joint at the top of the thumb. "Come on, save us some time. It's not worth it."

"Do your worst, boy. I will tell you nothing."

Sassacus tightened his grip on the man's neck and hand.

"God damn it," Bud muttered.

Pressing down with both hands, one on the hilt and one over the blade, he severed the man's thumb like a chicken wing, splattering blood over the table. The guard howled as he watched his thumb shoot off toward the edge of the table.

"Silence." Sassacus pressed his hand harder into the table to keep him from squirming.

In between screams, Bud stoically asked, "Now, can you see I'm serious?"

Gasping in horror, fixated on his severed thumb, the man howled, "Fuck all! You fucking bastard! I'm gonna kill you and your fucking whore of a mother and throw her in a ditch for the maggerts!"

"Good luck with that," Bud said and raised the knife over the man's forefinger and middle finger and chopped down violently. Another stream of blood poured across the table, staining the countertop crimson. "Now where's the witch?" he demanded, and raised the knife over the man's ring finger, pressing down until a tiny cut produced a drop of blood.

Staring at his disfigured hand, the guard bayed, "Wait!"

Bud pressed into the man's skin, cutting to the bone. "Where's the witch?"

"Fuck all! Stop! Her quarters are atop the tower."

"And what about Freydis, and the chalice?" Bud growled.

"I know nothing of Freydis, nor a chalice."

"Sorry, but you aren't convincing me." Bud placed the knife over the man's other thumb.

"Truly!" he cried. "I have not seen any of these things. Please…no more!"

Bud paused a moment, searching the man's eyes. He was defeated and filled with despair. Bud felt confident he had broken his will. It was a depressing revelation, but the remorse passed quickly.

"I suppose we'll find them with the witch," Bud said to Sassacus, then turned to the guard and asked, "How do we get to her?"

"The passage to her chamber is through the main corridor. It's at the end of the staircase that winds up the tower."

"How many guards are in our way?"

"Four guards on each level."

"Level?" Bud questioned.

"Yes. There are eight floors, including this one. The top floor holds the witch's chambers. I've never been past the third."

"How are the guards positioned?"

"On the lower levels, we are posted at four points," the sentry gasped, intently monitoring the blood pouring out of his severed joints.

"You see, that wasn't so hard now, was it? If you'd just said that in the beginning, you'd still have your goddamn fingers," Bud spat, peeved he had been forced to act like a monster. He quickly shook off the guilt, remembering the endgame and gathered Sassacus's attention with a stare. "Let's take him downstairs and throw him in a cell."

"We should kill him. He will alert the others," Sassacus warned.

"We can't kill him. I gave him my word. We'll just tie him up and gag him and knock him out. That should buy us enough time to find Freydis and get the hell out of here."

"Your honor may get us killed, but it is your honor," the Sachem agreed.

A sigh of relief puffed from the guard's lips as Sassacus grabbed his neck and forced him down into the stairwell. Bud slipped past and led Sassacus to his former cell and unlocked the door with the jailer's key. His stomach mewled with memories of hunger as he opened the door.

Sassacus shoved the sentry into the cell, whacking the back of his head, sending him tumbling into the wall. Bud knelt beside the man and sliced two strips of cloth off his shirt, while Sassacus restrained the guard. Pulling the rope from his pack, Bud handed it to Sassacus who bound the sentry like a calf and gagged him. Sassacus then pressed the butt of his axe against the sentry's temple; who groaned as Bud fashioned a gag out of the first strip and wrapped the other around the bloody stubs.

As they stepped out of the cell, Bud nodded to Sassacus and closed the door, locking it with the key. They walked toward the stairwell, and Sassacus raised his eyes and remarked, "Impressive. I underestimated your nerve. I wondered if you had the stomach for such things."

Bud huffed, "I was pretty much bluffing until he pissed me off."

"Then I would say it is best not to piss you off," Sassacus chuckled.

Inside the main hall, a cold draft brushed against Bud's face when he stepped into the middle of the artery. Skulking forward, he noticed silvery white pearls imbedded in the walls, glittering in the torchlight. A curious oddity, he thought, as he inhaled the feculent air flowing in and out of the ascending shafts. The outer walls had small passageways, sectioned five feet apart, leading into both sides of the corridor, and along the main hall, statuesque torches flickered, lanky flames swaying at the whim of the transitioning draft.

Upon reaching the second level, Bud heard slimy feet shuffling above, followed by hissing noises and low croaks. He stopped in the center of the hall and looked to Sassacus for direction.

"Into the tunnels," the Sachem advised in a low whisper.

Following, Bud listened as four Noctiss slithered into the hall. Once the creatures were well out of range, Sassacus crept into the hall and motioned for Bud. The corridor widened into a grand foyer similar to the one below. Black and red banners loomed under the ceiling, and a black portcullis with curved bars, like iron strands of seaweed, stood behind a twenty-foot high, black-planked gate. In the center of the room, an onyx statue of a Noctiss glistened under a waterfall of auburn water splashing down like liquid flames over its body. Bud's heart raced, and he put his hand on the hilt of his axe, until he realized the statue wasn't alive. The massive fountain overshadowed several sculptures of unearthly creatures with pointed heads and fat bodies. The creatures had long, gangly arms that took their knuckles to the ground. *Ancestors of the Noctiss?* Bud mused as he passed.

"This is the gatehouse," informed Sassacus, separating Bud from his curiosity. "Careful. There may be many guards here." He pointed toward the archway on the western side of the tower. "Into the tunnel."

Bud quickly followed inside the dark passageway. Then, as if to confirm the Sachem's insight, a dozen Noctiss shuffled into the hall led by one of abnormal size. The pack leader was twice the size of the others and wore studded leather armor from head to toe. Equipped with a six-foot bastard sword, a red cross as the hilt, the monster hissed an order and frothy slime dripped from its mouth.

Sassacus blinked, rubbing the back of his neck, and his biceps rippled as he squinted in disgust.

"Do you think—" Bud started.

"Yes," Sassacus answered. "Must be Nequt's Blood."

"How are we going to get past them?"

"We kill them all," Sassacus growled.

"What? They haven't noticed us yet—" Bud questioned.

"If we make haste, they will not. Time grows short. The guard spoke of four stationed at each level. Two each. We can surprise and kill them before they make a sound—fast, silent."

"Whoa. Timeout. Somebody is probably going to notice all these dead bodies a lot sooner if we do that. We can't start a war in here. We've got to stay hidden for as long as possible."

Sassacus frowned. "What do you suggest?"

Bud pointed up the dripping staircase. "Let's explore these side passages. It seems like they follow the same direction as the stairs. Maybe they go all the way to the top."

"And if they lead nowhere? If we are spotted in these passages, we will be trapped," Sassacus countered.

"I still have the fire orbs. They'd provide a bang in an emergency."

Sassacus scanned the foyer. Bud sensed the Sachem's desire to kill everything in the tower. He knew the giant was growing impatient and fighting his nature.

The Sachem spoke. "We use the side walls, but stay alert. We must not be trapped inside, fire orbs or no."

Bud nodded and slipped into the side corridor. The potted walls inside leaked black liquid through the cracks that streamed over thick black and green moss. The wet ground and steep angle made it difficult to find footing. Bud slipped with every other step. Tiptoeing the slope, he led with his lighter, wishing it were a flashlight or Tatoben's bow. After a short ascent, he found an iron gate sealing the path. Sassacus brushed him aside and grunted a condescending laugh at the blockade then wrapped his vice-like hands around the lock.

As he squatted, Bud stopped him, "Wait," placing a hand on the Sachem's shoulder. "Before we start making a whole bunch of noise, ripping shit apart, let me try a couple of these keys."

The giant agreed and stepped aside with a wave of his hand. Poking the keys around in the lock, Bud found a match on the third attempt, and the gate clicked and swung inward.

Inside the next corridor, Bud ducked to keep his head from scraping the ceiling. The cold water rushing down the sides of the walls moistened his clothing as he sloshed forward in the darkness. He noticed in the hall outside there were fewer banners, shorter in length, hanging from the rafters. Toward the center of the room, the statue of a naked woman, pouring water from a pitcher onto her feet, stood as a strangely erotic sight in the sterile environment. The sound of the splashing water masked their footsteps, and they stalked up and around the tower through the small corridors.

When Bud stepped into the last foyer, a hollow chill invaded his body. The room was eerily silent and housed a crimson door at the opposite end, carved and painted with Agni's maroon and black crest.

Sassacus stopped him. "This must be the witch's lair. Prepare for her magic. I have fought devils like these before. She will try to control your mind. Do not allow her inside," he cautioned as he pressed his hand to the door.

Bud nodded, drawing his axe and waited for the Sachem to enter.

"What is this?" Sassacus cursed, rubbing his hands along the edges of the frame. He banged his fist to the wood. "I see no handle."

"Magic?" Bud questioned.

"Curse these witches," barked Sassacus, and then, as if he had uttered the magic words, the door creaked open.

Inside, a woman draped in a black gown stood beside a high back chair. The onyx chair's gemstone studded frame sparkled maroon against black wings which extended up into the cone-shaped ceiling. Orange tentacles coiled around the bottom of the chair rooting it to the floor.

Bud recognized Freydis's voice as she spoke in a low voice to a woman seated in the onyx chair. Gently, she brushed out the woman's peppered hair. The woman made no sound, staring out the massive window. Moonlight passed through the breast of the stained glass Varrow looming above, pouring crimson light over the women.

When Sassacus noticed Freydis, he inhaled to make a call that she stifled with a whisper. "Enter, quickly," she beckoned in a low voice. "And keep your voices low. We mustn't disturb her."

Upon entering the small chamber, Bud heard the door close behind, and his ears perked to the sound of the old woman as she began mumbling inaudible Latin phrases. Her frozen gaze was focused outside the window on a vast black sea. It was as if the and water and jagged obsidian rock formations were calling to her like sirens. Bud became mesmerized by the streaks of silver poking through the water and the waves crashing thousands of feet below. Freydis continued brushing the woman's hair, as if massaging her chaotic thoughts into oblivion and said, "That is their homeland."

"What?" Bud blinked.

"The Noctiss," she answered then turned her attention to Sassacus.

"Freydis, I have come to free you from this prison," the Sachem informed.

"I am no prisoner, my love, and know that I have not abandoned the Pequot either. Beyond us, there are greater causes for concern—matters beyond the control of a swift axe or a timely bowshot. I am sorry for my secrecy, but I knew you would not approve of the decision I had to make, so I walked this journey alone."

"Journey? You came to this place willingly?"

"Yes, I have a duty to this woman."

"Your duty is with the Pequot."

"Yes my love, but this woman is not the evil you believe. She is a pawn to Agni's madness. He corrupts her mind with his lies, and her sanity wanes each day. When she is awake, she rambles endlessly, speaking of Earth, and in her dreams, she screams her terrors. She is a daughter of Istia, and she is the weaver who led a visionary to us, along with this one." She pointed at Bud.

"Yes, we have spoken of Earth, and of the visionary, but I have little control of their fates. I am here for you and the Chalice. Are you under the control of Agni as well as this witch?"

Freydis tittered, "No, my love."

"Then explain yourself woman! Enough mystery!"

"Quiet your barking," she chided. "You will wake her and bring the guards upon us." Freydis stroked the witch's wrinkled temple, blowing a hush under her breath. "I have been chosen for her."

"Chosen?" Sassaucus whispered.

"I am her vigil."

"What does that mean?"

"The Archons choose vigils to watch over the daughters of Istia."

"And they found you?"

"I found Viduata by accident. From the moment we settled in Idlewylde, I felt a tortured soul looming in the wind, filling my waking dreams. At first, I questioned my visions. Then, after time, I saw a woman's face with Agni's. It was Viduata, projecting her torment for someone to hear. I opened a thread of thought between us, but her mind was twisted and thoughts cluttered behind black walls. The task was maddening. For several moon cycles, I struggled with my decision to aid her, but as we drew closer to the Summer Solstice, her thoughts intensified. She began chanting what I now believe to be the *Istia's Escape*." She looked at Bud. "The portal he and Tsarina must have come through. Even before I was aware of her reach, I felt something grand was happening. It was then, I contacted Halcyon, and he explained the history of Earth and the line of Istia. He suggested I become her vigil, and I accepted."

"This does not explain why you would forsake your people and deliver our chalice to the witch? Did Halcyon advise you of this as well?"

"It was not for her. It was for Agni."

"Are you mad?" Sassacus cursed.

"No, my love. Think. A man as untrusting as Agni would not have simply let me into his tower and become a part of his war against the Cairn and the search for his father on Earth? *That* would be madness. I had to provide something of great worth to gain his trust," her face soured with guilt, "and this is where I knew you would disapprove."

"Yes," Sassacus growled.

"Shun me if you must, but if Agni controls the line of Istia, he will gain unstoppable power and the ability to pass freely between our worlds. I have gained loyalty in his eyes. In the days to come, my position here may tip the scales and save our way of life."

"How is our world threatened by one warlock? There are many warlocks here, and the Archons have kept order for centuries. Surely you don't believe Agni can defeat them with only these Noctiss."

"No, Agni's power would not stand against the Cairn alone. It is the power hidden on Earth that threatens us." She paused, searching his eyes for a reaction. "I realize you cannot understand," she looked to Bud, "but this one can imagine the power his world holds—great weapons of fire; machines that fly, swim, and travel at unimaginable speeds over land. All of these weapons would be at Agni's disposal if he were to secure a position on Earth. The Archons would not measure up against such things."

"That's about right," Bud agreed. "The lighter I gave you is just the tip of the iceberg. Imagine a lighter like that, exploding with a fire big enough to destroy an entire village and everything around it. I don't know how bad this Agni dude is, but I can tell you one thing, there ain't nobody like him on Earth."

Freydis confirmed, "Yes. Agni has become one of the most powerful materialists this world has ever known."

"And now he has an army of giant Noctiss." Sassacus said, derisively.

"Not an army," Freydis argued. "There are only a few, however I have created several batches of Nuppe's potion that Agni's first in command, Warzen, will put to use soon."

"What?" Sassacus snarled.

"Do not worry, I have a plan to taint them, if I can gain access to his alchemical lab when he is occupied elsewhere. Besides, the creatures are the least of our worries, my love. As you said, I do not believe they will tip the scales in Agni's favor. They will not hinder us any more than his recruiting of assassins and mercenaries. It will be his findings on Earth that will ensure his victory."

"Giant Noctiss won't help," Sassacus grumbled.

"Of course not. That is why I led him to believe it will take several months to concoct another batch. He also believes it requires a rare ingredient, found only in the Seffer Mountains— one that doesn't exist. Playing this falsehood, I sent his minions out into the cold, where surely some of them will die while searching for the herb. The mercenaries will be scattered, and this will hopefully purchase time for Bud to find Tsarina bring her here to open the portal."

"And if he doesn't?" Sassacus asked.

"For Earth's sake, he must."

"Why here?" Bud asked.

"Because Warzen has the Eye of Istia."

"What? Tsarina had it when she escaped." Bud stiffened.

"Sükh found her and ripped it from her."

"Where is she now?"

"From what I gleaned when he returned without her, his thoughts spoke of several warlocks from the Cairn who interfered with her capture. She fled into the fields of Jasmine with one of them. Sükh further complained to Warzen that he lost her in the mage's storm. If this is true, they would have returned to the Cairn, and she should be within those walls. I believe that is where you will find her." She paused and gave a concerned look. "But I fear for her safety. Spies hide within those walls, and they will seek to capture her once they find she is a daughter of Istia. That is why you must find her quickly and bring her here."

"If Warzen has the Eye, then how are we going to use it?" questioned Bud.

"I will take care of that when the time comes. For now, you must explain to Tsarina, she must come to us to open the portal. Once that is done, we will need the warlocks of the Cairn to retrieve Agni from your world, but remember, be careful of the people you trust inside the Cairn."

"How am I supposed know who to trust?" he asked.

"I'm sorry, but that is your burden. I have no names of the traitors."

"You should have told me all of this sooner," Sassacus admonished.

"I am sorry. Your wisdom is greater than mine, as always, my Sachem. But I was afraid for you and for our people. Please, I beg your forgiveness."

Sassacus gritted his teeth. "I will make peace with you woman, but never deceive me again."

"Never. I swear it." She closed her eyes, shedding a tear in relief.

"Come to me." Sassacus extended his arm.

With a smile, Freydis left Viduata's side and absorbed Sassacus in the center of the room. As they embraced, she gave a kiss with firm strokes of passion against his neck. She lowered her arms around his waist and comforted, "No matter my actions, know I always love you, more than you will ever know."

Bud stood in awe of their affection. His thoughts drifted to Tsarina, and he questioned if he would ever get to hold her again and speak to her in that manner. With each day they were apart, it seemed as if the soreness in his heart grew. He thought it a bit childish and foolish. He had only known her few days, but his feelings for her were undeniable and ever present. The nauseating feeling in the pit of his stomach forced him to speak. "Hey, I hate to break this up, but we need to get going before all hell breaks loose around here. Somebody, or some thing, is going to find those dead guards before long."

Sassacus agreed, cutting short the embrace. "Yes, we must go." He gazed at Freydis. "I do not like leaving you here, nor the chalice."

"Then take it." She pointed to the chalice resting on an onyx stand in the corner of the room.

"No. They will mark you as a traitor you for handing it to us."

"Warzen's mind is elsewhere, I can easily hide my thoughts and feed him lies. Once you are in the tunnel, I will call the guards and tell them you overpowered me. The distraction should provide you time to slip out."

"What if he does not believe you?" Sassacus questioned.

"There are dead guards here to signal the attack," she stated. "I know Warzen, and with this—" She tapped the jeweled hilt of her dagger and pointed it to her ribs.

Sassacus's face soured.

"Fear not, I will not scar. I will touch it only in the side. A wound of this size can be easily healed, but with this display,

Warzen's trust in me may even grow. I will be safe within these walls. And beyond all, my place is here until Agni is stopped. I promise I will send word of my progress in the days to come. Now go, before my eyes flood. Make your way to our people and ready them when the time comes for war. This is only the beginning. There are grave days ahead."

"The Pequot will be ready," he assured.

They embraced with a kiss before Sassacus grabbed the chalice and stuffed it in his backpack. "We go now. Is there a safe passage out?" asked Sassacus.

"The side passages that drain the rain water will hide your escape until you reach the bottom," she replied.

"Yes, we traveled those tunnels to reach you."

"That is the only way. Hurry, I will scream shortly after you leave and draw their attention."

"You are brave. Thank you," Sassacus murmured, a hint of guilt saddling his words. He placed his hand behind her head and gave a final kiss. Releasing her, he turned and walked away without looking back.

∞∞∞*For Tsarina*

Freydis's screams echoed from above as chilly water splashed Bud's shoulders. Wading through the slender corridor in darkness behind Sassacus, he crouched low each time they passed an opening to one of the main halls. After several minutes of slipping down the wet passage, the Sachem calculated, "We are close to the exit. I smell Noctiss."

Bud sniffed the putrid stench of Noctiss, sparking reflections of his incarceration. "You think they can smell us?" he wondered aloud.

"They have not yet, or we would be surrounded," Sassacus whispered confidently.

Nodding, Bud poked his head around the black wall, and dozens of Noctiss began filtering into the corridors. The Noctiss hissed battle cries as they stormed forward. Bud's hands trembled, and he readied his untested axe as he backed into the dark corridor with Sassacus.

"Protect your side," the Sachem barked, raising Galetaer to his chest.

The first Noctiss lunged at Bud with a wild swing of its hatchet, and Bud blocked it with the haft of Falchion. Returning the blow, he slashed the creature's leather-padded chest from top to bottom, and purple acidic blood spewed from the wound. He kicked the Noctiss, slamming it into another following close behind, while a third hacked at his shoulder. Spinning to avoid the blow, he stumbled into another set of Noctiss attacking from the hall. With a swift turn of his back, he dodged a vertical blow then whirled full circle, slicing the tip of his blade into the crunchy sternum that had crossed his path. Jerking his axe from the creature's chest, he directed the blade toward another oncoming hatchet. The head of his axe collided with the handle, slicing it in half as if it were made of papier-mâché. Pulling Falchion close to his body, he thrust the pointed spike of the axe into the stomach of the lunging Noctiss, while several more of the slimy warriors continued slithering in from all sides.

Hacking sounds of Galetaer chopping through sinewy muscles and bone, followed by battle cries from Sassacus, and the icy sounds of Galetaer's blade urged Bud to keep his arms up. *Protect your side,* he thought, as he switched hands, blocking a glancing blow with the shaft. Metal striking metal rang out as the haft bounced off the hatchet's blade. With his opponent stunned, Bud slipped an arrow from his quiver and plunged it into the heart of the Noctiss. Extracting and flipping the arrow in his hand, he slashed, swinging a right cross, carving a deep rut in the Noctiss's agape mouth, ripping through tendons and jawbone. Purple, acidic blood sprayed over Bud's arm, and the creature spun across the room. Clutching its unhinged jaw, it rolled backward into his battle mates, and inside the break, Bud scanned the room for an escape route. Every open space was flooding with hissing Noctiss. He feared his energy would wane, and the sheer numbers of the Noctiss would eventually overtake them.

"Back into the tunnel!" Sassacus ordered and dashed toward the side corridor.

Two Noctiss, blocking the exit, lost their heads after a swing of Galetaer passed swiftly through their necks, and Bud raced in behind, defending his flank from a clawing Noctiss.

"Go ahead, I will stop them from the rear," Sassacus shouted.

Clanging metal and the occasional freezing hiss of Galetaer echoed from behind as Bud stamped down the stairs. The frozen corpses were creating a barrier between them and the pursuing horde, and Sassacus quickly caught up to Bud.

"Can you see anything?" Bud asked.

"Nothing," Sassacus replied.

Curling down, Bud sprinted the aqueous slope until the tunnel opened into a long hall. When he emerged from the stairwell, he assumed his place behind Sassacus, and swarms of Noctiss leapt into the hall, emerging from every opening like hissing locusts. Bud felt his hands shaking as he reached into his pack for one of the orbs. The blast would likely kill them all, but it seemed their only choice for survival. The Sachem raised his axe over his shoulder and howled a battle cry that visibly set the Noctiss on their heels.

"If this is our fate, then let us die with honor," the Sachem charged and took a step toward the portcullis.

Bud reached back to hurl the orb over the heads of the Noctiss as Galetaer sliced through several in the front row. Suddenly, two flaming arrows sparked the forerunners of the horde into fiery auburn masses.

"What the hell?" Bud bayed, looking for the origin of the arrows.

"Stubborn Pequot who do not follow orders," growled Sassacus.

Tatoben stood across the hall, firing arrows rapidly at the Noctiss in Meatoc's path. The battle-master leapt into the middle of the burning pack, hacking with his axe, sending the black creatures flying into the center of the room as he approached Bud and Sassacus.

Bud shook the orb in his hand, allowing it to brew, and tossed it across the room into the pack blocking the portcullis. Sassacus charged the attacking horde, howling a furious battle cry, driving them back into the radius of the orb. Upon landing, it exploded, dismembering most of the Noctiss blocking the path, erupting their bodies into masses of hissing flames. As the burning carcasses sailed over the black rock, Bud spotted a giant Noctiss coming from the dungeon and fired an arrow into its chest. The goliath plucked the shaft from its leather breastplate as if it were a thistle and gave a loud hiss that turned Sassacus's head. The Sachem swiveled to confront the monster. "This one's mine!" he bayed.

Bud continued pumping arrows into the hides of the smaller Noctiss as they circled Meat, who was almost to the exit. Reaching the gate became priority, and Meat was heading the charge. Bud willfully tried to focus on Meat's path, but his eyes wandered toward the giant Noctiss and Sassacus. The mutant hoisted a ten-foot, poleaxe over his head and screamed an earsplitting hiss as it lunged forward, swinging the blade of his poleaxe down violently, missing the Sachem's head by inches. Sassacus ducked the blow and countered with an arching swing directed at the monster's knees. The cold blade of Galetaer passed through air as the giant Noctiss leapt high and gathered his poleaxe over his head with both hands. Crashing down, the tip of the poleaxe slammed against the stone floor, grazing Sassacus's cheek as he rolled to the side. Rising to his feet, the Sachem charged, but the end of the Noctiss's poleaxe bounced off the floor allowing a counter attack, and the creature hopped aside, easily fanning Sassacus's blow. Galetaer swung wide, spinning Sassacus in the opposite direction. Before the Noctiss could strike, Bud sent an arrow through its shoulder, sending it reeling backward.

In the midst of the fray, a loud shriek echoed through the hall, and Bud turned his attention toward the sound. Blue and purple scales shimmered under the opening portcullis, as Bingen entered from behind the flaming horde of Noctiss. The wyvern rose up on his hind legs like a stallion, shrieking another sonic cry that pierced the air. Grinding through the paralysis of the sound, Bud slid his bow around his elbow and covered his ears until the thunderous blast subsided.

White flames flickered inside the wyvern's nose like dancing demons as the beast expanded its chest, filling its lungs with the cool, stale air. Upon release, a vortex of alabaster vapor erupted from its mouth, plastering the center of the hall in ice. Meatoc, who was standing directly in the path of the wyvern, rolled to the side, bowling over several burning Noctiss. Bud darted behind one of the pillars, ice frosting his back.

In an instant, Bingen inhaled a second breath, and Tatoben stepped from his cover, firing two arrows into the wyvern's flared nostrils. As the arrows exploded in orange flames, the wyvern shrieked and snorted, allowing Meatoc a chance to charge from the side. The wyvern disintegrated the arrows with a blast of cold from its nose and hissed at the archer, paying no attention to Meatoc's axe. As the blade struck deep into the wyvern's leg, a distant, high-pitched scream careened into the foyer from the darkness behind. "No!"

Focusing on the cry, Bud turned and spotted Ethan ducking under the portcullis, scrambling toward the wyvern. The wiry handler unsheathed his sword in a fit of rage, and rushed Meatoc. "Stay away from him you filthy bastard!" the handler cried.

Taking a wild swing at Meatoc's head, Ethan threw himself out of position, and Meatoc kicked the young man to the ground, as he would a ruzzer rat in his practice rink. The wyvern shrieked upon seeing his master fall and lashed at Meatoc with its spiked tail, uprooting the giant from the ground. As Meatoc landed on his back, the remaining horde of Noctiss rushed toward the skirmish, hissing battle cries. Tatoben fired an arrow, merely as a distraction, that ricocheted off the wyvern's scaled forehead, and the wyvern's bright blue eyes turned toward the source of the attack. Meatoc bounced to his feet and gave a swift kick to Ethan's temple. The handler's head snapped backward, and his body went limp.

Across the room, the giant Noctiss's back veiled Sassacus's frame, as its muscular arms whipped the end of the poleaxe into the haft of Galetaer, over and over, with relentless voracity. Sassacus struggled to fend off the blows, and Bud anxiously waited for an opening between the bobbing heads of Noctiss horde to take a shot. Once they separated, he fired an arrow into the mutant's shoulder, allowing Sassacus a chance to duck and strike. Slamming the butt of Galetaer into its stomach, he lunged forward, but the creature remained upright and countered with a staggering blow to the Sachem's head. The haft of the poleaxe sent him stumbling backward in a semi-circle, and he shook his head, attempting to gather his balance. Continuing to apply pressure, the giant Noctiss thrust the butt of its poleaxe into Sassacus's spine, pummeling him to the ground. Tatoben sprinted toward his fallen leader, howling a shrill battle cry, as he loosed a flaming arrow into the back of the giant Noctiss's head before it could unleash the fatal blow on the Sassacus.

Bud heard a howl from Meatoc and spun, firing wildly at a Noctiss who had a hatchet buried in Meatoc's shoulder. The arrow found its mark in the center of the Noctiss's forehead, dropping it, and Meat gave a grin and ripped the hatchet from his hide. Bingen had turned his cold gaze from Meatoc to Tatoben from across the room, and a hot lump formed in Bud's throat as the wyvern leapt toward the archer. Bud fired an arrow at the wyvern, but the projectile merely ricocheted off the hardened scales of the beast's neck. He howled a warning to Tatoben as the shimmering reptile began to inhale. Tatoben, unaware, continued firing his arrows into the giant Noctiss, protecting the Sachem, and the wyvern unleashed a breath of white vapor, engulfing Tatoben in a cloud of ice.

"No!" Bud wailed.

"Tatoben!" Meatoc echoed, as the frozen corpse crumbled to the ground in a heap of shattered ice. Stau jettisoned from

Tatoben's remains, skimming across the stone floor, landing several yards from Bud's feet. He stared at the glistening bow for a moment, unable to react.

Meatoc unleashed a vengeful battle cry and charged the winged reptile, his axe poised overhead for a mighty strike. Bingen turned its frosty gaze upon Meatoc then flapped its wings several times, creating a vortex that staggered the giant. It lofted its scaled body into the air, skirting away from the wild slashes of the Pequot's blade.

Managing his horror, Bud scraped the silver bow off the ground and quickly knocked an arrow from his quiver. Almost as an afterthought, he howled the word, "*Stau!*" To his surprise, the arrow sparked an auburn flame around the tip. He drew the bowstring taught, raising it toward the sparkling head of the wyvern. When the creature inhaled, Bud fired the arrow into its maw. Bingen screeched, puffing a breath of frigid air, extinguishing the flame burning inside his mouth, but the arrowhead remained lodged in his pallet. His head thrashed back and forth as he plummeted toward the ground. The arrow had apparently hit something critical inside the wyvern's mouth, and it flailed in pain, crashing onto the floor. Meatoc charged the downed creature and hacked at its throat with his axe. The honed blade slashed through the light scales covering the wyvern's gullet, and frost began to form around the wound. Bingen looked at Bud as he choked a final breath of misty ice, and the wyvern's head slumped to the ground.

Sassacus called, rising from his knees, "Come, we must go!"

As if he thought to take on the remaining horde by himself, Meatoc snarled at the Noctiss then wisely spun and ran toward the portcullis. Bud fired several flaming shots into the pursuing frogmen, setting them ablaze, while backpedaling toward the exit. The dwindling band of Noctiss continued leaping after the party as Bud followed Sassacus and Meatoc, ducking under the half-open portcullis.

Sassacus clamored into the stall with the tallest stallion and mounted it bareback. Meatoc picked the next mare in line and followed Sassacus out of the stables. Bud hurried in last and grabbed onto the flowing mane of a muscular, black and silver palomino. He swung his leg over its spine and spurred its dappled belly. The stallion pranced forward out of the stall like a finely trained thoroughbred and exploded after the frontrunners.

Sassacus roared as he sped into the darkness with Galetaer raised to the sky, "To Idlewylde!" Bud's head and torso lurched backward as his stallion followed, dashing off into the swirling waist-high mist. Curling down the slope, the horses galloped over the black earth like apparitions, while darkness fought a waning moon. Shadows of obsidian rock formed around every curve, camouflaging the first head in a battle line of Noctiss. The heads sprouted between two crags, spooking the horses as they careened toward at full pace. Spurring his steed with a crack of the reigns, Sassacus pressed his horse to lower its head and ram through the wall of Noctiss. As the frogmen closed in on them with their poleaxes, Bud spurred his horse to keep pace with the Sachem.

Ahead, Sassacus and Meatoc choreographed their axes, slicing through rows of Noctiss. Meatoc shouted, "Pull your damned axe ruzzer!"

Mindlessly, Bud drew his axe from his waist and made a half-circular motion. The speed of his horse provided ample power to his attack, and two Noctiss caught his blade at the neck. Their heads shot over the crowd, and Bud's shoulder burned.

"Hit lower!" Meat shouted from behind.

Bud frowned, thinking the attack would surely take his arm off upon impact, but he followed Meat's orders and extended his axe toward the ground. His blow struck a Noctiss at the shoulder, and he struggled to hold on to the haft as it reverberated backward. The hard-hitting blow sent the creature flying forward, crashing into several of the others along its path. Wild slashes from the tips of the poleaxes brushed against Bud's legs as he spurred his stallion to accelerate. Inches out of touch, the spiked tips of the polearms poked through the air, heads shaped in the image of

Agni's raven crest with black horizontal blades as their wings. Bud glanced at the hissing band of Noctiss after punching through the line and raced to catch up with Meatoc and Sassacus. After they had put a safe distance from the horde, Bud noticed the Pequot were sharing several harsh words, and they glared at him.

Bud spurred his stallion to ride beside them. "Hey, I feel like I'm missing out on the party up here. What's up?"

"We must part ways," the Sachem informed, reining his horse to a full stop.

"What are you talking about?" Bud griped.

"There is no time to argue," Sassacus declared, as several blasts from shrill horns pierced the air. Soon Agni's guards will be on our hides. Meatoc and I will lead them from your scent to Idlewylde where we will defend our village. This fight is no longer for you. I have the Chalice, and you have fulfilled your promise to the Pequot. Go now, seek your woman."

"But I can help you fight—"

"No. Find Tsarina. Find her and take her to Freydis. There is nothing more you can do here."

Bud stared at the road ahead, his head spinning from battle. "Okay, but where do I go? I have no idea where this Cairn Rose is?"

Sassacus pointed the head of his axe toward a narrow path with cart tracks on the outer edges and short patches of green grass dressing the middle. "That is an old Dover trail which leads to a merchant road. Follow it south to Water Knorr on the coast. Disappear into the city and find someone to give you passage to the Cairn. Trade ships are fastest. Meatoc and I will cover your tracks and direct Agni's horde north. We crisscross the horses and make it look as if we are three. By the time they realize, if they do at all, you will be far down the trail, and we will be in battle."

"But—"

"This is the way," the Sachem commanded.

"Here then, take Tatoben's bow back to his family," Bud offered, and began removing Stau from his shoulder.

"No. Stau will avenge his death with you."

"I—"

"Go! You have your supplies, and your horse. Was that not our agreement?"

"Yeah, but—"

"Then ride swift! Find your woman," he charged.

Bud nodded. "Ok."

A stinging pain burned his chest as he kicked his heels into his mount, directing it toward the row of deciduous trees and the worn trail. Guilt weighed heavy on his body, and he sank into the back of his horse. The stallion's silver mane whipped across his face as he turned to watch Sassacus and Meatoc ride off toward their village. He feared for the Pequot against the wrath of Agni's army, but realized that without Tsarina, their battle, and all the Pequot deaths, would have no meaning. Bud began with a slow gallop under the silvery moon to steady his nerves then spurred his stallion into the mist.

FINIS

AUTHOR
B.W. ATKINS

Made in the USA
Columbia, SC
25 May 2017